It's a Twilight Christmas wedding and the sparks are about to fly!

"What's wrong?"

"Nothing," he said. "Just trying to figure out if I'm dead or dreaming."

"Neither." She breathed.

"That's what I was afraid of."

"I don't believe that for a second. You're not afraid of anything, Ryder Southerland."

"You are so wrong about that. You've got me quaking in my boots, Miss Priss."

"Why? What's so scary about me?"

"How damn much I want you."

"We can fix that," she said, and kissed him again.

He yanked her up tight against him. "You sure?"

"Positive."

"No going back."

"I don't want to go back." She bit his bottom lip, not hard, but firm enough to let him know she meant business.

"More," he growled.

Well, she didn't need to be asked twice . . .

By Lori Wilde

The Stardust, Texas Series

Love of the Game • Rules of the Game
Back in the Game

The Cupid, Texas Series

Love with a Perfect Cowboy
Somebody to Love • All Out of Love
Love at First Sight • One True Love (a novella)

The Jubilee, Texas Series

A Cowboy for Christmas
The Cowboy and the Princess
The Cowboy Takes a Bride

The Twilight, Texas Series

A Wedding for Christmas
I'll Be Home for Christmas
Christmas at Twilight
The Valentine's Day Disaster (a novella)
The Christmas Cookie Collection
The Christmas Cookie Chronicles:
Carrie; Raylene; Christine; Grace
The Welcome Home Garden Club
The First Love Cookie Club
The True Love Quilting Club
The Sweethearts' Knitting Club

Available from Harlequin

The Stop the Wedding Series

Crash Landing • Smooth Sailing
Night Driving

The Uniformly Hot Series

Born Ready • High Stakes Seduction
The Right Stuff • Intoxicating
Sweet Surrender
His Final Seduction
Zero Control

A Wedding for CHRISTMAS

A TWILIGHT, TEXAS NOVEL

LORI WILDE

AVONBOOKS

An Imprint of HarperCollins*Publishers*

First Avon Books mass market printing: November 2016
First Avon Books hardcover printing: October 2016

ISBN 978-0-06231145-0

16 17 18 19 20 QGM 10 9 8 7 6 5 4 3 2 1

This book is dedicated to Tomibeth Brooks, the first person to befriend me in yoga class. Your kindness touched me, and I thank you from the bottom of my heart. What a beautiful soul you have. Shine on!

Acknowledgments

I wrote this book during a time of personal upheaval. Four close family members were diagnosed with serious medical illnesses in a short span, all while I was embarking on a journey to complete a 200-hour yoga teacher-training program. Honestly, as I look back, I have no idea how I managed to write this book, care for my family, and complete my teacher training. I attribute it to the Grace of God, my exceptional yoga instructors, and my fellow students.

To the following people I owe a debt of innumerable gratitude.

To my teachers: Sandra Vanatko, who created a safe haven in Indra's Grace. She is a shining example of love in action. She walks the walk. John Stockberger, who challenged my misguided beliefs with a smile on his face and a twinkle in his eye, and who saved my creative life. Jenny Reitz, who inspires me with her steadfast devotion. Nancy Deison for her wisdom, calmness, and rocking hot yoga bod. Karen Henckell for her grace, and style. Lisa Humphreys for her peacefulness, and because she smells so darn good. Suzanne Rockrock, our cheeriest cheerleader, and lover of baseball. Thank you!

To my fellow students: Tara Tankersley, who is not only a fierce yoga warrior, but lots of fun to boot. Barbara Pursley for her commitment to animals and people alike. Caitlyn Rose, who is wise beyond her young years; I'll never be as poised as she is. Jamie Cowan for sharing her special blessing with us. Patrick Gass, the lone yang to our many yins. You brought balance to our class. Linda Crownover who gives the best hugs! Jan Hicks for her sense of adventure, and willingness to try anything. Marty Hungate, a natural teacher with a spellbinding voice. Roberta Kirkpatrick for being real and speaking from the heart, and for snorting during closing circle. Cheryl Lambert, who is the most caring, gentle soul I have ever met. Marcy Akers Freeman for being willing to leap and trusting the net will appear. Amy Magga for her self-contained sensuousness. Lori Powell for her beautiful smile and nurturing heart. Kathy Presbaugh for her go-hung attitude, and looking incredible in wheel pose. Erika Swyryn, whose planning and organizational skills gave so much to our family group. Tai Tipton, who lovingly shares what she's learned, and embodies the giving spirit of a true yogi. To Katherine Walker for her classy elegance.

And lastly, but certainly not least, Vickie Nelms, who is one tough, smart, gutsy cookie, and a badass pediatric nurse. Thank you for being my partner-in-crime in Costa Rica.

To each and every one of you, I send my deepest gratitude, and heartfelt blessings. I love you all!

A Wedding for CHRISTMAS

CHAPTER 1

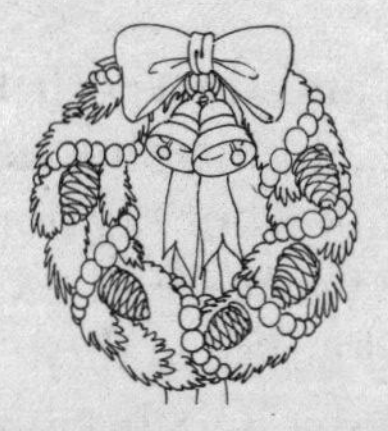

Los Angeles, California

December 23, 7:00 P.M.

Katie Cheek caught a glimpse of herself in the plate-glass window as she strode toward the front entrance of the old warehouse-turned-trendy-art-museum in downtown LA, and teetered in her six-inch platform heels.

Whoa!

She stopped. Stared openmouthed. Holy cow, who was that?

Vamp.

Smoking hot in a skintight, scarlet, designer sheath dress she'd borrowed from the closet of Gabi Preston, the woman she'd swapped houses with for the Christmas holidays. Just like in the movie *The Holiday*. Trading in her tiny yurt in the sleepy tourist town of Twilight, Texas, for a Malibu beach condo, knowing full well she'd gotten the better end of that bargain.

Across the street, a man whistled long and loud. "Yo, mommy, I'd love to find you in my Christmas stocking."

Katie blushed, and ducked her head to hide an involuntary smile, liking this new her, and freedom from the fishbowl of her hometown.

That's why she was here, to explore her options. And that included her sexuality.

She had changed a lot since high school. LASIK surgery dispensed with thick-lensed glasses. Braces corrected a severe overbite. Brazilian blowouts tamed her frizzy curls. Even so, she had never grown comfortable with catcalls and whistles.

Brillo hair, kids had called her, or other old standbys like four eyes, pencil-neck geek, and train tracks.

In public, Katie would laugh and pretend the name-calling didn't bother her, but when she got home, she'd cry to her mother.

Mom would give her a cookie, kiss her forehead, and say, "You won't always be an ugly duckling, sweetheart. One day you're going to turn into a beautiful swan. Just you wait and see."

The woman in the glass lifted her chin and triumphantly met her eyes. Today, decked out in Gabi's expensive clothing, no one could call her an ugly duckling.

People streamed into the entrance of the star-studded, red-carpet charity event—twinkle lights glittered, two huge Christmas trees laden with numerous ornaments flanked the doorway. The sounds of a band playing "All I Want for Christmas Is You" spilled into the street along with the air-conditioning. It felt strange, celebrating Christmas in warm weather among strangers.

But that was why she'd come here. To escape the claustrophobia of her hometown and the over-the-top, nonstop holiday festivities. Gabi had urged Katie to use her invitation to the charity ball, relax, have a good time, and enjoy herself. So here she was.

It was hard to relax among gold jewelry, Rolexes, Manolo Blahniks, and Rodeo Drive finery. Surrounded by the wealth, opulence, and celebrity of Hollywood, Katie felt her confidence wobble a bit, and the urge to run flooded her.

Outsider.

She didn't belong. *C'mon, swan, you got this.* She squared her shoulders and strutted into the event like she was the star attraction.

And people noticed.

Heads turned. Eyes popped. Several men murmured, "Who's that woman in red?"

Me, she thought proudly. *It's me.* Small-town, unemployed girl that everyone back home felt sorry for because her fiancé had died tragically.

But here in LA, over the course of the last three weeks, she'd transformed. No more bride-to-be turned almost-widow. She was free.

Guilt carved a slick hole in her belly. Why did letting go of the dream feel so disloyal? Was it because she'd started to come alive again? Was that so wrong?

Matt had been gone a little over a year, killed in

a boating accident, and although there were times when her emotions were still shaky, there were other times when she couldn't even remember what he'd looked like, or who she'd been when she was with him.

That was another reason she'd fled Twilight for the holidays. The house swap gave her a chance to discover who she was without a man or a job or a community.

She was three months from turning twenty-seven, high time to find her real place in the world. Sweep the stars from her eyes. If she'd learned anything this past year, it was this. Romantic fantasies were bullshit and she wasn't going to waste another second on wishes and regrets. She was going to live every day to the fullest.

Girl Next Door Gone Wild.

Well sorta. Wildish.

Inside the museum, she spied an actor she'd been infatuated with as a kid. An actor who reminded her a bit of the first real-life guy she'd ever had a crush on.

Ryder Southerland.

Ugh. Another memory she didn't want tromping in her head.

The actor looked worse for the wear. She wondered about Ryder. She hadn't seen the man in twelve years. How would he look today?

Forget Ryder.

Ancient history so old it had arthritis. Focus. Tonight have fun. Mingle. Dance. She studied the roomful of strangers, and anxiety sent her heart swooping to her feet.

Um, maybe she'd have a drink first. Beeline it to the bar. Yes indeedy.

But before she could put that plan in motion, her cell phone buzzed inside her purse. She almost ignored it, but what if it was Gabi feeling lonely in a strange town this close to Christmas, and needing to shot of confidence? Twilight, and the town's perpetual Christmas cheer, could be a bit hard to digest if you weren't in a happy-happy, joy-joy state of mind.

Stepping from the main flow of foot traffic, Katie pulled the phone from her purse and checked the caller ID. No, not Gabi, but rather it was Emma, her sister-in-law, who was married to Katie's brother Sam.

"Hello Em," she answered, scooting to a nearby alcove, and putting a hand to her other ear to block out the hubbub.

"Auntie Katie?"

It wasn't Emma, but her four-year-old daughter, Lauren, Katie's niece.

"Hi honey." Katie smiled. Lauren was fascinated with phones, and loved calling people. "Does your mommy know you've got her cell phone?"

"She's inna baffroom. I was gonna play Fruit Ninja, but I saw your pitcher on the phone and calleded you instead." Lauren sounded pleased with herself.

"That's so sweet of you to call me."

"Where are you, Auntie?"

"I'm in California."

"Where da?"

"Near the ocean."

"Oh." Lauren paused. "Dat's a long way off."

"It is."

"So you not gonna be home for Pop-Pop and Nanny's Christmas party?"

"I'm afraid not," Katie said. "But I'll see you later when I get home on Christmas night."

"But . . . but . . . it won't be the same," Lauren said, sounding years beyond her age.

"I know, but I'll bring you a present."

"From California?"

"From California."

"I miss you." Lauren's voice saddened. "You been gone a long, long time and no one plays tea party with me as good as you."

Katie's heart tugged. When she'd taken off to California for three weeks during the holidays, she never considered how it might affect her niece. "We'll play tea party as soon as I get home. I promise."

"Okay. Bye." Lauren hung up, leaving Katie a bit disoriented. Her body was in LA, but her mind and her spirit had traveled to Twilight.

She tucked her phone in her purse. Glanced around. Now what was she doing again?

Oh yes, getting a drink to steady her nerves. She snaked her way past people and art exhibits, looking for a cash bar with a short line, and finally found one. She queued up, took a deep calming breath, guilt prickling her for standing up Lauren on Christmas Eve.

"Buy you a drink?"

She glanced over to see a blond man in sunshades, fashionably ripped jeans, and crisp beige shirt with four buttons undone, showing off a shag rug chest. He sported impossibly straight, white teeth and a smile that rubbed her the wrong way.

"I'm good, thanks," she said, hoping to discourage him.

The guy couldn't take a hint. He stepped closer, crowding her space. "I won't slip you a roofie, I swear."

She hadn't considered that possibility. As a rule of thumb, people in Twilight didn't get roofied. But the look in his eye and his aggressive body language told her he wasn't above such a stunt.

The band shifted into a bouncy version of "Rockin' Around the Christmas Tree" and people started dancing around the exhibits.

Katie glued on a stiff smile, kept her voice light, but firm. "I do appreciate the offer, but I prefer to buy my own drinks."

"Cock tease."

"Excuse me?" Startled, she thought she must have misunderstood what he said.

"You heard me. You stroll in here, wearing a slut dress and fuck-me shoes, and you turn down my offer of a drink? What a stuck-up bitch." He snarled.

Stunned by the creep's verbal attack, Katie stood there with her mouth hanging open, her brain trying to process what was happening.

What shocked her was the fact that no one intervened. If this had happened in Twilight, half a dozen gallant cowboys would have jumped to her aid and challenged the guy.

Where was a knight in shining armor when you needed one?

Katie pivoted on her heels, rushed through the crowd. Maybe no one had spoken up because of the way she was dressed. Did people believe she was asking for that treatment?

No.

That was her old childhood insecurity talking. Plenty of other women were wearing form-fitting clothes and sexpot stilettos. Still, it disturbed her to think that the way she was dressed—the clothes she'd worn precisely because they made her feel empowered—had spurred the jerk's ugly behavior.

She found another bar, bought a glass of wine and gulped down half of it to calm her nerves, but it didn't work.

Shame. She was ashamed. She allowed the cruel man to make her feel ashamed.

In her mind she heard the voice of the grief counselor she'd visited after Matt's death. Dr. Finley had been kind, but with a no-bullshit approach to life. *The guy is a narcissistic, antisocial jerk. Don't let him define you.*

She wasn't, but she was done for the day. She'd had enough of glittery charity galas. Problem was, in the labyrinth of the exhibits, she'd lost her bearings. She deposited her half empty wine glass on the tray of a passing waiter and pushed through the crowd.

Where was the front entrance?

Rounding a corner, she glanced over her shoulder to make sure the creep wasn't coming after her, and smacked hard into a young woman holding a small plate of food.

"Oof!" exclaimed the woman. She had Angelina

Jolie lips that appeared to be courtesy of an excessive amount of filler, and an overly thin neck that made her head look like a lollipop on a stick. The woman fumbled her plate and spilled food down the front of Katie's dress.

The plate clattered to the floor, but thankfully didn't shatter. A big blob of something mushy and green, which Katie initially thought was guacamole, flipped into her cleavage, slid down into her bra.

Ugh. What a mess. She prayed Gabi's dress wasn't ruined.

The Angelina look-alike glowered. "Excuse you."

Katie raised her hands in apologetic surrender. "I'm sorry, I'm sorry. I should have been watching where I was going."

"Yes, you should have," the woman chided, but her tone softened.

The cold green mush that had settled between her breasts started burning her skin. A lot. Katie stared down, and saw a bright red rash spreading over her chest.

"Wh-what . . . is that stuff?" She gasped.

"Oh, dude," said Lollipop Angelina. "That's sick. Are you allergic to wasabi?"

Katie didn't know, but her breasts were ablaze. She had to wash it off. ASAP! "Bathroom?"

"Up those stairs." The young woman pointed at a metal staircase leading to a second level.

"Thanks." With energy born of pain, Katie flew toward the stairs in search of salvation, fanning her chest with a hand. But when she got to the steps, a red velvet rope was stretched across the bottom, and a posted sign announced "Closed for Private Party."

"BOLO. BOLO. Be on the lookout for a hot blonde in a red dress."

Personal bodyguard Ryder Southerland resisted an eye roll and muttered into the tiny microphone clipped to his lapel. "I know what a BOLO is, Messer, and I don't need an update every time you spy a good-looking woman."

"*Not* a hot chick alert. Repeat, this is not merely a hot chick alert, although she does sizzle. It's Ketchum's stalker."

Les Ketchum, the rodeo star turned country-and-western chart-topping singer, whom Ryder had been hired to protect. Two weeks ago Les had broken things off with a buckle bunny in possession of a mean streak who couldn't seem to take "Hasta la vista, baby" for the brush-off it was.

Ryder's entire body tensed, and he pressed a hand to the Bluetooth device that fed Messer's voice into his ear. "You sure?"

"Pretty sure."

"Where?" Ryder leaned over the balcony railing, scanning the well-heeled crowd milling in the art gallery below.

You'd think a hot blonde in a red dress wouldn't be that hard to spot, but since it was a celebrity-stubbed holiday bash, a surprising number of women were wearing red. And sun-drenched LA had a knack for manufacturing blondes.

"You got Ketchum in sight?" Messer asked.

"Yes." Ryder swung his gaze to his client, who was kissing a busty redhead known for her appearances in makeup commercials, underneath a bouquet of mistletoe. "Does your red-dress blonde look armed?"

"It'd have to be in her purse. That dress is sprayed-painted on. Couldn't hide anything underneath that."

"Can you still see her?"

"Negatory. She disappeared in the crowd."

"Stop talking, and freaking follow her."

"I'm trying, but some drunk sitcom actress just took off her top, and there's a hundred guys in my way."

This time, Ryder did roll his eyes.

Trite. His job was trite. Protecting spoiled celebrities from overly zealous fans who thought getting near them meant something special. But after four years in the Middle East, and an unpleasant bout of PTSD, Ryder was good with trite.

And working for his former platoon leader's personal security business in LA was a long sight better than crawling home to Twilight, where small-town minds had branded him disreputable years ago.

Pathetic.

He was twenty-nine years old, had been a decorated MP in the U.S. Army, and yet he couldn't shake the old childhood wounds, and the names he'd been called—bad boy, punk, troublemaker, delinquent, thug.

Ah, his youth. Those were the days.

There was only one family in the whole town he gave a fig about, and that was the Cheeks. The family who'd taken him in when his father kicked him out and no one else would touch him.

His favorites of all the Cheeks were his best friend, Joe, and Joe's kid sister, Katie. He hadn't talked to Joe since his friend had moved back to Twilight to take over his ailing grandfather's Christmas tree farm that summer. And it had been two years since they'd seen each other in person, back when Ryder had crashed at Joe's place, when he was living in Florida, for a couple of months after he'd been discharged from the army, and he was struggling to get his act together.

And as for Katie?

In his mind she was still the gawky fifteen-year-old who'd flung herself into his arms and kissed him. And that had been the last time he'd seen her, but he couldn't help wondering what she looked like today.

Head in the game, Southerland. Katie ain't nothing but a fond memory.

He leaned farther over the balcony railing for a better look, watching the circular metal staircase that led to the second story exhibits. The party was in full swing. The band blasted Christmas songs. People packed in close dancing, drinking, eating canapés served by tuxedoed waiters passing through the throng.

The crowd was eclectic. Young and old, trendy and traditional, dressed down and dressed up, an equal mix of male and female. The majority of them were wealthy, or plus ones of the wealthy. Ironic, how much money was being spent raising funds to benefit the poor. Why not just give the money to the homeless?

He scanned the three exits he could see, each one manned by museum security, and finally caught sight of Messer trapped in a bottleneck near the entrance.

He counted off the attractive blondes in red dresses, one, two, seven, a dozen. Was one of them Ketchum's stalker?

Concerned, he glanced back at Ketchum. The celebrity and his woman of choice were sitting on a bench near the restrooms, and they were in a liplock, hands all over each other. The second floor was reserved for special VIP sponsors, and Ryder guarded the threshold to their domain.

From his peripheral vision, he caught movement at the top of the staircase. A blonde. In red. Hurrying.

Hurrying, hell, the woman was full-on running.

Immediately, Ryder tensed, and his hand touched the Taser at his hip. He didn't want to use it, or the concealed SIG Sauer in his shoulder holster. Discretion was a big part of his job. Diplomacy another.

Besides, she was a woman. He was big, and she was small. Body block and chokehold ought to do it, and that was only if she was unreasonable.

He didn't want things getting messy.

In two long strides, he reached her, and for a split second, he was struck by the notion that anyone watching them might assume they were lovers rushing into each other's arms.

Except she showed no signs of slowing down, her gaze fixed to the spot where Ketchum sat kissing the redhead. This had to be the stalker, hyped up with rage, jealousy, adrenaline, and God knew what else.

Instinct, honed from numerous tours in the sandbox, took over, and he reacted without hesitation. It happened during the space of a single breath. Grabbing her by the arm, flipping her onto her back, falling atop her, pinning her to the floor in a four-point restraint.

"Stand back, people!" Messer shouted. Ryder felt rather than saw his colleague herding people down the steps. "Nothing to see here. Go downstairs and enjoy the party."

Ryder's hands manacled her wrists. His cowboy boots locked spread-eagle around her ankles. The woman was panting.

And so was he, because he realized not only was she not Ketchum's stalker, but he *knew* her.

Ryder peered down into her face. A familiar face despite the fact it had changed a lot over the past twelve years.

Katie Cheek.

What in the blazes?

All the air exited his body in one hard puff.

Her features were softer, thinner, and prettier than ever. The glasses were gone, and so were the braces, and instead of frizzy untamable, dishwater blond curls, her hair was straight and lush and golden.

Yes, she'd changed a lot, but he would recognize her anywhere.

Yep. Katie Cheek, all right.

It was his high school buddy's kid sister, all grown up, and curvy in the most dangerous places.

CHAPTER 2

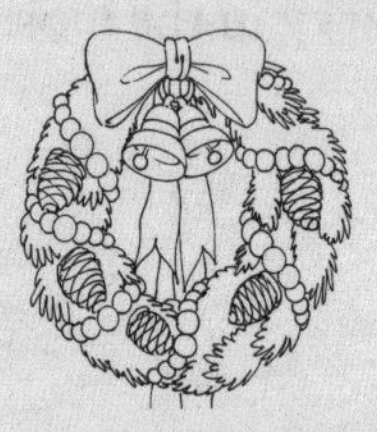

OMG, the boulder of a man lying on top of her, all hard muscles, tight sinew, and rugged sex appeal, was the first guy to ever break her heart.

Ryder Southerland.

Stunned, Katie stopped breathing, and thought, *Things that make my heart pitter-patter . . .*

1. Kittens.
2. Pretty boxes for organizing life.
3. Salted caramel anything.
4. Christmas morning.
5. Ryder Southerland.

Wham! Just like that, she was slammed into the past, dizzy, light-headed, her imagination tripped to the last time they were lying on the floor together. Except back then, she was on top.

She was fifteen, and had never been kissed. After all, who would willingly kiss a bony, knobby-kneed, four-eyed, metal-mouth, frizzy-haired wallflower?

Besides, boys like Ryder did not fall for girls like her.

Her parents had taken Ryder in after his dad kicked him out of the house for an indiscretion he never talked about, and he had been sharing the garage apartment with her older brother Joe. She'd spent countless hours daydreaming about Ryder and entertaining romantic ideas she knew would never come to pass.

Blistering sexual fantasies that confused the hell out of her and made her do dumb things like kiss her pillow and pretend it was Ryder.

It had been a brilliant, bone-sweltering July day, and Katie was standing at her bedroom window watching Joe and Ryder harvesting ripe juicy plums from her folks' backyard orchard.

Ryder leisurely stripped off his sweat-soaked T-shirt, giving her an unfiltered view of his hard, muscled chest, and her fifteen-year-old imagination fired wild and hot.

Swept away, she'd ended up sprawled on her bed, enthusiastically lip-planting a pillow.

"Whatcha doin', Miss Priss?" Ryder drawled from the doorway.

Miss Priss.

The nickname he teased her with because she was a rule follower who liked things neat and orderly.

Yeep!

Katie jerked her head around, saw him lounging against the door frame with one lazy shoulder, his arms dangling loosely by his sides, wearing nothing but cowboy boots and faded blue jeans.

That gorgeous bare male chest in *her* bedroom

sent Katie's imagination—and her pulse—into hyperdrive.

"Nothing!" Katie shot to her feet, simultaneously tossing her pillow over the other side of the bed. Oh God, what had he seen? Had she been moaning his name as she stroked the pillow, pretending it was his thick, wavy hair? "Nothing at all. What do you want?"

Panting. Seriously? She was panting?

One corner of his mouth curled up in a wolfish half smile. "Joe sent me."

"What do you want?" She knew she sounded bitchy, but it was the only way to keep from throwing herself at his handsome feet and kissing his cowboy boots.

The half smile curved into a half moon. "Do you know where your mom put the extra bushel baskets?"

"No idea," she said, feeling her face flush all the way into her hairline.

He cocked his head, and his voice bounced sly. "Were you kissing your pillow?"

"Nooo, no, no, no . . . I was just . . . I was just . . ." She gestured over her shoulder, her face hot, heart thumping.

"Yeah?" Half moon morphed into full-on smirk.

Dear God, please kill me now—lightning strike, swarm of locusts, flash flood. Name your poison. Anything. Get me out of this.

"Just?" he prompted.

"Um . . . um . . ." Frozen. Her mind was frozen. Deer in headlights on a ten-lane freeway were more limber than her vapor-locked brain.

Ryder cocked his head, studied her, his eyes full of mischief. "I could have sworn I saw your lips all puckered up and pressed against that pillow."

"Nope. Not me. You're seeing things."

"You know," he drawled, and for the first time she noticed he cradled a ripe red plum in his hand. "A pillow isn't the best thing to practice on."

She'd stared at him, mesmerized. "No."

"A pillow is too soft and pliable. You need something that feels more like real lips."

"How do you know?"

"Because I've done my share of kissing." He lowered his eyelids, stared at her in way that turned her knees to jelly.

Oh wow. Her heart fluttered, a crazed butterfly in her chest, her gaze hooked on his mouth.

"So what should I use?" she asked before she realized she was as much as admitting she'd been smooching her pillow.

"You need something firmer, fleshier. Say . . ." He held up the fruit. "This plum."

"Yes?" she whispered, barely breathing.

Her gaze hooked on to his face, mainly to keep from gawking at his naked chest as her adolescent hormones sent a million sensory messages galloping through her brain, none of them sane.

"It's perfect for your purposes." Ryder's mossy green eyes glistened, laser emeralds. "Plump and juicy, just like your lips."

Her lips?

She gasped inwardly, and forced herself not to reach up and finger her mouth. Was he talking about her lips in particular or was he simply referring to the collective "you" as in everyone's lips, all lips?

"Okay," she whispered, her voice coming out like warm mist. At this point she would have whispered okay to anything he said.

"Is there anyone in particular you're practicing for?"

You.

"No," she lied. "Just general all-round kissing. I figure it's probably a good skill to have, now that I'm in high school."

He nodded his head like that made sense, but narrowed his eyes. "No guy in sophomore biology class got you hot and bothered?"

The guy she wanted was in senior chemistry.

She shook her head vigorously, afraid he could see right through her. It didn't matter. A cool guy like Ryder would never look twice at her. If she weren't Joe's little sister, he probably wouldn't even bother talking to her.

"Katie?"

"Uh-huh?"

"Are you paying attention?" he asked.

Oh yeah. If a flash fire broke out, she'd get burned to a crisp because she couldn't focus her attention on anything else *but* him.

He had a reputation as a bad boy. She knew that. Had heard the rumors about the girls he kissed and other things he'd done. But that was not the Ryder she knew. Around the Cheek household, he was always kind, considerate, helpful . . .

Until right this minute.

Now, Katie saw that other side of him. The

side that skipped school, and sassed teachers, and sneaked off to the bushes behind the school with whatever girl he had on his arm that day.

How many times she'd longed to be that girl!

"You watching?"

"Yes." She breathed in a shallow rush.

"Soften your lips like this." He demonstrated, opening his mouth slightly, parting his teeth, and giving her a glimpse of his pink tongue.

She felt a hot thrill between her thighs, in the very core of her. Entranced, Katie couldn't move, couldn't even swallow. Part of her wanted to ask him to step out of her bedroom, but she couldn't unhinge her jaw in order to get the words out.

And then there was that other part of her that wanted to dispense with pillows and fruit altogether, fling herself into his arms, and kiss him like mad. But she was just a kid and he was her older brother's best friend looking at her like she was the funniest thing he'd seen all week.

Leisurely, he lifted the plum to his mouth.

OMG, Katie's own mouth was tingling. His lips hovered over the plum. Anticipation stole her breath, left her hanging, stunned and breathless.

Finally, after what seemed forever, his mouth came down on the smooth, red skin, and all the blood in Katie's body swamped to her pelvis. Deep inside she felt something tighten. Something she'd never felt before. It was both scary and glorious.

What she wouldn't give to be that piece of fruit!

"The best first kisses are soft and gentle," he narrated. "A quick, light touch down and then an immediate lift off."

"I see." Her throat narrowed to the width of a coffee straw and she could barely draw in air. "What about after?"

"After what?" He looked at her through sultry, half-closed eyelids fringed by jet black lashes.

Katie gulped. "Um . . . you know . . . after that first kiss."

"Good question." Humor simmered in those amazing green eyes, and the plum in his hand was shiny with moisture. "Are we talking a second kiss that immediately follows the first or a second kiss on a different occasion?"

"There's a difference?"

"Oh yeah." His voice was deep, throaty.

Katie shivered.

"You cold?" he asked.

"Yes," she lied. She was burning up.

He stepped to her closet.

Katie stood eyes wide, mouth hanging open, tense and thrilled and wondering what in the world he was up to. Her knees couldn't hold her up any longer, and she sank down onto a corner of the mattress.

He opened the door, peered in. Laughed.

"What?"

"I knew you were organized, but this . . ." He waved a hand inside her closet.

Feeling embarrassed, she drew her knees to her chest, hugged them, rested her cheek on her knees, and looked away. She knew what he saw. Everything labeled, pressed, color-coded, neatly folded or hanging on wooden hangers, the garments a perfect half inch apart. She measured with a ruler. Being neat made her feel in control, and as the youngest in a boisterous family of six children, she often felt out of control.

"OCD much?" he quipped.

Friendly as it was, his criticism hurt. Cold shame seeped through her bones. She respected his opinion, and didn't want him to think less of her.

"But I like it." He nodded. "After living with my stepmother in hoarder heaven, this closet is my idea of paradise."

She raised her head, skin heated, heart warmed by his analogy. Her closet equaled paradise.

He took out her favorite pink sweater, and came across the room to drape it over her shoulder. As he settled the sweater in place, his fingers lightly skimmed her shoulders.

Her stomach wobbled, and she forgot to breathe. Oh geez, oh wow, oh holy cow.

"How's that?" he asked, and patted her gently.

She had no voice, could not speak with him standing so close to her, touching her. He'd never touched her like this before. Oh sure, he'd slapped her palm in a high-five, or accidentally bumped her foot underneath the dinner table. But never so intimately, *never* when they were alone.

Katie realized then that she'd not ever actually been in a room alone with him. It felt like nine hundred kinds of wrong, and it made her heart pound so hard she could feel blood rushing through her head in a rhythmic throb of fast-paced, strobe-light energy.

His scent, part sweat, part ripe-plum sunshine, part peppermint from the gum he liked to chew. Did he taste of peppermint too?

He stepped back, looked jarred and out of place. He still held the plum clutched in his hand.

She cleared her throat, trying to clear away the dizziness of his nearness.

He tossed the plum in the air, caught it.

"The second kiss?" she prompted.

He touched the top of his tongue to the center of his upper lip, to the sweet part that bowed out slightly. "If the second kiss occurs after the first, you open your mouth a little wider, and lean in again."

"Show me," she said.

He winced, and a downdraft of fear passed through her. Was he upset?

"Oh." He blinked. "You meant on the plum?"

"Of c-c-course I meant on the plum," she stammered, realizing he thought she wanted him to demonstrate on her. She snorted for emphasis, mainly to still the rapid pounding. "You didn't think I wanted you to kiss me, did you?"

She added a laugh to show how silly that idea was, but it came out sounding kind of maniacal, like a cartoon villain plotting to rule the world.

"Um . . . no, no, of course not." He looked relieved.

His relief made her stomach churn. For sure he didn't want to kiss her. She was an ugly duckling, and he was the most handsome boy in high school. Her face burned. She wanted out of this conversation.

Now.

"I really don't know where Mom left those extra bushel baskets," she said. "But I could go look."

"Ditching your kissing lessons?"

"You don't . . ." She stirred the air between them with her hand. "This is silly."

"No sillier than you kissing your pillow."

"That's my point. It's all silly."

"You say that now. Until you're in a position to kiss someone you've been crushing on. Then you'll wish you paid more attention."

God if he only knew. Whenever Ryder was around, her attention was devoted to him, and him alone.

"Okay." She nodded like a serious student. "I'm listening. What more do I need to know?"

"Apply light pressure and suck."

"Suck?" she whispered so softly she wasn't sure he heard her.

"Just a little. Not as if you're trying to get a thick milk shake through a thin straw. More like you're trying to breathe him in. Watch." His mouth was on the plum again, that ripe, plump fruit.

A warm, tickling sensation started in the pit of her stomach, sank low and heavy as she watched him kiss the plum. It was a feeling she didn't fully understand, but it pushed up through her, from the bottom of her feet, spreading like rolling thunder to her spine.

And then something wild and crazy happened.

Or rather, *she* went wild and crazy.

Propelled by the novel feelings coursing through her, Katie launched herself at him.

Ryder was so startled he lost his balance. The plum flew from his hand and splatted against the wall, and he fell back on the floor with a loud thump, and she was lying on top of him.

And she'd gone at him like a feral animal—hard, lusty, and rapid-fire. Kiss. Kiss. Kiss.

A tommy-gun attack of kisses.

Cheeks.

Nose.

Forehead.

Chin.

Mouth. She kissed him smack-dab on the mouth.

Justifiably, Ryder freaked, jumped up, dumped her off his lap, and ran out the door as fast as he could run without a backward glance. The following day, he'd moved out of her parents' garage apartment, and joined the army. That's how badly he wanted to get away from her.

Embarrassment, bright and hot, burned through her, and she felt the wasabi sting again as she smacked back down into her adult body.

"Katie?" asked Ryder.

She blinked.

His concerned voice wasn't coming to her from the past. They were not in her childhood bedroom, but here in LA, at some nutty Christmas charity event in a strange museum.

He was still lying on top of *her*, pinning her to the ground. And, oh my Lord, he had an erection. A very big, hard erection.

Ryder stared into her eyes and she stared into his and she could tell that he knew she knew he had a boner. But he didn't look the least bit embarrassed about it, and she was blushing enough for both of them.

"Katie Cheek, is that really you?" He sounded incredulous.

"Yes," she whispered, happy to feel his erection ebbing.

"Holy hell, woman, what's wrong with your chest? You look like you've been dragged through a sticker patch and dipped in boiling water."

"Oh that." She splayed a hand over tender skin smeared with green goop. "It's the reason I was headed for the bathroom when you tackled me. Why *did* you tackle me?"

A muscular twenty-five-year-old in a tight black T-shirt, who looked as if could have been The Rock's stunt double, leaned over Ryder's shoulder to stare down at her. "That's not Ketchum's stalker."

"No shit, Messer." Ryder rolled off her, leaving Katie feeling strangely adrift.

"You thought I was a stalker?"

"My bad," the guy called Messer said.

"You okay?" Ryder asked, putting out a hand to help her up.

She stared at that big hand, afraid to touch it. Afraid of the fire he sparked inside her.

He didn't wait for her to make a decision, just grabbed her hand and hauled her to her feet. Macho Alpha Dude. Not much had changed in twelve years except he was bolder, brasher, more in charge and in-your-face.

And handsomer than ever.

She should have expected that.

"We have to get that stuff off your chest," he declared, still holding on to her hand. "Messer, you're on Ketchum. Call Davis in early as your backup. I'm taking Miss . . ." He shifted his gaze back to Katie, raised her left hand to examine it. "No ring. Is it still Miss?"

"Yes," she said, because she was so stunned she didn't know what else to say.

Ryder shifted his attention to The Rock look-alike. "I'm going to attend to Miss Cheek's wasabi problem, and then make sure she gets home safely."

"You know her?" Messer asked.

Instead of answering, Ryder snapped his fingers. "Ketchum. Go to it. There's a stalker after him."

"Will you be back before your shift is over?" Messer asked, pulling out his cell phone, presumably to call Ryder's replacement.

"No." Ryder leveled a long, speculative look at Katie. She shivered from head to toe. What did that look mean? "I'm done for the night. Come with me," Ryder said to Katie and hauled her toward the bathroom door marked "Women."

He kicked open the door. "Anyone in here? Everybody out. Security."

No one answered. No sound from any of the stalls.

"Looks like we're good to go." He hustled her inside, and then paused to lean half his body out the door to holler at Messer. "Clear the area except for Ketchum and his entourage, and block off the second floor."

"Yes, *dick*-tator," Messer called back.

"Now," Ryder said, turning his attention to Katie. "Let's get you cleaned up, sweetheart."

Sweetheart.

The fifteen-year-old in her thrilled to the term of endearment, while the almost twenty-seven-year-old resisted. "No," she said.

"No?" He sounded amused.

"You don't get to do that."

"Do what?" He maneuvered her over to the sink, turned on the cold tap, reached for a paper towel.

"Call me sweetheart. You haven't seen me for twelve years. I'm not your sweetheart. Never have been. Never will be."

"Oh." He grinned like he was on a fishing trip and had just hauled in a prize specimen.

"Oh?" She sank her hands on her hips. The burning at her chest had ebbed into numbness. "What does that mean?"

"You've gotten bolder. And pricklier."

"Yes, well, things change."

"I like it." He winked. "Now hold still."

"Messer was right. You are a dictator."

"Sweetheart, I'm just trying to take care of you."

"Not your place," she said, snatching the paper towel from his hand. Not because she didn't want him to dab the soothing water on her excoriated skin, but precisely because she did.

"Independent streak too. Gotta tell you, Miss Priss, I'm really into this new you."

Miss Priss. The old nickname he'd given her. He'd remembered.

"I'm not new. I just grew up."

"Yes." His eyes lit up with appreciation as he watched her scoop wasabi from her cleavage. "Yes, you did."

The rough paper towel scratched against her sore skin, and Katie hissed in her breath. She leaned forward over the sink, splashed cooling water over her chest and neck. Ah, much better. She thoroughly cleaned herself off, and then straightened to reach for another paper towel, but Ryder was already holding one out for her.

"Thanks," she said grudgingly.

"Welcome." His roguish grin was incorrigible.

She gently patted her skin dry, but it was only when she'd finished up and caught Ryder staring at her that she realized she'd gotten her dress damp, and her puckered nipples were clearly visible through the wet fabric of her clothes.

Dammit.

"Do you remember the time you kissed me?" he asked.

Double dammit.

How could she ever forget that? It had been a defining moment in her life. The very next day Ryder had joined the army, getting as far away from her as he could get.

"Nope," she said.

"Sure you do. It was—"

"You rejected me."

"Hell yes, I rejected you. You were fifteen and it was your first kiss and you were my best friend's little sister and I was living in your parents' house. What would you have me do, woman?"

Woman. Why did that one word sound so sexy coming from him?

"One of my most embarrassing moments," she said. "I felt ugly and stupid and ashamed."

He stabbed his fingers in his hair, blew out his breath through puffed cheeks. "You had nothing to be ashamed of."

She chuckled nervously, not brave enough to meet his eyes. "I was fifteen, who knows what the hell I was thinking? I'm sure I had some silly romantic notion that you would kiss me back, sweep me up in your arms, carrying me to your white charger, and we would gallop off into the sunset."

"That's exactly what I wanted to do with you, and more . . ." His eyes strayed over her body. "So damn much more. But you were my best friend's little sister. Still are, for that matter."

"Do shut up, Ryder," she said, because her entire body was lit up like the proverbial Christmas tree. "If you'll step aside, I'll be on my way."

"I'm not letting you go off like this. You need ointment for that burn."

"I can stop at a drugstore. Surprise! I know how to do that."

A bullish look came over his face, and she remembered he was a Taurus. Stubborn as the day was long. "I'm driving you home. No arguments. This is not the safest part of town for you to be driving in late at night."

Honestly, she was a bit relieved to have him offer. The high heels were killing her feet, and her wet dress drew attention to her nipples, and she didn't want to whine, but the wasabi burns were pretty uncomfortable. How did people eat stuff that hot? Plus she'd had that half glass of wine and not enough time for it to wear off before she got behind the wheel.

"Where are you staying?" he asked.

"Malibu."

He shook his head. "That's too far. My apartment is only a few blocks away in the heart of downtown. I've got ointment, and Benadryl. I'll fix you up, and you can sleep on my couch."

"I'm not waking up to Christmas Eve morning with you."

"Duh." He blinked sheepishly. "I'm being an idiot. You've got someone else."

No. No. She did not. But she didn't tell him that.

"You still have that boyfriend?" he asked.

"What boyfriend?"

He shrugged. "I don't know. Joe mentioned once that you had a boyfriend you were living with in a yurt. That doesn't sound much like you."

"Fiancé," she said. "Matt was my fiancé and he died. Last year."

"Shit, Katie. I didn't know. I'm sorry."

"Not your fault."

He winced. "I hate that I didn't know. I could have sent my condolences."

"Why would you? It's not like we kept in touch or anything."

"No," he said. "But I care about what happens to you."

His words squeezed her lungs, caused her blood to warm and her heart to pump wildly. Ryder cared?

He's just being polite. Don't read anything into it.

Ryder snapped his fingers. "Hey, wait a minute. It's Christmas. Why aren't you home in Twilight?"

She waved a hand. "Long boring story. Short version, I needed a break from excessive Christmas celebration and I swapped places with a friend for the holidays."

"Like in that movie with Cameron Diaz?"

"Yes, like that."

"Switching things up. Good place to start. You can elaborate on the way to my place." Before she could think of a good reason why not, he took her hand.

Holy Santa Claus! Ryder Southerland was holding her hand! It felt so good that she didn't resist.

He led her down the stairs and out a side exit to where a big black Harley was parked.

"You still have the Harley?" she asked, pulling her hand away from his and cradling her arm against her side out of his reach.

"Only vehicle I've ever owned." He puffed his chest out with pride, ran a hand over the smooth chrome.

"Of course," she said. "What else would a lone wolf drive? But I'm putting my foot down. I'm not getting on that machine in a dress. I'll go to your apartment *only* for medical attention, but we're taking my BMW."

"My, my. A place in Malibu. A BMW. Miss Priss has certainly come up in the world." His tone was both sarcastic, and amused.

"It's not my place or my car," she reminded him.

"Doesn't matter, you're living the life."

She wasn't sure what he meant by that. She pulled the car keys from her purse, dangled them from her index finger. "Let's go."

"Fine," he said, snatching the keys from her hand. "We'll take your wheels. But I'm driving."

CHAPTER 3

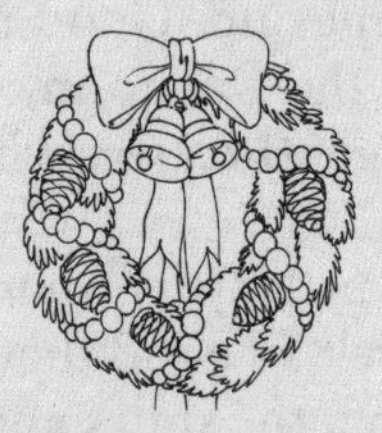

It started off innocently enough.

Okay, scratch that. Anyone who'd believe that line of bull was dumb enough to buy a bridge in Brooklyn, sight unseen.

Truth?

The minute they walked into Ryder's apartment in downtown Los Angeles, Katie knew she was not going to resist if he made a move on her. She, however, would not make a move on him. The last time she'd done so, things had not turned out so well.

There was no denying the pulsing sexual tension throbbing between them. Every time he looked at her, she could feel her cells tingle and vibrate. Damn, but she wanted him.

To distract herself, she glanced around the apartment.

The decor was modern, masculine, steel and metal, silver and chrome. But there were no pictures on the walls. No throw pillows on the couch. Not even a television set. Ultra-minimalist to the point of monkish.

She should have liked it. The effect was a tidy, efficient, no-nonsense style, but there was too much emptiness. Cold. Distant. Untouchable.

This was how Ryder lived his life?

A sharp spike of sorrow pricked her, but the sensation staggered away when he took her hand and led her toward his bedroom. A fine punch of fear/excitement combo and a galloping pulse vanquished the sadness.

She balked at the bedroom door, digging in her heels.

"It's just a bedroom, Katie," he said. "We have to pass through it to get to the bathroom where my first aid supplies are. I'm not going to force myself on you if that's what you're afraid of."

"I didn't think that."

"Would you feel more comfortable waiting in the living room?" He let go of her hand.

"That's not it."

"What is it?" He cocked his head and studied her intently.

Would he be surprised to discover the nice girl he called Miss Priss wanted a hot, hard fling?

She couldn't believe it herself, but the more she looked at him, the more she thought, *Oh yeah*. She could go there, and no one would ever have to know. It was a once-in-a-lifetime chance to have sex with her fantasy man.

Wasn't that the real reason she'd agreed to come to his apartment with him?

So why was she balking at the door?

Why? Because the fantasy of him was one thing, reality was quite another. What if the reality didn't live up to the fantasy? It would ruin a perfectly good daydream.

Take a chance. Risk it. Just do it.

She'd always been such a rule follower. The good girl. Well, except for the time she'd thrown herself at him. That had been out of character, and it had formed her future relationship with men. After his rejection, she made sure never to take the lead in any of her relationships.

"Have a seat." He nodded at a plush leather chair positioned across from his California king–sized bed. "Or not. Suit yourself."

He disappeared into the en suite bathroom, and she scurried to the leather chair, sank down into the plump cushion.

The room smelled of him. Masculine. Sandalwood. Rich.

She glanced around. It was another pristine clean, minimalist room. A bed. A chair. The dresser. A clock. A desk with a laptop computer and a satellite radio. That was it. She thought, *That bed needs mussing. I should so muss that bed with him.*

Nervous with the silence, she leaned over and flicked on the radio. "Santa Claus Is Coming to Town" trickled out.

Ryder came back into the room, sunburn ointment in one hand, a medical glove on the other.

An electrical thrill ran through her—charged and erotic.

He sank down on his knees in front of her, uncapped the ointment, spread a little bit on his gloved hand, and leaned forward to rub the salve gently over her tender skin.

His touch rocked her.

"How's it look?" she asked to keep from thinking about just how much he affected her.

"Like a bad sunburn. I didn't know wasabi could do this."

"I might be allergic," she said. "I'm allergic to horseradish."

"Then why were you eating wasabi?"

"I wasn't." She waved a hand. "It's a long story."

"I'm not going anywhere." His husky voice sent a wave of goose bumps undulating over her skin.

Was than an invitation? She studied the top of his head as he bent over her breasts and wondered what a random stranger would think about this scene if they were to walk in right now. Say a maid, maybe?

"You don't have a maid, do you?"

"I do, but I'm pretty sure Carmen is not going to pop in unannounced at nine P.M. on the eve of Christmas Eve."

"She might be very conscientious. Your place is very clean."

"She's not *that* conscientious."

"How did you know I was worrying about someone coming in on us?"

"Because I know you. You care too much about what other people think."

"That was twelve years ago. You don't know me now. I might have changed. I might be a completely different person."

He rocked back on his heels, studied her with amusement she found irritating. "Are you?" he asked. "A completely different person?"

"No," she mumbled. "I still care too much about what people think."

"Why were you at the party alone tonight? That's a bold move for a gal who cares too much what people think about her." Nonchalantly, he recapped the ointment, and stripped off the glove inside-out with a swift, practiced movement.

"More of that long story. Let's not get into it. Let's just call it fate."

"I like that." His eyes twinkled.

She sucked in a breath. Her chest jutted up against his palm. He took one look into her eyes and she took one look into his.

Snap. Crackle.

Sparks!

There was nothing clean or simple or organized or tidy about what she was feeling now. She felt messy and wild and out of control. Hormone pandemonium. Pushing her forward headlong.

Muss. Fuss. Chaos. Oh my.

"It's been a long time since I've seen anything that looks as good as you," he said.

"Even with these wounds?" She waved at her reddened chest glossy with the sheen of ointment.

"I was in the army, I'm attracted to wounds."

"Which explains a lot about you," she said, her temperature scaling to heights she'd not felt outside the throes of a fever.

"Katie," he croaked.

"Ryder." She exhaled his name on a sigh.

Their gazes fused. He moistened his lips. Her body moistened in secret places.

He held his arms wide.

She fell into them, scooting off the chair to join him on his knees on the floor, threaded her arms around his neck, tugged his head down, and pressed her lips against his.

Shocked by her impulsiveness, she immediately drew back. Had she gone too far?

He didn't take his mouth from hers, but his body tensed, and she sensed his mind retreating, backing up, reevaluating. Second-guessing himself or her or both?

"What?" she whispered. "What's wrong?"

"Nothing," he said. "Just trying to figure out if I'm dead or dreaming."

"Neither." She breathed.

"That's what I was afraid of."

"I don't believe that for a second. You're not afraid of anything, Ryder Southerland."

"You are so wrong about that. You've got me quaking in my boots, Miss Priss."

"Why? What's so scary about me?"

"How damn much I want you."

"We can fix that," she said, and kissed him again.

He made a rough, masculine noise of frustration, yanked her up tight against him. "You sure?"

"Positive."

"No going back."

"I don't want to go back." She bit his bottom lip, not hard, but firm enough to let him know she meant business.

He growled and she felt the sound vibrate out of his chest and into her, a deeply primal sound of want and need. It was a dark sound. A feral sound. A sound that lit her up like a circuit board.

"More," he said.

Well, she didn't need to be asked twice. She parted her teeth, kissed him deeper, slipped her tongue over his, pressed closer, ground her pelvis against his erection, heard him groan.

Good Christmas, but she was turned on.

His hands went around her waist, his palms spreading down and out to cup her fanny and tug her closer until there wasn't a whisper of space between their bodies.

She could feel his wildness, the bad boy of Twilight, Texas.

But there was something more. An inner steeliness that was new, control that came from the military or maturity or both. He was seasoned. Tempered. She could taste it on him.

He was working hard to keep his passion in check. She knew it didn't come naturally to him. Was he doing it for her? Because she was special? Or because he still saw her as Miss Priss and assumed she was sweet and innocent?

Phooey on that.

What? Did he think she'd been living in a nunnery? She was almost twenty-seven years old. Okay, so she hadn't slept with that many guys. If she went to bed with him, he'd be number four, a modest number for women her age.

Maybe she was a little on the sweet and innocent side, but the only way to cure that was to act in a not so sweet and innocent way. She was as entitled to her sexuality as the next woman. What was wrong with simply wanting to have a great time?

Katie claimed his mouth again, making it her own. She was the untamed one now, chaotic, in a sexual tailspin. She ate him up, tasting and sucking and licking.

Please. Strip my clothes off. Throw me on the bed. Do me. Hard and long. Make me whimper and moan.

Still he let her take the lead, holding steadfast to her fanny. Not moving. She knew he wanted to. He was not the kind of man who easily gave the reins to anyone, under any circumstances. But here he was, deferring to her.

Dammit. She was not a china doll. Screw this self-control stuff. She'd provoke a reaction out of him one way or another.

She yanked his jacket off his shoulders, and flung it across the room. He grunted, stood looking down at her like he'd been hit by a cyclone.

Good. She wanted to shock him.

She pulled the tail of his shirt out of his waistband, skimmed her palms up underneath the hem, ironing her hands along the heat of his taut abdomen, felt the burn of his bare skin.

Hot.

Damn.

Tamale.

Twelve years ago this ugly duckling would never have captured his attention. That hadn't stopped her from doodling "Mrs. Ryder Southerland" in her diary. Back then he'd been lean and gangly, narrow-hipped and long-legged.

He was still long-legged, but there was nothing gangly about him now. Filled-out and full-blown man. Ever muscle in his body was hard and big, but not bulky. Not an ounce of fat.

She dug her fingertips into his flesh, enjoying the feel of his solidity.

He hissed in a breath as if he'd been scalded, and swayed on his feet.

She moved to his belt buckle, surprised by how expertly she thumbed it open.

Two big strong hands went to her shoulders. "Katie," he said in a gravelly voice. "Do you have any idea what you're doing to me?"

She tipped her chin. "Pretty sure, unless that's a gun in your pocket."

He groaned again, pulled her into his arms once more, pressed his head against her forehead, stared into her eyes until they were both cross-eyed, and giggling.

"What is going on here?" he whispered.

"Hopefully, we're about to have sex."

"I'm talking about the ramifications."

"The only ramification I foresee is hot sex."

"I don't want to hurt you, Katie."

"Do you mean physically or emotionally? If you mean physically, I'm a lot tougher than I look, and who ever minded a few rug burns or bruises in the pursuit of pleasure? If you mean emotionally, get over yourself, mister. I'm no longer that pathetic fifteen-year-old who had such a crush on you."

"You were not pathetic. You were a sweet kid."

Sweet.

He was still seeing her as that awkward teen when she wanted him to see her as a red-hot firecracker. She was just going to have to show him.

Katie kissed him again, as firmly and fiercely as she could. "You taste anything sweet about that?"

"Katie," he said in a quiet, serious tone. "I don't have anything to offer a woman like you."

"I'm not asking you for anything beyond tonight, and frankly it's a little ego-y of you to assume that I want anything more."

He shook his head. His eyes were unreadable. Kid gloves. He was handling her with kid gloves, and it pissed her off.

"But hey." She wriggled away, still on her knees, and waved at the door. "You're free to say no. I could go. I'm sure it wouldn't be all that hard to find someone willing to spend the night with me."

"Over my dead body." He growled.

"Then step up to the plate," she said, barely about to contain herself. Need popped out on her like freckles.

"You want sex?" he asked, his tone darkening along with his irises.

"Yes!" She thrilled to the flicker of wildness she saw in his face. Not fully housebroken after all. "Take me."

"Is this what you want?" He got up, taking her hand, taking her with him, dragging them both to their feet. He spanned her waist with his hands, picked her up off her feet, and tossed her onto the mattress.

"Yes." She laughed nervously. "Yes."

He hesitated, desire and honor warring in his eyes.

"Come and get me," she said, and it was like waving a red flag at an angry bull.

He made a beastly noise, charged the bed, any scrap of self-control gone. In that moment he was exactly what she wanted—something wild, something wonderful, something just a little bit dangerous.

His mouth crushed hers, kissed her long, deep, and vigorous. Kissed her like he'd been waiting his entire life to devour her.

She was into it, one hundred percent.

Then abruptly, he moved back, took it all away again.

"What?" she whimpered.

"You think you can handle that?" He said it like he didn't believe she was up to the challenge.

This was so on.

She used a word then that would have gotten her grounded when she was fifteen. A succinct, dirty word that started with an F, and she added "me" to it.

An I-didn't-expect-that expression of startled surprise lit up his eyes.

"What? You didn't think I knew words like that? I have four brothers. I hung out with you and Joe, for heaven's sake."

"Heaven's sake?" One eyebrow curled up, a question mark. "Now that sounds like the Miss Priss I remember."

"I haven't been her in years."

"Trying to convince yourself you're something you're not?"

She ground her teeth. "That's pretty insulting, Southerland. I'm not a virgin. I was engaged, and even before Matt, I had boyfriends. I had sex.

Did you think I was sitting at home drying up and pining because you ran away from me when I kissed you?"

"No." He hung his head.

"I like sex," she said. "I like it a lot. And I haven't had any for over a year, so excuse me if I would like to have sex with a handsome guy." When she finished her speech, she was breathing hard, chest yanking up and down in a jagged rhythm.

And so was his.

But he didn't say a word. He was on his hands and knees on the mattress, looming above her, dark and silent and mysterious.

Katie notched her chin up. "In case you haven't noticed, Ryder, I'm a full-grown woman in charge of my own sexuality. We're not kids living in my parents' house. Look at me. See me for who I am today. Right here. Right now."

His eyes glittered in the dim lighting.

She wasn't quite sure what was happening to her, but she knew one thing, she did not want to be put up on a pedestal. She wanted a man who would let her be in control when she wanted to be, and take the lead when she didn't. A man who could both respect any boundaries she set, but yet wasn't afraid of her. She wanted someone wild and earthy. A sensual man who knew how to live in the moment.

She wanted a man like Ryder Southerland. Had wanted him for a long time now.

"Well?" she demanded. "Are you in or are you out?"

Nothing.

Not a word. Not a peep. Not a movement.

"I'm not that sweet kid you used to know. Actually, I never was. I like to talk dirty in bed. I make noise too, sometimes really loudly. And I want to do it with you."

Still, he said nothing.

Was he shocked? Had she shocked him? Actually, she'd shocked herself being so forward.

"I'm human. I have needs," she muttered, more to herself than him. "I'm allowed to ask for what I need. Just as you are allowed to turn me down." Her pulse galloped in her ears, a hundred horses' hooves. "Are you hearing me?"

He was a jungle tiger, staring down at her, trying to decide if she was worth eating or not.

Katie suppressed the hard shiver that gripped her spine, but he saw it. He knew.

"I want you, Ryder," she whispered. "Take me now before I explode. Take me, or I'm walking out that door."

Chapter 4

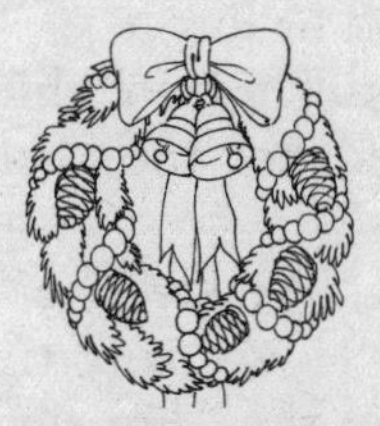

The woman had no idea how much restraint it took for him not to rip her clothes off and sink his body into hers without any preamble or warm-up. And Ryder didn't want to do that.

Hell, he was just a man, and she was a beautiful woman begging him to make love to her.

God, he was wound up. Crazy. She was driving him batshit crazy with lust.

But he couldn't forget she was his best friend's little sister. She was a good girl, who'd grown into a mighty fine woman, but that didn't change the fact she was sweet and kind and nice, and the last thing on earth he wanted was to taint her.

He knew she'd had a crush on him when she was a teenager, and he couldn't shake the feeling she was trying to live out some girlhood fantasy by taking him to bed.

If he were a smart man, he'd get up off this mattress and get her the hell out of here as fast as he could.

Apparently, he was quite stupid, because when

she locked her sexy legs around his waist, he surrendered to his cravings, and kissed her.

Christ, he was sunk. One taste of her sweet lips, one whiff of her flowery scent, one sound of her soft whimpers and he lost it.

She wanted him. She'd told him so.

And he wanted her too. Far more than was smart to admit.

He pulled back. "You're sure?"

She groaned. "How many times are we going to have to go over this? I'm single, and well over twenty-one. I'm a woman with needs. You're a man with needs. No one else ever has to know about this."

"What happens in LA stays in LA?"

"Exactly."

Still, he hesitated.

"Stop thinking of me as the girl you once knew. I'm not the same person. You've put me in a box and tied me up in a neat little bow."

"I thought that was the way you liked things. Neat and tidy."

"Don't restrict me with labels."

Was that what he was doing? Guilty. He'd compartmentalized his past, and Katie along with it, shoved it away in the back of his mind. He of all people should know better than to slap a label on someone. Look how he'd been labeled, judged, dismissed as a punk and a troublemaker.

And once the labels had stuck, he'd felt an obligation to live up to them. Dumb. What a dumb kid he'd been.

Not much smarter now, Southerland.

Using those powerful legs, she tugged him down on top of her, hugging him tight, as she sniffed his neck.

Hell, she wasn't the only one fulfilling childhood fantasies. He'd always seen the potential in her, able to look past the gawky exterior to the woman she would become. But now that woman was in his arms, potential fully realized, and it was a complete game changer.

She was not only the quintessential girl next door—wholesome, peppy, generous, reliable—she was brave and honest and sexier than any woman he had ever known.

Bit of an overstatement?

And he'd known a lot of women. Still, he could not remember being stirred to this level. He studied her through heavily lidded eyes. Not an overstatement. Not by a long shot. His engines were revved and ready to rock.

"Well?" she said a bit rudely. "Are we doing this thing or not?"

He smiled. Okay. If this was what she wanted, he was in.

"That was like pulling teeth." She exhaled, and went to work on the buttons of his shirt. "Let's get naked."

He laughed. Her enthusiasm was contagious. Damn, but she was fun.

Her hot palms skimmed the planes of his abdomen, and her touch was so amazing, he had to close his eyes for a moment to collect himself.

"You okay?"

"Terrific." He growled, opened his eyes, and

dispensed with her dress as she efficiently relieved him of his shirt, stripping her down to her bra and panties—a red bra and panties that matched her dress.

Brick house. The woman was stacked.

Have mercy.

His mouth went dry, and he realized he was staring, but couldn't seem to stop. Amazing. She was absolutely amazing.

"Let's get rid of that bra," he said.

"Yes." She giggled. "Free the girls."

Once "the girls" were freed, Ryder cupped them in his hands. They overflowed his palms. Hard to believe that skinny girl he remembered had grown so voluptuous. Her stomach was flat and smooth, her thighs taut.

Perfection. She was sheer perfection.

None of the other women that he'd been with could hold a candle to the beautiful woman in his arms. She exceeded his wildest expectations. It was as if he'd been waiting his entire life to be with her.

Hell, maybe he had.

He'd left Twilight partly because of her. Because of the inappropriate feelings he had for her. She'd been like a little sister to him, and when he'd started having wicked thoughts about her, he knew he couldn't stay in Twilight.

The feelings were still there. Not just there, but stronger than ever. Completely dismantling him.

Unbelievable. He'd gone to work today as usual, nothing out of the ordinary, and then on the turn of a dime, everything had changed, and he was living out his wildest daydreams.

Him. Katie Cheek. In bed together.

Amazing.

He kissed her. Everywhere. Mouth. Chin. Cheek. Forehead. He feasted on her. Earlobes. Neck. Breasts. Those beautiful, beautiful breasts. He touched her. Caressed. Massaged. Kneaded. Smooth flesh. Tender skin. Soft hair. He tasted her. Salty. Sweet. Hot. Moist.

Reverently, she ran her hands, lips, and tongue over his body, exploring him the way he explored her. Full throttle. No holds barred.

And when she wrapped her velvet hand around his erection, it hit him like a concrete wall.

No dream. He was truly here, in Katie's arms, making love to her. Stirring the chemical soup that started simmering the day he'd used a plum to teach her how to kiss.

Did she have any idea how long he'd lusted after her?

Tenderly, he eased her off him, and slid from the bed to kick out of his shoes and shuck off his pants. She flipped over onto her belly, rested her chin on her stacked palms, her sweet rump in the air, watching him with a gleam in her gorgeous brown eyes.

He wished he had his cell phone so he could snap a picture of her, a forever souvenir of this momentous occasion.

When he stripped off his boxer briefs, she sucked in an audible breath. He met her gaze. She smiled coyly, whispered, "Impressive."

A chuckle bubbled up from the bottom of his lungs. He knew he was an average-sized guy, maybe a little wider than most, certainly nothing extraordinary. But he was pleased that she was pleased. Her approval was a helluva turn-on.

"Come here," she said, and crooked her finger at him.

Bam! He was in her arms again, their legs entwined, and they were kissing her hotly, deeply. Her glorious breasts rubbed provocatively against his chest. Incredible.

And when she pressed her luscious mouth to his granite erection . . .

"Katie." He sat up; her name was a gasp in the dark.

Laughing, she pushed him back, and returned to kissing, licking, and flicking that wicked tongue of hers. Her long blond hair tickled against his skin, driving him absolutely mad.

God, she was so damn beautiful—the feel of her soft mouth on him, the sight of her naked body, that heavenly face, and that naughty wink when she paused long enough to glance up and catch him watching her.

She made him feel so good.

Scary good.

But damn, he wanted this to be about her, not him. "This isn't what I want," he croaked, desperate to break the spell while he still had some strength of will.

For the first time, she looked at a loss. "I did something wrong. What did I do wrong?"

"Not a damn thing, sweetheart. You're perfect. But I want to look into your eyes." He reached down, slid his hands under her armpits, and hauled her up to his chest.

Somehow, she was still wearing those scarlet panties that looked so dramatic against her creamy white skin. He hooked one finger around the waistband and slowly tugged them over her hips to her ankles. She kicked them off with one graceful riffle of her foot.

Ryder flipped her over onto her back, and knelt between her spread legs. He inhaled her feminine perfume, touched her gently. She came unspooled, a soft gasp slipping from her lips, and he laughed.

"Oh you." She sighed. "You."

"Me." He crowed proudly, and touched her again, pressing firmer on her most sensitive spot. "Me."

She moaned softly.

Ah. She was so responsive, so ready for him.

"I have a condom in my purse," she whispered.

"No worries. Got one in my wallet." He scrambled for his pants, found his wallet and the foil package inside, returned to bed.

She leaned over his shoulder, kissing his arm as he rolled on the rubber. "Hurry," she said, managing to sound both adorable and hot. "I want to feel you inside me."

The minute he had the condom in place, she shoved him onto his back and straddled his hips, ready to sink down . . .

He caught her around the waist, held her suspended over him, holding her off, making her wait.

"Hey," she protested, and stared down into his face.

"You slide down this pole, there's no going back."

"I know." She wriggled. "That's the point. What part of 'I want you' do you not get?"

"Just wanted to make sure."

"Are you going to make me beg?"

He smiled, and didn't let go of her waist, but he did ease her down slowly. He could feel the heat of her body, and then, dear God, her soft, wet warmth as she fully sheathed him.

Their gazes locked, fused, ignited.

He felt as if he were the hero in the best romantic movie ever made. He'd dreamed of this moment more than a few times over the years. But the fantasy couldn't begin to compare to the real thing.

Releasing her, he reached his hands up to cup her face with his palms and slowly eased her head downward so he could steal another kiss. She rocked back slightly, tilting her pelvis to take him deeper inside her.

Ryder groaned inside her mouth, rough and needy.

Eyes still welded to his, she began to rock slowly back and forth, sliding up and down. The pleasure was so intense, he lost his breath, his chest muscles seized up, and he simply floated in the moment, not caring that he couldn't breathe.

"Ryder," she whispered. "Inhale."

He sucked in air, and with the movement, her body rose up, and they created a beautiful rhythm together. Rocking and breathing in perfect timing. Moving as one, a duo no more. Her body enveloped his in her silky cocoon.

It was no longer he and she. Him and her. It was the two of them. Together. Melded.

Us, he thought mindlessly. *Us*.

Their joining was unbelievable. Yes, he had daydreamed about getting it on with a grown-up Katie Cheek, but his fantasies didn't began to compare to what was happening between them. Not even close.

He clutched her around the waist again, flipped them over as one unit, settled more deeply into her sweet, lush body.

"This is . . . you are . . . amazing." She exhaled the last word on a husky whisper.

Overcome by pleasure, Ryder couldn't even speak. He was too busy focusing on the incredible sensations shooting through him. Restlessly, he ran his palms over her satiny skin, traveling up to tangle his fingers in that silky blond hair.

She stilled beneath him.

Aw, had he done something wrong? He opened his eyes, peered into her face. Her eyes were closed, a peaceful smile spread across her lovely face. "Are you all right?"

"Splendid."

"You stopped moving. Did I hurt you?"

She opened one eye, peeked at him slyly. "I didn't want to come yet."

"You're already close."

"Very close. But I want to savor this moment."

He throbbed inside her and, impossibly, felt his shaft grow even harder, the urge to push toward climax so strong he could barely contain it.

Slowly, she started moving again, shifting her hips up to meet him. He closed his eyes, fought hard to keep things slow and easy.

Lost the bid.

An untamable force pushed him harder, faster, fiercer. He heard the roar of white noise inside his head. The room disappeared. Even the bed disappeared. Nothing existed but the two of them. He had not ever experienced such powerful pleasure, such blood-pumping rapture. It felt as if his skull had cracked open and his soul spilled out to surf a wave of ecstatic vibration.

Making love to Katie was more exhilarating than skydiving. More pulse-revving than driving a Lamborghini at top speed. More bone-thrilling than rafting class six whitewater rapids. His heart felt like a drum beaten by the most skillful shaman pounding out a primal tempo—primitive and elemental.

His mouth was hers. Her mouth was his. Her hands. His. On faces and cheeks. Shoulders and thighs. Buttocks and back. Feet and knees. All over kisses and caresses.

They were a never-ending circle of limbs and lips. She began where he ended and vice versa.

He heard a moan. Thought it was Katie. Realized, slightly embarrassed, that it was he. Losing it. Losing his last shred of control.

"More," she whispered fiercely. "More, Ryder. Give me more. Please, please."

He groaned. Loudly. He couldn't hold back any longer, and at her urging, quickened the pace and deepened the rhythm. He was unraveling. No going back now.

"Katie," he called her name. "Kate. I . . . I'm . . ."

She came undone, gasping, panting, squeezing him with her inner muscles, crying out his name on a long, keening sigh.

Her release rippled through him, a rocking wave of joy.

It was the most magnificent, stunning thing that had ever happened to him.

She gripped his shoulder, clinging to him like he was a life raft in a vast expanse of turbulent ocean, and cried tears of breathless pleasure.

Pride pushed against his rib cage. He was the one who'd dismantled her.

A grin lit up his face, quickly followed by the rumbling heat of the rocket-fueled orgasm blasting out of him. His chest muscles locked down tight, squeezing the air from his lungs. All the blood drained from his brain, leaving him dizzy and empty-headed.

Beautiful.

She was so damn beautiful.

He drifted in fuzzy euphoria of release, hugged Katie tightly in his arms. Nuzzled his face against her neck, smelled her scent mingled with his. Intoxicated. He was drunk on her.

He looked down into her face and she smiled up at him, sweet and blissful. The good girl next door again. And even though he was a grown man, at heart, with her, he was still that bad boy.

And the last thing he'd ever wanted to do was ruin her.

Aw shit, aw hell. How was he supposed to deal with this?

Don't panic.

She was smiling and he was smiling, and he felt fresh and clean and new. But that's where the fear came in. He wanted more of that feeling. Wanted more of her. The feeling was overpowering. Insane.

He rolled over, falling onto his back beside her, staring at the ceiling, trying to catch his breath and right his upside-down thinking.

"Wow." Katie exhaled audibly. "That was . . . you were . . . we were . . ."

"Dynamite?"

"Atomic."

"Nuclear."

"Thermonuclear."

"Radioactive."

"Okay, can't top that one." She leaned over to kiss along his chest, lazily swirling her index finger around his nipple.

"Baby, you top them all." Ryder bit his lip, surprised at how sappily happy he sounded, afraid of saying too much, of expressing some thought he hadn't fully explored yet.

"Really?" She laughed, and added, "I don't believe that for a second."

"Don't undersell yourself, woman. Best sex of my life."

Her face flushed pink, and her lips parted, softened. "Oh Ryder, you don't have to lie."

Shit, was she really that clueless to her own sexual power? He sat up, drew her into his lap.

Her eyes turned somber.

Things stumbled a bit, shifted. Their earlier synergy dissipated along with the afterglow, and he didn't know how to get that mood back.

"So," he said, waving at the clock on the bedside table. Five minutes after midnight. It was officially December twenty-fourth. "What are your plans for Christmas Eve?"

"Ryder . . ." Her voice was soft, sad. She scooted all the way across the bed from him, tugged the sheets up to hide her naked body.

"What?" He smiled brightly as if that could alter her tone and her feelings.

"You're not thinking there's going to be more—"

"No." He shook his head and his heart leapfrogged. "I would never assume that."

She looked disappointed, but said, "Of course not. I knew you weren't the kind of guy to make this anything more than what it was. That's why I wanted this with you. Precisely because I knew you weren't the kind of guy who gets hung up on emotions."

He made a face, blood back in his head again, pounding out a tomahawk of a headache. "Me? Pah, no way."

"Whew, good. Because for a minute there you had me believing you thought we were going to hang out and stuff. This isn't . . . it . . . can't . . . be that."

He wanted to ask her why the hell not, but the

earnest expression on her face answered the question for him. He was a hot lay. She'd tapped him because he was familiar. He was lucky to have gotten this much from her. He wasn't going to push or make demands.

"Tonight is tonight. Only," she expounded.

He made a derisive noise, lied. "I don't want more."

"You sure? Because the last thing I want to do is hurt you."

"C'mon, girl, I'm a big boy. I'm fine."

"You sure?"

"Rolling stone, babe. That's me."

"Always moving on." She sighed.

Damn, why did she sound so wistful when her words made it clear this was a one-time thing? Was she secretly on the fence? Or worried that he was feeling more for her than he should be?

Because he was. Screw him, he was feeling such big feelings he couldn't begin to catalogue them all. But damn if he was about to tell her that.

"Don't read anything into this," he said. "But I think you should spend the night. It's late, and a long drive to Malibu. Plus you had a Benadryl . . ."

"But I don't have anything to sleep in."

"I'll get you one of my T-shirts."

"No toothbrush either."

"I keep new ones on hand. For impromptu guests."

"Oh good."

Things were disintegrating right before his eyes. Going from the best night of his life to the most awkward.

"Well then," she said. "I accept your invitation to spend the night."

"It wouldn't hurt to toss the covers one more time," he said, treading cautiously. He didn't want to scare her off. "Since you're staying."

She paused. Considering. "I suppose I can agree to that."

"Then what are you doing way over on that side of the bed?" he asked.

She grinned, tumbled back into his arms, and things were easy again. But he didn't trust it. Not for a second.

Chapter 5

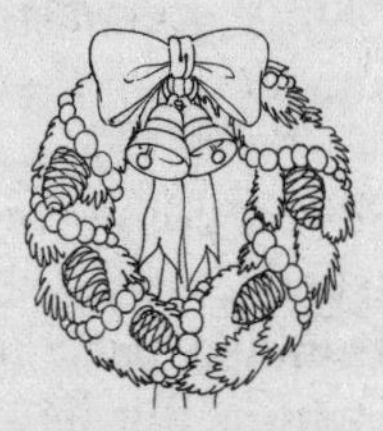

On Christmas Eve morning, Katie woke to a fried-egg sunrise—over easy, buttery, bright.

And wrong. Wrong on so many levels.

Primary among them, she was in bed with Ryder Southerland, and his big, thick arm was thrown around her waist.

She stared up at the ceiling, and a helpless smile overtook her face. Yes, last night had been amazing, and she was sweetly sore in the right places. But now it was morning, the dawn of reality, and consequences.

Time to move on before things got messy.

Except how did she do that with this slab of a man blocking her way? Aw, it was really cute how he was holding on to her like she meant something to him. Her heart flip-flopped.

Watch it. You're reading way more into this than he intended.

Guys like Ryder were allergic to commitment, and despite how she'd acted last night—everyone was entitled to cut loose once in a while—she wanted what her parents had, what her brothers and sister and their mates had.

True love. A home. Family. Commitment.

She was not ever going to have that with Ryder.

Crap! She needed to get out of here fast, before her imagination took root and that schoolgirl crush she'd had on him turned into something she could not handle.

Out of bed. Out of his house. Out of his life.

Best thing for them both.

Now for the tricky part, easing out from under that arm. She pressed her body as deeply into the mattress as she could and scooted, just an inch. Paused. Held her breath. Waited.

No reaction.

She wriggled a bit more. In the process, his hand shifted from her rib cage to her breast. At his touch, her nipples hardened instantly.

Oh boo, settle down, nipples. No more action for you.

Her recalcitrant nipples grew even tighter.

Fine. Get hard. Be frustrated. I'm still out of here.

Except Ryder made a possessive noise and pulled her up flush against his chest. His eyes were closed. His breathing hadn't changed. He appeared to be asleep.

But oops! At least part of him was awake. Jutting hard and proud against her fanny.

And damn her, she wanted to slip under the covers and stroke him fully awake with her tongue. How had she gotten herself into this fix?

A glass of wine. A glob of wasabi. Finding herself in her dream man's bedroom getting her breasts rubbed with ointment.

Oh yeah, that's how she'd gotten herself into this.

This was her first one-night stand, and she was uncertain of the protocol. One thing she knew for certain, she wanted to be gone before he woke up and they had to talk about what happened.

Talking, she feared, would kill the whole fantasy.

She wasn't scheduled to fly home until tomorrow, but she could not stay in LA one second longer. No siree. Time to make like Cinderella and get out of here before it all fell to ashes.

Who was she kidding? It was already ashes. The flames of their sexual fire had burned out, leaving only a cold, leaden knot of shame in her stomach.

It could so easily be kindled, whispered the part of her that had landed her here in the first place.

To what end? Sure, they could have sex again, but what after that? Last night, she thought he'd been about to ask her to spend Christmas Eve with him, but maybe she had imagined it.

She ached at the thought of staying. Briefly imagined building a life in Los Angeles, but couldn't dredge up how it would look beyond spending time in Ryder's bed. She was a small-town girl, deeply rooted in Twilight, Texas. Her family had lived there for generations. She couldn't conceive what life would be like without the constant support of her family and friends.

How had Ryder managed it?

She bit her bottom lip. He was so independent.

He'd never been the kind of man who needed anyone's permission or approval. He charted his own course, blazed his own trail.

Nope. He was not the man for her. No matter how much she might wish otherwise. They were just too different. She valued order and family and social commitment. He valued . . . well, she didn't really know what he valued.

Let it go. You already know what you should do and where you should be and it's not here.

And the clock was ticking. The longer she lingered the later it got, and the later it got the more likely he was to wake up. And if he woke up they would have to have that awkward conversation.

Up. She had to get up.

Inch by inch, she eased away from him, stopping when his breathing turned shallow, waiting until it deepened before moving again. Finally, she was free from the weight of his arm. She eased off the mattress. He murmured something.

She cringed, her back to him, and slowly swung her head around to see if she was busted.

His eyes were closed, his breathing deep, but he was still muttering. Talking in his sleep.

"Miss Priss," he mumbled, and smiled, and her heart fell to her knees. He looked so adorably boyish she could eat him right up.

She stayed rooted to spot, watching his face, battling a barrage of feelings—wistfulness, regret, guilt, tenderness—but underneath it all she felt a tiny flicker of joy that she would nourish for years.

From now on, whenever she thought of Ryder Southerland, this was the picture she would recall.

His body relaxed, a soft smile on his face, his hair ruffled, her nickname on his lips.

Her heart hopped from her knees right on up to her throat. "Merry Christmas, Ryder," she whispered. "Have a nice life."

Then Katie found her clothes, and got the hell out of there while she could still walk away.

Usually, great sex relieved pent-up tension and made him feel invincible. Typically, Ryder would jump from the bed, take a cold bracing shower, and go conquer the world.

But the morning after the most stupendous sex of his life with Katie, he ended up feeling like someone had dipped him in blue paint and left him to dry in a corner of the damp tropics.

Why?

He should be hollering like Tarzan, beating his chest and letting loose with an invigorating jungle cry. Instead, he was sulking like a teenager, staring into a bowl of milk-soaked cornflakes, watching them go limp and soggy.

What the hell?

No woman had ever slipped off after a night with him.

Eh, his ego had taken a pounding. That's what this gummy mood was all about. He'd had silly plans of making an omelet and serving her breakfast in bed. That's what he got for making plans and having expectations. He knew better, and yet he'd let himself get excited about the morning with Katie.

Shake it off. You had a great night. No need for anything more.

But he couldn't, which troubled him more than anything else. Even if she didn't live in Texas, and his work currently had him staying in California, they would make for a mismatched pair. She was the quintessential good girl.

And he'd been born to push boundaries.

Testing limits had gotten him more detention than anyone in the history of Twilight High, although his friend Joe had come in a close second, but it had also snagged him the head quarterback position both his junior and senior years.

Surprisingly, limit testing had come in handy during his job as military police in the army. Primarily because he knew just how those other boundary pushers ticked and he'd earned the moniker "snake charmer" because of his knack for defusing explosive situations.

But last night with Katie, that had been a boundary he shouldn't have pushed. "Got your feelings hurt because she ran out on you?" he muttered under his breath.

Yeah, kind of.

"Stop feeling sorry for yourself." He leveled a hard-edged stare at himself in the mirror. "You had a great night. Be grateful."

It was good she was gone. What a relief. No small talk. No polite chitchat necessary. He should be happy she slipped out. Yes indeed, best thing all the way around.

But his mind kept churning. Should he call her? At least make sure she was all right, and had made it back safely to where she was staying in Malibu?

He thought about how she'd switched homes

with someone like a heroine in a romantic Christmas movie, and smiled. Katie Cheek had moxie. He'd give her that. He reached for his phone to call her.

Leave her be.

Maybe a quick text instead? Just to make sure she'd gotten back to where she was staying in one piece.

But he didn't have her phone number. He could call Joe, but then he would have to explain why he wanted her number, and that would fly over like a lead balloon. How did you start that conversation?

Um, hey Joe, your sister and I hooked up for one wild night, and it sure was sweet. And once wasn't enough. So if you'd just shoot me her phone number . . .

Ryder scratched the back of his neck. He could already feel Joe's fist punching his face in. Joe was very protective of his baby sister. All Katie's brothers were.

Once, Joe had caught him eyeing Katie when she'd bent over in a pair of shorts, and he'd smacked Ryder hard on the shoulder. "Not cool, dude. That's my sister."

He'd violated an essential guy code. *Do not have a one-night stand with your best friend's kid sister.*

And if you do, for hell's sake, never let him find out.

Right. No calling Joe or Katie either.

Still, he couldn't help worrying about her. Call him an idiot, but he was going to pay for one of those telephone lookup services. He went to his computer and did a search on her.

"Dumb ass," he told himself as he waited for the search results. "She snuck out for a reason."

But that didn't stop him from calling her number. It rang several times and went to voice mail. Ryder started to leave a message, but couldn't figure out what to say that didn't sound desperate, and hung up.

At noon, he was to help deliver gifts and food to needy families through his volunteer work at a community center. That would keep his mind off Katie. Then he would drive Les Ketchum up to the singer's place at Big Bear for the man's holiday celebration. That would keep Ryder's mind off the fact that he had no one special to spend Christmas with.

He was headed out when the doorbell rang, and he found Clara Kincaid, his elderly next-door-neighbor, standing there with a box of Christmas cookies in her arms and a twinkle in her eye.

"Merry Christmas!" Clara thrust the cookies into his hands. "Pecan sandies. Your favorite." She paused and eyed him curiously. "You were leaving?"

"To deliver toys." He clutched the box of cookies in his hand, the only Christmas gift he was likely to get this year. It might sound sappy, but he liked the hell out of Clara and treasured their interactions. She was like the grandmother he'd never had.

"I'm still tickled by the thought of you playing Santa."

"Don't rub it in," he grumbled with a smile. "It's

what I get for agreeing to volunteer at my boss's charity event."

"I think it's sweet. Make sure you get someone to take your picture in the Santa suit." She made a motion of snapping a camera button.

"Over my dead body."

"Oh, you act so gruff." Chuckling, Clara went up on tiptoes that were clad in camouflage green footie socks to pinch his cheek. "But I know you're just a big old campfire marshmallow inside."

"Shh, don't let that get out." He pressed a fist against his lips, cradled the box of cookies in the elbow of his other arm. "People will be asking me to volunteer for all sorts of things."

"Ooh." Clara clapped her hands, her face luminescent. "You'd make an adorable Easter bunny. No, no . . ." She dissolved in peals of laughter. "The Tooth Fairy. I can just see you with shiny iridescent wings and a pink tutu."

"Go ahead. Make fun. Glad to be the butt of your joke if it lightens your day," he teased.

"Such a grand gesture." She sighed, pressed her palms together, and tucked them under her chin, and batted her eyelashes as if she was a besotted teenager. "I see why you have to beat the women off with a stick."

"Hey, I've never beaten women off—" He clamped his teeth together realizing she'd gotten him to say something unintentionally risqué. "Clara, you naughty thing."

She giggled.

"Behave," he teased her. "Or I'm not going to give you your Christmas gift."

She bounced exuberantly on the balls of her feet. "You got me a present?"

He turned to the stainless-steel coffee table, set down the box of cookies, and opened the drawer to pull out a box wrapped in silver foil and topped with a matching bow.

"I can't believe you bought me a gift. That is nice of you." Clara clapped her hands, reached for the package.

Watching her open it, Ryder felt his heart soften at the grandmotherly woman's glee. She'd taken him under her wing when he'd hit LA two years ago, and he'd grown fond of their daily conversations, usually taking place in the courtyard as he was coming or going from work.

"My, my!" Clara exclaimed. "What a beautiful shawl." She took the colorful garment from the box, flung it around her shoulders in a dramatic gesture. "You remembered me."

How could he forget her? Clara was the only person close enough to him to warrant a special present. The precious few others on his list got generic gift cards.

"I saw it in a shop window and I thought it looked like you." He shrugged like he hadn't spent four hours walking around a shopping center searching for the perfect gift.

"It is so *me*." Clara rubbed the soft material against her face and smiled as if he'd given her a pocketful of gold. She looked so happy Ryder felt a strange punch in his gut.

"If you don't like it you can—"

"Hush! I love it. Thank you so much."

"You're welcome." He shrugged again, slightly embarrassed. "Where are you spending the holidays?"

"Becca and Will are coming to get me. We're headed to Kyle and Kim's house. It will be my first time seeing the new baby," she said, referring to her latest great-grandchild, who had been born two weeks earlier.

"That should be fun."

"Every Christmas should have a baby in it," Clara hugged the shawl tighter around her, lowered her lashes, and looked at him speculatively. "So, are you going to be spending the evening with that lovely young woman who was here last night?"

Ryder startled. "Um . . ."

"She's the sweetest thing," Clara went on. "Not like those other women who've trotted through here."

His pulse jumped, and he pressed a palm to the nape of his neck. "You talked to Katie?"

"My, yes. She was passing by and saw that someone—probably Mina Jackson's Siamese—had knocked over my Christmas cactus. Darling girl righted the pot and scooped up the spilled dirt and patted back into place so gently. I spotted her and invited her in for coffee and some of those pecan sandies."

"She came in for coffee?" Ryder said, feeling slightly appalled, and not really sure why.

"She did, and she is so lovely. Really, Ryder, you must not let this one get away. She's special."

"I think it's too late for that."

"Why?" Clara bristled, drawing herself up tall. "What did you do to Katie?"

Wow. Katie must have really impressed his neighbor for her to throw him under the bus. "First-name basis with her?"

"She told me to call her Katie."

"When was that?"

"When she helped me change the lightbulb in the kitchen."

"If your lightbulb needed changing, why didn't you call me? That's what I'm here for, Clara."

"I know." She went up on her tiptoes again to pat his cheek. "But you've been so busy guarding Les Ketchum I didn't want to bother you."

"But you'll bother Katie?"

"I didn't ask. She offered when I told her it was out," Clara said mildly, but he could tell by the way she gave him the once-over that she wasn't pleased with him. "So what did you do to her?"

"I didn't do anything to her," he groused. "She's the one who did it to me."

Clara cocked her head like a pert parrot. "Oho? What did she do to you?"

"Ran out on me this morning without saying good-bye."

Clara hooted. "Shoe's on the other foot for once, huh?"

He shrugged, tried to look like he didn't care.

"I like her even more," Clara mused.

"Whose side are you on?" Ryder asked.

Clara drummed three fingers against her chin. "The side of love."

"You can stop hoping for that. Katie and I are . . ."

"What?" she prodded.

He shook his head. "Incompatible."

"Uh-huh." Clara nodded as if he was totally full of shit. "Whatever you say."

"You're patronizing me?"

"Nope. Just not contradicting you."

"But you don't agree?" Ryder shifted his weight, getting irritated. He needed to be on his way. They were waiting on Santa at the community center.

"I'd say any woman who gets you this hot and bothered is worth her weight in gold."

"Who says I'm hot and bothered?"

"You haven't stopped talking about her since I brought her up."

"Clara," he said, deepening his voice. "I'm not going to let you ruffle my feathers. Thanks so much for the cookies. I've got to head out."

"Sure, sure." Clara bobbed her silver head. "I know how you are. Don't like to face your feelings. I'll just scoot on out of your way. Thank you so much for the shawl. I love it." She patted his arm. "Please try to have a good Christmas, and give some consideration to exploring what's going on between you and Katie."

"There's nothing going on!"

Clara's smile turned naughty. "Then why are you yelling?"

"I'm not . . ." Purposefully, he regulated his voice to a whisper. ". . . yelling."

"Okay, but I still say you're a fool, Ryder Southerland, if you let a quality woman like Katie slip through your fingers. And let's face it. You're not getting any younger, champ, and in my opinion it's better not to wait until you're too old to throw a ball to your kid before you have one."

"I have no plans to have children." He ushered her toward the door.

Clara looked horrified. "Why not?"

"I'm not the paternal kind."

"Nonsense." She sank her hands on her hips and glared at him over the rim of her glasses. "You'd make an amazing father."

Because he had such a terrific role model? Right. "Clara, I've got to go."

"Children are God's greatest blessings."

"I'm sure they are." He shooed her out the door. "For other people."

"Oh Ryder, Ryder, Ryder." She clicked her tongue. "Whatever am I going to do with you? When you have kids yourself you'll finally understand just how much love they bring."

"Have a merry Christmas." He waggled his hand at her.

"Okay, I'll stick a pin in it for now, but this conversation is *not* over."

"Merry Christmas," he repeated, locking the door behind them.

Clara spread her arms, to draw the shawl more tightly around her. "You too. Although I doubt you will, since you're working."

"I like working."

"I know. You like it too much. That's the problem."

"With the way you nag me, I swear, you could be my real grandmother."

"Oh no, dear. If I were your grandmother, I'd

box your ears for not spending the holidays with Katie."

"She has family to be with."

"Exactly," Clara said, waved a hand over her shoulder, and disappeared back into her apartment.

Clara's parting quip rang in Ryder's ears as he dressed up as Santa and delivered toys to underprivileged families. He had no one special to spend Christmas with. Although that had been true for the last twelve years, somehow, this year, it bothered him.

When he got back home, he tried texting Katie using the phone number he'd looked up.

She didn't reply.

Face it. She made it clear she didn't want future contact.

Or, here was a thought. She was off enjoying Christmas Eve with other people and not near her phone.

But he'd made an attempt. He wasn't going to bother her again.

He poured himself a whiskey, plunked down in a chair at the window, and watched his neighbor's Christmas tree lights blink, blink, blink. Finally, he swallowed the remainder of the whiskey in one big swallow, picked up the phone, and called again.

This time, he did leave a message on her voice mail. "Have yourself a merry Christmas, Katie Cheek," he mumbled, and hung up.

CHAPTER 6

Twilight, Texas

December 1, one year later

Out on the streets of Twilight, the annual Dickens on the Square parade came up Ruby Street to the town square, a procession of favorite characters—Scrooge, the Christmas ghosts, one-shoed Miss Havisham in her bedraggled wedding gown, Tiny Tim, the Artful Dodger, Mrs. Gamp. With the festival, Christmas in Twilight officially began. Three weeks of nonstop celebrating.

Toying with the snowman pendant on her necklace, Katie stared out the window of the top floor office above Ye Olde Book Nook on the west side of the square and remembered the year she played Little Dorrit, and Ryder Southerland had saved her from getting crushed under the wheels of Santa Claus's float.

She'd been playing her part, Little Dorrit in rags, when she'd seen her brother Joe coming out of Rinky-Tink's ice cream parlor, with his new friend, a tall, black-haired boy who rode the bus to school and looked like he didn't give a damn what anyone thought of him.

They were eating ice creams cones, and it struck Katie as wrong. Her sense of fairness ruffled. Mama had said they couldn't have any snacks, it would ruin their dinner, and here was Joe licking away.

Incensed, Katie had sunk her hands on her hips, forgetting that she was supposed to be Little Dorrit, and jaywalked right across the street to address the injustice. So intent was she on her indignation that she didn't notice the float turning onto the square off Ruby Street.

But Ryder noticed.

His face had gone white as a Christmas ghost, and the next thing she knew, he'd thrown his ice cream cone over his shoulder and was tearing into the middle of the road to shove her out of the way of the Santa float, complete with a giant bobble-head Rudolph and his flashing red nose.

She ended up on her back in the gutter, staring up into Ryder's green eyes, gaping like a landed guppy because he'd knocked the air from her lungs.

He stared at her somberly, but there was no judgment in his eyes about her dumb-assedry. Her gramps's preferred terminology when anyone did something foolish.

"You okay?" he'd asked, just as he had when

he'd knocked her down last year at the museum gala. Seemed the man had a habit of tackling her.

Truth was, sleeping with Ryder last year had changed her. She dreamed of him. A lot. And not just at night.

Sometimes she'd be in the midst of organizing a client's space, and hot waves of memory would flood her body, spreading up from her pelvis to her stomach, chest, and neck. Settling at last in her head, a mental orgasm pushing loads of feel-good-hormones through her brain and blood.

Always connected to thoughts of Ryder.

If anyone noticed a change in her, she would smile pertly and shake her head, the movements setting off widening circles of intense pleasure reverberating throughout her cranium along with a joyous throb that pulsed to the beat of Ryder's name.

It was freaky and disconcerting and scarily enjoyable.

Reliving the orgasmic waves that had overcome her after the night they made love—sometimes it happened when she was shopping at the grocery, stopping at a red light, thumbing through her outgoing mail while standing in line at the post office.

She tried to suppress it. Shutting down her thoughts every time his name popped brightly in her head like a neon sign. But then hot frustration would swamp her womb, intense and heavy, and her pulse would pound at a terrifying clip.

What was happening to her? She had no word for it. Could not define it.

The problem kept her awake at night, her body lighting up as she lay in bed, her mind helplessly wandering to thoughts of Ryder. It was as if by making love with him, she'd plugged into a powerful electrical current that she could not unplug from, even when their bodies were separated.

What craziness was this? What was the cure?

When it happened at night, she came utterly, completely awake. Nothing could coax her eyes closed. Not music. Not warm milk . . . and later, not a glass of wine. One phrase kept rotating through her head.

I am alive!

She'd been asleep for so long. Moving through life without really planning anything, allowing the wants and desires of other people to push her this way and that.

Until California.

And Ryder.

Katie sighed, fingered her lips, and turned away from the window and the memory.

"What's that smug grin all about?" Sesty Langtree asked. "Plotting on how you're going to body check the other women at Gabi and Joe's wedding so you can snag the bouquet?"

"Huh?" Katie blinked at her office mate. "Nooo." She shook her head. "I have no interest in getting married."

"Ever?"

"Not in the foreseeable future. No candidates on the horizon."

"Hmm," Sesty mused, but didn't elaborate.

"No hmm. There's no hmming."

Sesty was married to retired NASCAR driver Josh Langtree. Since their businesses dovetailed, Katie and Sesty had decided to save money and rent office space together on the Twilight town square. Sesty was an event planner, and over the course of the past twelve months, after returning from her house swap adventure in LA, Katie had been steadily building a reliable reputation as a professional organizer.

"No always-a-bridesmaid-never-a-bride blues?" Sesty asked. "How many times have you been a bridesmaid, by the way?"

Katie stopped to count it off, ran out of fingers. "A dozen I think. Maybe it was thirteen. But don't forget I was almost a bride once myself."

"Oh spit." Sesty slapped a palm over her mouth. "I'm such an idiot. I was teasing. I didn't think about Matt . . . Just tell me to shut my big gob."

"It's okay," Katie reassured her. "It's been two years. I'm at peace."

"Time heals all wounds?"

Katie shrugged. Perhaps it did, but a large part her acceptance of Matt's passing had come from the personal journey she'd been on since last Christmas and that wild night of unbridled sex with Ryder.

That night had brought her to the realization that before Ryder, she had no idea what great sex was. Maybe she and Matt had not been the best fit after all. Maybe, if he hadn't been killed, they might not have made it to the altar anyway.

It was a lot to digest, and the understanding had changed her.

This past year had been one of empowerment and discovery. She'd started her own business, sold the yurt and small farm Matt had left her, bought her own cottage three blocks off the square, and agreed to be Gabi's maid of honor for her and Joe's upcoming December wedding.

Of course she'd agreed to the maid of honor thing before she'd known Joe was going to ask Ryder to be his best man. Or that Ryder would accept.

She'd been fretting about it for months. In a couple of weeks, Ryder would be coming home to Twilight for the wedding.

Just thinking about seeing him again had Katie shifting restlessly in her seat. She'd left things a bit messy between them, slipping off as she had and not returning his text or calls. Ghosting wasn't normally her style, but with Ryder she had no self-control, as clearly evidenced by their night together.

But when she'd played his message last year, and heard his husky voice wishing her merry Christmas, and sounding so darn lonely, she almost broke down and called him back.

At the time she told herself not returning his call was the best way to make a clean break. It *would* have been a clean break except for Gabi and Joe getting engaged and insisting on having their best friends in attendance.

Now she had an encounter to dread.

Would Ryder make a thing of seeing her again? What if he made a thing of it? He was scheduled to be in town in time for the bachelor party, which was the weekend before the wedding.

A week. He'd be in Twilight for a week.

All she had to do was get through the week of the wedding, and then Ryder would go back to guarding celebrity bodies in LA, and all would be well.

The door opened, and their shared assistant, Jana Gerard, bopped inside. Jana paused, sank her hands on her hips, glanced around the room, and swiveled her head back and forth.

"What?" Sesty prompted.

Jana paused for dramatic effect. She was a willowy brunette, but the ends of her hair were dyed a shocking color of neon yellow and braided in creative designs. A zoo full of tattoos decorated her body—parrots, cheetahs, zebras, chickens, snakes, an elephant. Today, she wore red leggings, a black pleather mini-skirt, tie-dye T-shirt that couldn't begin to compete with the tattoos, and a faux fur white jacket. She had multiple piercings—ears, nose, tongue, eyebrow—and loved shocking people.

At first, Jana's appearance had startled Katie and put her off. It wasn't so much the tattoos and piercing and vibrant hair as the mess of Jana's overall look. Chaotic. Disorderly. Unharmonious.

But now that she knew Jana, and understood that she was not only an amazing assistant but also a goodhearted person who used her appearance as a shield, Katie hardly noticed her looks anymore.

"You two." Jana's head bobbed, and the expression on her face said she'd written them off as lost causes. "Both of you so perfect with your organized files and your up-to-date spreadsheets and your color-coded everything. Makes me want to come over there and toss your things."

"You wouldn't dare," Sesty said, hunching protectively over her desk.

"You're right." Jana sighed. "I'd have to clean it up, and if I didn't put everything back just-so, it would drive you wacky. Although . . ." She pointed a finger at Sesty. "I must say you have loosened up a lot since you and Josh got hitched. Regular sex agrees with you. Keep it up."

Jana turned toward Katie, hands planted on her hips again. "You, on the other hand, seem to be vying for organizational sainthood."

Katie smiled, not letting Jana get to her. "Tidy space, tidy mind."

"At least Sesty now has photographs on her desk and plants in her window and, shocker, I see paper clips mixed up with banker clips in the holder. And OMG, the rug is slightly askew. Take a lesson, Cheek. Relax. Get laid. You'll be happier. Right, Sesty?"

"I'm perfectly happy," Katie said mildly, despite the strange tension running along the bottom of her stomach.

"Uh-huh. Sure you are."

"I am."

"Jana does have a point," Sesty piped up from her desk on the opposite side of the open room. "You can't always be in control of everything all the time. Believe me, I've tried."

Oh, but she wasn't in control. Not by a long shot. Katie thought about the last time she'd had sex. A year ago. With Ryder. And shivered.

Hard.

Sesty and Jana both stared at her.

"What?" Katie said, hearing a defensive note in her voice. "I'm cold."

"Or thinking about all the sex you're not getting." Jana laughed.

"Could we stop talking about sex, please?" Katie asked.

"Because you're not getting any—"

"Do we have any new business to discuss?" Katie gave Jana a pointed that's-enough stare.

Jana liked to stir things up, but she knew when it was time to zip it and get down to work. She reached for her notebook computer, turned it on, and came to sit in the white swivel office chair parked in front of Katie's desk.

"We got a call from Wanda over at home health," Jana said. "They have a patient whose house is so cluttered they can't go into the home to take care of him until the place is cleaned up. The doctor is planning on releasing him from the hospital on Monday, so they're in a time crunch. They want you to come wave your magic wand and make it all better."

Katie sucked in a deep breath, held it a long moment. Katie and Wanda both volunteered together at the free clinic on Thursdays. A call from home health services meant only one thing. A hoarder. Katie hated to judge, but working with hoarders wasn't easy. It took not only great organizational skills, but also exceptional people skills. Plus it didn't hurt to have a degree in psychology.

"Hey," Jana said, reading reluctance in Katie's silence. "I told them your schedule was pretty full just in case you wanted to wriggle out of this one."

"Thanks." Katie let out a sigh.

"But they said the place is so filthy they can't allow the patient to go into that mess with an open wound. He's a diabetic with complications. It was all TMI for me." Jana made a face, wriggled her hands like she was shaking off mud. "But that's the deal. If it doesn't get cleaned up, he'll have to go to a rehab facility, and his health insurance might not cover it."

"Did you ask them to contact Dr. Finley?" Katie asked. "This might be more of mental health issue than lack of organizational skills. Get the patient some help for the hoarding behavior, and hire a cleaning crew."

"Wanda already talked to Dr. Finley. She referred her to you. The hoarding apparently came from the patient's wife. She recently passed away, and he just didn't know how to get started clearing it all out."

The second Jana said that, Katie realized who the home health patient was, and the bottom dropped out of her gut. There was only one person she knew of in Twilight who had recently lost a wife with hoarding tendencies.

Jax Southerland.

Ryder's estranged father.

"Call Wanda back and tell her unfortunately our schedule is booked. Refer her to Lisa Allbright in

Jubilee. I know Lisa will sometimes drive to Hood County for referrals," Katie instructed.

"I thought you were keeping your work schedule light during December. You should have openings," Sesty said from her side of the room. "In fact, don't you only have the one job this month? Helping Marva Bullock downsize?"

Katie smiled, sunshine and rainbows, and in the perkiest voice she could muster answered, "Yes, and I want to keep my schedule light. Maid of honor duties and all."

"It's not like you to run away from a challenge." Sesty tapped her chin with the end of her ink pen. "What's up?"

"I need time. You know how nutty my family gets about Christmas. And Gabi and Joe's wedding, as if Christmas isn't busy enough . . ."

All true. But mostly because Ryder was coming home for the wedding, and under the circumstances, the last thing she wanted was to be working for his dad. It was bad enough they had to see each other at wedding functions. She was not compounding things by agreeing to organize the Circle S. Even though she could probably be in and out before Ryder got to town.

"Excuses, excuses," Sesty said. "I think you're nervous to be that close to Ryder. Hanging out in the home he grew up in."

"Why would I be nervous about that?" Katie kept her voice bland, but her pulse was hopping like crazy.

"I don't know." Sesty pushed back her chair. "But every time Ryder's name comes up you get antsy."

"Antsy? I don't know what you mean."

Sesty nodded at her. "You chew on the cap of your pen."

Katie jerked the pen cap out of her mouth.

"And," Jana added, "your spine goes all stiff as if someone jammed a stick up it."

Katie slumped.

"Not to mention you shake your foot like a paint mixer." Sesty pointed.

Dammit. Katie pushed down on her knee to still her shaking foot.

"What did happen between you and Ryder in LA last year?" Jana asked.

"Um," Katie said, ignoring Jana's question. "You two might not have anything to do today except overanalyze my body language, but Marva is waiting on me. Catch you later."

"You can run but you can't hide," Jana taunted as Katie picked up her purse and rushed out the door, wishing like hell she hadn't told them she'd seen Ryder last Christmas when she was in LA.

Luckily, she hadn't been dumb enough to tell her friends what had happened between them. *That* was none of their business. But clearly, her body language had given her away. She'd have to be more careful, especially when Ryder was in town.

At the idea of seeing him again her stomach weakened and her knees wobbled. Outside on the street, she stopped to take a deep breath. Last year, after his call wishing her merry Christmas—which she'd never answered back—she'd never heard from him again.

And that was good. Very good.

But then darn it all, Joe had asked Gabi to marry him and she'd said yes, and Katie had agreed to be maid of honor before she learned Joe had asked Ryder to be the best man.

Buck up. You can handle this. It's just a week.

All she had to do was stay as far away from Ryder as possible for the week leading up to the wedding. Yes, they'd probably see each other every day over the course of that week, but she would make sure never to be in a room alone with him.

And while Sesty and Jana might suspect something, they didn't know anything for sure. It was up to her to play her cards close to the vest, and maintain a poker face.

Marva Bullock answered the door on the second ring of the bell. She smiled at Katie, but it was a tight smile, full of tension and worry. "Is it ten o'clock already?"

"I'm a few minutes early."

"No worries, come in, come in." Distractedly, Marva waved Katie into her living room stacked high with moving boxes. The new construction was a replica Craftsman-style house, about half the size of the Tudor that Marva and her husband, G.C., were moving out of. It was an adorable cottage, but it didn't begin to accommodate all of the Bullocks' belongings. Something had to go.

With her rich brown skin, ebony hair plaited in cornrows, and athletic body, Marva, the principal at Twilight High School, looked a decade younger than her fifty-five years. Her two children, Ashton and Kiley, were grown and gone, and G.C. had recently retired from his job as an electrician.

"Lots of change going on." Marva shook her head, and sank her hands on her hips. "I know downsizing was the right thing to do, but I can't shake the emotional attachment to the house the kids grew up in. I miss it so much already."

"Is it the house you miss?" Katie asked. "Or Ashton and Kiley?"

"Both. I can't really separate them. We brought Ashton home from the hospital our first week in the old house." Marva swiped away a tear with the back of her hand. "I didn't expect to feel so mowed down. I know moving is the right thing, but it's tearing my heart in two."

"Letting go of the past opens you up to the present moment," Katie said, thinking of the calm place she'd come to after Matt's death.

"How did you get so wise so young?"

"I'm repeating what my mother told me when I was grieving Matt. I'm not saying I'm any good at taking my own advice."

"Letting go feels like a betrayal." Marva ran a hand over a box filled with mementoes. "Of the memories our family made in that house."

"You'll make new memories here." Katie moved to a box marked "Pots and Pans." She picked up the heavy crate and headed toward the kitchen.

Marva trailed after her. "I know, but . . ."

Katie set down the box, turned back to Marva, and gave the woman her full attention. She knew moving into a new home was in the top ten most powerful life stressors. She'd gone through the same emotions last year when she'd sold the yurt and bought her first house.

"I feel . . ."

"What?" Katie prompted.

"Blank. Empty. The remarkable thing about my feelings is that they are so inconspicuous. Like white paint."

Katie glanced around at the white kitchen, at the house full of boxes that as of yet had no personality. A house might just be wood and nails, brick and mortar, but symbolically, a house represented the place where you belonged.

Or didn't.

For some reason, an image of Ryder popped into her head. He was a man without a home. He had an apartment in LA, a place to lay down his head at night, but that's all it was.

Katie nibbled her bottom lip and wondered what that felt like. Never putting down roots. Never really belonging anywhere. Did he, like Marva in her current upheaval, feel blank and empty? She shivered.

"Are you cold?" Marva asked. "I can turn up the heat. Or make us some tea."

"I'm good. Ready to get down to work." Katie rolled up her sleeves. She picked up a small flat box with "Junk Drawer" written on it. "What's in here?"

"The contents of my old junk drawer."

"Well, we'll fix that." Katie smiled. "Find a place for every item in it and, voilá, no need for a junk drawer."

"Honey," Marva said, placing a hand on Katie's shoulder. "Everyone needs a junk drawer."

"But a junk drawer defeats the purpose of a place for everything and everything in its place."

"But it does have a place." Marva laughed. "The junk drawer."

Katie took a deep breath. How to say this without ruffling feathers. "Having one junk drawer sounds good in theory, but inevitably, it leads to junk drawer creep."

"Okay, I'll bite. What is junk drawer creep?"

"The junk drawer will migrate, and multiply. You'll have two drawers, then three, and before you know it, all the drawers are junk drawers."

"I see what you're getting at," Marva said.

"You do?"

"Yes, and I still want one junk drawer."

Feeling frustrated, Katie let her shoulders sag. "But why if you know it can lead to junk drawer creep?"

"To remind me that life is messy, and that I'm not perfect and it's okay to let go just a little."

That notion went against everything Katie stood for, so she just smiled and nodded and said, "Maybe I will have that cup of tea."

"Great." Marva moved toward the single-cup coffee/tea maker on the counter, the only small appliance that had been unpacked. "What kind of tea would you like?" Marva spun a carousel rack of tea pods. "Peppermint, chamomile, Earl Grey."

"Chamomile," Katie said.

Marva took her time, getting out a lemon and

slicing it neatly. Pouring cream into a special little pitcher, and arranging the napkins just so.

"Are you stalling, Marva?" Katie asked.

"That obvious?" Marva laughed. "This is such a challenge. Indulge me?"

"Of course." Katie nodded, and sat down at the kitchen table.

Marva bustled around, and a few minutes later slid across from Katie with two steaming mugs of tea and a plate of cookies. "Store-bought," she apologized. "No time for baking."

"I love store-bought cookies." Katie crunched one of the crisp ginger snaps. "Mmm."

"How could you love store-bought when your mom is such an extraordinary baker?"

"That's probably *why* I like store-bought. They were forbidden in our house." Katie laughed. "I used to sneak Oreos into my bedroom in my schoolbag."

"Forbidden fruit does hold its appeal," Marva said. "Speaking of forbidden fruit, how are you feeling about Ryder Southerland coming home for Joe's wedding?"

Katie schooled her features to remain neutral and nonreactive. She wasn't sure she pulled it off. "I have no feelings at all. Why do you ask?"

"Didn't you used to have a crush on him when you were teenagers?"

"How many kids have you seen come and go through Twilight High?" Katie asked, answering a question with a question to steer the topic away from her puppy dog crush on Ryder. Ancient history, and weren't they just talking about letting go of the past?

"Heavens." Marva sipped her tea. "It must be thousands."

"All those kids and you can still remember who had a crush on whom?"

Marva cocked her head. "I'm pretty sharp, but you're right. I don't remember everyone. But I could never forget Ryder."

Katie leaned forward, careful to make sure her knee wasn't bobbing and her spine wasn't overly stiff, nothing to give herself away. "Why not?"

"He caused me more trouble than any other kid in my tenure at Twilight High."

"No kidding?" Katie cradled the teacup in her palms.

Marva's lips tipped into a soft smile. "Although your brother Joe was a close second. Those two hellions running together were a principal's nightmare. But Ryder was much harder to corral than your brother because he didn't have a stable home life. With Joe, all I had to do was pick up the phone, and your parents would whip him into shape."

Katie had not ever considered Ryder from the point of view of authority figures. No matter what trouble he got into, she'd always been one hundred percent on his side.

"It's not that Ryder was a bad kid," Marva continued. "Not deep down. Not at heart where it counts. But he was wild and undisciplined and acting out. He pushed every envelope, broke every rule, defied every edict. Stubborn young bull."

Katie didn't remember him that way. She remembered him taking up for the underdog and being fiercely loyal to her family. And she remembered him with unruly hair and a proud jut to his chin, fists clenched at his sides, ready to fight against whatever injustice the world dished out.

In those moments, he looked so alone that the earth mother inside her wanted nothing more than to draw him into her arms and promise him everything was going to be okay.

But she hadn't dared. Not only had she been a shy ugly duckling, but also Ryder had scared her. He was the kind of boy who cussed and got into trouble on a daily basis and carried a sharp knife.

And yet, a part of her couldn't help feeling they had a special bond because he'd saved her life, pushing her out of the way of that float. Whenever he winked at her and called her squirt or Miss Priss, she felt as if she could conquer the world.

"Such a shame." Marva clicked her tongue.

"About what?" Katie set her teacup on the table, her palms still warm from the heat of the liquid.

"You haven't heard?" Marva's eyebrows spiked up on her forehead.

A prickle of sensation crawled the back of Katie's neck. "Heard what?"

"Jax has to sell the Circle S."

Katie put a hand against her mouth. "Oh, that's a shame. What's happened?"

Marva scooted closer and lowered her voice, as if by speaking more softly she could blunt the news. "Jax is completely broke, worse than broke. He's over a hundred thousand dollars in credit card debt."

"How did that happen?"

"This is all hearsay, and I probably shouldn't be repeating it, but from what I've heard, Twyla kept the books. And after she died, Jax discovered the woman had over eighty credit cards and she'd been juggling them to pay the bills each month, writing advance checks on one credit card to pay off another, and it just kept spiraling. On top of that, he's got both his and Twyla's medical bills."

Marva paused a moment to let it sink in, then finished with, "Looks like Ryder was right all along."

"Right about what?"

Marva drew back, studied Katie for a long moment. "You don't know why Jax kicked Ryder out of the house when he was sixteen?"

"I thought it was because Ryder and Twyla couldn't get along, and Ryder called her a disrespectful name."

"That's true, but there was a lot more to it than that."

It was Katie's turn to lean forward. She rested her elbows on the table and her chin in her open palms. She'd heard the rumors about Ryder's estrangement from his father, but he never spoke of it, and bristled when other people brought it up. So no one talked about it in his presence, and her parents refused to let anyone gossip about him behind his back.

Marva lowered her eyelids. "I'm only telling you this because it might shed some light on Ryder's past for you now that he's coming back to town and you'll see him at the wedding."

Katie nodded. Part of her wanted to ask Marva to not tell her, but her curiosity got the better of her and she sat there listening.

"I heard that Twyla accused Ryder of taking out credit cards in her name and running them up with purchases, and for stealing two thousand dollars she kept stashed around the place," Marva said.

Yes, Katie had heard accusations that Ryder was a thief, but she hadn't believed them for a second. He was the most honorable man she'd ever known, and she knew a lot of honorable men.

"I'm ashamed to say I believed Twyla." Marva shook her head. "But now it looks like she made Ryder the scapegoat for her uncontrollable spending sprees."

Katie's heart broke for Ryder. Wrongly accused. Thrown out of the house at sixteen. Estranged from his father for the past thirteen years.

Her heart broke for the senior Southerland as well. Caught between his wife and his son. She imagined Ryder's father was in a rough place emotionally, wrestling with tough revelations, dealing with the fact that Twyla had been lying all along and he'd alienated his son because of her lies.

"Jax is going to need a lot of community support. The Circle S has been in his family for four generations. Not to mention how much help he's going to need cleaning the place up to sell it."

Katie's cell phone rang. She reached to turn it off since she was in a conversation with Marva. But Marva waved a hand. "Go ahead and answer it. I'm getting another cup of tea. Do you want a refill?"

Shaking her head, Katie answered the cell phone to the honey-dipped voice of Wanda Wright, the home health coordinator. Wanda greeted her with an exuberant "Hello, Katie, it's Wanda."

"Hi," Katie said, wishing she and Wanda didn't know each other so well from their volunteer work.

"I know you're busy and I hate to pester, but I took Jana's advice and called Lisa Allbright. But she's out of town and we're desperate to get at least a few rooms in a livable condition before Jax Southerland is dismissed from the hospital on Monday."

"This is Thursday. There's no way I can sort through an entire house by Monday."

"Just the living room, kitchen, master bedroom, and bathroom," Wanda bargained. "We've got a cleaning service over there now, and they're wading through the kitchen, but there's just so much stuff. Besides the obvious trash, we need someone to comb through the junk and figure out what can be thrown or given away and what needs to be kept and where to put it."

Katie tightened her grip on the cell phone.

"You're our last hope," Wanda said. "Is there any way you can take on this project?"

Katie glanced up to see Marva standing in the doorway watching her with a just-do-it expression on her face.

She did love a challenge and this project sounded like it could be her biggest task to date. Besides, it was still two weeks before Ryder came back to Twilight. With her crew, and the parameters, she should be in and out of the Circle S by Monday.

"Please," Wanda begged. "I'll owe you big-time."

How could she refuse? This was Ryder's dad, after all. And even though he'd treated Ryder shabbily, the man was his father. He was sick and needed help.

"All right," Katie agreed. "I'll do it."

But as she hung up, she couldn't help wondering if she'd made a big mistake.

CHAPTER 7

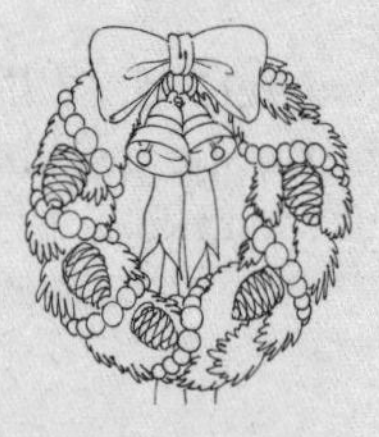

Homecoming.

The word had a nice ring to it.

Homecoming.

The word was supposed to stir good memories of the place where you'd been hatched and spent your formative years.

Homecoming.

The word suggested forgiveness, acceptance, unity.

But for Ryder? Not so much.

The second his Harley hit the Twilight city limits sign, his lungs squeezed tight, and the air tasted thin, and all he could think about was how good it had felt to drive in the opposite direction thirteen years ago when he'd fled to the army.

He could have said no when Joe had asked him to be his best man. Should have told him no. Why hadn't he told him no?

Ryder cruised the main drag of Ruby Street that led to the town square, and his gut kicked. He saw folks fishing off the pier, a woman in a pink tracksuit walking a greyhound puppy, a kid struggling to fly a Batman kite in the whipping wind. But he didn't see what he really wanted to see.

Searching.

He was searching for something, and it wasn't until he saw a shapely blonde and his heart leapfrogged into his throat that he understood why he was scanning his surroundings so intently.

He was on the lookout for Katie.

The blonde turned her head to laugh at something the man she was with had said, and disappointment contracted Ryder's stomach. No. Not Katie.

Fool.

Yes, he knew that. But it didn't stop him from feeling disappointed.

Some kids standing on the corner eyed his bike, but no one waved. He didn't expect them to. Few would recognize him. He'd changed a lot in thirteen years. No longer that punk kid with a two-by-four-sized chip balanced on his shoulder.

He lifted a hand, waved. People waved back.

Ryder smiled. Maybe coming home wouldn't be as bad as he feared.

Yeah? Who was he kidding?

He'd learned from reading the Twilight, Texas, Web site that his stepmother had died. No one had called him to let him know that Twyla had passed away. Not Joe. Not Katie. Not even his father.

A familiar feeling of isolation washed through him, but Ryder didn't indulge in self-pity. He was a man of action, not reflection.

But driving down the streets he hadn't traversed

in thirteen years stirred more feelings and a flash flood of memories he couldn't resist or control.

The town, which had been such a straitjacket in his formative years, now seemed quaint and receptive in maturity. As a teen, he'd loathed Twilight, vowing never to return once he got out. It symbolized everything that was rigid and suffocating about growing up in a small community.

And he'd kept his promise.

Until now.

He passed the Sweetheart Park, and the Sweetheart Tree with the names of lovers carved into the trunk of the old pecan. His name was carved there too, but he hadn't been the one doing the carvings. Several of the young women he'd dated had taken a pocketknife to the thick bark and cut out tributes to the fickleness of young love.

"Amanda & Ryder."

"Jodi loves Ryder."

"Kristy + Ryder = forever."

"Darcy and Ryder XOXO."

Everyone knew your business because it was right there on the skin of the tree for all the people to see. No privacy. No keeping things to yourself. No freedom to simply be. Someone was always weighing in and offering unsolicited advice on how you should live your life.

Ryder zipped past the fountain of the town's founders, Jon Grant and Rebekka Nash, clasping each other in a forever embrace. On Halloween one year, he and Joe had TP'd the statue, and that had caused an uproar among the town council.

Passing through the place where he'd grown up,

Ryder was struck by how little things had changed. Same yellow-white twinkle lights outlining the historic stone buildings on the square. Same mistletoe hung from the quaint streetlamps, inviting lovers to kiss beneath them. Same banners in the window advertised the Christmas Tour of Homes. Same holiday music blaring over the outdoor speaker system, serenading customers as they shopped.

Visitors walked the streets, peering into store windows, stopping at kiosks, or buying snacks from street vendors. Signs urged tourists to snag tickets to *Rudolph the Red-nosed Reindeer* at the Twilight Playhouse. Encouraged them to pluck a name from the Sweetheart Cherub Tree and make a needy child's Santa dreams come true. Advised them not to miss the cowboy Christmas concert at the local musical venue.

The environment made him inexpressibly nostalgic for the kind of idyllic childhood he had not had. Something about the unchanging sameness stirred up personal memories, and set them to whirling despondently like fake snow in a Christmas globe.

Then, at the corner of Ruby and Market streets, in a building that was reportedly haunted by the ghost of Jesse James, sold John Wayne memorabilia, and housed an old soda fountain at the back of the store, he caught a glimpse of his reflection in the long plate-glass window.

A lone man in a black leather jacket straddling a vintage Harley, and wearing mirrored sunglasses that cast him as mysterious and untouchable. A man apart. Separate. Distant.

He no longer belonged here. Had he ever? He might be a fourth-generation Twilightite, but he'd forever felt like an outsider.

Not forever, whispered a voice at the back of his brain, *but ever since Mom died.*

His heart thumped hollowly in his chest, an echoing rhythm that sent tingling ripples of self-doubt vibrating through his cells. He hadn't called ahead. His plan was just to show up, but now that he was in the process of executing the plan it felt disjointed and wrong, catawampus and inappropriate.

The split-second snapshot of his reflection, wearing the bad-boy suit of armor the town had branded him with all those years ago, rattled him. Stole his breath and left him wondering who he was and questioning why the hell he was here.

Joe's wedding, remember? And to check on his dad after finding out about Twyla.

Oh yeah, those reasons. Reasons loaded with emotional landmines. Honestly, no shit, he'd rather be back in the sandbox of the Middle East. At least there he knew where he stood. Everything was enemy.

Here? Friends could be enemies. Enemies could be unexpected allies. Nothing was as it seemed.

Ryder's fingers tightened on the handlebars.

This wasn't going to be fun. No fun at all.

But then Katie came to mind, and damn if he didn't smile. Talk about fun. Now there was a playground, and what a sweet diversion from his issues with his father.

You can't just pick up where you left off. She

never returned your call. She's not interested. Drop it.

What if she'd never gotten the message? What if he had the wrong cell phone number? What if she had just been waiting for him to call, and assumed he was the one who wasn't interested?

Ryder shook his head, shook off the past. He wasn't the type to overthink things. Why was he doing it now? She'd made it clear she didn't want anything more to do with him. He could handle seeing her again, and he could keep his mitts off her. He would. Because it was what she wanted.

But what if she'd changed her mind? What if she missed him as much as he missed her?

If that were the case, she would have contacted you. Put Katie out of your mind. You're here to see your father first. Wedding second. Leave her be. She's got her life and you've got yours and you two will never be compatible. Not for the long term. Not possible.

Ryder slowed as he passed through the center of town, and pulled over when he reached the marina. Unlike the rest of Twilight, this area had changed. A conference center and hotel had been built since he was here. A boardwalk constructed. Picnic tables and benches added.

Shutting down the engine, he sat on the bike, looking out across the lake, unsuccessfully trying to stifle the conflicting voices in his head. The thoughts had followed him all the way from California, through the Arizona desert and the mountains of New Mexico. Now here he was back in Twilight and still feeling rudderless. And he hated it.

Stop thinking about Katie, you've got bigger fish to fry. Twyla's death. The condition of the ranch. Dad. Yeah that. Not easy.

For the longest time, he stared out across the lake, watching fishing boats bob on the water. As the sun edged past the midpoint of the sky, Ryder started the Harley, hit the throttle, and headed for the place he did not want to go.

Fifteen minutes later, Ryder passed the wide-open iron gates of the Circle S. His heart was in his throat as the old farmhouse came into view. Even from a distance, it looked forlorn, like a great white elephant dying alone on the plains.

There were no cattle in the pasture. No farming equipment in the field. Not even a pickup truck parked in the driveway. There was a silver Camry underneath the carport. Not a vehicle his made-in-America proud dad would drive. But perhaps it was Twyla's car.

His cell phone vibrated in his pocket, and he chuffed out a sigh of relief at the interruption. He slowed, pulled over onto the yellowed grass, plucked the phone from his pocket, and smiled when he saw the caller ID.

"Hello Clara," he said. "How are you?"

"Fine, fine. But I miss you."

He might not want to admit it, but it felt good to hear his neighbor say that. Not too many people missed him. Clara might be the only one.

"Trask will change your lightbulbs, and take out the trash for you," he said, referring to the other bodyguard who sublet his apartment for the month Ryder would be in Twilight. He'd sublet it more so

Clara would have someone to turn to if she needed help with anything, than to have someone keep an eye on his place.

"It's not the same," Clara said in a small voice. "Trask is too chatty. I miss your quiet."

"Do you want me to speak to him? I'll speak to him."

"No, don't do that. He is who he is. How are things in Twilight?" she asked. "Have you seen her yet?"

Ryder thought of Katie. No point in stirring that pot. "Just got here . . . so no, haven't seen her yet."

"But you will see her."

"I have to. We're in a wedding together."

"She's so nice."

"You spoke to her all of ten minutes."

"Doesn't matter. I have a sixth sense about people. I can tell right off the bat whether they're good folks or not."

"You're too trusting, Clara."

"Maybe. But if I hadn't trusted you, we would never have become friends. You like to project that badass, don't-touch-me persona, but I can see straight through you, Ryder Southerland."

Ryder shifted uncomfortably on his seat. "Listen Clara, I was just about to drive up to my dad's house, so . . ."

"Oh my, your first big meeting in thirteen years. Are you nervous?"

Yes, but he wasn't going to admit it. "No."

"Well, you should be. This is big. I'm nervous for you. I've been sitting here knitting like a fiend. You know how I knit when I'm nervous."

"You can stop knitting. No need for drama."

Clara snorted as if he was as dumb as a box of rocks. "Tend your garden, Ryder."

He wasn't even going to ask what that meant.

"Gotta go now, honey," she said kindly. "My granddaughter is taking me Christmas shopping."

"Wait," he said, not wanting her to hang up. If she hung up, he had nothing to do but walk up to that door and knock on it. Clara was his touchstone and as long as they were talking, he had a connection to his ordinary world.

But Clara had already hung up.

Gulping, Ryder disconnected the call and shifted his attention back to the farmhouse where he'd grown up, but which felt so alien.

Time to man up.

Heaving in a deep breath, Ryder sped down the dirt road to the house and crossed the threshold into his past.

The condition of the outside of the house hit him hard. The front porch sagged and the house needed repainting. The blinds in the front windows were smashed and mangled from objects inside being shoved against them. The welcome mat was worn bare and filled with dirt. The glass in the lamp was shattered, and a busted lawn chair lay turned upside down against the railing.

Sad.

Knocking on that door was harder than Ryder thought it was going to be. He hadn't seen or spoken to his father in thirteen years. How would this go down? His arm was a fifty-pound weight, and he rapped like he was a knuckle-dragging ape.

But when the door opened, his jaw unhinged, because the eyes he stared into weren't his father's, but the last person he expected to see at the Circle S.

Katie answered the door because she was expecting Jana. Seeing Ryder standing there took her last breath.

He wasn't six inches away from her, but it felt as if there was an invisible glass wall between them. He was dressed in cowboy gear, looking a long way from the badass biker she'd slept with in LA the previous December. The Western-style shirt, complete with mother-of-pearl snaps instead of buttons, fit him like it had been tailor-made for his rugged, masculine form.

A black Stetson—but of course, what other color would the town bad boy wear?—was cocked back on his head, revealing a headful of tousled dark hair. He'd grown it out from the conservative haircut he'd worn the last time she'd seen him.

Katie approved, even if the cut did make him look less like badass military man and more like the hot young teen he'd once been.

Except now he was a lot more dangerous. The hard look in his eyes, the stern set to his jaw. He was not happy to be here, and from his tight body language, even more unhappy to find her in his father's house.

Hey, not any more unhappy than she was to be here.

She'd been dreading this moment since she learned Ryder was going to be Joe's best man. She'd had a year's notice. She should have been more prepared for the impact of seeing him again.

She was not.

He said nothing.

Neither did she.

Katie gulped.

Ryder didn't move a muscle. Didn't even blink.

"You look incredible," he said so softly she wasn't sure she heard him.

Her cheeks warmed at his compliment, and her heart beat faster. *Watch it.* She tucked an errant strand of hair behind her ear. She was in work clothes. Jeans, long-sleeved T-shirt, apron, and sneakers. Nothing sexy about that, and yet he was looking at her like she was filet mignon.

"Do you want to come in?" she invited as if it were her house instead of his.

"What are you doing here?" he asked.

Unable to peel her gaze from the bad-boy, biker cowboy on the front porch, she moistened her lips with the tip of her tongue. "Working."

"What kind of work?" He scowled.

"Organizing things." She raised a hand to hold on to the door, needing something, anything to give her support beneath the onslaught of his enigmatic green-eyed stare.

Quizzical eyebrows shot up on his forehead.

"It's my job," she answered his unspoken question. "I have a business helping people get organized. I started it after my grandfather had to move to a retirement community following his car accident, and Joe bought Gramps's Christmas tree farm, and we had to go through his things, and it turned out I sort of have a gift for it and . . ."

Oh gosh, she was saying too much. Babbling. Shut up. Just shut up.

Katie clamped her mouth closed.

"Where's my father?" he asked, suddenly in motion, muscling across the threshold, shattering the invisible glass wall with his broad chest, coming straight at Katie, nothing between them but air.

She leaped aside, getting out of the way before he touched her. "He's not here."

"Where is he?"

"At the hospital."

Ryder pulled up short. "What's going on?"

"He had an episode with his blood sugar."

"What do you mean?"

"Your father's a diabetic." She put a palm to her mouth. "You didn't know?"

"I haven't talked to him in thirteen years, Katie, what do you think?"

Katie nodded, wished she wasn't in the middle of his family situation. "After Twyla died, Jax didn't take care of himself. Stopped taking his medication. If a neighbor hadn't come by to check on him—" She broke off. It wasn't really her place to fill him in on the details of his father's condition.

Plus, she was breathless to see him again. She'd forgotten how big and powerful he was.

"Who?" he asked. "What?"

"Hondo Crouch's wife, Patsy, found him passed out in his easy chair. He almost died."

Sharp silence descended between them.

"I'm sorry," she said.

Ryder cursed under his breath, and for a flicker of a second, Katie saw a flash of hurt in his eyes, but he quickly squelched it. No room for weakness in Ryder Southerland.

Katie wasn't sure what to do. Or say, for that matter. So she just stood there, waiting for him to make the next move.

"Not your fault." He grunted. "Or your problem."

"Kinda is. It's my job."

"Dad?" Ryder called, trucking into the living room, as if looking for his father, unconvinced she was telling him the truth.

"He's not here." This would be the perfect time for her to exit, but her purse was in the kitchen and her car keys were in her purse. No running away this time. Reluctantly, she trailed after Ryder.

His shoulders were so broad he was having trouble squeezing down the path made narrow through the towers of piled junk. He moved like a bulldozer, plowing over stuff, shoving boxes aside, sending them crashing and spilling.

Katie cringed, and her pulse ticked fast and heavy. "Wh-where are you going?"

Ryder whirled around to glare at her, his face a mask of anger. She shrank back, bumped into a top-heavy stack of boxes, and sent them toppling.

He grabbed her hand, pulled her toward him, out of the way of the crashing boxes. Held her close, his arms encircling her waist. "You're trembling. Was it the falling boxes or did I scare you?"

"Both," she admitted. "You look so mad."

"Not at you, Katie." His voice turned pillow soft. "Never you."

"Oh," she said, because she didn't know what else to say. "Oh."

He stared into her eyes, gently this time. "I forget," he said, "how scary I can look."

"It must be a shock," she said. "Coming home to find your father in the hospital and . . ." She waved an arm. "This."

"Yeah. It was a disaster when I lived here," he said. "But it's worse now. Much worse."

"You stepmother had . . ." She wanted to put this delicately. ". . . issues."

"That's a kind way of putting it. And that's why Dad hired you. To sort all this out?"

"Actually, home health hired me. If I'm not able to get the place cleaned up before he's discharged on Monday, he'll have to go to the rehab hospital. Home health won't come into a place this—"

"Filthy," Ryder finished for her, so she didn't have to.

She smiled at him kindly, knowing this was a stab in his heart. From everything she'd heard about Ryder's mother, she'd been a sweet, loving woman who'd kept a meticulous house. "It must hurt learning your father was living in such terrible conditions."

"His choice." Ryder swallowed visibly, his arm still around her waist.

She felt overwhelmed, and anxious to create some distance between them as memories of last Christmas floated through her head, but there was nowhere to go.

If she stepped backward she would slide into a Rascal scooter stacked high with old newspapers. If she stepped to the right, she'd fall into a well-worn La-Z-Boy recliner with blankets piled on it. If she stepped to the left, well, there was no left to step toward. On that side of the room the boxes reached the ceiling. The other rooms in the house were in the same condition, if not worse. This was the most challenging mess she'd ever undertaken to sort out and organize. She had dropped by to get the lay of the land after agreeing to take on the project. Tomorrow her crew would arrive and they would roll up their sleeves and get down to serious work.

"Why didn't you call and tell me Twyla had died?" Ryder whispered, his palm pressed into her spine. "Why did I have to find out from the online newspaper?"

"I . . ." She cleared her throat. "I didn't feel it was my place to interfere."

"Or you didn't want to talk to me."

Well, that too.

"I thought we were friends."

Friends.

Were they friends? It certainly didn't feel like it. There was too much chemistry between them. Too much yearning for this feeling to be anything close to friendship. She wanted him. Just as much as she had wanted him a year ago. Maybe even more.

His eyes were sharp, and full of pain.

"I'm sorry," she said. "That I didn't tell you. That I didn't call you back when you left that message on my voice mail—"

"You have nothing to apologize for," he said. "Not your circus. Not your monkeys, right? You set the rules. I should have honored them." He let her go, stepped back, but then wobbled as he stepped on something and lost his balance.

She put out a hand to stabilize him, but he flicked his wrist, deflected her touch, and she couldn't help feeling slightly rejected.

"I'm here now," he said. "I can deal with this." He arced his arm wide, indicating the chaos around them.

"You'll need help."

"Just show me how to get started and I can take it from there."

Katie started to argue. Even with her accomplished team and a cleaning crew, she knew getting the place livable before Monday was a feat. Ryder going at it by himself didn't stand a ghost of a chance.

But she nodded and said yes. Some things people had to figure things for themselves.

Chapter 8

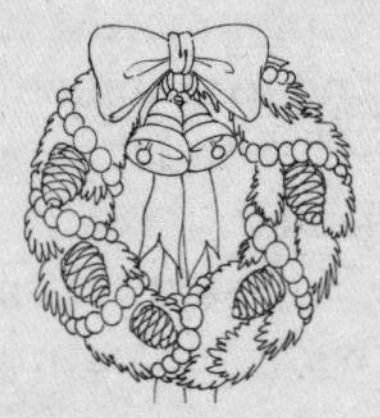

"Let's get to it." Ryder rubbed his palms together.

"Now?"

"No time like the present."

"Don't you want to go see your father first?"

Ryder winced. "I'd rather get started on this."

"When are you going to see him?"

"Later."

"Sooner is better."

"Later." He growled.

"Have you seen Joe?"

"Later." He grunted.

"Oh, it's like that, is it?"

"Yeah." Cleaning the house was the perfect way to sweep his feelings under the rug. Bonus, he was here with Katie.

"So tackling this mountain of mess is easier than tackling the emotional messes."

"You got it," he said. She'd nailed him. The woman could see straight through his bullshit. He unbuttoned his sleeves and rolled them up. "Where do we start?"

She looked at him like she wanted to prod and poke. He leveled her a let's-get-down-to-business stare and her expression shifted, mouth tightening, eyes softening, as if she felt sorry for him, so she wasn't going to say what she really wanted to say.

Damn. He hated when people felt sorry for him.

"I've made some progress in your father's bedroom." She inclined her head toward the back of the house. "Although progress in this house is a relative term. Translation? It means I can actually open the bedroom door without knocking over a dozen things in a convoluted Rube Goldberg chain reaction."

He laughed. She was funny. Plus laughing was better than the alternative: yelling in anger. Not at her, but at his father, at Twyla. At the hurt kid he'd once been who lashed out at anyone, and everyone who tried to help him. And at the absent son he'd become.

She smiled and canted her head in a way that made him think of sunshine glinting off diamonds, and crooked her finger at him.

"How long have you been doing this for a living?" Ryder asked, following her as she inched her way through the thin trail leading from the living room and down the hall to the master bedroom. Stuff was stacked to the ceiling—old newspapers and magazines, paper bags, plastic milk jugs, clothing, cardboard boxes. Funky smells assaulted them at every step. It stunk of musk and dust and yuck.

Damn, Dad, how the hell did you live in this?

"Ten months."

"Is this your worst case?"

"My most challenging," she said, reframing it in a more positive light. He liked that. "Yes."

Ryder grunted when the tip of his boot connected with an orange so rotten it was greenish-white, and it disintegrated into oozy mush.

"What?" she asked, turning.

"Hit a challenge."

"Here." Katie plucked a pair of vinyl gloves from the pocket of the green and white checkered apron she had tied around her waist, tossed them to him along with a Ziploc freezer bag. She was prepared. This was nothing new.

"I'm thinking a Hazmat suit is in order." He put on the gloves and bent to peel the fuzz blob formerly known as an orange off the toe of his boot, and dropped it into the Ziploc bag along with the gloves. "Now what?"

"I've got a large plastic trash bag in the bedroom. You can discard it there."

"God, Dad," he muttered under his breath. "How did it come to this?"

"Living with a hoarder is an uphill battle. It's easier to turn a blind eye," she said, her voice rich with sympathy and understanding.

"Blind, deaf, and mute too." Ryder wished he could have a big scoop of that sympathy for his father and his stepmother. Right now, all he felt was pity and disgust. "Or he's actually going blind."

"Could be," she said. "Who knows? Uncontrolled diabetes can lead to blindness. But I don't know the specifics of your father's condition."

"Shit." He shoved a hand through his hair, looked at the unmitigated ruin all around them, felt bleak. Yeah, he could see how his father might choose to ignore the mess once it got this bad. Helpless in the face of so much work. How did Katie do it?

"What's wrong?" she asked.

"I should have come back sooner."

"What would you have done?" Katie asked. "You can't rescue people who don't want to be rescued."

"Maybe he did want to be rescued." Ryder chuffed out his breath. "I mean, c'mon, who wants to live like this?"

"I'm sure Twyla didn't even want to live like this. From what my counselor has told me, hoarding is a mental illness. A form of OCD." Katie eased past a treadmill still in the box parked in the hallway.

"You're seeing a counselor?" That pulled him up short. Katie seemed so well-adjusted. She had such a supportive family. Why would she need a counselor? He stopped, so did she, and she squeezed around to look at him.

"For a time," she said. "To help me put my life back together after Matt died."

His gut kicked at the thought of how rough things must have been for her after her fiancé died. And damn if for a split second there, he felt jealous of a dead man.

"Did you ever see a counselor?" she asked.

"I had a few mandatory sessions when I was in the army."

"And?"

"It helped."

"But you didn't keep it up?"

"My PTSD was mild."

Her eyes cradled his gaze. "I'm sorry you suffered."

"Everybody suffers, look around."

Katie pushed open the door to his father's bedroom and stepped in as far as the small area she'd cleared would allow. Ryder moved in behind her. If he leaned forward an inch, he would be touching her. God, how he wanted to touch her, find comfort in her soft warmth.

"Progress, huh?"

"Warned you. I've made piles. Keep, donate, and throw away." She indicated each heap with a flap of her hand.

"How long did it take you to get this far?"

"Three hours," she admitted. "But my crew is on another job. They will be here tomorrow, and things will go much more quickly."

"Until then looks like it's just you and me," he said.

She forced a smile, but it was a ghost, thin and faded, as she echoed, "Just you and me" in a voice that said the idea scared her.

Hell, he was scared too. "Tell me what to do."

Katie shifted her weight. She looked uncertain, as if unsure how to proceed with him here.

He tightened his jaw. He was determined to be part of the process, even though he wasn't sure why he gave a damn. "I'm not leaving."

She fidgeted, didn't meet his gaze. "You want to know how I work?"

"Love to see you in action. Give me a crash course in organization."

She turned to meet his gaze, but shifted as far away from him as the debris would allow. Too close for comfort? "Obviously, this goes beyond the scope of organizational problems. In fact, I usually don't wade into hoarder territory."

"Why did you this time?"

"Because it was your father."

The muscles of his chest torqued. What did she mean by that? He wanted to ask, but couldn't bring himself to dive that deep. Not today. Not yet. "Teach me."

Katie straightened and cleared her throat. She looked like a passionate math teacher he had in school, serious about her topic. "Organization isn't really about keeping things neat and clean."

"No?"

"Well, it is, but that's not the bottom line."

"What is the bottom line?" he asked.

"Getting truly organized is about taking stock of your life, facing your fears, and letting go of the things that no longer serve your highest good."

"Sounds kinda airy-fairy to me."

"It's not. Getting organized and staying that way is actually very earthy and grounding. Take this for example." She picked up a box with faded lettering and old-style advertising circa 1980-something, Ron Popeil's Pocket Fisherman. The box had never been opened. "It has no emotional value."

"Except to Twyla."

"It wasn't the product that provided the emotional value to her. It was the accumulation of stuff. She was trying to fill an emotional hole in her heart."

"What hole was that?"

"I don't know. She was your stepmother."

"What a waste of money," he muttered, not even trying to guess at Twyla's mental landscape.

"Hundreds of unopened boxes here. Besides hoarding, it looks like your stepmother had a shopping addiction as well."

Yeah. Ryder knew all about Twyla's shopping addiction, and her denial of it. His stepmother's issues were the reason he and his father had gotten crossways in the first place. What hurt most was that his father had taken Twyla's side, choosing to believe her lies over Ryder.

It still hurt.

"Clean out the junk, and you clean out the inner demons," Katie went on.

"Twyla had a hell of a lot of inner demons." Ryder sank his hands on his hips, felt a familiar roil in his stomach whenever he thought of his stepmother. She'd poisoned the well of his childhood and even though she was dead, the pain lingered. But he forgave her. Felt sorry for her, in fact. The woman had not lived a happy life.

"Hoarders do hoard because in a weird way, the junk makes them feel safe. Getting rid of stuff makes them feel vulnerable, defenseless. That's why it's so hard to get them to let go. It's not about the stuff but rather the way the stuff makes them feel."

"So for you, cleaning is like what? A religion?" He eyed her curiously, tried not to notice how well she filled out the cute red long-sleeved T-shirt she had on.

"Not cleaning per se, organizing. Although I suppose the two go hand in hand."

"I'm a minimalist. Keep things lean. That's my motto."

"I noticed." She cut her eyes at him, stared at his biceps.

Ryder hid a grin. She was still interested in him whether she wanted to be or not. "Makes it easier to move on. Prevents a guy from getting entrenched."

"You don't ever feel the need for something more solid? For roots?"

"I was raised with this crap. What do you think?"

"But not always, right? I mean before your mother died. She wasn't a—"

"Hoarder. No."

"Twyla probably considered herself a collector," she said gently.

"Collectors have a system," he said. "A purpose. There's no sense to this madness."

"I'm sure this made sense to Twyla."

"Yeah, maybe. In crazy town."

"We don't know what was going on inside her head."

"Nothing normal."

"Ryder," she chided. "You gotta let it go. The past is over, and hard feelings become their own form of mental clutter."

"I don't know," he said, lowering his eyelids and his voice seductively. "Not all *hard* feelings are bad."

"You're out of line, mister," she whispered, but there was a flare of interest in her eyes. He wasn't mistaken about that.

"Are you peeved because I won't fit neatly into one of your boxes?"

"This rebel-without-a-cause thing might have been hot when you were seventeen, but now . . ." She shrugged. "It's kinda sad."

He laughed like he wasn't bothered, and he spied a flicker of disappointment in her eyes. Was she disappointed in him? Quickly, he shifted things, picking up a green canvas zippered bag with a caricature logo of Katie, a broom in her hand, and the words "Fresh Start." "What're these?"

"My branded packing cubes. They're for stacking and organizing the items we're going to retain. As I mentioned before, we've got three piles here." She pointed as she turned to each mound. "Throw away, donate, keep and organize. We do one category at a time. I like to begin with clothing."

"Mmm, okay." He glanced around at the heaps of items stacked and stuffed every which way. "How do you find anything in this rubble?"

"I admit that can be a challenge," she said. "But trust the system. Whatever we come across that isn't clothing gets moved aside until we're ready for that category."

"Oh, this is going to be hilarious to watch," he said.

"Don't think you're getting off scot-free." She handed him another pair of vinyl gloves. "You're in this with me."

"Do I get a discount for helping?"

"You get good son points," she said. "Work off some of that bad-boy karma."

"Ouch, you sure know how to hit a guy where it hurts." He chuckled.

"Here." She thrust a large cardboard box in his hand, which was full of what looked like garage sale finds. "Start digging."

"Couldn't we just throw the whole room away and call it a day?"

"Have some sensitivity. It's your father's entire life here."

"Then shouldn't he be the one sorting through this stuff?"

"Normally, yes. But I don't think he's physically or emotionally strong enough for that right now," she said. "This is where we start. See what's salvable for charity. Anything ripped, pilling, worn, age-faded, or stained gets discarded."

"You're the boss." He shook his head, shrugged, stared at the insurmountable task in front of them.

"The items we want to keep will go into color-coordinated cubes. Blue for pants, green for shirts, black for undergarments, brown for shoes."

"Aren't you carrying this just a little too far?"

"I didn't tell you how to do your job, did I? And frankly, I could have offered some constructive criticism, like don't tackle the wrong person," she teased.

"Point taken," he said, and fished a pair of blue jeans from the cardboard box. "Pitch? Donate? Or keep?"

"Are they your dad's size?"

"How the hell do I know that?"

Katie sighed and sank her hands on her hips. "He's about a thirty-eight-inch waist."

"These are thirty-fours."

"Donate pile. Unless they're ripped—"

"Pilling, worn, age-faded, or stained, yada, yada, I get it." Ryder put down the box, unfolded the jeans. "I wear a thirty-four."

"Donate pile." She snapped her fingers and pointed at the appropriate pile.

"What if I want them?"

Katie rolled her eyes. "Seriously? Are you going to give me grief about every single item?"

"Not this," he said, pulling a hideous purple and orange muumuu from the cardboard box. "Definitely trash. This thing should never have been created."

"Ack! That's a top designer." She grabbed the muumuu from the "toss" pile. "It's in pristine condition. Someone somewhere will want it. Your father needs the money. We can sell it."

"How am I supposed to know high-fashion designer duds from Wal-Mart clothes?"

"This isn't working. Explaining things to you is going to take three times as long." She made shooing motions toward the door. "Out."

"You're throwing me out of my own place?"

"It's your father's place," she said. "You haven't been home in thirteen years. Go. Shoo. Get."

"I'll do better," he said, wanting to stay. "Show me how it's done. I'll be good. I promise."

She pushed up her sleeves, waved him aside, dove into a big cardboard box. Bam. Bam. Bam. She was through the box in under a minute flat and that included neatly folding the few clothes she was keeping. "And that's the gold standard."

She handed him another cardboard box stuffed with clothes.

"You know," he said, "I'm more of a visual learner. You went at it so fast, it would help to see that again in slow motion."

"Watch closely."

He lowered his head.

"Eyes on my hands, not my ass."

"Spoilsport."

"Listen up. Here's how to clean out a hoarder's haven."

"The gospel of Miss Priss. I remember your closet . . ." He paused, met her gaze head-on, added, "And that pink sweater."

"You remember that sweater?" Her cheeks flushed. She thought their time together in California had gotten her past this silly shyness, but here she was feeling foolish and embarrassed all over again. In LA it had been easy to pretend she had a whole new persona. But here, surrounded by their past, it was a lot harder. The old roles were back—the prim ugly duckling and the rebellious bad boy.

"How could I forget? Two minutes later you launched yourself into my arms and kissed me."

"Learning how to get organized is life-changing magic," she went on, as if he hadn't said anything, babbling to fill the air so she'd stop talking about her most embarrassing moment. He knew her. She babbled when she got nervous. "It will change your lifestyle and your perspective. You'll feel freer, richer . . ."

"You're preaching to the choir, honey," he said. "I lived in this house with Twyla. I saw firsthand how holding on to stuff can weigh you down, warp your beliefs, and cloud your judgment. But I like how you think. Keep talking. What do you love about this job?"

A helpless smile ran away with her face, curling her lips up to her cheeks. The woman had found her passion. "The alchemy of creating order from chaos. Taming the . . ."

He stared at her, his gaze hooked on her lips. He recollected what those lips tasted like, both salty and sweet.

"Taming the . . . taming the . . ."

"Uh-huh?"

"Wolf."

"Wolf?" He chuckled.

"Um, um . . . I meant taming this wolfish mess."

"Sure you did," he said, pleased that he'd hijacked her brain. "Because most messes are wolfish."

"You're making fun of me."

"What can I say?" He grinned wickedly. "Being back in Twilight brings out the bad boy in me."

"There is *nothing* boyish about you."

"Glad you noticed." He stepped closer, drawn irresistibly by the sight of her in those skinny jeans, her blond hair pulled up in a bewitching ponytail that swished whenever she nodded or shook her head. Her T-shirt was sliding off one shoulder, revealing the strap of white cotton bra.

God, how he wanted to kiss her.

"Look," she said in a serious tone that told him he was too close for comfort. "I really don't have time to teach you my trade. In order for your father to come home on Monday, this place has to be halfway decent. So I'd appreciate it if you'd just get out of my way."

"No," he said.

"What?" She jerked her head up.

"I'm not leaving. My father is in a helluva mess."

"Yes, and I'm straightening it out. So shoo." She waved him away.

"Not leaving."

She looked stumped, chuffed out a breath, finally said, "All right. If you really want to help, bag the things in the throwaway pile, and take them to the dump."

"As you wish."

"*The Princess Bride*? Really?"

"It's your favorite movie."

"You remembered that too?" She interlaced her fingers and held them up to her chest like a knotty shield.

"I remember a lot of things about you." He lowered his voice and his eyelids.

She nibbled her bottom lip, offered him a wobbly smile, and he realized she was as nervous about being near him as he was being near her.

It touched him. Right down to the center of his bones.

And it occurred to Ryder that maybe coming home wasn't going to be as difficult as he feared, and that's when he saw THE BOX.

Chapter 9

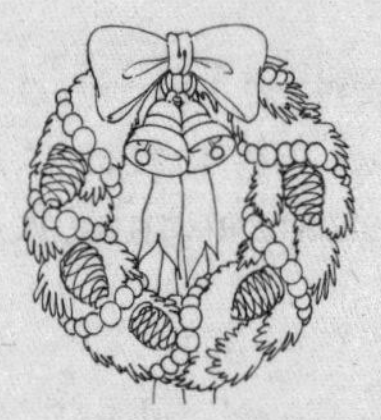

The small black jewelry box was the first thing Ryder ever stole.

Reaching down, he curled his hand around the box on the nightstand that was peeking from underneath a pile of newspapers, flicked it open with his thumb, and stared down at the silver heart pendant necklace.

His heart cracked into a million brittle pieces.

"Ryder?" Katie asked, concern in her voice.

He swayed on his feet. The room narrowed, and Katie disappeared.

A familiar nightmare came to him, right smack in the middle of the day while his eyes were wide open.

It was the one about his mother.

His body jerked as if he'd taken a pugilist's fist to his solar plexus. His heart pounded. The daymare clung to him like spiderwebs, sticky and binding. He heard the sounds of Katie moving toward him, but he raised a palm, warning her off.

Stay away. I'm no good for you.

Caught in the grips of a terrible memory, the last

thing he wanted was for her to touch him, and try to make everything all right.

Nothing would ever be right. Not for him. Not in this lifetime.

In his mind's eye, he saw his thirty-year-old mother, how she'd looked the morning of the accident, this very necklace around her throat. The necklace he'd bought her for Mother's Day with money earned from helping his father around the farm. Mom, smiling and waving him off to school, having no idea it was the last day of her life.

Or that her young son would be the instrument of her death.

It was at noon on that same day when Great-Aunt Delilah came to pick him up at his third grade classroom. She'd been crying, and when she whispered something to his teacher, tears misted her eyes too.

"I've come to take you to my house," his great-aunt said.

He didn't want to go. He wanted to stay at school with his friends. He didn't know his aunt well. Only from family get-togethers, and he'd never stayed at her house by himself.

"No," he'd said, sensing in his bones something was terribly wrong.

"You have to go with your aunt," his teacher said kindly. "Get your things, Ryder."

He balked, digging in his heels, crossing his arms over his chest. "No. Mama told me never to go with strangers."

"I'm not a stranger," said his aunt, who smelled like clove cigarettes, and the koala bears at the zoo.

Her too-red lipstick was smeared at the corner of a mouth that sagged with age. "I'm your father's aunt. Your great-aunt Delilah. I know you remember me. Stop being so stubborn."

"No."

Under her breath, she muttered, "Spare the rod, spoil the child."

"You're scaring him," his teacher said, and he liked her more than usual because she said that.

"I'm sorry." Great-Aunt Delilah sighed and dabbed at her eyes with a tissue. "I'm upset. Not thinking clearly. Please Ryder, your father sent me to get you."

"You have to go with her," his teacher said firmly, and cut a nervous glance at Delilah. "Something's happened at home."

The way his teacher looked at him, with fear and sadness in her eyes, spurred him to sink his hand into Great-Aunt Delilah's outstretched palm, even though he didn't want to.

She took him to her house and fixed a peanut butter sandwich on stale whole wheat bread, and chocolate milk, but the milk was slightly soured. Blinky, his mother called it. When the milk was blinky at home, she'd mix it with old breadcrumbs and give it to the chickens.

Chicken food. His great-aunt was feeding him chicken food.

He took one sip and pushed it away. "I want to call my mama."

"You can't," she said, smoking one of her funny brown cigarettes and pacing the green linoleum floor.

"Why not?" he challenged, crossing his arms over his chest. He felt sick to his stomach, but determined not to throw up.

"Your father will be here after a while and you can talk to him."

Yes. Dad would straighten this all out. Clearly, there had been a mistake. They'd laugh about it, and Dad would take him home and Mom would be waiting with Blue Bell vanilla ice cream and homemade chocolate chip cookies.

Day turned into night and his father didn't come. Great-Aunt Delilah fed him a frozen dinner she nuked in the microwave and let him eat it on a tray in front of the television, and watch *The Three Stooges*. A show Mama wouldn't let him watch.

There were lots of phone calls. Great-Aunt Delilah took them in another room, whispering low and frantic. A couple of times, she caught him pressing his ear to the door trying to overhear her conversations, and she shooed him away with pursed lips and a worried frown.

The cold, sick knot in his stomach twisted even tighter.

Finally, when it was time for bed, his father showed up at the back porch looking shattered, his hair was every which way, his eyes bloodshot, his shoulders stooped.

Ryder ran to throw his arms around his father, but Dad put a palm to Ryder's head, holding him in place, not letting him come closer than arm's length, even though Ryder pedaled his legs hard. Fresh fear bubbled up inside him and he started to cry even though he didn't quite know why.

"Mama," he said. "Where's my mama? I want my mama."

"Sit down, boy." His father took him by the elbow and maneuvered him none too gently into a kitchen chair.

What was wrong? What had he done? Why was he being kept from his mother?

"Mama." He bawled like a baby. "I want my mama."

"Your mama is gone," his father said, in a rough voice.

"Gone where?" Ryder demanded.

"She's in heaven with the angels."

"No." Ryder shook his head violently. "No. She's at home. Baking cookies."

"She's dead, son. Like Max."

Max was his collie that had gotten run over the previous summer. Ryder pouched out his bottom lip. "No, no, no."

"She fell off the back porch," his father went on, his jaw clenching tighter and tighter. "Tripped over that goddamn Tonka dump truck I kept telling you not to leave lying around. She tripped and fell wrong and broke her neck."

"Stop lying!" He whaled at his father, pummeling him with his fists.

"I told you if you left that truck lying around someone would get hurt. I told you, I told you, I told you . . ." His father collapsed onto the kitchen table, sobbing brokenly. "You killed her. You killed her."

Great-Aunt Delilah rushed across the room to lay a hand on his father's shoulder. "That's enough,

Jax. I know you're hurting, but he's only a boy. He didn't mean to leave that truck out. He didn't mean for it to happen."

"No! No! No!" Ryder slapped his palms over his ears to drown out the screams. His screams. His mother was dead and it was his fault.

He went nuts then. Ran around the room. Pulled his hair. Knocked things off the counter. A toaster. Cups. Towels. Smashed a canister. Gritty sweet sugar dusted him.

Dad grabbed him and held him until Ryder's screams dissolved into helpless tears.

"I love you, son, I'm sorry I said those things. I'm sorry, I'm sorry, I'm sorry." He squeezed Ryder hard. "I love you and everything is going to be all right."

But they both knew that was a lie. Nothing would ever be all right again. His father blamed him for his mother's death, but no more than Ryder blamed himself.

For two weeks Ryder stayed with Great-Aunt Delilah, through his mother's funeral and the long days that followed. He began to think his father was never going to come take him home, and he would have to live there forever.

Then one morning Great-Aunt Delilah woke him up for school. He blinked his eyes open, saw she was wearing the heart necklace, *his* mother's heart necklace.

Ryder had grabbed for her throat, trying to yank the necklace from around her neck. "No," he yelled. "You can't wear it. It's not yours. It's my mama's."

Stunned, Great-Aunt Delilah staggered back, clutching where Ryder's fingernails had raked across her skin, her feeble lips quivering. "You . . . you attacked me!"

"You stole my mama's necklace!"

"Your father gave it to me." She fingered the necklace. The silver heart his mother had loved so much shining in the light flooding in through the open curtains. "It's mine now."

Feeling utterly betrayed by the world, Ryder had acted out in school, scrawling the dirtiest words he knew in black marker down the hallways. The principal called his father. Jax had spanked Ryder, stood there while he cleaned the marker off the walls. Told him the heart necklace belonged to Great-Aunt Delilah now. She'd wanted something special to remember his mother by, and she deserved it for taking care of Ryder.

Ryder hated that, but he had a plan, and at least Jax finally took him home.

One Saturday when he knew Great-Aunt-Delilah would be at the beauty shop, he walked two miles into town, slipped into her house, and reclaimed his mother's necklace.

When his father found the necklace under Ryder's mattress two weeks later, he'd called Ryder a thief, and took the necklace away from him again.

In a mad fury, Ryder had gone on a stealing spree, taking candy from the convenience store, pilfering his father's loose change, filching money from the collection plate at church.

Bad seed, people called him. Rotten to the core.

Punk. Thug. Troublemaker. Rabble-rouser. Hooligan. Thief.

Labels. Defining him.

And Ryder had striven to live up to them all.

Not knowing what else to do with his troubled son, Jax decided what Ryder needed was a new mother, and he'd married Twyla. Twyla's husband had divorced her after the baby boy she'd been carrying was born dead and the doctors told her she could never have more children.

In Jax's mind, Ryder needed a mother, and Twyla needed a child to love. On the surface it was a win-win situation.

Except things had not turned out that way.

Ryder and Twyla had resented each other from the beginning. He wasn't the son she'd lost and she wasn't the mother he missed with every breath in his body. He was no angel. He did things on purpose to set Twyla off. Their tumultuous relationship came to a head when he was sixteen, and she accused him of stealing two thousand dollars from her drawer and running up her credit cards.

Ryder tried to tell his dad how ridiculous her accusations were. Why would he charge sewing patterns and pantyhose and collectible dolls from the Franklin Mint?

His father had taken Twyla's side when she claimed Ryder had charged those things just to make her look bad. Jax stood by Twyla. Ryder had a reputation as a thief, after all. And Jax kicked him out of the house.

Ryder had nowhere to go, and the only people in town who gave him a chance were Joe's parents.

The Cheeks had taken him in, no questions asked, and it was the first time since his mother died that Ryder had felt like he was part of a real family. If it hadn't been for the Cheeks, he would have ended up . . . well, nowhere good, that was for sure.

Because of Joe and his family, Ryder cleaned up his act. Improved his grades. Started trying to live down his reputation. The year he lived with the Cheeks had been happy, normal. Whenever he was with them, he'd felt loved and respected.

Then Katie had kissed him.

And ruined everything.

He knew he had to go. Because her kiss stirred feelings he had no business feeling. Not for his best friend's kid sister. Not when she was fifteen and he was almost eighteen.

So he'd joined the army, and it ended up being the best thing for him. In the service, he'd found redemption. Going from bad boy to decorated soldier. In the eyes of the U.S. government, he was a good man.

But in his heart, Ryder feared his shadow side that lurked untamed and dangerous. He *knew* what he was capable of, and that was why he kept to himself, avoided entanglements. Things were safer that way.

"Ryder?" Katie whispered. "Are you all right?"

He blinked at her, felt himself come back into his body, back to the reality of the filthy room and the black velvet jewelry box in his hand. He dragged his palm down his face.

"Fine," he said. "I'm fine."

"Where did you go?"

"Nowhere." He shook his head, tucked the box into his front pocket.

"Is there anything I can do?" she asked, concern brimming in her eyes.

"I'm fine." He gritted his teeth.

"You're not."

He ignored that. "You're right. I'm not up for this job."

"Too many memories?" She nodded toward the box in his pocket.

"Yeah."

"Do you want to talk about it?"

"No."

"You sure? It seems like you're in pain."

"I'm fine," he insisted, sliding steel into his voice.

She took his irritation in stride. "All right."

They stood watching each other. Him guarded, her open.

"You need to go see your father," she whispered.

"I know," he whispered back. "Tomorrow. I'll do it tomorrow."

"Do you want me to go with you? I'll go with you if you want."

He started to say no. He meant to say no. He should have said no. But instead, he latched on to her gaze and murmured, "Would you?"

CHAPTER 10

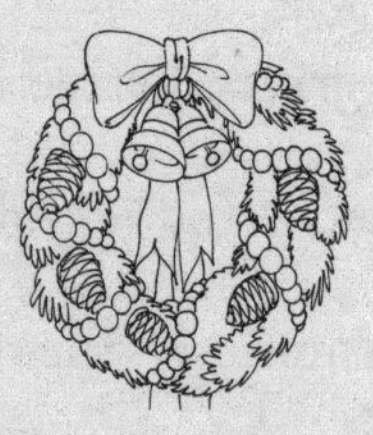

Katie didn't know what had happened to Ryder, and she didn't know anything about PTSD, but she knew a lot of people who had been in the military suffered from it, and it was clear he'd had some kind of flashback.

When he'd opened the small jewelry box, his eyes went glassy and his entire body trembled. She'd called his name several times, but it was as if he couldn't hear her. She'd been afraid to touch him. So she'd waited for him to snap out of it.

He still seemed dazed. If it would help, she would certainly go with him to see his father.

"Sure." She smiled, letting him know he was not alone. "Whatever will help you get through this."

"Thanks." He nodded.

"What time tomorrow?"

"Noon? We could grab lunch afterward."

"Sure you don't want to do it today?"

He shook his head. "I've been on the road for two days straight. I need a break before tackling *that* mountain."

"Oh gosh, I hadn't even considered that. Driving from LA on a motorcycle through the desert has got to be exhausting. And here I am putting you to work. Why don't we just call it a day?"

"No," he said. "It's not the physical exhaustion. I need a good night's sleep before dealing with my dad. Besides, I like to start what I finish."

Katie glanced around the chaos, thought, *Hoarding: a persistent difficulty discarding or parting with possessions because of a perceived need to save them.*

Twyla Southerland certainly fit that description. Katie stood in the small area they'd cleared, hands on her hips, flummoxed at how they were going to sort it all out.

Just looking at the mess made her feel claustrophobic.

And to think Ryder had grown up in this. No wonder the guy was a minimalist. Because his stepmother, and by association, his dad, held on to so much—frank language warning here—*shit*, Ryder had reacted by keeping his life bare bones.

No roots. No attachments. Nothing to weigh him down. And apparently that included relationships.

To Katie's way of thinking, neither extreme was healthy. Too much attachment to material things led to, well . . . *this*. But total detachment could leave you anchorless, empty, and lonely.

Yes, she liked for her surroundings to be clean and tidy, but there were objects that brought her joy. Like the spelling bee trophy she'd won in fifth grade, after having struggled in spelling so miserably in fourth grade. Or the last photograph of herself with her grandmother as they were sprinkling sulfur on their shoes to ward off chiggers when they went blackberry picking the June afternoon Katie finished her final day of high school. Or the little yellow rubber ducky that Ryder had given her after winning it at the Texas State Fair the year he lived with her family. She kept it on the side of her bathtub. Matt had tried to get her to throw it away when she moved into the yurt, telling her there was no space for silly knickknacks, but she'd vetoed his veto of the yellow duck.

The litmus test for whether something stayed in her life or not was simple.

Did it bring her joy?

Even functional items had to put a smile on her face—like her days-of-the-week underwear, or the designer handbag she'd splurged on because it would last a lifetime.

"You with me?" he asked.

"That could take until midnight," she warned. Or longer.

"I'll get better at sorting," he promised. "We'll speed up. How much do you charge for overtime?"

"It's a set fee."

"A bonus then."

"Let's just see how it goes," she said.

"All right," he agreed.

They tackled the task with renewed zeal and by five, they'd made it through half the room, which was much better than Katie thought they'd do.

They were taking a short break, when Katie's cell phone rang. It was her niece Lauren.

"You're invited, Auntie Katie!" Lauren said in her childish singsong.

"Hello, kiddo. Where am I invited?"

"To Pasta Pappa's for pizza. Everbody comin'. You too."

"Aw, thanks for inviting me, but—"

"Please, please, please," Lauren begged. "You gotta come."

"Okay, I'll be there."

"Yay!" Lauren squealed, and yelled, "Auntie Katie's coming."

Lauren's mother, Emma, got on the phone. "You don't have to come if you've got other plans. I know how Lauren can strong-arm people into accepting an invitation."

"Are you kidding? I'd love to come. I have to swing by the house for a shower first, but I'll be there."

"See you at six at Pappa's?"

"I'll be there." Katie hung up.

"You've got a date," Ryder said.

"Yes. My family's going out for pizza. Wanna come?" Part of her wanted him to say yes, another part of her hoped he'd decline. They were already too close for comfort.

"I'm going to stick around here. Work on whittling this down."

She didn't argue. "All right. See you tomorrow."

"Tomorrow," he echoed, reached up to rub his shoulder with one hand, winced.

"Something wrong?"

"Crick in my shoulder. Slept on the ground last night in the desert."

"Good grief, why didn't you get a motel?"

"Well, for one thing I was in the desert and there were no motels around. For another, I like camping."

"In December?"

"I don't mind being uncomfortable." He kept kneading his shoulder. "We don't grow when we're in our comfort zone."

She grinned at him. "So you're growing a whole lot right now."

"Yeah." He laughed ruefully. "I guess I am."

"Sit down," she said, indicating the clearing on the floor.

"Why?"

"I'll give you a quick neck massage."

"You don't have to do that."

"I know I don't have to, but I'm offering."

"You have a dinner date."

"In an hour. There's time to give you a five-minute massage."

He must have really been hurting, because he said okay and sat crossed-legged on the floor. She knelt behind him, knees digging into the carpet so old and dirty it crunched.

Katie had no more than touched the wall of hard male muscles than she realized what a colossally bad idea this was. His outdoorsy scent penetrated her senses, seeped into her bones. She was unprepared for the onslaught of sensations that zinged through her palms, her wrists, her elbows. She swallowed against the desire rising up in her throat. Gulped it back. Felt her belly tremble and her knees weaken.

And when he groaned at her kneading, she almost

came completely undone. He moved his neck from side to side as she massaged him. Grunted when her thumb hit a knotted trigger point.

"Harder?" she whispered.

"Oh yeah."

Using her knuckle, she put as much pressure into the knot as she could exert.

"That's it, sweetheart. You've got it."

Sweetheart.

They both froze at the word, both decided to ignore it.

Blood churning with numerous sensations, all of them wild and crazy, Katie rubbed his shoulder a few minutes. "There. How's that? Help any?"

"Helped. Yes. Good."

She hopped up, heat spreading throughout every cell in her body, tingling and throbbing. "I'm glad. Gotta go."

Zigzagging around him, she darted for the door.

"Katie?"

She stopped, turned, her pulse jumping strangely at his earnest tone of voice. "Yes?"

"Thank you for the neck rub."

"Of course," she said. "My pleasure." Realizing a fraction too late just how that sounded, and how unfortunate the word choice was on both their sides, and yet how true it was.

Her face heated, and she opened her mouth to try to mitigate things, but Ryder's sultry smile was on her, hot and sexy.

"Mine too," he said, smooth as sipping whiskey.

Katie felt her pupils widen and her body vibrate and she couldn't take a second longer in his presence. Pulse galloping, she fled, as she latched on to one shocking thought.

The last year had not lessened her desire for him. Not one whit. In fact, if anything, she wanted Ryder more than ever!

After Katie left, Ryder grabbed a beer from the cooler on his Harley and went out to stand on the back porch. The last rays of the sun bumped up against the horizon, cooling off the temperature fast. He huddled deeper into his leather jacket.

White-faced Hereford cattle grazed in the field beyond. Not Jax's animals. Not anymore. His father had sold off his herd and leased the land out to others to run their cattle on. According to Joe, anyway. Ryder didn't know firsthand. He hadn't talked to Jax since he'd come to tell him he was joining the army and his father told him he was a damn fool.

Sadness torqued his chest, and Ryder stared out across the land spreading out as far as he could see, except instead of seeing the topography he knew so well, he saw Katie in his mind's eye.

Her stunning brown eyes, smooth and soothing as high-quality milk chocolate, her pert high breasts, her curvy, feminine body. Every drop of testosterone inside him heated and stirred, intense and demanding. He wanted her.

Desperately.

More than he'd ever wanted any woman.

God, how he wanted her again, but having a one-night stand with her in LA was a far cry from an affair in the bosom of her friends and family. In LA, she'd been exploring, trying on a new identity.

Here? She was herself. Good girl next door, and no matter how you spun it, in Twilight he would always be the reckless bad boy who took risky chances, and damn the consequences.

He couldn't taint her. Wouldn't do anything to cause her harm or damage her reputation. And if that meant keeping his hands off her forever, then that's what he would do.

Katie sat through the lively family dinner, an automatic smile posted on her face, saying almost nothing, allowing the conversations to wash over her, her mind still dazed from her afternoon with Ryder.

Only her niece Lauren noticed she wasn't her usual self.

"Auntie?" Lauren asked, leaning over to pat her knee as they sat side-by-side in the huge circular family-style booth at Pasta Pappa's. "Is sumpthin' wrong?"

Intuitive kid.

"No, sweetheart, nothing's wrong."

"You look sad."

Katie pushed her smile up higher. "Just tired, I guess. I had a busy day."

"Me too," Lauren said, then launched into a tale of everything she'd been up to in kindergarten.

Grateful for the distraction from her thoughts, Katie sat and listened to her niece. She was so lucky. What a lovely life she had. She was with

Lauren, Emma, Sam, and Sam's son from his first marriage, Charlie, who was almost a teenager. Her parents, Lois and Bill Cheek. Her older sister, Jenny; and Jenny's husband, Dean; and their three children, Haley, Sophie, and Oliver, all under the age of five. Jenny and Dean had had fertility problems. Jenny didn't have her first child until she was in her late thirties, but once they got their family started, they took off.

The evening wound down early with so many kids to get to bed, and by seven-thirty, Katie was on her way home. But she couldn't get Ryder out of her mind, and the thought of him working by himself in that miserable house saddened her. Without planning, she turned the car toward the Circle S.

She was two miles out of town headed west when her tire blew.

Crap.

Carefully, she steered the car over on the shoulder of the road and shut off the engine. If she called one of her brothers or her father they'd want to know what she was doing out here when she was supposed to be headed home. She didn't pay for roadside assistance because she had so many family and friends who would help her in case of an automobile emergency. Now she wished she'd sprung for the service.

She pulled out her phone, trying to figure out whom to call, and saw that her phone had died. Sighing, she took out her charger and plugged it in, drummed her fingers on the dashboard while waiting for it to charge.

Headlights appeared on the horizon in front of her. Maybe it was someone she knew, and they would lend her a hand in changing her tire.

No, not headlights.

Headlight. One headlight.

A motorcycle.

What were the odds it was Ryder? She crossed her fingers. Please, please.

The motorcycle whizzed.

Yep. It was Ryder.

Immediately after passing her he slowed, made a wide U-turn, and came back. Her heart bumped and jumped. Ryder to the rescue. Her hero.

A knight in shining armor stepping from the pages of a romance novel. Appearing out of the darkness with that flashing smile, big masculine muscles, and ability to use a jack, ready to slay tire dragons for her. She'd melted like the tenuous snowflakes on warm asphalt.

Her Sir Galahad.

Okay, maybe not Sir Galahad, since he was supposed to have been pure of heart, body, and mind, but one of the knights of the round table.

His strength, and the sheer force of his presence, dispelled her fears and made her feel safe in a way she had not felt before. As if he would never let anything happen to her.

It was a dangerous thought. He wasn't *her* chivalrous knight. Not *her* man. She had no claim on him. She'd known him as a child. Had one mad night with him a year ago. That's all it was. All she wanted it to be. Looking at him, feeling his self-assured energy, she knew it would be far too easy to get spun up in the vortex that was Ryder Southerland.

Even now, one small part of her cried, *Who cares? He's a handsome creature. Let him sweep you away, turn you inside out, and use you all up.*

No. She'd just found herself. She finally knew what she wanted in life and where she was going. She wouldn't abandon her hopes and dreams and ambitions for a pretty face and a hot body that would disappear as soon as the wedding was over.

C'mon. One night wouldn't hurt. In fact, look how much stronger she'd been after that night with him in Los Angeles.

She'd come home resolved to put the past behind her and turn over a new leaf, and she'd done it. She'd started her own business, sold the yurt, bought her house. She'd stopped running to her family every time she got into a bind. She was standing on her own two feet and she loved the independence.

Why would she get involved with another bossy alpha man who would insist on having everything his way?

Good grief, she was getting ahead of herself. The man hadn't even made a pass at her.

She rolled down her window as he approached the car, as if he were a state trooper and she were a reckless speeder.

"Hi," he said.

"Hi." She wriggled her fingers, slumped sheepishly down in the seat.

"What happened to your dinner date?" He bent down, placed his palms on his knees so they'd be eye-to-eye.

"Over already," she said. "They had kids to put to bed."

"Ah, the constraints of parenthood."

"Those little suckers do put a damper on the nightlife."

"And you're out here west of town because . . ." His voice trailed off, but his eyes stayed zeroed in on her.

She wasn't going to explain herself to him, especially when he was wearing such a smartass, knowing grin. She didn't have to explain herself to him. "I had a blowout."

"So I see. Pop the trunk and I'll change it for you."

"Thanks," she said.

"Least I can do after that neck rub."

Katie glanced away, unable to hold the heat of his gaze, and hit the trunk latch release button. The trunk raised. Ryder straightened, walked to the back of the car. Katie let out a breath held so long her head spun.

She waited a moment, until she regained her composure, and got out to check on him.

"Get back in the car," he said kindly, but firmly. "It's dangerous standing on the side of the road."

"You're here."

"I'm changing the tire."

She folded her arm over her chest, snuggled deeper into her coat. "I'm staying."

"Then stand out of the way." He gestured toward the tall grass off the shoulder.

"I could hold the flashlight for you," she said, picking up the flashlight lying on the ground.

He grunted, acted as if he was about to argue, nodded curtly instead. "Only because there's no traffic. If cars start coming, you go stand over there by the fence."

"All right," she agreed.

He jacked up the car, worked the lug nuts with the tire iron, his hands moving rapidly, muscles bunching as he worked.

"Where were you going?" she asked.

"To find a place to spend the night. That house isn't fit for man or beast."

She almost told him he could stay at her house, but managed to bite her tongue in the nick of time. "Jenny and her husband run the Merry Cherub, but they might not have any availability since it's Dickens on the Square weekend. In fact you might have a hard time finding any accommodations this weekend."

"Worse comes to worse, I can sleep outside on the ranch in the sleeping bag. The only reason I didn't want to do that in the first place is because I didn't want to aggravate the crick in my shoulder. Especially since you massaged it out so well."

"The KOA might have some cabins for rent. They're bare bones, so they're the last accommodations to go during the festival."

"Thanks for the tip." He put the spare on, tightened the lug nuts in under a minute.

"That was quick," she said. "Thank you."

"My pleasure." A smile curled his lips. Was he mocking her?

He stowed the flat tire in the truck, along with the jack and tire tool. He took the flashlight from her hand and escorted her back to the car. Opened the door, said, "In."

"You're pretty bossy."

"Comes in handy for a bodyguard." He closed the door. The window was still down. "Buckle up."

She complied, even though his bossiness was getting on her nerves.

"First thing tomorrow," he admonished, "stop and get a new tire. You can't keep driving around on that donut. Got it?"

"Um, who died and made you the boss of me?" She jutted out a defiant chin even though she had every intention of following his advice.

"You have a thing for organization," he said. "I have a thing for protection. Get steel-belted radials. The best they carry." He named the size and brand he thought she should buy.

"Stand down, Southerland. I'm not in the army, and you're not my commanding officer."

He looked flummoxed. "I'm just trying to take care of you."

She threw both hands in the air. "Surprise! I managed to get to be almost twenty-eight years old without your help. I think I can manage getting a tire put on my car."

"Why are you being so testy? I'm not telling you anything one of your brothers wouldn't tell you."

"Exactly. I have four brothers, I don't need a fifth." She drove off, leaving him on the side of the road shaking his head.

Nothing about this day had gone the way she'd planned.

CHAPTER 11

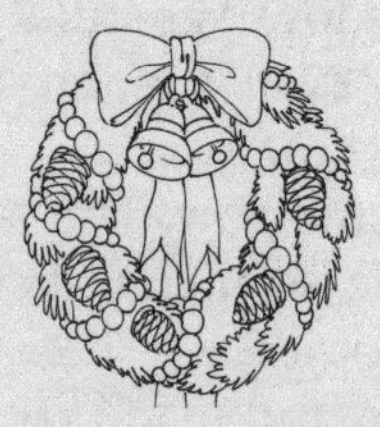

An arousing sex dream, featuring none other than Ryder Southerland, jerked Katie awake at five A.M. the following morning. Her heart thumped hard and she was hot and damp all over.

The image of him was imprinted on the backs of her eyelids—tall, broad shoulders, hard muscles. Masculine nose. Bossy jaw rough with stubble. Dark eyes the color of trouble. Sable hair. Sunburnished skin.

Making love to her.

Katie gulped, pushed her hair out of her eyes with a palm. She'd been having this sex dream about him at least once a month, but as the wedding drew closer, the dreams increased in frequency.

After each one she was left wrung out, overwhelmed and restless, achy and frustrated.

Fanning herself, she sank back down on the mattress, her mind frolicking back to the sex dream. God, it had felt so real. In the throes of it she'd actually thought it *was* real. That she was with Ryder in a medieval castle, and her body sang with electrical joy.

"Shake it off."

If she got this worked up over him in a dream, how was she going to make it through organizing the Circle S and the wedding? Three weeks. The one week she'd worried about had turned into three weeks.

"You'll handle it," she told herself, hopped out of bed, wriggled and jiggled her body, expelling the excess sexual energy.

Just a dream. No biggie. Didn't mean a darn thing. It wasn't like she didn't have a dozen different things to keep her busy. Like getting a new tire for her car.

The little bungalow she'd bought all on her own was so much more comfortable than the chilly yurt on a winter morning. It had been a long time since she'd arisen at this hour. Not since Matt. She was by nature a night owl. Because of meadowlark Matt, she'd adjusted, but left to her own devices, she'd go to bed after midnight and get up around eight.

So go back to bed. The tire store wasn't open yet. Wouldn't be until seven. But she was wide awake now.

She opened the closet door for her bathrobe where she kept it neatly hung on a hook, no draping on the back of a chair for her. A place for everything, and everything in its place.

Inside the closet, she caught sight of her green bridesmaid dress, reminding her of Gabi and Joe's wedding. Ryder was only here for the wedding.

Temporary. His appearance in Twilight was temporary and he would be gone again. Back to where he belonged.

"Do not forget that," she admonished her reflection as she brushed her teeth.

But as she brewed herself a cup of coffee, she remembered the taste of his skin—salty, delicious, mysterious.

He was so damn virile.

Yeah, and that was part of the problem, wasn't it? If he crooked his little finger and sent her one of his sultry stares, she'd come running.

No. Not anymore. The old Katie might have been a pushover, but the Katie that had come back from California last year was fundamentally changed. Most everyone she knew had noticed, and commented on her transformation.

She was damn proud of herself too, and she wasn't about to go back to the girl who molded herself into the person that whatever man she was with wanted her to be.

No more tornadic men for her. No getting swept away. Thank you very much.

She spent the early morning cleaning her house, which was already basically clean, but some dust had gathered. She cooked herself a hot breakfast for once, and took a walk around the town square. At seven, she headed to the tire store, and by eight, she was at the Circle S, arriving just ahead of her crew.

Thank God, she and Ryder wouldn't be alone together today.

They chatted a little. He'd ended up spending

the night at the KOA cabin she'd recommended, and Ryder decided he wanted to go see his father at noon. Katie had confidence in her crew, and knew they could handle the job without supervision for a few hours.

By lunch, Katie, Ryder, and her team of three, Alice Wright, Sia Montoya, and Newt Haus, had finished Jax's bedroom and were three-quarters of the way through the living area. Progress! The cleaning crew home health had hired would come in after they'd finished their job.

They broke for lunch. Alice, Sia, and Newt headed out to eat, Katie and Ryder to the hospital. They took her car because it was more convenient than the motorcycle and in better shape than Jax's twenty-year-old truck.

"All that damn junk in the house Twyla spent hundreds of thousands on, and Dad had to drive a POS." Ryder grunted.

"Your father had a hand in it," Katie said. "He could have put his foot down. He didn't. Either he didn't care that he drove an old truck, or bucking her wasn't worth the fight."

"I'll never understand that man," Ryder muttered from the passenger seat. "Never."

She glanced over at him. The pain in his voice was raw and real.

He was staring out the window at the rolling fields as they drove into Twilight, the lake dotted with fishing boats, Froggy's restaurant with a blinking sign out front advertising "Best Fried Catfish in Texas." A proud boast that wasn't far off the mark.

"The catfish is damn good," Ryder said. "But I always liked Froggy's fried chicken better, and the peppered cream gravy they serve with it."

"Me too," she admitted. "Yummy."

She almost suggested they stop for a meal, but she couldn't wrap her head around the idea of sitting across from him, chitchatting idly, when he was in the midst of processing some deep emotions.

Acutely aware of the vigorous warmth radiating off his body, and the tight way he held himself, as if he'd come completely unwound if he allowed himself to relax, Katie cleared her throat.

"Is it that hard?" she asked.

"What?"

"Being back home?"

He barked a laugh, a harsh, hollow, humorless sound. "This isn't my home."

She didn't know what to say to that, so she didn't say anything, just sent him positive mental vibrations and hoped for the best.

"It *is* a quaint town," he admitted after a moment, his tone easing.

"I like it," she said. "When I was a kid, I used to imagine I'd live in a big city someday, lots of hustle and bustle, no one up in your business. But last year, after my stay in LA, I changed my mind. I'm a small-town girl at heart. Twilight is my home. Always will be."

They drove past the square, where the annual Dickens event was in full swing. Storybook characters come to life, and strolling the courthouse lawn. She saw the historical buildings, constructed in the 1880s, through fresh eyes. Appreciated the Old West flavor. Admired how things rarely changed. That was the appeal. The sameness. It was something you could put your trust in. Knowing that home was always home, no matter where you went, or how far you roamed.

Ryder, however, did not feel the same way.

The sky held a few fluffy white clouds, and the weather was mild. Crisp and clean and cool. It could have been a happy day. But it wasn't. Ryder was tense. His jaw tight, arms a barrier over his chest, eyes hooded.

"Do you remember the time you pushed me out of the way of the Santa float?" she asked, hoping to lighten his mood.

"How could I forget?" he said, with a genuine laugh that lifted her spirits. "I lost my ice cream because of you."

"You saved my life."

"You're overstating."

"I'm not. I froze. If you hadn't shoved me out of the way . . ."

"Someone else would have."

"Why is it you're happy to take the blame for your mistakes, but you don't own the good things you've done?"

"Maybe because there's a lot more bad than good."

"I don't believe that for a second, Ryder Southerland."

She pulled in the parking lot of Twilight General Hospital, and killed the engine. Impulsively, she reached across the seat to touch his hand. "It's going to be all right."

He swung his gaze to meet hers. "I wish I had your optimism. I love that about you."

Love.

Emotion clotted her throat. She knew he didn't mean *love* love. It was just a turn of phrase. She pressed her lips together, trying to ignore the leap-frog sensation jumping in her stomach.

"Well, then," she said brightly. "Let's do this thing."

He nodded, ran both palms down the length of his thighs. Opened the car door. Unfurled his long legs. Got out.

She joined him, coming to stand beside him in the parking lot. "I'm here for you."

"Thanks." He gave her a half smile. "I'm glad to have a friend."

Friend.

There was that word again. Did friendship exclude sex?

Oh gosh, why was she even thinking like that? He was here to see his estranged father for the first time in thirteen years. She needed to clean up her mind, and be present for him.

She linked her arm through his, was both amazed and pleased when he didn't pull away.

But at the reception desk, he uncoupled their arms, and asked what room his father was in.

They were silent in the elevator. Standing side by side. Facing forward. Watching the numbers light up their way to the third floor. She noticed Ryder's breathing quickened the closer they got to his father's hospital room. She tried to imagine what he was feeling, but she couldn't. She was lucky. She and her family were close.

How she wished she could bottle her family's love, and inject it into Ryder. A vaccine for the childhood that had left him ripped apart, and raw, but too stubborn to admit his vulnerability.

At least he allowed her to come with him. That was something, right?

Ryder rapped his knuckles lightly against the door of his father's hospital room, which was slightly ajar, and toed it all the way open.

Katie trailed behind him, realizing her heart was fluttering.

"Hello, Dad," Ryder said in a tension-filled voice.

Katie heard a rustling sound, peered around Ryder's side to see the older man cranked up in the bed, a copy of the *Fort Worth Star-Telegram* in his hands, glasses perched on the end of his nose. An IV snaked from a needle in his forearm to a bag of liquid hanging from a pump. His right foot was out from under the sheets, propped on a pillow and swaddled with bandages up to the ankle.

Jax Southerland calmly turned the page as if the son he hadn't seen in thirteen years hadn't just walked into his room. "Pork bellies are up."

Huh? Katie shook her head, wondering if she'd heard wrong.

Ryder sauntered over and plunked down in the chair next to the bed. "You don't keep pigs anymore. Cattle or chickens either, for that matter."

Jax peered at him over the top of the newspaper. "How do you know?"

"Been to the ranch."

"Permission was not granted."

"Tough shit. I went anyway."

Jax snorted. Thumped the newspaper with a thumbnail.

Katie sank her top teeth into her bottom lip, hovered near the door, and wished she had not come.

"Sit down, girl," Jax commanded, and waved at the remaining chair. "You're not a damn ghost."

Not knowing what else to do, Katie sat. She looked at Ryder, but his face was unreadable, his eyes murky and expressionless. He and his father had that stony stare in common.

A long moment passed. The clock on the wall ticked. Jax studied the paper. Ryder didn't move. Katie tried to breathe silently.

"What's wrong with the foot?" Ryder asked.

"Ulcer on big toe. I went around with a rock in my boot for a whole day and never knew it. Damn diabetes."

"You should take better care of yourself."

"And you should go straight to hell."

Ryder flinched, but only for a second. "I suppose I deserved that."

"You did."

"Why didn't you tell me Twyla died?" Ryder asked.

"Well, let's see. I had no idea where you were or how to contact you and I know you hated her guts and she pretty much hated yours and the two of you made me miserable for, oh, approximately half my life . . . and then you sashay in here like I owe you something, like you're special."

Katie gulped, fisted her hands on her knees. She wanted to cry. For Ryder. For the boy he'd been. For the fact that his father couldn't forgive, and maybe Ryder couldn't either, and the wall between them was never going to come down without some kind of major earthquake, and she couldn't do anything to fix it.

Ryder rested his left ankle on his right knee. The gesture looked casual enough, but it put Katie in mind of a rattlesnake rearing up to strike.

Oh dear, why *had* she come? Why was she trying to smooth things over between them? Make things tidy and right? It was none of her business. What was wrong with her?

"You make it sound like you weren't the one who threw me out, threw me away," Ryder said evenly. "And I didn't hate your wife, old man. I felt sorry for her. There's a difference between pity and disdain. And how much *are* pork bellies up?"

"Enough to make me wish I was in futures." Jax flipped another page of the paper, did not glance up.

Was it just her, Kate wondered, or did this conversation have a split personality?

"Your timing was always for shit," Ryder said.

"Yeah, too bad I timed a diabetic coma to coincide with Twyla's heart attack. Otherwise, I'd get up and kick your ass."

"You want some water?" Ryder asked, moving to pour a glass of water from the yellow plastic pitcher on the bedside table into a matching yellow plastic glass. "Your lips look dry."

"Changing the subject, huh?" Jax squinted at his son. "You know I could kick your ass if I wasn't laid out flat in this bed."

Katie almost laughed at the notion of the withered man in the bed sparring with Ryder.

"You comfortable enough?" Ryder's voice was steady, loose, but his body was stiff. "Need an extra pillow?"

"I need for you to get the hell out of my room. You're not invited. Not welcome."

"So I guess this means it's going to come as something of a shock that I'm moving in with you," Ryder said.

"The hell you say." Jax's face turned beet red and he sat straight up in bed, sputtering and gasping. "You can't . . . no . . . no way. I . . ." He dissolved into a coughing fit, held out a hand.

Ryder rushed to his father's side. "Dad?"

"I'll take that water now."

Ryder slipped the glass of water into his father's hand, waited for him to stop coughing, and settled back against the pillow, pale and winded. "Are you all right?"

Jax glowered. "You're not moving in."

"Yes, I am." Ryder's tone was mild. "You don't have any say in the matter. You didn't take care of your blood sugar. I'm staying until you get sorted out." He gave his father a curt salute. "See you at the ranch on Monday." He nodded to Katie. "Let's go."

She jumped up and followed him into the corridor. "What in the hell was that?"

"My relationship with my father."

"My God, you two are dysfunctional."

"That's about the size of it."

"C'mere." Katie opened her arms.

"What?" His eyes widened in surprise, showing real emotion for the first time since they'd walked into the hospital.

"Bring it in, Southerland." She flapped her arms at him. "Like it or not, you're getting a hug."

He raised his hands. "I'm good. I'm fine. I promise."

"Well, I'm not fine. After seeing that exchange, *I* need a hug." Moving quickly before he could sidestep her, Katie enveloped him in her embrace, felt the heat of his hard muscles, the quickness of his breathing.

"There," she said, patting his shoulder. "There, there."

And to Katie's happy shock, Ryder hugged her back.

CHAPTER 12

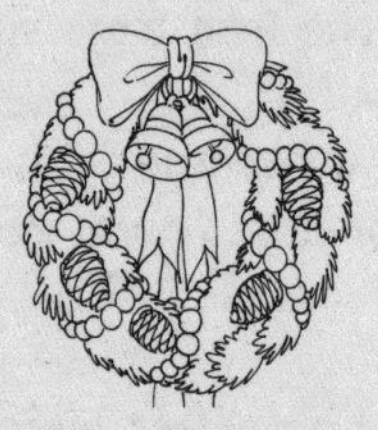

The impulse to stay wrapped in Katie's arms was so overwhelming, Ryder didn't know if he could force himself to step back.

If a familiar voice hadn't hollered, "Ryder Southerland, you son-of-a-dog!" he might very well have kissed her in the corridor of Twilight General Hospital.

What a big mistake that would have been. The hug was bad enough. Especially when that familiar voice belonged to her brother Joe.

Katie was the one who jumped free, hopping a yard away from him, planting a big smile on her face, whipping her hands behind her back as if they hadn't just been wrapped around Ryder's waist.

"Joe," Katie said, and rushed toward her brother. "What are you guys doing here?"

An attractive, petite woman stood next to Joe, and she was watching everything with fascination.

"Meredith had her new baby," the woman said.

"We just came from seeing her. Can you believe it? She had a girl this time. Lenora Elizabeth. Six pounds, seven ounces. Now she's got two babies under the age of two."

"That's on top of two six-year-olds," Joe added.

"Who's Meredith?" Ryder asked.

"Hutch Hutchinson's wife. You remember Hutch," Joe said.

Brian "Hutch" Hutchinson had been a few years ahead of him and Joe in high school. "He was Delta Force, right?"

"Until his team got ambushed. He was the sole survivor." Joe shook his head, a woeful expression on his face. "Sad story."

"But he got his happily-ever-after with Meredith and the kids," Joe's woman said.

"Hey big guy, get over here." Joe yanked Ryder into a bear hug. What was with this huggy family? "Damn it's good to see you."

Keeping one arm around Ryder's shoulder, Joe latched his other arm around the cute woman at his side. "Ryder, this is my bride-to-be, Gabi Preston. Gabi, my best friend in the whole world, Ryder Southerland."

"It's so great to meet you," Gabi said warmly, and shook Ryder's hand. "I've heard so much about you. We weren't expecting you for another two weeks."

"Why *are* you here two weeks early?" Joe asked.

"I read about Twyla on the Twilight Web site," Ryder said. "Why didn't you tell me she died?"

Joe stuck his hands in the front pockets of his

jeans, ducked his head, and looked chagrinned. "I didn't think it was my place."

"Yeah. I get that." Ryder forgave him. He would forgive Joe just about anything.

"Did you guys come to see the baby too?" Gabi asked Katie.

"We didn't know about the baby," Katie said. "We came to see Ryder's dad."

"Your father is in the hospital?" Joe asked. "I didn't know. Gabi and I have been caught up in this whirlwind of wedding planning . . ."

"It's okay," Ryder said. "I don't expect you to keep tabs on him. Lord knows I don't."

An awkward silence fell over the group.

Then they all started talking at once, chatting about Christmas and the wedding. A nurse came out of one of the patient rooms and glowered at them. "Shh, this is a hospital. People are sick. Take the lively conversation elsewhere."

"We're sorry," Katie apologized. Perky Gabi turned and led them to the elevators.

"Hey," Gabi said once the elevator doors closed behind them. "We were going to grab a burger at Kelsey's. You guys want to come with?"

Katie shot a glance at Ryder. Trying to gauge his receptivity?

Part of him longed to go out to dinner with the group, but another part of him, the damaged part of him that had just brushed up against Jax, wanted to go somewhere and lick his wounds. He needed time alone to think, to process his interaction with his father, and decide his next move.

But Katie was looking at him with hopeful eyes,

and damn if he didn't want to spend more time with her. He felt better whenever he was with her, and right now, he could use all the good feelings he could muster.

Ryder nodded. "I am starving."

"Me too," Katie gifted him with a huge smile that stretched his heart.

"Yay!" Gabi clapped her hands. "I'm so glad you came into town early, Ryder. We all are going to have so much fun!"

He cut his eyes at Katie and she cut hers back at him and an electric thrill ran through him, the likes of which he hadn't experienced since last Christmas when she'd ended up in his bed.

It scared him, that thrill, because he'd be gone in a few weeks, after he got things settled at the ranch, after the wedding was over, and then where would he be?

He knew the answer—back in LA by himself, and lonelier than ever.

"Okay," Gabi said to Katie in the restroom at Kelsey's Pub. "Why didn't anyone tell me Ryder was drop-dead handsome? The two of you are going to make the most awesome maid of honor and best man photographs ever."

"Why are you drooling over Ryder?" Katie said, feeling a wee bit jealous. "You've got Joe."

"Not for me, silly." Gabi bumped Katie with her hip. "For you."

"Don't be ridiculous. Ryder is a family friend."

"That hug you were giving him at the hospital went way beyond friendly." Gabi grinned.

"I was comforting him. You should have seen how his father treated him after not having seen him for thirteen years. Shameful."

"Uh-huh. Sure you were comforting him." Gabi winked. "I'll make certain to toss you the bouquet."

"I'm being serious, Gabi. Ryder and I . . ."

Gabi might be her best friend, but she hadn't told her about hooking up with Ryder when she'd been in LA last year after they swapped places. She hadn't told anyone. Gossip like that would have been all over Twilight in half an hour. Not that Gabi would have spilled her secrets, but in small towns, even the walls had ears.

"Oh," Gabi said, catching on, and motioning toward the bathroom stalls just in case someone was in there. "Gotcha. Mum's the word. We'll talk later."

"There's nothing to talk about," Katie murmured.

"Really? I could have sworn you two were sparking."

"Nope. Not us. No sparks. Just old friends."

"Well pooh. That's a shame."

"No shame. It's all good."

"So Ryder is from LA, right?" Gabi asked.

Katie could practically hear her mental gears turning. "He lives there, yes."

"Joe said he's a bodyguard."

"Personal security."

"For celebrities?"

"I suppose."

"Hmm. You didn't happen to run into him while you were in LA, did you?"

Katie put a finger to her lips. Shh.

"OMG!" Gabi let out a squeal, then silently mouthed, *You did run into him*.

Um, more precisely, he'd run into her, tackled her, to be exact. Katie's face heated. In fact, her whole body flushed. She wet a paper towel and pressed it to the back of her neck.

"Getting hot and bothered?" Gabi whispered.

"Shh." Katie sighed. She needed a lot more than a damp paper towel to cool off the fire Ryder stirred in her. "Later."

"I'm coming over tonight, with a bottle of wine."

"What's Joe going to say about that?"

"I'll tell him we have wedding stuff to discuss. Which we do."

"Tonight's not good."

"Why? Are you going to hook up with—"

Katie plastered her palm over Gabi's mouth.

"Sorry," Gabi mumbled around her palm.

"Come by the house later," Katie hissed, and lowered her hand. "But this is for your ears only."

"I knew it!" Gabi said. "I knew there was something—" This time she slapped her own palm over her mouth. "Maybe I'll bring vodka, instead of wine, and we'll make salty dogs. It sounds like it could be that kind of night."

"So are we going to talk about what's going on between you and my sister?" Joe asked Ryder as they went to the bar to get a round of drinks for the table.

"Huh?" Ryder played dumb, keeping his tone mild, belying the hard squeeze of his gut. "I don't know what you're talking about."

"What's going on with you and Katie?"

"Why would you even ask that?" Ryder went on the offensive. Best defense, in his estimation.

"I saw that hug she gave you in the hallway. It was—"

"You know your sister. She's a hugger."

"It looked unnatural to me."

"No, not at all," Ryder lied smoothly, but felt bad about it. Technically there was nothing going on between them. Not now anyway. "She saw my reunion with my father, and she was feeling sorry for me."

"Ouch," Joe said. "Seeing your father again was that bad?"

"Not as bad as when he called me a worthless thieving bastard, punched me in the face, and threw me out of the house when I was sixteen." Ryder motioned to the bartender that he wanted a pitcher of draft beer and four glasses. "I suppose we're making progress."

"But then there's the way Katie looks at you." Joe paused. "Or rather, doesn't look at you. It's not kosher."

"You're saying that because she doesn't look at me that means something?"

"You're weird around each other." Joe rapped his knuckles against the bar.

"Hell, Joe, when have I had time to be around your sister? I just got into town. You saw us at the hospital, in the car, and when we walked in here."

"I don't know when you came into town. You might have been here for days. You weren't supposed to be here for two more weeks. Why *are* you here two weeks early?"

Ryder straightened, felt a surge of panic. Had Katie told Gabi what had happened in LA? Had Gabi then leaked it to Joe? Was that where this was coming from? "I told you. I found out Twyla had died and came home early."

"You rushed home because the stepmother who hated you died."

"She was a human being, Joe. I'm not happy she died too young. She wasn't even sixty. I came to pay my respects, and to see my father."

Joe frowned. "Something fishy is going on between you and Katie. I don't know what it is, but it's something."

"You're imagining things."

"So you two haven't gotten crossways with each other? You're not mad at each other for some reason?"

Oh, was that what Joe was hammering at? He thought Ryder and Katie had a falling out. Ryder tried not to look as relieved as he felt. "No."

"Look." Joe punched Ryder lightly on the shoulder. If his buddy had known what Ryder had done with his little sister last Christmas, Joe would punch him.

Hard.

And he would deserve it. Ryder had violated one of the most cardinal guy rules: never mess with your best friend's sister. He had that punch coming.

"I want this wedding to be perfect. Gabi deserves perfect. Whatever is going on between you and Katie, fix it." Joe poked Ryder's shoulder with the knuckle of his index finger. "Got it?"

"Loud and clear." Ryder rubbed his shoulder,

gave Joe a loopy grin to hide the uneasiness sliding through him. Joe was going to be pissed when he found out what he and Katie had been up to behind his back.

"Make a gesture of goodwill," Joe continued. "Reach out. Take her to lunch. Just the two of you."

"We're good. I swear."

"I insist," Joe said.

"Gabi put you up to this, didn't she?" Ryder hitched his thumbs at the waistband of his jeans.

"Yeah."

"You're off the hook. You can tell Gabi you had a word with me."

Joe narrowed his eyes. "You're not going to take Katie to lunch, are you?"

"Nope."

"Something *is* going on between you two, and don't bother denying it. Every time I mention Katie's name your breath gets shallow and the vein at your jaw jumps."

"WTF, man? You staring at my jaw veins?"

"It's your tell."

"My *tell*?"

"You know, a physical tic that says you're suppressing your feelings." Joe gazed pointedly at Ryder's jaw.

"I bet it's jumping now." Ryder slapped a palm over his jaw.

"Other side." Joe gestured, laughed.

"Laugh it up, fuzz ball." This time, Ryder punched Joe's shoulder.

"So this thing with Katie—" Joe picked up the

pitcher of beer the bartender put on the counter while Ryder snagged the four frosted beer mugs to carry back to their table.

The more Joe talked about Katie, the antsier Ryder got. That night in Los Angeles was imprinted in his brain. Thinking about her, about that night, about how he'd like to repeat it again and again, made him feel both guilty and horny as hell. The power of his desire scared him and he was not in the mood to examine why, especially with Joe.

"There is no *thing*." Ryder snorted.

"You sure? Because—"

"Tiny Tim coming at you," Ryder said, as much to derail the topic of conversation as to warn his buddy about the exuberant five-year-old dressed in Dickensian attire, who'd come bursting through the door, running at full speed through the bar, a white walking cane tucked underneath his arm.

Joe leaped out of the way in the nick of time.

Tiny Tim whizzed between them, sending people scattering in all directions. On his tail came Bob Cratchit, hollering for Tiny Tim to get back here right this minute, or he was going to get coal in his Christmas stocking.

"So," Joe said, picking up the conversation without missing a beat, "if you won't take Katie to lunch, Gabi is going to insist on having you two over for dinner. She's not happy unless the people around her are happy."

"Katie's happy. I'm happy. See?" Ryder stretched a smile so wide it hurt his face. "Happy, happy, happy."

"Actually, you look kind of constipated."

"Look, leave me and Katie alone. We're fine. F-I-N-E."

"That's not what Katie says."

"What?" Alarm shot through him. "What did Katie say?"

"Gotcha." Joe pointed a finger. "I knew something was going on between you two."

"Katie didn't say anything?"

"No."

The restaurant sound system was playing "Santa Claus Is Coming to Town," the same song that had been on the radio the night he and Katie made love, admonished them to be good for goodness' sake.

Too late for that one. He was at the head of the naughty list.

Joe and Ryder stared at each other, and an odd look crossed Joe's face, and in that instant Ryder knew his friend had finally put two and two together. "*Oh.* Oh, I get it, you and Katie . . ."

"There's no me and Katie." Ryder made a face. "She's your sister and she's your fiancée's bridesmaid and she's organizing my dad's house. That's the extent of our relationship."

"Okay then. I'll tell Gabi everything is under control." Joe set the pitcher of beer down at their table.

"Good." Ryder held his breath.

"Great." Joe stuffed his hands in his front pockets. "Want me to pour you a beer?"

"Never thought you'd ask."

Joe hovered with the lip of the pitcher over the mug, met Ryder's eye. "'Cause if there's a problem between you and Katie, I'll let you off the hook.

Consider yourself unhooked. I can get one of my brothers to be my best man. Just say the word and you're free. Gabi and me, we got a good thing going here, we don't need any drama."

Shit. Ryder could feel the vein in his jaw jumping now. "You think I'd cause trouble?"

"No, but . . ." Joe cleared his throat. "I'm handling this badly. I know coming back to Twilight is a strain for you, and if it's easier on you to just skip it and go back home, all you have to do is say the word."

Ryder blew out his breath. "Level with me, Joe. Do you want me out of the wedding?"

"No."

"Does Gabi?"

"No."

"Then what's the problem?"

Joe rested a hand on Ryder's shoulder, looked him squarely in the eyes. "I love you like a brother. I hope you know that, but you've got this lone wolf thing going on. I know that's part of who you are, and I admire the hell out of your independence."

"But . . ."

"A wedding is a team effort. You've got to be part of the fold, at least for a little while. I know you don't like this town. I know there's hard feelings here—"

"And?" Ryder clenched his teeth, his fist, and his pride.

"You need to take a good look in the mirror and decide if Twilight is really where you want to be right now. If it's not, then walk away. No harm. No foul. No hard feelings."

CHAPTER 13

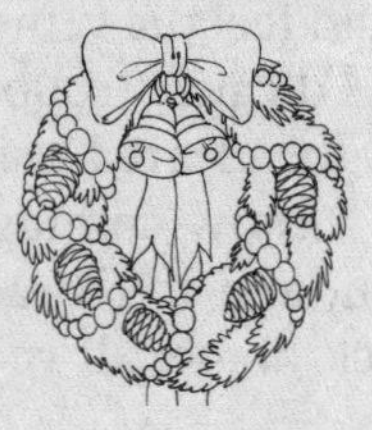

Blindsided.

Ryder felt completely blindsided by what Joe had told him. It stung, and he wasn't going to pretend it didn't. Was he too much of a lone wolf to be Joe's best man?

Hell, he'd been through a damn war, survived his crappy childhood. He'd been part of a team plenty during his eight years in the military. He knew how to come into the fold, as Joe put it, whenever he needed to.

So why was Joe giving him an out?

Dammit. If he were smart, he'd take the out. Jump on his Harley and head back to LA, especially after that oh-so-tender reunion with his father.

Smart choice. Forget all about Twilight and the people in it. He'd almost convinced himself that was what he was going to do, but then Katie and Gabi came back from the ladies' room.

He was sitting at the table across from her, sipping beer and pondering his options, and he could see his own dismal reflection in her lively brown eyes.

She telegraphed him the most brilliant smile, like the sun coming out after a season of monsoon rains, and he thought, *No, not gonna do it. Not gonna run away from that smile.*

Joe was right. Despite his military service, he wasn't good in groups, and he did keep people at arm's length, even his old army buddies. He was afraid of getting sucked in. Of getting too invested. Of getting hurt.

Shit. That sounded cowardly.

Was he a coward when it came to intimate relationships? He'd never been engaged. Not even close. The longest he'd had a steady girlfriend was eight months, and she'd broken things off because he wouldn't commit. The longest friendship he'd ever had was with Joe, and he hadn't seen him in two years.

Wow. The epiphany struck him like a two-by-four upside the head.

What kind of person was he? Closed off. Isolated. A hard nut no one bothered to crack.

Lonely.

Yes, he prized his independence. Had been damn proud of the fact that he didn't need anyone. Self-reliant. Autonomous. Free.

But he now saw a long path stretching into the future where he became more and more cut off from people, grew less and less capable of loving someone.

What were the lyrics to that song? Freedom's just another word for nothing left to lose?

It pulled him up short. What was he in the process of becoming? Did he want to be that person?

He knew at once what he was going to become if he left town now.

Fuckstick.

He would turn into Jax. He'd be like that ornery old man in the hospital bed. Shut down. Dug in. Entrenched. Unable to forgive or see beyond his own nose because he was too afraid to acknowledge he'd been wrong.

If he stayed here in Twilight, and tried to sort things out with his father, no matter how hard that might be, and deepened his relationship with Joe, and with Katie, how would that change him?

A thrill rose up inside him, a kid on Christmas morning kind of thrill. And he knew then what he wanted. Had wanted it since last Christmas when he'd taken Katie to bed.

He wanted *her*. He couldn't fully define what that meant. Not yet. But he wanted her. Damn, how much he wanted her.

Katie's gaze was hot on his face. Those eager eyes that moved him in ways he had not ever been moved before.

Ryder gulped. If he stayed, what personal dragons would he have to slay? Bigger question. Was he up to the challenge?

He had two choices. Stay and see this through. Or bow out. This was his opportunity to leave Twilight, and his father, and his past behind forever. All he had to do was go.

But that meant letting go of his friendship with Joe. That also meant leaving Katie behind.

Briefly, he closed his eyes, unable to bear the intensity of her stare. He would be around her a great deal over the next few weeks, during the most romantic time of year. Was he truly prepared for that much closeness?

Do or die, Southerland. Do or die.

He opened his eyes, glanced over at Joe.

Ryder had never been fully committed to anything but the army, certainly not a person. But he was all in. His poker chips stacked in the middle of the table for the taking. He'd reached the point of no return. He was invested. Committed. To being Joe's best man, to mending fences with his father, to seeing where this thing with Katie could lead.

"Something you need to say, buddy?" Joe asked, his question heavy with innuendo.

"Yes," Ryder said.

Every eye at the table was trained on him as if they all knew there was weight in whatever he was going to say next.

"What's that?" Joe pressed his lips closed.

"When and where do I go to get fitted for my tux?"

"Who wants to play trivia?" Katie asked, once they'd eaten hamburgers and were finishing off the pitcher of beer.

Ryder seemed so intense, and after the miserable visit he'd had with his father, she was anxious to lighten his mood. Mindless pub trivia might be fun. The man could use some fun in his life.

She reached for the controller sitting in a charging dock in the middle of the table, which was used to answer the questions appearing on the computer monitors mounted throughout the pub, and tried not to feel shaky.

She felt as if Ryder had just made a monumental decision of some kind, but she could not pinpoint why she felt that way, other than there was a shift in him. His smile seemed lighter, while the look he gave her had more heft to it. His expression sent a shiver rocking up each bone of her spine.

Perhaps she was imagining it. Or projecting. Her feelings for him had deepened, so she assumed his had too? Not smart to assume. Not smart at all.

Gabi took a sip of beer and told Ryder, "Katie is a trivia fiend. You'll win if you're on her team, but don't play against her."

Katie leveled her gaze at Ryder. "Well?"

"Can't," he said. "My head's Swiss cheese when it comes to fun facts."

"Or anything fun for that matter," she quipped.

"Boo-yah." Joe laughed. "Skewered."

"Remind me again why I'm hanging out with you, cheeky Cheeks?" Ryder grinned.

"Because they're awesome," Gabi said.

"You're too serious, Southerland." Joe poked him in the ribs. "Lighten up. Jump in with both feet and let my kid sister mop the floor with you."

Ryder snapped his fingers at Katie. "Gimme."

"You're going to play?" She giggled.

"If you give me the controller."

"It's all yours." She slapped the controller into his palms, her fingertips accidentally brushing over his skin in the process.

His nostrils flared as if he'd caught a whiff of her

lime and lavender cologne, and he blurted, "You smell edible."

"You think this is good, wait until you get a whiff of the Christmas scent I'm wearing to the wedding," Katie said. "Smells like chocolate chip cookies."

"Mmm," he said, lowering his eyelashes and licking his lips. "Can't wait."

Not her imagination. He'd come to some conclusion about her. Katie just wished she knew what it was.

"Log in," she directed.

"Huh?" His eyes were latched on to hers.

"For the trivia. You need a username."

"Oh yeah. Right." He punched letters into the controller's keypad. On the TV monitor popped up the username Wasabi.

Katie's cheeks heated.

"Wasabi?" Joe said. "What the hell kind of username is that?"

"Katie's allergic to wasabi," Gabi said. "She found that out when she was in LA after we swapped houses last year."

"Did she now?" Ryder drawled, his voice thick and sultry.

Katie stared at him, into him, and felt her body loosen and sway. *Hush!* She sent him a mental chastisement with her eyes. *Hush or they'll figure out something went on between us last year.*

"She did," Gabi chattered away. "She was at a charity gala with my invitation, and some woman accidentally spilled it down the front of her dress and Katie got this massive rash from it."

"You don't say." Ryder never took his eyes from Katie's face. His smile was wickedly conspiratorial.

"Truth. Right, Kate?" Gabi bobbed her head. "She was still broken out when she got home."

"Truth," Katie murmured, her mouth gone excessively dry. She took a sip of beer. It didn't help, so she took another one.

"You guys doing all right?" their busty waitress asked.

"Yes," Gabi said. "But bring another a pitcher. We're celebrating." She raised a hand to indicate Ryder. "An old friend has come to town."

"And a good-looking friend he is too." The waitress lowered her eyes, and lobbed Ryder a come-hither stare.

Katie took another sip of beer to wash down her jealousy. She had no claims on Ryder, none at all. She was the one who made it clear their sexual relationship was a one-time thing.

Ryder leaned closer to her, churning her senses and lifting her hopes. He looked straight at her. Not even a passing glance at the attractive waitress. And underneath the table, his knees touched hers, and he did not move them away.

Boom-boom went her heart. *Whoosh* sailed her hot blood through her veins. *Thrillfest!*

Oh God, he was driving her crazy. Right smack-dab around the bend.

"So," Ryder said. "What do I get if I win?"

"You won't win," she assured him. "My house and my life might be tidy, but my mind is an attic stuffed full of trivial information."

"That's because you're such a bookworm. Since

you're so brilliant, and I'm trivia impaired, I think a handicap is in order."

"All right," she said. "You get ten points added to your final score."

"Fifty."

"Twenty-five."

"Done."

He reached out his hand, and she shook it, and felt a million blessedly wonderful electrifying things.

"Now," he said, rubbing his palms together. "What do I get if I win?"

"I'll pay for your meal."

He considered it a moment, shook his head. "Nah. I can pay for my own meal. Let's go for something a little more creative."

"What do you want?" she asked, suspicious of the possibilities.

"Hmm." He tapped his fingers on that rock-hard chin of his. "How about you make me a home-cooked meal?"

Joe made choking noises. "You're taking your life in your own hands, buddy. This one here can't boil water without burning it."

"I'll take my chances." Ryder's gaze didn't budge from her face.

"You always did like to live dangerously." Joe topped off everyone's mug with fresh pitcher of beer the waitress brought back.

"Cooking makes a mess," Katie said.

"And she hates anything messy," Gabi told Ryder.

"I'll wash the dishes afterward," Ryder offered. "Home-cooked meal? That on the table?"

"Since I'm not going to lose, okay," Katie said.

"Don't you get it? With Katie's cooking, even if you win you lose," Joe pointed out.

"I believe she's up to the challenge." Ryder peered into her eyes.

"The man is living in a fantasy world," Joe whispered to Gabi.

Katie gulped, but didn't drop Ryder's gaze. She could handle the heat. "What do I get if *I* win?"

"A ride on my Harley."

"Who says I want one?"

"You used to beg me for a ride when you were fifteen."

"That was a long time ago," she said.

"You still want it." His green eyes lit like flames, singeing her from the inside out.

She did. Oh yes indeed. She wanted to straddle that big machine, strap her arms tight around his lean waist and rest her head against his broad shoulders and fly down the highway with a hot engine pulsing between her legs.

"It's December. Too cold for a motorcycle ride," she said.

"Not if you have the right gear."

"That's the thing. I don't. Have the right gear, that is."

"Sure you do. I'll fix you up. That is, if you win."

"How about you stop talking and let's get to it?" Katie challenged and waved at the monitors throughout the bar displaying the startup screen for the next game. "We're live."

"Sassy. I like that." His big thumb stroked the controller.

"You guys playing?" Katie asked Gabi and Joe and reached for a second controller.

"We're spectating this round." Joe slung his arm around Gabi's shoulder and drew her, chair and all, closer to him.

The monitor above their table scrolled the instructions and the rules of the game. People throughout the bar could join the game and pick which team they wanted to be on. Katie was on the red team, Ryder on the blue.

The first category was potpourri.

"I hate potpourri," Gabi said. "It's such a mixed bag. You never know what you're going to get."

"Like a box of chocolates." Joe kissed her forehead.

"Actually, no, not like a box of chocolates. In every box of chocolates I've ever bought they have a diagram drawn into the lid telling you which chocolate is which, so if you bother to read the lid, you *do* know what you're getting in a box of chocolates." Gabi planted a palm in the center of her husband-to-be's chest and rested her head on his shoulder.

"You're saying Forrest Gump's mother was yanking his chain?" Joe ran his fingers through Gabi's hair.

"Yup." Gabi sighed contentedly.

"Don't look," Katie told Ryder. "They're getting sickening."

"You're just jealous," Joe said. "'Cause you're not in love."

"Hmph." Katie grunted and poked Ryder in the ribs with her elbow. "First question is about to come up. Eyes on the screen. It moves fast once the questions start. Speed counts. You get extra points—"

The first question popped up. *What year did Masters and Johnson publish their seminal tome* Human Sexual Response*?* Along with the question were four multiple-choice answers.

Some yokel in the back of the pub snickered loudly. "Semen-al."

Ryder guessed wrong. Katie got it right.

"How did you know that?" he asked.

"I watched a television show about Masters and Johnson."

"Guess I'm behind the eight ball on pop culture questions. I don't own a TV," Ryder said.

"I know—" Katie bit her tongue. She was about to say, *I know, I was in your apartment*, but then realized where she was and who she was with and finished lamely, "—no one who doesn't have a TV."

She need not have worried. Gabi and Joe weren't listening. They were deep in the throes of a passionate kiss.

"Jesus," Ryder said. "Save something for the honeymoon."

"Jealous," Joe mumbled around Gabi's lips.

"You both just missed answering the second question when you weren't paying attention," said the waitress, who dropped by to see if they wanted anything else, and they all ordered coffees.

"Darn it," Katie said. "We gotta focus."

"At least we're even," Ryder said.

"We're not even. I aced the first question. You're down by one. Ooh, new question." Katie bounced on her seat, read the screen. *The first rubber condom was produced in what year?*

What was with these questions? When did potpourri category get so sexy? Katie had no idea, punched in an answer at random, and got it wrong.

Ryder, however, got it right.

"Lucky guess," Katie accused.

"Yes." He grinned impishly. It felt good to see him having fun. "But it still counts."

"These are hard," Katie grumbled.

"That's what condoms are for," Gabi teased.

Which land mammal has the largest penis to body ratio?

Seriously? But she knew this. She'd heard this fun fact on a morning radio talk show. Rapidly, she clicked "barnacle" as her choice.

The monitor turned red. Indicating she'd guessed wrong. No. No way. She knew it was the right answer. "Hey! I was robbed. The barnacle *does* have the largest penis to body ratio."

"I'm not even going to ask how you know that," Gabi mumbled.

"The barnacle might have the largest penis," Ryder said. "But the question asked for a land mammal." Ryder had nailed it, answering with African elephant.

"Oh yeah." Katie's cheeks heated and she avoided meeting anyone's gaze, particularly Ryder's, training her eyes on the screen. The next question was about chewing gum, thank heavens, and both she and Ryder got it right.

"Neck in neck," he said, leaning in so close she could smell his woodsy aftershave.

She grinned at him, and he grinned back. "Might end up a draw."

"For sure," he murmured. "The draw is a given."

Gabi snapped her fingers from her perch in Joe's lap where she'd migrated. "You're missing the questions again."

The game continued, and Ryder quickly lost his edge as the category changed from potpourri to Katie's wheelhouse, books and authors. She aced every single question in that round.

Ryder scored one. He'd known Poe was the author of "The Pit and the Pendulum." "I only know that one because of you," he said.

"What do you mean?"

"You gave me a book of Poe's short stories to read."

"I did?" She wrinkled her nose.

"You don't remember?"

"I gave a lot of books to a lot of people."

"And here I thought I was special."

You have no idea how special! "I'm impressed," she said, "that you read it. From what I remember you weren't much of a reader."

"I . . ." He cast a sidelong glance at Joe and Gabi, and from his expression she could tell he wanted to say more, but not in present company.

What was on his mind? His demeanor had certainly shifted from how he was when they'd gone to see his father to now. It was as if a switch had been flipped.

The topic of the third round category popped up. Military. Ryder chuckled, rubbed his palms together, and said, "You are so dead."

But Katie had once worked for Lockheed Martin, an aerospace company with military contracts. She knew a thing or two about the military. She missed a few questions, and Ryder gained on her, but in the end, her score beat his.

She did a little victory dance in her seat. "Get the Harley tuned up. Looks like we're going for a ride."

"Um," Joe said. "I believe you owe the man a home-cooked dinner, although why he would want that from you is beyond my understanding."

"What do you mean? I won." Katie waved at the scores on the screen. "Katydid beat Wasabi."

"You spotted him twenty-five points, remember?" Gabi knocked her fist gently against Katie's noggin.

"Oh yeah. Pooh."

Ryder's smile turned devilish. "Can't wait for that delicious meal."

"She might cook for you, but if you're holding out for delicious, you're going to be waiting a *looong* time," Joe joked.

"Enough, brother," Katie said. "He gets it. I'm a terrible cook. But a bet is a bet. I'm going to fix the best meal I know how."

"What?" Joe laughed. "Take-out chicken from Froggy's?"

Ryder got to his feet. "We'll arrange a time for dinner later," he told Katie. "For now, I'm going to go back to the KOA. No way am I spending the night at the ranch until Katie works her magic and cleans up that hell hole."

Katie hopped up, grabbed her jacket from around

the back of her chair. "You're gonna need a ride back to the ranch to get your Harley."

"That's okay," Joe said. "We'll take him to the ranch. It's on our way, and that way you won't have to make a special trip out of town."

Curses. Foiled in her attempt to get Ryder alone to discuss those meaningful looks he'd been sending her.

The half smile he gave her was contrite, as if he felt the same way. "Guess I'll see you tomorrow," he said.

"Yep. Back at it." She made a gung-ho gesture with her arms like she was ready to tackle the world.

Question: Was she ready to tackle the interesting feelings stirred up inside her after spending another day with Ryder?

CHAPTER 14

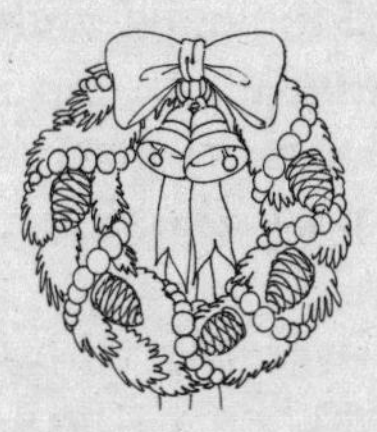

"Tell me everything that happened in LA."

It was seven P.M. that same evening and Gabi was standing on Katie's front porch, a bottle of vodka in one hand, and a carafe of grapefruit juice in the other, and her overnight bag thrown over her shoulder.

"And don't even try to pretend that you and Mr. Pure Sex Walking didn't hook up last Christmas," Gabi went on. "I picked up on the innuendo over trivia."

Katie arched an eyebrow. "Am I to assume you're spending the night?"

"Yes. Drinking will be done." Gabi jutted out her chin, and stood her ground. "Slumber party!"

"No sleeping ever gets done at slumber parties." Katie could tell her friend was not going to be dissuaded. "I have to get up early tomorrow and wade through Jax Southerland's shambles of a life."

"You're not punching a time clock. You're the boss."

"My crew arrives at eight. I need to be there to let them in."

"We'll be in bed by midnight," Gabi vowed. "I promise."

Katie held the door open wide, feeling grateful, despite a sigh rising up in her. Gabi was such a good friend. She was so glad she'd responded to Gabi's Pinterest post those fifteen months ago. "C'mon in."

Gabi trooped over the threshold, and headed straight for the kitchen to mix up the cocktails. Resigned to talking about Ryder, Katie trailed after her.

"So . . ." Gabi had to stand on tiptoes to reach the glasses on the top cabinet shelf. "Start from the beginning . . ."

"It's kind of a long story."

Gabi dumped sea salt in a saucer, dampened the rims of the glasses, and rotated them in the sea salt. She measured out a shot of vodka in each glass, filled it with grapefruit juice, bitters, stirred vigorously to mix and served it over ice. "We're drinking. You're dishing. Spill it."

"Where's Joe?" Katie asked, stalling.

"Joe and Ryder are cutting down trees at the farm as we speak. Bonding. Doing guy things. Probably talking about us."

"But it's dark."

"You know how well the Christmas tree farm is lit, and I think they just needed to work off some stream. We invited Ryder to spend the night with us instead of wasting money at the KOA. I've got nowhere else to be but here."

"You're not going to let this go, are you?"

"Nope." Gabi pushed the salty dog into Katie's hand. "A toast."

"To what?"

"Our hot guys."

"Ryder's not my guy."

Gabi rolled her eyes. "Okay, to hot guys in general."

"To hot guys." Katie clinked her glass with Gabi's, and then took a long swallow of the tangy citrus drink.

"Now, back to Ryder. Details. I want details. When did the attraction begin?"

"Ryder lived with our family during his last year of high school, after his dad kicked him out."

"I know. Joe told me . . . Continue."

"I had a secret crush on him." Katie mumbled, staring into her glass at the grapefruit pulp clinging to the ice cubes.

"Well of course you did. What red-blooded American teenage girl wouldn't have a crush on a hottie like Ryder?"

"Hey, watch it. You're about to marry my brother."

"Just a statement of fact. I've got eyes. But my heart belongs to Joe always and forever. Rest assured, I am not lusting after your guy."

"He's not *my* guy," Katie protested.

Gabi took a pull off her straw. "Okay, so you've been crushing on Mr. Pure Sex Walking for over a decade, and—"

"You make it sound like I've been mooning over him for thirteen years. It's not like that. I was engaged. I was with Matt . . ." Katie fished an ice cube from her glass, sucked on it.

"And yet you still fantasized about Mr. Pure Sex Walking from time to time."

"Yes, but fantasies are fantasies for a reason," Katie admitted sheepishly. "And stop calling him that."

"Why? Ryder *is* sex walking—those muscles and sinew, that thick tanned skin, his lanky movements, eyes that ooze bad-boy charisma."

"Nothing is going to come of this relationship, so don't even try to play matchmaker. We hooked up. Once. And that's how it's going to stay. A one-time thing."

Gabi hopped onto the bistro barstool beside Katie. "How come?"

"Seriously?"

"Seriously. I want to know."

"Well, for one thing, I'm T-ball and he's major league."

"Oh, shut the front door." Gabi snorted. "He is not out of your league."

"You said it yourself. He's pure sex walking and I'm certainly not."

Gabi snorted and rolled her eyes. "You are smoking-hot gorgeous. Ryder would be lucky to have someone like you."

"Smoking-hot gorgeous?" Katie swept a hand at her faded mismatched pajamas, hair pulled back in a sloppy ponytail, and fluffy pink bedroom slippers. "You have a generous definition of gorgeous."

"Girl." Gabi flapped a hand. "Pretty is from the inside out. Clothes and makeup aren't what make a woman gorgeous. It's her smile, her laugh, her heart, her humility. You've got all that times ten."

"Guys are more superficial."

"That's a bit sexist. Painting all guys with the same brush."

"You're right. It's just that men, in general, are so visual. The pretty package is what lures them in. That's how I snared Ryder in the first place. I was wearing that snug-fitting red sheath dress of yours."

"Katie Cheek, stop it. Ryder knew you when you were a skinny teenager with braces and thick glasses and frizzy hair. You didn't hoodwink him by cleaning up nice and putting on a designer dress. He knows the real you."

That thought thrilled her so much she didn't dare entertain it for long in case she started believing it. "Mom's been showing you the family picture albums again, huh?"

"What can I say?" Gabi shrugged. "I asked to see Joe's baby pictures for the wedding video, and I got deluged with the entire Cheek family history. I'm not completely sure your mom remembered which baby was which, so she threw all the pics at me."

"I think after the first couple offspring, she might have lost track." Katie laughed. "Six kids are a lot to take care of."

"And your mom makes it look easy, but back to the high school crush. You were swooning over Ryder as a wide-eyed fifteen-year-old, but feeling inadequate. I'm guessing he had no idea how you felt about him."

"I think he got an inkling there at the end." Katie pressed a palm to her face. Her forehead sweltered from embarrassment. To cool off, she downed the rest of icy salty dog, felt her head spin pleasantly.

"How so?"

"I kissed him," Katie confessed, and told her the kissing-the-plum story.

"Ooh, that sounds sexy. No wonder you threw yourself at him. Kudos to you for being brave enough to go for what you wanted."

"I didn't plan it. The kiss was completely impulsive."

"Many of the best kisses are." Gabi smiled, her eyes faraway, as if remembering an impulsive kiss or two of her own.

"And stupid. Very stupid."

"How do you mean?"

"I actually launched myself at him and knocked him to my bedroom floor . . ." Katie went on with the story. "And when I attended your fund-raising gala in LA, he was there guarding Les Ketchum, and he saw me racing up the stairs, my chest burning from wasabi reaction, and he thought I was Ketchum's stalker, and he tackled me."

"Knocking you to the ground."

Katie nodded. "Spread eagle. He pressed me into the floor. I'm not a big believer in coincidence, but I . . . I think we both considered it fated somehow that we ended up in the same place, in the same position we were in the last time we were together, and we simply got swept up in the moment."

"Been there." Gabi smiled wickedly. "With Joe."

"Eww." Katie plugged her ears. "You're talking about my brother. TMI."

"Getting swept away can be fun." Gabi giggled.

"It might have been fun," Katie said, and hardened her jaw. "But it certainly wasn't smart. If I had known you were falling for my brother at the same time I was in LA getting tackled, I certainly wouldn't have hooked up with Ryder that night."

"Why not?"

"Because now there's a reason for him to come back to Twilight. If he wasn't serving as Joe's best man, I wouldn't ever have to see him again."

"He would have come back anyway, Katie. He had to check on his dad after his stepmother died. But I still don't get why you're ruling him out as a serious love interest."

"It's way too complicated."

"How so?"

"For one thing, Ryder lives in LA and I'm Twilight all the way. You've met my family. We're entrenched in this town and each other's lives."

"He's from here. Maybe he'll move back. Especially now that his dad is widowed and alone, they might make up."

"Those two mix like matches and gasoline." Katie shook her head. "I don't ever see Ryder coming back here for good. This town was not very nice to him. There's nothing for him here."

"*Ahem.*" Gabi cleared her throat and stared at Katie pointedly.

"What?"

"You. You were here for him."

Katie grunted and shook her head. "What man

would give up his job and LA for Podunk, Texas, and me?"

"I gave up LA for Joe."

"Yes, but you were looking for small-town life."

Gabi made a noise of impatience. "Dammit, Katie, you're a wonderful person and I'm so proud to call you my friend, but I swear sometimes you don't give yourself enough credit. Let your light shine, woman. Maybe Ryder agreed to be Joe's best man because he *wanted* to see you again. Ever considered that?"

"No." Katie swiveled from side to side, shaking her body as well as her head for emphasis. "He came for Joe."

Gabi rolled her eyes. "I have half a mind to thump you."

"Ryder did not come back home for me," Katie insisted.

"How do you know?"

"Because when Ryder and I . . ." Katie paused, caught her bottom lip between her teeth. Normally, she'd be more circumspect, but the salty dog slipped the parking brake off her tongue.

Gabi scooted to the edge of her seat, breathed deep. "Yes?"

"When we, um . . . um . . ."

"Did the deed?" Gabi finished gleefully.

Katie nodded, and couldn't stop a modest smile from curling at her lips. "I made it clear that our hooking up was a one-time thing. No strings attached. I told him it could *never* be more than that. Ever. And he agreed."

"And you said that because you figured that's what he wanted?" Gabi asked.

"Because it was what *I* wanted."

"Really?" Gabi folded her arms over her chest in an I'm-not-buying-it expression.

"Really," Kate said, not buying it herself. But hey, she talked a good game.

"Geez." Gabi stabbed a hand through her hair. "That's surprising. But a girl has a right to change her mind. You could change your mind. You're not stuck with the no-strings edict."

"It's more than that," she confessed.

"What?"

"I didn't leave things on a positive note between us. I don't think there's much hope of changing the rules this late in the game."

"Why? What happened?"

"I snuck out on him the morning after. Slipped out of his bed and ran away without even leaving a note. I'm not proud, but I did it."

Gabi winced. "Do you think you hurt his feelings?"

"I don't know." Katie shrugged. "I felt really bad about running off without a conversation, but I couldn't face him in the light of day."

"Sex was that bad, huh? I can see that would be a dilemma. Here the guy you've been crushing on since high school is lousy in the sack."

"No," Katie whispered. "The sex was that *amazing*. Mind-blowing and life-altering doesn't even begin to cover it."

Gabi grinned as if she'd just found a real diamond in a box of Cracker Jacks. "I know what that's like. Joe is—"

"Ugh!" Katie clamped her hands over her ears again. "TMI. TMI."

"Sorry." Gabi chuckled. "I couldn't resist."

"I get it. You and my brother have fantastic sex. Let's move on."

"Okay, wait." Gabi held up both palms. "Hold the presses. I have to make sense of this. You ran out on Ryder because the sex was over-the-moon?"

"I guess you could say that."

"Why? Why would you hamstring yourself like that? Why close down a world of possibilities? Is something wrong with him that I can't see?"

"Yes," Katie whispered.

"What?" Gabi lowered her voice too as if they were coconspirators worried about being overheard by nefarious spies.

"He's the white unicorn."

"The what?" Gabi's brow furrowed.

"You know, the fabled white unicorn. The fairytale creature every little girl dreams of catching, but once she does she realizes it's a fantasy for a reason."

"And what reason is that?" Gabi asked, eyes wide, head tilted with curiosity, a few grains of sea salt clinging to her upper lip.

"Once you capture the white unicorn, the fantasy is over."

"I see," Gabi said in a tone that said she didn't see in the least.

"Here's another way of looking at it. If you capture the unicorn, tame it, you change it, and it's no longer the beautiful creature you once longed for."

"You're saying Ryder's wildness is the very thing that attracts you?"

"Yes. I can't change him. I won't even try."

"So when you were in LA, you took a walk on his wild side, but you knew that while it was a fun place to visit, you couldn't live at that level of excitement. And if you were to attempt to tame Ryder, it would destroy who he was at his core, and that's why you told him no-strings attached. Not because you didn't want strings, but because you knew strings would bind him."

"Exactly." Katie clutched her hands in her lap, looked down, and noticed with surprise that she'd been chewing on her thumbnail. She hadn't done that in years. Not since she'd left her ugly duckling phase.

"I'm not sure I agree with the reasoning, but you know Ryder better than I do."

Automatically, she brought her thumbnail to her mouth, but forced herself to clasp her hands together.

"I get that you don't see Ryder as a forever kind of guy. You don't want to change him, whatever. But why can't you just enjoy his company, and then let him be on his way?" Gabi asked. "Nothing wrong with having great sex with someone you trust. Enjoy yourself."

Katie's heart pitched at the question. Rolled. A tiny boat on a turbulent ocean. She ran an index finger around the rim of her glass, collected salt, and licked her fingertip. "Because," she said, "if

I have sex with him, I'm gone. It would kill me to lose him. I couldn't take the grief of it. After losing Matt, I'm too raw, too scarred."

"What are you saying?"

"I lied when I told him no strings attached. I didn't really know I wasn't telling him the truth, but I was denying it to myself, but after we had sex . . ." Katie hauled in a deep breath, didn't say another word.

"What?" Gabi prompted, curling her fingernails into her palm. "What is it?"

"When I got home from LA and looked around at my life—the yurt, the farm, my past with Matt—I realized it was just a place I'd drifted into, not because I was desperately in love with Matt and wanted to be with him, but because I couldn't have what I really wanted. And if I couldn't have what I really wanted, what was the point? I might as well have Matt and be what he wanted me to be."

"What did you really want?" Gabi asked.

Katie laughed, a dull, lifeless sound. "What do you think?"

"Ryder?" Gabi ventured.

Silently, Katie nodded, felt a riff of emotions sing through her—sadness, regret, doubt, fear.

"Oh my," Gabi whispered.

"Yes," she said. "When I opened the front door at the ranch yesterday afternoon, and found him standing there, it was like a freight train hit me. And I finally understood what I felt for him was no schoolgirl crush. I'm in love with that man and have been for half my life."

"Wow." Gabi placed a palm over her heart. "Wow. I don't know what to say to that except I think it's time for another round of drinks."

Groaning, Katie shook extra Tabasco into the Bloody Mary she was mixing. Was it enough? Should she add more? Maybe she should be adding more vodka instead. But the thought of adding more than the teaspoon she'd already put in turned her stomach.

She'd never in her life drunk alcohol at seven o'clock in the morning, but it felt as if a twenty-piece marching band was tromping around inside her skull. If this was what a hangover felt like she was glad she skipped the hard partying in college.

Joe once told her the cure for a hangover was more alcohol. She wasn't so sure about that, but right now, she'd try anything to make the pounding stop. Unfortunately, this was her first time concocting a Bloody Mary and she was winging it.

"What are you doing?"

Katie jumped, shot a guilty gaze at Gabi, who bustled into the kitchen. "Hair of the dog. Which sounds kinda gross when you think about it."

"More booze is not the solution."

"Joe said it worked. Ouch, ouch." Katie clasped her head. "Shh."

"Joe can be an idiot sometimes," Gabi said. "I love him to pieces, but he is a guy, after all. And when it comes down to it, what do guys know about affairs of the heart?"

Gabi took the Bloody Mary away from Katie and dumped it down the sink.

"Hey . . ." She started to protest, but shifted her voice to a whisper. "Damn, I have to stop shouting."

"You're not shouting. Is this your first hangover?"

"That obvious?"

"Here." Gabi guided her to a chair, got a package of frozen peas from the freezer, wrapped them in a kitchen towel, and pressed it into Katie's hand. "Put this on your head."

"Thanks." Katie put the ice pack to her right temple where it was pounding the hardest, hung her head. "I just wanted to say I'm sorry. I drank too much. I'm ashamed and I'm sorry. Please forgive me."

"No need to apologize to me. It was my fault. I'm the one who brought the vodka over. I just had no idea we'd have so many deep topics to cover."

"Yeah." Katie massaged her temple. "Could you just forget all that stuff?"

"Too late. You already confessed to being in love with Ryder." Gabi set a glass of water and two aspirins in front of Katie. "Here, take this. And drink all the water. It's the best I can do."

"You could make me another Bloody Mary."

"Alcohol got you into this situation. More is not going to get you out."

"I know, but I'm miserable."

"You're lovesick. That's what you are. Take the aspirin."

The minute the water hit Katie's stomach, she got let out a groan, and that made her head thump harder. "Oww. I'm never ever drinking again."

Gabi took pity on her suffering. Gently, she

touched Katie's arm. "I know what it's like to be in love and believe it's not going to work out."

"It's not going to work out. It can't."

Gabi opened her mouth as if to argue, but shut it without saying anything.

"Oh God, and now I have to go over to his father's house and try to make sense of that chaos and Ryder will be there. Top that with a hangover and it's all too much."

"Shh," Gabi said. "Give the water and aspirin time to kick in, and as for the other stuff, just know that it will all work itself out the way it's supposed to."

"Thanks." Okay, it was trite advice, but it was the only thing Katie had to hold on to. Hope was good. Right?

"Come on," Gabi said. "Grab your jacket. I'm taking you out for breakfast."

CHAPTER 15

"Up and at 'em." Joe flung Ryder's blue jeans at him. "Breakfast at Perks."

"Perks?" Ryder blinked up at his buddy from Joe's living room couch, where he'd spent the night.

"Coffee shop on the square, makes bitchin' sausage croissant sandwiches. Truck's leavin' in five." Joe clapped his hands.

Yawning, Ryder sat up. He'd slept like crap, his restless mind filled with thoughts of Katie. How she'd looked last night playing trivia. How his heart lit up every time their eyes met. She was so different from the women he dated. She was so open, and unguarded, offering her feelings and smiles so freely. She led with her heart, and if he had a lick of sense he'd stay as far away from her as current circumstances allowed. He didn't want to be the one to break that tender heart.

"What?" Ryder asked. "We can't stick a piece of bread in the toaster and be done with it?"

"You need to get out and about. Make new friends in your community."

"For one thing," Ryder said, sliding into his jeans, "it's not my community, and I don't need any new friends. I won't be in town for that long. For another thing, when the hell did you become a morning person?"

"When I got the Christmas tree farm from Gramps. Farmers don't get to lie around in bed all morning. Chop-chop. Let's go."

Ryder ran a hand through his shaggy hair—he needed to schedule a haircut before the wedding—pulled on a T-shift, jammed his feet into his cowboy boots, and grabbed his jacket to follow Joe out the door.

"Why are you limping?" Joe asked as they climbed into his truck.

Pine needles were strewn across the floorboards, and the cab smelled like Christmas. The radio spun Bruce Springsteen's "Santa Claus Is Coming to Town." Unlike most folks, Ryder got little enjoyment from Christmas music, or Christmas in general, ever since his mother died. The only time he recalled being truly happy near Christmas, after his eighth birthday, was last year when he wound up in bed with Katie. Because of that night, he liked the hell out of this song.

And while Bruce sang about being good for goodness' sake, he thought about Katie, and ached all over.

"The limp?"

"Huh?" Ryder leaned down to rub his left shin. "Was I limping?"

"I wouldn't have mentioned it if you weren't."

"Shrapnel. Sometimes when I sleep in a cramped position it acts up."

"You were wounded in the war? I didn't know that. Why didn't I know that?" Joe drummed his fingers on the steering wheel. "You should have told me."

"Minor." Ryder shrugged.

"Shrapnel in the leg doesn't sound minor to me."

"Soldiers came back with body parts blown off, or didn't come back at all, some of them from this very town. I'm damn lucky, and I know it."

"I don't say it often enough, hell, we don't talk often, but thank you for your service."

"Knock it off," Ryder said, rubbing his palms together in front of the heater vent. "I was just doing my job."

"A job that entailed keeping my farmer ass safe."

Ryder didn't like being called a hero or thanked for doing what he'd been paid to do. It embarrassed him, but apparently it made people feel good to tell members of the armed forces that their service was appreciated, so he gritted his teeth and accepted it.

The coffee shop on the town square was packed. The store was decorated for the holidays, complete with three large Christmas trees that crowded the already cozy space. Lively conversation hung in the air along with the scent of strong coffee and bacon, as they joined the line waiting at the counter to place orders.

"Those trees came from my farm," Joe bragged.

"No kidding?"

Joe named off each variety of the trees and detailed what section of his farm they'd been grown in with a big grin.

Ryder shook his head, disarmed by the changes in his friend. "I can't see you as a farmer. You were the one who could never sit still, and now here you are watching trees grow for a living. What happened to the ADD?"

"Found ways to deal with it, and here's the kicker, working the land settles my butt right now."

"I thought you'd always be footloose and fancy-free. In fact, didn't we make some kind of pact when we were in high school?"

"Change comes to us all, buddy." Joe laughed joyfully, and listening to him warmed Ryder from the inside out. "And change is a good thing, a great thing. I'm happier than I've ever been in my life, and expect things to keep getting better after I make Gabi my wife."

"You are different." Ryder cocked his head to study his friend. Gabi had turned Joe's life around, a complete one-eighty. Funny. Ryder saw marriage as something that stunted, rather than nourished, but he had to admit a lot of that was based on Jax and Twyla.

"Can you ever see yourself becoming a rancher?" Joe asked.

"No way in hell."

"So when your dad passes away, what's going to happen to the Circle S?"

"Jax is only sixty. He's not going anywhere anytime soon."

"Twyla was only fifty-seven," Joe pointed out. "And your father is a diabetic who is not taking care of himself. One day, that ranch is going to be yours."

Ryder snorted. Why was Joe hammering on this? "Hell, for all I know he wrote me out of the will when he kicked me out of the house."

"But if he did leave it to you, what would you do with it?"

"I'd sell it in a heartbeat."

"For real? But it's been in your family for generations. All that family history." He shot Ryder a heavy look.

"Too much history," Ryder said, thinking of his mother.

"That's a shame," Joe mused. "It truly is. Around here many of the old ranches are being split up, and sold off by the heirs. End of an era."

"It takes a lot of hard work and money to run a ranch." Ryder massaged the bridge of his nose with his thumb and forefinger.

"Next," said the pixie-haired barista whose name tag identified her as Brittany. She winked at Ryder, but it bounced right off him. He wasn't a flirt, and he wasn't interested.

He and Joe collected their food and found a table someone was just vacating. The second they sat down, a loud male voice hollered, "Hide your women and lock up your money, that swine Ryder Southerland is back in town!"

Ryder cringed. He didn't have to turn around to know who was speaking. Tumley Hudson owned the ranch next to the Circle S. He'd been trying to buy Jax out for as long as Ryder could remember and he'd hated Ryder ever since Tumley's daughter asked Ryder to the prom and he'd turned her down because he wasn't going. The man was a snapping turtle when it came to holding grudges.

"You could always sell the ranch to Tumley," Joe mused, taking a bite out of his breakfast sandwich.

"Not funny." Ryder growled.

A heavy hand smashed down on Ryder's shoulder.

He glanced up into the face of the grizzled old coot who had brandished a shotgun at Ryder when he was eleven, for taking a shortcut home from school across his property. Tumley had served in Vietnam, and couldn't seem to let go of the anger that war had stirred in him.

"Hey boys." Tumley glanced over this shoulder at "the boys," a group of older men sitting in the corner watching the exchange with amusement. "Should we call Sheriff Hondo and give him a heads-up that this riffraff is on the loose?" Tumley grinned, flashing a mouthful of nicotine-stained teeth.

On the surface it was a joke. Ha. Ha. The bad boy returns to the town that done him wrong and he has to take whatever shit the locals dish out or prove he deserves the reputation. But Tumley's fingers were biting into Ryder's shoulder, and there was nothing friendly about that smile.

"Would that be the same Hondo Crouch who used to be a heroin addict?" Ryder asked evenly. He knew Hondo had cleaned up his act after he'd returned from Vietnam, but it didn't hurt to remind Tumley that Ryder wasn't the only one in town with demons to live down.

Tumley raised his fists and took a boxing stance, his eyes flinty. "Dissing Hondo, whippersnapper? Them's fightin' words."

Joking? Or not?

Ryder estimated the odds of a fight breaking out in the coffee shop. Not that he couldn't take Tumley with his hands tied behind his back and his legs shackled, but he didn't want to cause a ruckus. Plus Tumley did have a gang of the old guard as backup. And while he might be a senior citizen, Tumley had served in that mess of a war that had ruined many a man, and he'd come out of it a survivor. He had Ryder's respect for that if nothing else.

Joe's eyes narrowed and he fisted his hands, ready to come to Ryder's defense.

Ryder shook his head. *Easy. It's all good. I can handle the likes of Tumley Hudson.*

Joe nodded, unclenched his fists, went back to his sandwich, but kept a watchful eye on the senior citizen standing between them.

"Sorry about your stepmama." Tumley's voice softened and he sounded sincere. "And I'm sorry about your dad being laid up in the hospital. But he's an ornery old bastard, so I know he'll pull through."

"Thanks," Ryder said, and exhaled, not knowing if he could or should trust Tumley's sympathy.

"I'll let you get back to your breakfast." Tumley returned to his seat.

Leaving the sweat that had popped up on the back of Ryder's neck drying in the cool air.

"What was that about?" Joe muttered.

"Who knows? Probably just showing off for his posse. Tumley is a loudmouth. You could park a 1973 Cadillac Fleetwood in his jaw and still have room for a Volkswagen."

Joe laughed. "Let's talk about something else. For instance . . . what's going on between you and Katie? Before the trivia game last night I thought you guys were pissed off at each other, but then you two were giving each other heated looks and I started to realize something else was going on."

"Don't know what you're talking about." Ryder took a sip of coffee that was already going cold.

Joe dabbed at his face with a napkin. "Just what are your intentions toward my sister?"

Ryder didn't know why, but irritation bubbled up inside him. Maybe it was the exchange with Tumley, and the fact his muscles were still twitching for action. Or maybe it was the realization that while the chemistry between him and Katie was stronger than ever, and so was the swift undercurrent keeping them apart. Or maybe it was because he was scared to death of the feelings he didn't dare name.

"I don't know what the hell you're talking about. I don't have any intentions toward your sister. No feelings for her at all."

"Oh shit," Joe murmured, eyes widening as he gazed over Ryder's shoulder.

And before Ryder ever turned around, he knew whom he was going to see standing behind him.

Katie.

Dread filled him as he swiveled his head to take her in. She wore old blue jeans, a fluffy blue sweater over a white T-shirt emblazoned with the same

"Fresh Start" logo on her branded packing cubes. She had on fleece-lined boots and . . . sunglasses?

Why was she wearing sunglasses inside the coffee shop?

He couldn't read her eyes because she was wearing the sunglasses. Couldn't tell how much his words had hurt her.

Gabi was standing beside Katie, staring at Ryder with a fierce you-are-a-total-butthead expression on her face. But she quickly replaced it with a soft smile for Joe and moved over to kiss her husband-to-be.

"Hey Trouble, how are you this morning?" Joe cupped her cheek with his palm.

"Trouble?" Ryder asked, because he was having problems gauging just how much trouble he was in. His heart was pounding and his mouth was dry and he was scrambling for something to say that would make everything all right between him and Katie.

"His nickname for me." Gabi patted Joe's chest. Then to her bridegroom, she said, "We didn't know you guys were coming here."

"No, but I knew *you* were planning on treating Katie to breakfast, and I just had to see you before going to work. I missed you."

Gabi plunked down in the empty chair beside Joe. They gazed into each other's eyes, and interlaced hands.

Ryder offered a sheepish smile to Katie, who still hadn't reacted. "Have a seat," he invited, sweating bullets and pulling out a chair for her with his foot. "Join us."

"Coffee," Katie muttered. "I need coffee."

Because of the sunglasses, he couldn't see if she was looking at him or not, but she sidestepped the chair he'd pulled out, and headed for the counter.

"Hey." Panicked, he reached out to snag her elbow as she brushed past, stopping her.

She froze. Glared hard at his hand as if it was the nastiest thing she'd ever seen.

"Katie," he murmured, feeling like a giant shitheel, and wishing that every person in the place wasn't eyeballing them. Another downside of being the town bad boy with a dangerous reputation. Everyone kept tabs on you. He wanted to hustle her to one side and have a private conversation, but there was no room in the place.

"Yes?" The Sahara was wetter than her tone.

"I swear I didn't know you were standing behind me."

"Clearly," she said, her smile strong but her voice stringy, and she wrenched her elbow from his grip, tucked it tight up against her side. "But that's all right. Good to know how you actually feel, which is, oh, right, nothing."

He let her go. What else could he do? Tackle her? Make her listen to him? And tell her what? The truth? That he was so scared of his feelings for her he denied them?

"I'm sorry," he said. Which was unusual for him. He rarely apologized. He was of the school of thought that apologies showed weakness.

"Let yourself off the hook, Ryder." She readjusted her sunglasses, compressed her lips into a straight line. "It's perfectly fine. I don't have any feelings for you either."

"Oh," he said, knowing it was total bullshit, but unable to call her on it in front of everyone. Funny, even though he knew it wasn't true, it stung anyway. Dammit, why had he been so worried about admitting to Joe his feelings for Katie?

Maybe because he wasn't exactly sure himself just what those feelings were.

"If you'll excuse me," she said. "I'm in desperate need of coffee. Now *that* I have strong feelings about."

Ryder cringed and watched her walk away with a you-can't-touch-this strut, back pockets swaying, not letting him get her down. God, how he admired her pluck.

"Don't take it personally," Gabi leaned over the table to whisper to him. "She's got a hangover."

"Katie?" Joe sounded puzzled. "My sister? She hardly ever drinks. To my knowledge, she's never had a hangover in her life."

"She hasn't," Gabi confirmed. "This is her first. Hence the sunglasses indoors."

"What caused her to drink too much last night?" Ryder asked.

Joe and Gabi both stared him squarely in the face, looking at him as if he were an utter moron, and simultaneously said, "*You.*"

CHAPTER 16

Katie grabbed her coffee from the barista and lit out the back door of Perks. No way was she walking past Ryder again.

She sat in her car, listening to her heart thump erratically, realizing she was going to have to go to the Circle S and face him.

No. She couldn't. Not today. Not with this hangover. Not until she'd had a chance to sort herself out.

Tears pushed at the backs of her eyes, but she blinked them away. It was okay. She was going to be okay. Nothing had changed. She been in love with Ryder for years, and he wasn't in love with her. Status quo.

Except she'd actually admitted to herself—and, egad, to Gabi—that it was far more than a high school crush gone on too long. She was in love with the man. Always had been, probably always would be.

So yeah, she was not going to the ranch today.

She did something she'd never done in the ten

months she'd owned her own business. She took a sick day. Because she was sick.

Sick at heart, that was.

She phoned Jana and asked her to go meet the crew and stick around to help them.

"Extra pay?" Jana asked.

"Of course."

"Double time?"

"Time and a half."

"Done."

Feeling blue, she drove home, intending on going back to bed for a couple of hours to see if she could sleep off the hangover. Once inside the house, she sank down into a kitchen chair in front of the bay window that looked out over the big backyard. She admired how green the yard was, planted with pines transplanted from Joe's Christmas tree farm. She had forgotten to turn the Christmas lights off when she went to bed last night, and hadn't remembered them when she and Gabi left this morning. The lights twinkled a fairy-dust glow over the yellowed blades of grass.

And then she spied the cat.

She took off her sunglasses for a clearer view. It sat statue-still. An orange tabby, scrawny and big-eyed, underneath the pine tree closest to the back porch. The cat switched its tail, stared straight at her, and meowed so loudly she could hear the plaintive cry through the double-paned glass window.

She moved to the fridge and poured up a saucer full of half-and-half she used for her morning coffee. Careful not to spill it, she carried the saucer to the back porch and set it down. Stepped back into the doorway, pulling her sweater around her against the crisp December air.

"Here kitty, kitty," she crooned.

The tabby lowered its head, crept toward the porch on lithe paws. Its gaze swung from her to the saucer of milk, and back again. Poor little thing was so hungry that survival won out over its natural wariness.

Once he reached the saucer, he crouched with muscles tensed, ready to spring away if she made a threatening move. Up close, she saw that yes, it was indeed a he, and the poor guy was so thin his ribs were visible beneath his skin. He looked young too, not quite a kitten, but he hadn't fully grown into his cat-ness.

He stretched his pink tongue out as far as he could, lapping up the half-and-half. She wished she had some cat food to give him, and wondered if there was a can of tuna in the pantry.

To her surprise, when the milk was gone, he did not dart away, but instead curled into a ball with his tail wrapped around him, lowered his eyelids halfway, and began to purr.

Katie lowered into a squat, but otherwise did not approach the cat. He raised his head and contemplated her a moment.

"Hey kitty." She rubbed her thumb against her first two fingers in a circular motion. "Where did you come from?"

The tabby's whiskers twitched.

"Not the talkative type, huh?" She smiled, felt the cool wind burn her cheeks. "I know something about strong, silent guys. You take your cream where you can, and then don't give us girls the time of day."

The cat eyed her.

"I know what you're thinking," she told the cat. "Ryder is just not that into me. And why should he be? He's a man of the world and I'm a small-town girl. Which is fine. Totally. I don't care. Not really. Okay, I do care. All right, yes, dammit, I stupidly fell in love with him, but that's on me."

The cat meowed.

"Yes? You already knew that? I know he doesn't love me. I don't even know if he's capable of love. Losing his mom when he was a kid seems to have knocked the love bone right out of his body. Unfortunately, I can't avoid him. I'll be seeing him over and over again during all the wedding festivities. And annoyingly, it's Christmastime and we'll have to do all that happy-happy, deck-the-halls stuff together too."

A tear trickled down her cheek and she closed her eyes, took a deep breath. How did you fall out of love with someone?

"What do you think?" she asked the cat, and opened her eyes. "Any advice?"

But the tabby had disappeared.

"Hey kitty, where did you go?" Had he darted under the porch? She bent lower to peer through the gaps in the boards. "Here kitty, kitty. I'll get you more milk."

Nothing. Silence.

Disappointed, she got to her feet, scanned the

yard, but that cat was nowhere in sight. "That's right, get your fill and run away."

She picked up the empty saucer, opened the door, and felt a cold draft blow through her legs as she stepped back inside. Katie moved toward the sink. Saw the orange tabby sitting on the kitchen counter, contentedly licking his paw, and she let out a startled shriek.

"Holy shit, how did you get up there?" she exclaimed, and slapped a palm over her mouth. "I thought you'd disappeared. By any chance are you Harry Houdini reincarnated?"

The tabby swished his tail.

"And by the way." She snapped her fingers. "Get off the counter. You could have fleas."

Harry shot her a haughty expression that said, *It's winter, stupid*, lifted his tail, and walked cockily over the counter.

"Hey, you could still have fleas even though it's winter. This is Texas, and while it gets cold, it never stays cold for long."

He turned his head, sauntered over to where she'd deposited the saucer in the sink, sniffed at it.

"You're still hungry. Hang on. Let me check to see if I do have a can of tuna." She rummaged through the pantry. "No tuna, but here's a can of baby food meat and gravy for when I babysit my sister Jenny's kids. Will that do?"

Harry meowed.

"I take that as a yes." Katie scooped him off the counter and set him on the floor. He protested with a loud meow, but when she put the baby food on the saucer and set it beside him, he changed his tune and got all purry again.

"Stick with me," she said, "and you'll eat like a baby king."

She knelt on the floor beside him, softly stroked his matted tail. She'd not ever had a cat. Growing up, Joe had been allergic, and later, Matt had not cared for cats, but Katie had always adored them. "I've always wanted a cat. I wonder if you belong to anyone. Maybe you have an owner who loves you and you got lost. Maybe you have a chip. Looks like a trip to see Sam is in order."

Harry eyed her suspiciously.

"Don't panic. Sam's one of my brothers. He's a vet. He'll take care of everything." She called her older brother's house.

Emma answered in her bubbly voice that never failed to cheer her up. "Morning, Katie."

"A stray cat showed up at my back door," she explained.

"Sam's already at the clinic," Emma said. "He's got a busy surgery schedule this morning, but if you hurry over, I'm sure he could squeeze you in."

"Um . . . how do I transport the cat over there?" Katie said.

"Hang on." Emma laughed. "We have a million cat carriers. I will swing by and drop one off for you."

"You're a lifesaver," Katie said.

"Isn't that what family is for?"

"It is. I don't know what I'd do without you guys." She thought of Ryder, who had no family other than the father he didn't get along with, and she felt sorry for him.

An hour later, Sam finished examining Harry with a shake of his head. "He's not feral, but no one's been taking care of him either." He scowled. "No chip and he hasn't been neutered. Looks like someone might have dumped him."

"How terrible!" Katie pressed a palm to her throat. "Who would do that?"

"Hopefully not anyone in Twilight. He needs vaccinations. Are you considering keeping him?" Sam said it like the idea of Katie owning a pet was completely foreign.

At her brother's pointed tone, Katie raised her chin. She hadn't been considering keeping the cat, but Sam's question issued a challenge. "You make it sound so farfetched. People get cats every day. Why can't I get one?"

"You absolutely can."

"But?" Katie sank her hands on her hips.

"You're just such a neatnik. I can't see you with a litter box in your house."

"Maybe you need glasses," Katie joked. "I used to live on a farm, remember? We had chickens and cows."

"Outside animals. Livestock. That Matt mostly took care of. You've never had a house pet."

"First time for everything."

"You really want to keep him?" Sam stroked the tabby's thin spine. "Just making sure. He's young, and well-cared-for house cats can live fifteen to sixteen years or longer."

"Harry picked me. I'm all in. Do whatever needs to be done."

"I'll only charge you for the medication. Family discount." Sam's familiar smile was back. "Leave him here for the day, and we'll take care of him. You can pick him up this afternoon."

"Thanks." She headed for the door, leaving Harry in the best hands possible.

"Katie," Sam called.

She paused with her hand on the knob, looked back. "Yes?"

"You're going to love having a cat."

Because that was apparently her fate? If she couldn't have the man she loved, was the universe telling her she might as well give it up and become a crazy cat lady?

When Ryder finally got Joe to drop him off at the ranch, he vowed never again to be without transportation around lovebirds. Between feeding each other from their plates, and stopping for long, deep smooches, it took Joe and Gabi forever to finish eating breakfast and drive him back to the Circle S.

There was a van parked in the driveway instead of Katie's silver Camry. Her crew, he figured, and bounded up the porch steps, his palms sweaty, anxious to have a word with her, but uncertain of what he was going to say.

You could start with I'm a complete dumb ass, please forgive me.

The person who met him in the entryway wasn't Katie, but a funkily dressed young woman with multiple tattoos and piercings. She introduced herself as Katie's assistant, Jana. She told him Katie wasn't coming in that day, but she'd be back on the job tomorrow.

If he felt like a snake belly before, he sank two rungs lower. She'd skipped out on her job because she didn't want to see him. Cursing himself under his breath, he whipped out his cell phone.

"In the meantime," Jana said, and shoved a large plastic garbage can at him, "Katie said to put you to work clearing out your old bedroom."

"Hang on a minute." He held up on finger while he dialed Katie's number. Would she answer? He held his breath.

It rang once. Twice. Three times.

Ryder wasn't particularly good at groveling, in fact, he couldn't remember a time he had actually groveled, but he was going to grovel now. Just when he thought the call was going to go to voice mail, he heard Katie pick up. *Thank you*, he sent a silent prayer up to the heavens. Now was his chance to redeem his sorry ass.

"Yes, neuter him," she hollered.

"What?" Ryder exclaimed, feeling his balls draw up tight against his body.

"Not you," she said. "I was talking to Sam."

"Your brother?"

"You know any other vets from Twilight named Sam?"

"Um . . . no. But I don't know all the vets in Twilight."

"There you go."

Confused, he stabbed fingers through his hair. "There I go where?"

"Did you need something?" she asked.

"You're not here."

"Here where?"

"The Circle S. You're supposed to be here."

"No, I'm supposed to be here. My assistant, Jana, is there in my place."

"I'm beginning to feel like Abbott in 'Who's on First,'" Ryder mumbled. "Or was it Costello?"

"Where's the confusion? You're there and I'm here."

"Yes, but why are you there and not here?"

"I'm here, you're there."

"Okay, let's forget the here and there stuff, and get down to brass tacks. Come to the ranch. I'm sorry. I didn't mean to hurt you. I'm an idiot. Please forgive me, and come back to work."

Katie laughed. "You're an idiot all right. Get over yourself, Mr. Ego. You are not the reason why I took the day off."

"The hangover excuse isn't cutting it. I upset you and I know it. We need to talk, Katie. Face to face. Sort this out."

"I found a stray cat in my backyard," she said. "He needed medical attention, so I brought him over to see Sam. Sam's gonna neuter him, and I want to be here when he comes out of anesthesia."

"You're keeping the cat?"

"Yes."

"Huh?"

"What?"

"Nothing."

"It's something or you wouldn't have said huh."

"I don't see you as a pet person," Ryder explained.

"Why does everyone keep saying that? I love pets."

"You love cleanliness and order more."

"I'm adaptable. Some things are worth sacrifice. The cat is worth putting up with kitty litter and hairballs. Sheesh. Give me some credit. First you think I'm a big crybaby because you don't have feelings for me, and now you think I shouldn't have a cat because they make messes."

"Katie."

"Yes?"

"I do."

"Do what?"

"Have feelings for you," he mumbled.

She caught her breath. "What?"

"I have feelings for you," he said, raising his voice.

Wait? What? Really? Her heart crashed drunkenly through her chest. "That's not what you told Joe."

"I lied to your brother, because he's your brother and my best friend, and lusting after you felt wrong and because . . ."

"What?" she prompted when he couldn't continue.

"We need to do this face-to-face. This is not a conversation for the phone."

"You called me."

"I need to see you."

A long silence passed. Ryder was aware of Jana still standing there with the oversized garbage can, staring at him hard and listening intently to his side of the conversation.

"I'll be at the ranch tomorrow. The conversation will keep until then. In the meantime, Jana is in charge, do whatever she says."

"Katie, I—" He started to argue.

But she had already hung up.

Chapter 17

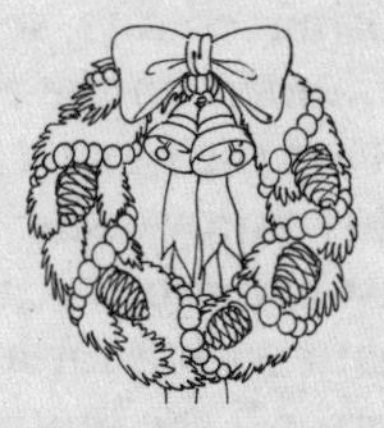

Katie picked Harry up from Sam's office that afternoon, and took her groggy new roommate home.

"Okay," she told Harry once she got him settled in on a pillow. "Here's the deal. You didn't catch me on my best day. I'm feeling a little sorry for myself, but I promise you my pity parties are always short-lived. I'm going to eat some ice cream and watch a silly movie. You can lie on the couch with me while you recover."

Harry swished his tail as if that was okay by him.

She took a pint of cherry cheesecake ice cream from the fridge—the stash she normally kept to satisfy her that-time-of-the-month cravings—and turned on a frivolous comedy on Netflix, making sure it was *not* a romantic comedy. She was not in the mood to watch people fall in love. She wanted jokes and pranks and pratfalls, and lots of them. Harry crawled up in her lap to sleep and purr contentedly.

Life was good. Who needed men? She had

movies, a cat, and ice cream. What more could she ask for? She would worry about Ryder tomorrow. After she had a good night's sleep and woke with a clear head.

Just as the closing credits scrolled across the screen, a knock sounded on the front door.

Taking care to ease the freshly neutered cat from her lap back to his pillow, she apparently didn't get to the door fast enough, because the impatient caller knocked again with a rat-a-tat staccato.

"Hold those horses," she muttered.

She yanked opened the door to find Ryder standing on her front porch, a big brown paper bag from Froggy's in his hands, looking frazzled, but still incredibly delicious. His motorcycle was parked in the driveway. She'd been so busy laughing at the comedy she hadn't heard him drive up. She wasn't forewarned, nor was she prepared for the sight of him at her doorstep.

Oh Lord, she was in trouble.

The sleeves of his red plaid Western shirt were rolled up, and the top two buttons were undone, giving her a tantalizing glimpse of his tanned chest. He was disheveled—hair mussed, beard stubble ringing his jaw, clothes rumpled.

Her heart sloshed because she was so damn happy to see him. Wow, she was pathetic or what?

"Is that fried chicken?" she asked, because it seemed the most sensible thing to focus on.

"Straight from Froggy's." He offered her his charming bad-boy grin.

"Get in here." She grabbed him by the elbow and dragged him inside, but not before she darted a quick glance up and down the street to see if any tongue-wagging neighbor gossips were outside watching, or peeking around curtains.

"Scared Gladys Kravitz is going to see us together, and spill the beans?" he teased.

"You know the grapevine in this town has eyes and ears all over the place."

"I do. I've been a victim of vicious slander a time or three, yes."

"It's not slander if it's true," she said.

"Touché." His grin grew more disarming. If that grin was an industrial-strength vacuum, she'd be buck naked right now, completely suctioned of all her clothes.

"So you'll put your motorcycle in the garage?"

"Won't that look worse? Like you're hiding me from view. Like you're ashamed of me. Are you ashamed of me, Katie?"

The sound of her name on his tongue set her lips to tingling. Terrific. She couldn't be in the same room with him without tingling, shivering.

"Right." She pressed her palm to her forehead. "Good point. Why do you have to have the same vehicle you had when you were seventeen? Everyone in town knows that Harley."

"For one thing, I love her."

Yeah, he loved his motorcycle, heart and soul. Why not her? Maybe if she made noises like an ironhead engine he'd have feelings for her. *Vroom. Vroom.*

"For another thing . . ." His voice deepened along with the look in his eyes. "I don't commit to many things, but when I'm committed, I'm all in."

"I see." She gulped.

"Relax about the gossips," he said. "I have reason to be here. We're in a wedding together, remember? Your brother is my best friend. We have things to discuss."

"They'll ponder why we couldn't discuss those things over the phone. To make me feel better about it, could you go put the Harley in the garage?"

"Why do you care what they think?"

"Because it will get back to my mom and that's a conversation I do not want to have."

"Why not?"

"I can hear it now. Yes, Mom, I boinked the bad boy you took into our home. Yes siree, I'm doing it with my foster brother. Proud of me, Mom?"

" 'Doing'?" he said. "Don't you mean 'did'? It was only the one time, Miss Priss. Just the way you wanted it."

"Well, technically it was three times." She skimmed over her Freudian slip. "During that one night."

"Does that make it better or worse?"

"The chicken smells really good," she said, hoping to hijack the topic and fly it to the food.

"Looks like you've already eaten," he said, staring at the ice cream carton in her hand.

"Oh that." She thrust the carton behind her back, having forgotten she was still holding it. "I thought I would eat dessert first tonight."

"That does not sound like the rule-following Katie I know." He stepped closer.

"No?" She didn't back up, kept standing there

clutching the ice cream carton like it could save her life.

"But that's not the first time you've surprised me. I'm beginning to think I might not know you as well as I thought."

"Maybe not."

"Maybe it's time we get to know each other all over again." He took another step toward her.

She raised her chin, hooked her gaze on his lips, and thought insanely, *Kiss me, kiss me, kiss me.*

He leaned in.

She held her breath, closed her eyes.

And he dropped a kiss on her cheek. No, it was too quick to qualify as a kiss. It was a peck. He'd given her a peck on the cheek.

What the hell?

No way was she letting him get away with a peck.

To surprise him again she wrapped her arms around his neck, dropping the ice cream carton to the floor, pulled his head down, and gave him a bona fide kiss.

Long. Hard. Hot. Moist.

Was it stupid? Hell to the yeah. Did she care? No. Because how much more broken could a heart get? She was already in love with him, and he didn't love her back.

C'mon, under those circumstances, what's the worst that could happen? Great sex? Sign me up.

When she pulled her lips away from his, Ryder grinned as if he'd dug up a treasure chest in his backyard and it was filled with gold. "What was that for?"

"You looked like you needed it. Spending the day sifting through Twyla's mess must have been exhausting."

"It was," he said. "But you kissed it and made it all better."

"Glad I could help." She was feeling uncertain now, but didn't want him to know.

"Take this." He handed her the Froggy's bag. "Dinner is part of the apology."

"You don't have to apologize, Ryder. You're entitled to your feelings. Or lack thereof."

"I do have feelings for you, Katie." His eyes turned stormy. "And I hate that I hurt you."

"You are entitled to your feelings," she repeated, "and you're not responsible for mine. That last part took me a long time to learn."

"I was responsible for hurting you. I said something that wasn't true."

"What is the truth, Ryder?"

He paused, glanced around the room as if looking for rescue.

"Hey," she said. "It's my turn to apologize for putting you on the spot. Seems like you're not real familiar with feelings in general. But you were a solider. You had to go to war. I get that you got used to suppressing your feelings."

"Katie . . ." He swallowed so savagely his Adam's apple jumped. "That night we shared was special to me—"

"We could do it again," she interrupted, and then paused to let him consider it. When he didn't immediately respond, she added, "If you want to. But no pressure."

Dear God, had she just propositioned him?

"I'm pretty beat," he said. His eyes looked tired, and she noticed he was favoring his left leg. "And hungry."

"Oh," she said, feeling deflated. She'd started having visions of him whisking her off to bed and eating fried chicken off her naked belly, but apparently they were not riding the same train of thought. "Did I do something wrong?"

"Aw." He smiled. "There's the good girl. I knew she was still in there somewhere."

"What are you talking about?"

"The people-pleaser thing. You think it's your fault when people aren't happy. It's not you, Katie. It was never you. In my book, you can do no wrong."

She touched her lips, wanting to believe him, but not sure she did.

"I'm pooped. Today, besides digging through ruins of my childhood at the ranch, I went to talk to my father's doctor. Dad is facing some tough challenges. If that wound on his toe doesn't heal, he could very well end up losing his foot or even the whole leg. That's what it's so important for him to come home to a clean place."

"Do you want to talk about it?"

"Let's eat and I'll"—he raked an appreciative gaze over her body—"see if I can rally and take you up on that offer."

"We don't have to. I . . ."

"I *want* to."

"All right," she said, and took the food into the kitchen, stopping long enough to scoop up the ice cream carton.

Ryder trailed after her. "Nice house."

"I bought it this summer."

"Putting down roots."

"Finally got my act together. I was in flux what with Matt dying and getting laid off from Lockheed."

"Matt?"

"My fiancé."

"Oh yeah. I forgot his name."

"Anyway, swapping places with Gabi, going to LA, meeting up with you . . . it changed me. Made me realize I'd been drifting along in life, letting other people steer the boat. I took the helm for the first time in my life. Started my business, bought this house, and I'm truly happy."

"It shows," he said. "Your face . . . you shine. I'm glad for you."

"Thanks." She smiled and ducked her head, suddenly feeling shy in the face of his praise. "Could you go stash the Harley in the garage now?"

"Yes, Miss Paranoia. I'll go stash it. I won't sully your reputation."

Whew. She felt better knowing the Harley was out of sight, just in case someone from her family happened to drive by.

Ryder dashed outside, and came back a few minutes later to lean his butt against the kitchen counter, watching her as she got plates down from the cabinets. Sunflower and lemongrass Fiestaware that matched her yellow and green kitchen. She set the plates on the counter and turned around to open the paper bag, but Ryder took her elbow.

"What—"

Drawing her into his arms, pulling her against his chest, tipping her chin up, he kissed her, planting his mouth over hers, solid and seeking.

The sudden rush of energy dizzied her. She fisted his shirt in her hands to keep from falling over. His arms tightened around her, and he deepened the kiss until they were both breathless and trembling.

"Now that makes up for this morning," she said, and stepped back so she could study his face. His eyes were swampy with desire, and they triggered a chain reaction inside her. Detonating her nerving endings in a series of tiny bomb explosions until her entire body was ablaze.

"I am sorry," he whispered. "I hurt you and there's no excuse for that."

"You didn't know I was standing behind you." His words had hurt her that morning, but it wasn't his fault. She was the one who'd let her fantasies go wild with impossibilities. Ryder was who he was. That's *why* she loved him. The last thing she wanted was to change him. She accepted him for who he was. Her white unicorn. The beautiful creature she could not possess. For the very act of possessing him would forever change who he was.

"I should not have said it. I didn't mean it."

"Did you see your father today?" she asked.

"For a couple of minutes."

"How was he?"

"They came to treat his wound while I was there so I didn't stay long."

"In other words, he was the same."

"He was better. At least physically. Mentally,

emotionally . . ." Ryder rubbed a palm down his face. "That's another story."

"It'll take time. He's got a hard callus over his heart." *And so do you.* She rubbed a hand over Ryder's shoulder, felt his taut muscles. "What I want to know is how are *you*?"

He smiled, but didn't mean it. "Fine."

"Tell the truth. This can't be easy."

"Not much in life is easy. Except being with you." He tugged her close again. "I missed you all day."

She leaned against him, trying not to read too much into his sweet talk and hot kisses.

He was saying nice things, and making her feel both wanted and needed, but she knew he would not stay in Twilight, and she was as rooted here as that hundred-year-old elm tree in the front yard. She should untangle herself from his arms, but she didn't because he smelled too damn delicious.

Or maybe it was just the fried chicken.

He tightened his grip around her waist and kissed her forehead. "God, you feel good."

"I missed you too," she confessed, even though that was probably a bad idea. Dangerous stuff, letting him know how much he meant to her. That gave him all the power.

Who was she kidding? He'd had the all power from the beginning.

She pulled his head down and gave him another kiss on the lips. Hoped he was getting the message. *Stop kissing forehead and cheeks, buddy. Lips. Kiss the lips.*

One palm slid down her spine to spread out over

her bottom, his fingers sinking into the flesh of her buttocks.

He ran his tongue over her lips, and she loosened her jaw, tipped her head back farther, allowed him deeper inside her.

Falling. She was falling. Falling straight into him, heart and soul.

"Hey," he said, wrenching his mouth from hers. "What's that brushing against my leg?"

"Oh." She glanced down, laughed. "That's Harry."

"Ah, the cat you rescued. I was beginning to think you made him up. Harry as in Harry Potter?" Ryder squatted to scratch the orange tabby behind the ears.

"As in Harry Houdini. He's a sly one. Stealthy."

Harry pressed his head against Ryder's palm and purred like a sports car engine.

"He likes you."

"I like cats."

"Have you ever had a cat?"

"Barn cats on the ranch when I was growing up. Never a pet of my own."

"I have a feeling he's going to fill the empty hole in my life," she said.

"You've got an empty hole? Wait . . ." He laughed. "That came out wrong."

"Not hole. That's the wrong word. Space. There's space in my life for more."

"More what?"

"Love."

"Oh," he said, and then again, "oh." His tumultuous eyes met hers, and she saw something there she could not name.

Her heart hammered, and she dropped her gaze. Turned away. Hurried over to the counter. "Chicken's getting cold."

"I like cold chicken."

"You're in luck. So do I."

"I know," he said.

He'd gotten up and was headed for the sink to wash his hands after petting Harry, orange hairs clinging to his shirt, his eyes heavy-lidded and sultry.

"Hey, why do you have a compass on your counter?" He dried his hands on a cup towel and picked up the antique compass from its spot next to the flour canister.

"It was Matt's."

"He meant a lot to you."

"I didn't keep it because it was Matt's. I kept as a reminder not to ever lose sight of who I am again."

Ryder glanced from Katie to the compass in his big palm and back again. "Matt robbed you of your identity?"

"No." She shook her head. "I allowed myself to get caught up in his dreams and ignored my own. I put my needs aside for his."

"What are your dreams, Katie Cheek?" Ryder asked, stepped closer. "What are your plans for filling those empty spaces inside of you?"

"To eat chicken." She laughed because she couldn't begin to tell him what was in her heart.

He laughed too, a sound as wobbly as her own. "Remember the night we fought over the last piece of cold fried chicken in your mom's refrigerator?"

She did indeed. She'd awoken in the middle of the night hungry for her mom's leftover fried chicken. She'd padded into the kitchen to find Joe and Ryder with their butts sticking out of the fridge.

Joe had sunk his teeth into a juicy chicken leg, when Ryder, who was holding the last piece, a breast, her favorite part of the chicken, looked up and saw her standing there.

"I was coming for that," she'd said.

"Too bad," Joe gloated. "We beat you to it. You snooze, you lose."

Ryder had glanced at the chicken and then back at her. Katie had given him an award-winning smile, and fluttered her eyelashes.

"Aw, hell," Ryder said.

"Don't you dare give that to her." Joe snorted. "Have some self-respect."

Katie's stomach growled loudly. "I'm so hungry," she whimpered, and placed a palm over her stomach.

Ryder hesitated.

"Don't fall for it. She uses that poor little youngest thing to get everything she wants." Joe picked up an apple. "Here, have a Golden Delicious."

"I was dreaming about that chicken," Katie said.

"Tough. We beat you to the punch. Suck it up. You want the apple or not? 'Cause if not, I'll eat it too."

"Here, take it." Ryder had thrust the chicken at her. "I can't take any more of those pitiful eyes."

"We didn't fight over the chicken," she corrected him now. "You gave me your piece."

"Did I?" He sounded dubious. "That doesn't sound like me."

"You did. But this time, it's share and share alike." She dug around in the paper bag, pulled out the fried chicken and containers of buttered green beans, mashed potatoes, cream gravy, and buttermilk biscuits.

"I missed Froggy's something fierce when I was in the Middle East," he said. "After my mom died, me and Pop ate there so much Floyd MacGregor started reserving a table for us."

Katie didn't know what to say about that. She couldn't remember having heard Ryder speak of his mom. She knew it was a tender topic. When her family had taken him in, her mom had warned them not to bring up his mother, and no one ever had.

"That must have been such a rough time for you," she said, trying to calm her pounding heart.

He shrugged. "I barely remember her now."

Katie didn't know whether to keep talking or shut up. The only thing she knew about Ryder's past came from Joe, and Joe didn't spill much.

"I'll take the dark meat," he said. "I know white meat is your favorite."

"Don't do that."

"Do what?"

"Defer to me. There are two chicken breasts. We can both have one."

"What's wrong with giving you what you like?"

"It spoils me."

"And?"

"Being the youngest, my family did that to me my entire life. It made me . . ."

"What?" he asked, looking interested.

"Complacent. I thought I'd get everything on a

silver platter, and I drifted through life. Until . . ." She swallowed. Why was she telling him all this?

He leaned in, watching her divvying the food on the plate. One breast for him, one for her. One leg for him, one for her. Two scoops of potatoes for him, two for her. Making it come out equal.

"Oh," he said. "I almost forgot."

She raised her head, met his frank gaze. "Forgot what?"

"I found this when I was cleaning out my old room." He reached in his back pocket for his wallet, opened it up, and passed her a pink envelope that smelled faintly of cotton candy. His name was scrawled on the front in her penmanship.

At the sight of the envelope, her heart tripped, stumbled to her stomach. "You kept it."

Chapter 18

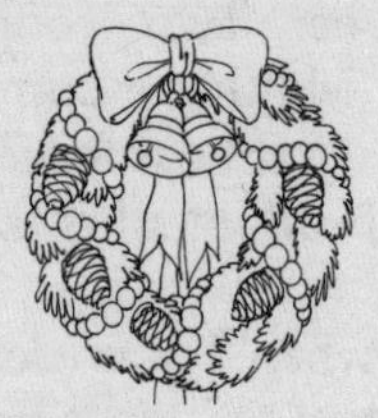

A tender smile tugged at his lips. "Of course I did. You were the only one who ever handmade me a birthday card."

"It was dumb."

"I thought it was awesome."

"I wanted to give you something special."

"And you did." He thrust the card into her hand. "Open it."

She didn't have to open it. The memory was imprinted in her brain forever.

But because he was standing there looking expectant, she slid the flap back, took out the folded piece of paper, filled with teenage drawings of hearts and flowers and smiley faces. God, what a dork she'd been.

Some of the glitter and rhinestones she'd stuck on with Elmer's Glue had fallen off, the pink paper age-dried crisp, the red ink faded. But she could still read the girlish proclamation, "Happy birthday to my favorite guy."

Her face heated. "I was a silly kid with a crazy crush."

"You were sweet," he said. "The card was sweet."

"Cheesy."

"No way."

"You don't have to be nice about it. I know I was a huge nerd."

"For months I carried this card around in my wallet. Even took it with me to basic training. Every time I looked at it, I felt a little less . . ."

"What?" she prompted when he didn't go on, and her heart gave a bunny hop of hope. For what, she had no idea.

"Lonely," he finished, looked chagrinned, and shrugged. It was adorable, the big, burly alpha guy all sheepish and vulnerable.

She stared down at the dopey card decorated with the dreams of a starry-eyed fifteen-year-old. "I still can't believe you saved it."

"I didn't have a lot of good things to remember about my childhood," he said. "This was one of them. Your family was one of them. *You* were one of them."

Why was he looking at her like that? What did it mean? His eyes were soft, and special as Christmas morning.

She shifted her gaze away, unable to bear the poignancy of the moment. *I'm doing it again. Getting swept away. Losing myself.* She shouldn't be smiling about it, but she was. Oh crap. Where had he put her compass?

Katie's pulse hammered, and her mouth went

dry and her toes curled inside her fuzzy socks. He was looking at her in such a way that she couldn't think straight, so she offered him a casual smile, and turned back to the food.

"Sit down." He guided her to the kitchen chair, and fool that she was, she let him. "I've got this."

He rested his hands on her shoulders and kissed the top of her head, and Katie wriggled at the hot brand of his lips on her scalp.

"Hmm," he said, his voice dropping as he dipped his head close to her ear. "You smell like purple flowers."

"Lavender." She shivered at the prickle of his breath against her skin.

"Cold?"

"Ticklish." She slanted her head away from him, but his mouth was at her ear, his breath warm on her skin, and she forgot everything else in the world.

She closed her eyes and inhaled heavily at how good his body heat felt against her skin. "I thought you were hungry," she said, feeling the corner of the envelope poking from her pocket into the small of her back, and shivered again.

"Starving," he said and stepped back.

Katie exhaled audibly and straightened her spine, surprised to find just how hot and melty her body had become.

"Whoa!" Ryder exclaimed, and she turned her head to see him dance, off balance, around Harry, who'd appeared out of nowhere to trip him in the middle of the floor. "Where did he come from? I'm beginning to see why you named him after Houdini."

"He's probably hungry. Let me feed him." She got up to give the cat half rations per Sam's post-surgery instructions.

While she was feeding Harry, she heard a lighter strike behind her, smelled a whiff of spiced apples. Turned her head to see Ryder had lit the kitchen candle that was casting soft yellow light over the room. He switched off the overhead light.

"What are you doing?" she asked.

"Creating a mood." He pulled his cell phone from his pocket, opened up a music app, riffled through a playlist to find Justin Timberlake singing "Rock Your Body." The hot Billboard song burning up the charts the same summer he'd left for the army.

The same summer she'd kissed him.

"You had this planned. My favorite takeout. My favorite song . . ."

"Your favorite guy," he said, added, "I hope."

"Ryder," she whimpered helplessly.

"Katie." He held out a hand to her.

She gulped, but took it.

He pulled her close, spun her around the room, waltzed with her to a rock song.

"I had no idea you could dance."

"Learned while I was in the army," he said.

"Impressive, but we're out of step to the beat."

"I know."

"Well, as long as you know."

He stopped moving in the middle of the kitchen, and they stood there surrounded by the smell of fried chicken and apple crisp candle and each other; the sound of their past stroking their ears as they gazed deeply into each other's eyes.

What was going on here? She was too scared to hope, and yet how could she not?

"I truly am sorry I was too much of a coward to tell Joe how much I want you."

"You weren't cowardly," she said. "You were just avoiding a black eye. We both know Joe has an infamous punch. He might have reacted poorly to hearing you wanted to take his baby sister to bed."

"Here's the real deal, Miss Priss, I'm not good enough for you. Joe knows. I know it. Everyone in this town knows it, but I swear I must be the luckiest bastard on the planet because for some bizarre reason, you seem to want me too."

She shook her head. Ryder didn't think he was good enough for *her*?

His personality was a vortex, big, sweeping, commanding.

She was getting sucked in again. Letting a man drive the relationship. If she'd learned anything over the past year, it was that she couldn't keep taking a backseat. Not if she wanted to live life on her own terms.

But honestly, this was what she wanted. She wasn't deceiving herself about that.

Was she?

"Enough apologizing," she said. "If you really want to make things up to me, shut up and kiss me."

Splaying a hand to the nape of her neck, Ryder speared his fingers through her hair, brought her head closer to his, capped her sweet mouth with his, and took his time exploring.

Or rather tried to.

She had no patience for his leisurely pace. She met his lips with a force that rocked him back on his heels and stole the air from his lungs. A soft little moan, and a hot, fervent kiss that left him thinking, *At last*. He had her again at last.

Everywhere she touched him, he caught fire. His lips, tongue, gums. Hands, arms, palms. Fire. Hot, beautiful fire.

She pressed her body against him. God, she had such a perfect body. Curving and soft, but strong too. Womanly and earthly and heavenly and impossibly in his arms. Her breasts were squashed against his chest, her thighs melded into his.

Her frantic fingers worked the buttons of his shirt. She wanted him as much as he wanted her, and Ryder let out a laugh of pure joy over that. She was so much damn fun!

She wriggled her hips against him, made a noise of frustration when one of his buttons refused to yield. Finally, she just yanked and the button snapped off, shooting across the room and landing to the floor with a ping.

"Sorry about the shirt." She chuffed and jerked it off his shoulders, tossed it to the floor.

"Screw the shirt."

"No, screw me!"

Holy shit. Ryder got harder than he'd ever been in his life. What a sweet little firecracker. She had changed since last year. Had grown bolder, more fiery, more beautiful. So beautiful he didn't know if he could stand it.

He took her mouth again, held her hands between his palms, and kissed her as thoroughly as he knew how. Kissed and kissed and kissed until they had to come up for air, panting like guppies.

She moved to go back for more, but he raised a hand. "Wait."

She looked horrified. "No, no, you're not backing out now. You can't back out now. Not when you've got me all charged up and wanting you so badly I can't remember my own name. What is my name again?"

He laughed again, tickled by her eagerness. "No, not backing out. I just have to warn you."

"About what?" She slapped a palm over her mouth. "Do you have a venereal disease?"

"Good grief, no. Do you think I would let things get this far if I had a disease?"

"Sorry. I had to ask."

"Smart girl. Don't apologize for it. I get an annual physical and my doctor checks out everything and I'm careful."

"Then why are you interrupting? Things were just getting good."

"That's why I'm interrupting."

"Listening. Spit it out."

"I don't want you to be disappointed."

"Huh? No chance of that, buddy. I have a great memory and last year was amazing. I expect more of the same. So let's get after it." She wriggled against him again.

He caught her wrists. "Slow down. Or if you

don't I'm not going to last eight seconds. I haven't had sex since I was with you."

She paused, blinked up at him. "You haven't had sex since me?"

"No."

"Why not?" She looked sincerely puzzled.

"Because I didn't come across anyone who interested me as much as you did."

"Really?" A trill lifted her voice on the last syllable. "That is so sweet."

"Not really. It means I have a hair-trigger response. The first time is going to be a dud, just warning you."

"Or"—she rubbed her palms with glee—"I could take care of you first, then we move on to act two where you give me lots of foreplay until you recover."

"I can't argue with that logic." He groaned and gathered her to him.

"Wait." She held up a palm. "Now that we've taken a break and had time for common sense to settle in, there's something else we need to talk about."

He tightened his grip on her. "What's that?"

"This is a causal thing. No strings. Three weeks of fun. And then you can scamper on back to LA."

"No strings," he said, just repeating what she'd said, but she seemed to think he was agreeing with her.

"Glad we're on the same page," she said. "And one other thing."

"Yes?" He braced himself. What was she going to say next?

"We keep it a secret from family and friends. We

don't need everybody weighing in on our business. Especially Joe and Gabi."

She was ashamed of him. The thought rolled like a marble around in his head.

"Agreed," he said, surprised at how ragged the word came out when he forced it past his teeth. "A secret affair."

"Perfect!" she exclaimed, and jumped into his arms. "Now follow me into the bedroom, and bring the chicken. We'll need a snack for later."

Chapter 19

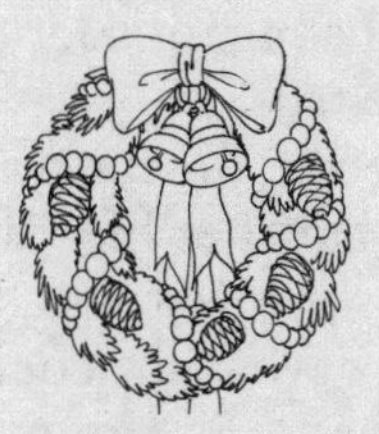

Thank heavens he'd agreed to keep their affair a secret. Katie couldn't handle it when he left if everyone knew and kept asking her about him.

She plugged in the bedroom Christmas tree, turned to see Ryder standing in the doorway looking at her like she was a diamond. She flushed with pride and happiness.

"Christmas tree in the bedroom." He laughed as the light from the tree that sat on a spinning stand, cast their in faces in the glow of multicolored twinkling lights. "You're a true Cheek. A Christmas tree in every room."

"I had a couple of bah-humbug years, but I snapped out of it after last year." She met his eyes. "With you."

"I refilled your Christmas spirit?"

"You did."

"I'm honored."

"Oh, you just think you're honored now. Wait until I get finished with you, mister."

The curtains were open and the full moon shone silvery through the window. Combined with the twinkling Christmas lights, it created a magical spell that took her breath. Ryder was so handsome, and he was with her again. Her deepest Christmas dreams had come true.

How seductive the dream was. To be with the man she'd loved half her life. She knew he didn't love her the way she loved him, but he didn't have to. She would take what she could get.

She took his hand and drew him to her bed. They finished undressing each other, garment by garment. Taking their time.

Once they were naked, she knelt before him, took him gently in her mouth, and he let out a groan that stoked her own arousal. She felt like a goddess, strong and empowered.

And he was right. He barely lasted ten seconds. She giggled when he collapsed on the bed, panting and wrung out.

"Katie . . . that was . . . you were . . ."

"Shh. No talking. Slow and easy. We've got all the time in the world."

Ryder gave as good as he got and then some. He touched her in all the right places. Lighting her up. Generating heat.

Flipping her over onto her stomach, he trailed damp kisses down her back, pressing his hot lips to each vertebra, his tongue following the curve of her spine, traveling south to kiss the dimples that sat at the top of both buttocks.

Her skin burned, alive with sensation.

She wriggled beneath his magnificent mouth,

ticklish, but loving the sweet torture. She moaned into the pillow, wanting desperately to flip over and kiss him, but he kept one hand splayed to her shoulders, holding her in place while he playfully nibbled her butt.

"Ryder," she whispered. "I want to see your face."

He paused as if considering her request, then said firmly, "Not yet."

She made a noise of frustration, but he ignored her, plying that wicked tongue of his over her soft curves.

If it had felt amazing, she would have said to hell with alpha macho male shit, and flipped herself right over whether he liked it or not.

But the man clearly knew what he was doing.

Goose bumps, both external and internal ones, chilled her in a pleasant way. Bossy, bossy man. Why did she find that so appealing?

Vortex.

She was letting herself get swept up into his vortex again. She had to stay on guard if she didn't want to lose sight of herself. But, oh, getting swept away felt so wonderful. Letting go. Enjoying the ride.

His tongue laved the juncture between her butt and her upper thigh, a spot that turned out to be surprisingly sensitive. No man had ever explored that part of her before and she felt like virgin territory, mysterious and new.

Oh, you are so weak, she told herself.

But it was the best kind of weak. Open, vulnerable, ready for wherever he might take her.

Finally, he flipped her over onto her back, and positioned himself on his side next to her. He propped his head up on his elbow and gazed down into her eyes.

He looked as stunned as she felt, surprised to the center of his being that this was working out so well. That they were so good together.

At least that was her impression. Katie hoped she was right.

But when it came down to it, what did she really know about him? Yes, his father was well-known in town. Yes, she'd had a massive crush on him when she was a teenager, and yes, he'd lived with her family for eleven months.

Thirteen years ago.

She knew that boy. She did not know this man.

And he scared her a little.

Not because she didn't feel safe around him, precisely because she did. He made her feel safe and protected in more ways than one. She trusted him implicitly.

It was herself she did not trust.

Why did she gravitate to strong alpha males? The kind of guy who made it hard for her to get her opinion in edgewise. The kind of guy who had his way of doing things and expected everyone else to fall in line.

Being with Ryder was much more than an ongoing series of novel sensations. He had awakened in her a deep sense of connection, the ultimate mystery of sexuality itself. Joining with him created such a blissful state, she felt as if angels had descended and enveloped them in boundless joy.

He stirred her to sensuous, tender rapture. A limitless ecstasy that took her breath. Blessed. She felt huge blessings for having known him even though she could not say for certain what was actually taking place between them or where it would lead.

At one point, he got up to retrieve a condom from his pants pocket and the fun began in earnest.

He sank into her and she immediately felt pulled upward and outward from the very core of her entire being. Her body hummed with heightened sensation, streaming heat through her veins, muddling her brain.

Masculine energy flowed from him into her, heightened her senses—brightening colors, accentuating sounds, filling her with an intense *knowing* that there was so much more to the world than met the eye, so much more to him.

The knowledge was so pure, so achingly raw, she feared she would disintegrate altogether.

In sweet, slow-motion ecstasy, he took her to a place, a world, an insular universe made just for the two of them, full of light and warmth and happiness.

This sweet apex of suspension seemed to last for hours as he stroked and kissed her in every way imaginable.

And then suddenly the orgasm was upon her. Huge and spectacular.

It consumed her, ate her whole from the inside out, swallowed her up in a blinding heat. Exploded her consciousness and rocketed her to a place where nothing existed but sweet bliss and the powerful hum of *I am!* She hadn't had many lovers, but this was hands down the most incredible sexual experience of her life. Even topping that passionate night in his apartment.

He'd transported her to a beautiful place made of light and joy, and she had the craziest thought that this was her real home. Here in his arms, with his body inside hers.

She struggled to manage the flow of sensory phenomena flooding through her. Immediately, she felt sad, because it was so lovely, so amazing, she knew it could not last. Doubted she would ever feel anything this intense again.

No matter what happened, she would always be grateful for the gift of this miraculous now.

Katie did not know how he felt about her, but she'd moved into a moment of complete awareness and what she felt for him was utter unconditional love. She gave her love to him freely, without any strings or expectations attached. Love poured out of her. No hesitation or reservations.

Her heart swelled and in that sweet bliss, she swam in an ocean of acceptance and light. Ecstasy flowed around her, inside her, bubbling from somewhere deep within her, and she gave it all away.

To Ryder.

Everything that had held her back or caused her problems dissolved in that rapturous instance. The walls she'd built around her melted. The old ideas, opinions, misguided beliefs, habits, rules, strategies she'd learned from her family, teachers, and community burst like soap bubbles.

All resistance dropped away. All fear vanished. She was no longer a separate individual grasping and anxious, but part of a magnificent whole. The two of them merged. One.

They were rocketed into another level of consciousness, leaving earth, bound for the stars in an explosive roar, clinging to each other, fused, moving at warp speed, headed for the heavenly light.

Something sacred was going on here. Something she could not explain or rationalize. It simply was something divine.

Together, they sparkled and flowed in perfect union, riding long, slow, pulsing waves of pleasure, and in the moment where they burst together in simultaneous bang, Katie thought, *I am.*

It was an intoxicating, blissful state of grace they'd found inside each other. The ultimate orgasm to end all orgasms. True, unified oneness.

And then she felt the condom break.

"Don't panic," Ryder said, trying to convince himself as much as Katie. "You're probably on the pill or something, right?"

Wide-eyed, Katie shook her head. "No. I don't have a partner so I thought why expose my body to chemicals unnecessarily? And with you . . . well, this was completely impulsive. You and me weren't even supposed to happen."

Ryder blew out his breath, pressed a palm to the nape of his neck. "Still not the end of the world. Women can only get pregnant a few days out of the month. Where are you on your cycle?"

"Um . . ." Katie bit her bottom lip. "That's kind of hard to say. My cycle isn't terribly regular, but I'm supposed to get my period next week."

Ryder paced the immaculate bedroom wearing only his blue jeans. Katie huddled on the bed, sitting cross-legged beneath the covers. She was so beautiful it stalled his heart. "If you had to hazard a guess?"

She rolled her eyes up and to the left as if mentally counting off the days. "We should be okay."

Should be.

"Okay," he said. "We're not going to borrow trouble. We're not going to worry until there's something to worry about."

"Sounds like a plan," she whispered.

Briefly, it occurred to him that he might suggest the morning after pill, but immediately shut down that thought. She was a savvy young woman, and she hadn't brought it up. He wasn't about to say it, even if the idea of a baby scared the hell out of him. "Good. We have a plan."

She pulled her knees to her chest underneath the covers, rested her chin on her knees, her brown eyes looking dark and vulnerable in the glow of the twinkle lights on the Christmas tree.

A tender, mushy feeling swelled in his chest. He'd never thought much about kids before. Why would he? He never saw himself as the marrying kind. But a baby? With Katie? Well, that wouldn't be the end of the world, would it?

No, having a baby with Katie wouldn't be the end of the world for him, but for that baby?

Disaster.

Hell, what did he know about being a parent? He'd lost his mother when he was eight. In reality, he'd lost Jax too because his father had turned into a cold and distant man. He'd had no role model. Had no idea how to be a good father.

Shit. Shit. Shit.

"Ryder," Katie called to him in a calm voice. "Take off those blue jeans, and come back to bed. The damage, if indeed there is damage, has been done. You might as well get some sleep."

She was so strong and brave. So accepting and trusting. And at peace. She had the kind of peace he longed for but had never known.

The lone wolf in him wanted to jam his feet into his boots and run away as fast as he could. Escape into the night. Go back into the cold. Alone. The way he'd always been. The way it was supposed to be. The way that felt safe.

"Ryder," she said, her voice gentle as a touch, and she held her arms wide. "Come here."

His heart was thrumming, the wolf panting, dying a little inside.

But she was smiling, full of love and kindness and warmth, and God help him, he could not resist. Ryder shucked off his jeans, crawled up onto the bed, and let her envelop him in her embrace.

And when she held him against her breasts, softly stroked his hair, and told him everything was going to be okay, he almost believed her.

Last night that fat Christmas moon had whispered to her, *Surrender, give up, let go, and bathe in my silvery glory.* This morning, the sun said, *Oops, idiot, you did it again.*

But this time had been different.

This time the condom broke.

Katie shouldn't have smiled—she was in deep trouble here and she should be worried about that—but smile she did. Couldn't help herself. Ryder had made love to her again. The grin stretched her mouth as wide as it would go. Curling up cheekbone to cheekbone.

"Hey, sleepyhead."

Aw, that warm, rich voice of his was as seductive as the tropics. Katie opened one eye to see Ryder standing over her, a steaming cup coffee in his hand. He looked so peaceful she thought that maybe the condom hadn't broken and she'd dreamed it all.

She yawned, stretched her arms over her head. "For me?"

"Heck no, get your own," he said, and pretended to drink from the mug, but then chuckled and held it out to her. "Yes, for you."

She scooted up in bed, curled her fingers around the warm mug. He'd fixed it just the way she liked it. Lots of sugar and cream.

"You're spoiling me."

"You deserve it." His grin turned loopy. "Plus I'm hoping to tempt you into getting naked again."

"Is that all you ever think about? Getting naked?"

He raked his gaze over her tousled hair and makeup-free face. "With you? Pretty much."

"You're not . . . upset?"

"About the condom?"

"Yes, about the condom."

"I Googled it. If your period starts next week, the odds are in our favor."

She noted he hadn't mentioned the morning after pill. If he had done an Internet search on condom breakage, surely he'd come across the morning after pill. Should she mention it? Her heart hammered. She knew the morning after pill was just added birth control and nothing more, but she couldn't bring herself to suggest it. Hated for him to think she wanted to get rid of any baby they might have created together. If she was pregnant, so be it. Let the chips fall where they may.

Fear sent her stomach into a nosedive.

"Like you said," he went on, smiling brightly. "Why worry unless there is something to worry about?"

"Excuse me. Who are you and what have you done with Ryder Southerland? Where did you get this optimism?"

"It's you, babe. It's your positive attitude that's turning me around."

It wasn't that she didn't love this new easiness to his smile, but rather she didn't trust it to last. Was he putting up a valiant front to keep her from freaking out? Knowing Ryder and how protective he was, probably.

"Whatever it is, I'm happy to see that big grin. We've got a long day ahead of us at the Circle S. And remember, no matter what goes on inside this bedroom, to the world outside these walls you and I are not together."

His smile vanished, and his voice came out sharp as peanut brittle shards. "Message received, loud and clear."

The minute she said it, she realized how it

sounded. That she was ashamed of him. That's not how she meant it. Not at all. She simply wanted to keep their affair a precious secret between the two of them for a while before the town started gossiping and meddling. But she worried that apologizing and over-explaining would just make it worse.

She reached out a hand.

He turned his back.

Helplessly, heart aching, she watched him walk away.

Chapter 20

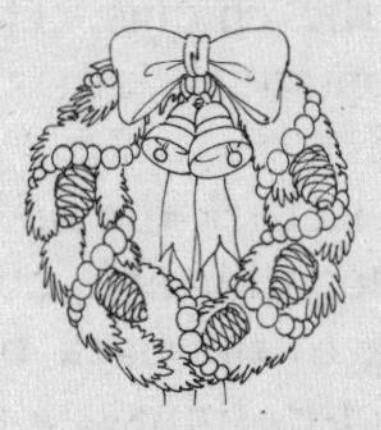

After Katie's crew left the Circle S late Sunday evening at ten o'clock, it was just the two of them.

Miraculously, they'd made the deadline. Jax could come home when his doctor dismissed him from the hospital tomorrow morning. The ranch house was straightened, organized, and spotlessly clean for the first time in over twenty years.

The job had taken a total of a hundred and eight man-hours that included Ryder; Katie; her team of three organizers; Jana's pinch-hitting; a six-person cleaning crew; a carpet, drapery, and furniture steam cleaning service; and a group of high school boys Katie hired to move the heavy stuff to the barn.

Yes, much of the junk they'd shifted out of the house was stuffed into the barn awaiting the next stage—either hauling it to the dump, holding a garage sale, or taking it to Goodwill. Katie would continue to help with that, although it might take a few weeks since her maid of honor duties were gearing up, but that could wait. The house was the main thing.

Standing in the living room surveying Katie's handiwork brought a lump to Ryder's throat. He couldn't believe the change. The difference was shocking. The woman was amazing. In more ways than one.

He'd managed to tuck the broken condom incident and that uncomfortable conversation they'd had this morning to the back of his mind, filing it under things-not-to-think-about-until-you-have-to-think-about-them, and neither one of them had spoken of it again. They hadn't even been around each other much, keeping busy in separate rooms to avoid lingering looks, and sly, helpless smiles.

Yes, he felt like her dirty little secret, but it was hot. The forbidden. It whetted his desire for her, stoke his longing.

Katie collapsed onto a living room sofa that smelled of the floral fragrance used by the steam cleaners. "I'm pooped."

Ryder plopped down beside her. "Me too."

They looked at each other, and smiled.

"Hey you," he said, reaching out a hand to her.

"Hey yourself." She popped her palm into his, and when he squeezed it, she squeezed back.

"We make a good team," he said.

"We do."

"How tired are you?" he asked.

"Bone weary."

"Me too." He rubbed his thumb over her palm. "Wanna do it?"

"God," she whispered. "I thought you'd never ask! I can't stay all night. I have to go home and check on Harry, plus I don't want anyone to see my car in your drive overnight."

"I live in the country," Ryder said, as if he really did live here.

"You still have neighbors."

"A quickie?"

"Perfect." She sighed.

"I'll get the condoms."

"Wear two," she said. "Just in case."

They made love on the couch, staring into each other's eyes. Her heart beat crazily, full of love for him, wishing they had more time. Not just for tonight, but forever. In less than three weeks the wedding would be over, his father would be settled, and he'd be back in LA.

Unless you're pregnant.

What would he do if she was pregnant?

Hell, what would she do if she was pregnant?

She stomped out that thought. Nothing to worry about yet. Right now, she was enjoying the beautiful ride. The thrill of his mouth at her nipples, the feel of his thumb stroking the inside of her thigh.

Yes.

Oh yes.

"Yes!" she screamed, and came in his arms.

And then it was his turn.

Ryder held her as they drifted down together. Their bodies quaking with the aftereffects.

As she closed her eyes, listening to the rhythm of their comingled breathing, she thought, *If I died now, I'd die happy.*

But she had to get up and go home. Her rules. She'd set them. No one to blame but herself.

The next morning, Katie returned to the ranch. She had offered to drive Ryder to the hospital to pick him up since Jax couldn't very well hop on the back of the Harley, and the man's old rattletrap pickup was unreliable.

"Are you worried this will set tongues wagging?" Ryder asked a bit sarcastically when she came to pick him up.

"No," she said. "I'm just giving a client a ride home from the hospital."

"I see."

"Are you mad at me?" she asked.

"No," he said. "Frustrated. I wanted to wake up next to you, smell your hair, and smother you with kisses."

"Rain check," she said.

"When? Tonight?"

"Can't. I promised Jenny I'd babysit, and it will be your first day alone with your dad."

"Why do you think I want to get out of the house?"

"It'll be okay. Maybe not comfortable. It's a long road back to each other, but you guys will get there if you don't give up on him."

"I love your optimism. I wish I had a teaspoon of it."

Love.

She wished he wouldn't throw that word

around. It made her heart hop painfully every time he did.

"This is the first step," she said.

"To where?" he asked.

"Home."

To her delighted surprise, Ryder didn't say, *This isn't my home.*

Because of his instability on his bandaged foot, Ryder and Katie escorted the cantankerous old man—Jax had bitched about the hospital staff all the way home to the ranch—into the house.

He stopped stock-still in the entryway, his eyes bugging, jaw dropping slack.

Katie shot Ryder a triumphant look as if certain they'd astonished and amazed him. Uneasiness prickled the back of Ryder's neck. The same prickle of warning he used to get when on patrol in Afghanistan. Uh-oh.

"What the hell did you do!" Jax howled.

"We cleaned your house." Katie's eyes twinkled. "Isn't it pretty?"

Jax snarled, turning on her. "You moved my stuff. Where's my radio? Where's my Carmex? Where's my ball cap? Where's the TV remote? Why does it stink like roses? You ruined everything, you stupid twit."

"Enough." Ryder snapped, grabbed Jax by the shoulder, and whipped him around to face him. "Don't talk to Katie that way. Don't you *dare*."

Katie laid a soft hand on his arm. "It's okay, Ryder. Jax is feeling displaced by the changes. It's understandable."

"What she said." Jax jutted out his chin, wrinkled his nose at Ryder.

"I don't give a damn, you don't get to call her names." Blood boiling, Ryder fisted his hands at his side.

"Fine." Jax pulled his spine up tall, wobbled a bit unsteadily in Katie's direction. "I apologize for calling you a twit."

"I accept your apology," Katie said smoothly. "Now would you like me to show you where everything is?" She moved into the living room, Jax trailing after her. "Your radio is right here next to your easy chair."

Furious, Ryder gritted his teeth. Katie might have forgiven the old bastard, but Ryder hadn't.

She led Jax around the room, opening drawers and lifting lids on decorative boxes, showing him where the living room essentials were stored. "It will take you a while to learn where everything is, and I know it will be frustrating at first, but once you do it will make life so much easier. A place for everything and everything in its place."

"How am I supposed to keep it like this? Too much damn work." Jax snorted.

"A cleaning service will be coming out every week," Katie told him.

"Well who the hell is gonna be paying for that?"

"I am," Ryder said. "Whether you like it or not."

Jax grumbled and fussed. He didn't like this, and he wanted that moved. And where had she put the empty milk jugs he was saving? And the newspapers? And the twine?

"Those items are going to be recycled," she said.

"That's my stuff! You can't just waltz in here and take my stuff. That's theft. I'll file a police report." Jax chuffed.

"The items aren't missing." Katie was so calm. She spoke slowly and made eye contact with Jax the whole time, giving him her full attention. "They're stored in the barn for now. Nothing except trash has been thrown away."

"You better not be lying." Jax narrowed his eyes at her. "Some of that is my wife's stuff and she'll be hopping mad."

Katie looked at Ryder, stricken.

"Dad." Ryder stepped closer to his father. "Twyla's passed away. That's why I'm home. Why we did all this."

"I know, I know." Jax waved a hand as if shooing a fly away from his ear. "I just got confused for a minute when I thought about how mad she was gonna be. Guess it don't matter now."

Then as if all the air had been let out of him, Jax collapsed into the easy chair with a heavy thump.

Ryder inclined his head and studied his father, wondering how long the old man had been like this. He'd been a hard man, and unforgiving when Ryder was a kid, but there was a new layer here. Cognitive impairment of some kind. A disconnect. Was it a mental illness? Or was Jax showing the early signs of dementia? Could it be complications from the diabetes? Or even some of the medicine he was on?

Then again, Jax had just lost his wife of twenty years. And his house altered to the point of unrecognizable. Most anyone might be disoriented under those circumstances.

Ryder made a mental note to revisit these questions with Jax's doctor.

"Dad," he said. "Sit here and rest. I'm going to walk Katie to her car."

"You're leaving?" Jax sounded alarmed.

"Yes, Mr. Southerland. I have other clients, but I'll be back to help sort through the things in the barn when you're feeling better."

"What if I need something? How will I find it?" Jax spread both hands over the arms of his easy chair and sat up straight.

"Ryder's going to be here to help you."

Jax swung his gaze to Ryder. "You're gonna be staying here?"

"In my old room."

Jax paused to think that over, moistened his lips, finally nodded. "Okay."

"I'm walking Katie to her car," Ryder reminded him. "I'll be right back."

"Turn on the Weather Channel, will you?" Jax asked.

Ryder flipped on the TV, then took Katie's arms and walked outside with her.

"Wow," she said. "You've got your hands full."

"I shouldn't have waited so long to come home." Ryder pulled his palm down his face.

"Under the circumstances, I can see why you didn't."

"Thanks for your help. You were great with him. When he called you names . . ." Ryder shook his head. "I'm sorry for that."

"It wasn't your fault. And truly, Ryder, I do understand. It's not easy for him. His whole life has been turned upside down. Be patient with him."

"Can I call you if I'm ready to yank my hair out by the roots?"

"By all means." She leaned in, and for one hopeful minute he thought she might kiss him. "I'd hate for you to lose that lush head of hair."

"Ah, now we get down to it," he teased. "The real reason you like me. I have a full head of hair."

"Yep, it's those luscious locks, babe," she teased back. "Lose them and I'm gone."

He leaned in toward her, but it must have been too close for comfort, because she stepped back. Not being able to touch her was driving him up the wall. All he wanted to do was touch her. Stroke her. Kiss her. Lick her.

Stop it! He was making himself hard just thinking about what he couldn't do to her.

Why was she insisting on keeping their romance a secret? It gnawed at him. Was she ashamed of him?

"We could always sneak up to my bedroom and get naked," he said.

"Be serious."

"I am serious."

"You're incorrigible."

"Not the first time I've heard that."

"Probably won't be the last." She laughed.

"When can I see you again?" he asked.

"I'll have to let you know. Tomorrow I volunteered to be an elf in the Santa diorama on the square."

"Katie." He touched her arm. "I'm here with my

father, you've got to give me something to look forward to."

She hinted at a smile, removed his hand from her arm. "Self-control, Ryder. You've got it in spades. Call on it now."

"If you can get away even for a few minutes, let me know." He pressed his palms together. "Please. Call. Text. E-mail. Carrier pigeon. Any time, day or night. I'll be there."

She laughed and sank her hands on her hips. "I have to say I really like you this way."

"What way?"

"Groveling. Ta-ta." With a wave of her hand, she hopped in the Camry and drove away.

"Ryder!" Jax hollered from the front door.

He sighed, headed toward the house. "What is it, Dad?"

"They've got a new weather girl on channel 10. When did they change out the weather girl? Too many changes. I want the old weather girl back. Call the TV station and tell them to put her back on."

"I have no control over the weather girl, Dad."

"Then what good are you?" Jax slammed the door.

Ryder smacked his forehead with the heel of his hand. Dad home. No Katie. It was shaping up to be a very long day.

Chapter 21

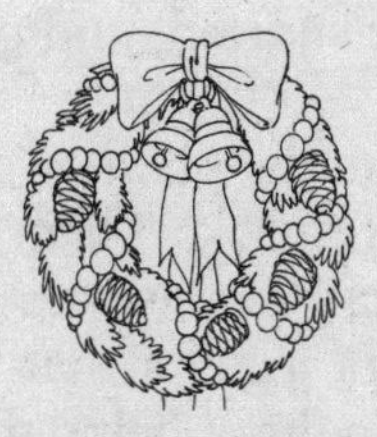

At five P.M. on Tuesday afternoon, six days after he'd roared back into town, Ryder got the text he'd been waiting for from Katie.

Want to see me? she texted.

Yes! he texted.

Come play Santa.

????

She texted a smiley emoji. *Diorama Santa bailed. Need a new one. You?*

Be right there.

A stringing of dancer emojis appeared on his phone screen.

"Dad," he called to his father, who'd been napping in his easy chair. "I gotta go out for a while."

"Where?" Jax scowled.

"Town square."

"Why?"

"I'm playing Santa."

"Why would you wanna do that?" Jax growled.

"For fun," Ryder said.

Jax gave him such a startled look it made Ryder wonder if his father even knew what fun was.

"Do you want me to bring you anything back from town?"

"Pigskins." Jax snorted, and promptly fell back asleep.

Ryder made sure the phone was near Jax, along with water and a snack. Then he took off, surprised by how excited he was to be playing Santa. It wasn't the Santa gig that had him charged up, but rather the thought of being near Katie again.

The diorama was set up in a temporary plywood structure erected on the courthouse square. The building contained Santa's sleigh and a North Pole scene. Already a line of kids and their parents had formed.

Katie was waiting with the Santa suit. She looked adorable as an elf in green tights and long green tunic sweater, and he felt like a kid again.

"The regular Santa is a lot bigger than you, so you'll have to pad. We've got pillows. And cinch the belt tight so your pants don't fall down."

He ducked into the small dressing room. "Hey," he said. "Can you help me?"

She popped her head into the dressing room. "What is it?"

He pulled her all the way in, and shut the door. Kissed her hard.

"Ryder." She glared, but underneath it, he saw a smile. "Stop it."

"Did you get your period yet?"

"No. But it's not due for a couple more days."

"You'll let me know?"

"Yes, yes, of course. I have to get back out there. Hurry. The kids are restless."

The next three hours passed in a blur of kids on his lap and laughter, tears, and sticky fingers. Kids tugged his beard and drooled on him and asked for everything in the world, greedy little grub worms. He was going hoarse from too many ho, ho, hos, and his thigh was slightly damp from what, he didn't really want to think about. But damn if he wasn't having a great time.

And most of it had to do with the gorgeous elf manning the camera, snapping photographs for eager parents.

"Last one," Katie told him as she scooped a red-haired three-year-old off his lap and gave her back to her mother. "We're closed," she told some stragglers who'd wandered through the door.

"Oh no." The mom's face fell. "I had to wait until I got off work. I'm so sorry."

"Santa! Santa!" Twin four-year-old boys jumped around. "Santa! Santa! We want Santa!"

"Santa's been up on that sleigh for three hours without a break," Katie said. "I'm sorry, but we closed at nine."

"It's okay, Elf Katie," Ryder called in his best Santa voice. "C'mon boys." He waved the twins over.

"Oh thank you!" The mom put her palms together in supplication. "Thank you. You have no idea how tough it is being a single mother of twin boys."

The boys each took a leg and jabbered away at him, and he let them have a full ten minutes of his attention. When the family left and everyone else was gone, Katie locked the door—which consisted of nothing more than on old-fashioned clasp lock—and came to climb up on the sleigh beside him.

"That was a very nice thing you did for that mom and her twins."

"No big deal."

"It was to them."

"It was fun."

"You mean that."

"Don't sound so surprised."

Her face broke into a massive smile. "I can hardly believe you're the same guy who tackled me for running up the stairs in Les Ketchum's direction last year," she said.

"Why's that?"

"You've changed so much."

"How?"

"For one thing, you smile more."

"I do?"

"Yes, and you look less . . ."

"Less what?"

She shook her head. "Never mind."

"No." He put a hand on hers to keep her from backing away. "I want to know."

"Stressed. You're relaxed. Easy. An adjective I would never have used to describe you before."

Ryder peered into Katie's eyes, saw his own reflection in her brown-eyed stare. God, he admired the hell out of her.

"So this security firm you work for in California," Katie said. "You really like it?"

"Suits me." He shrugged.

"And you miss it?"

"Yeah," he admitted, wondering what she was getting at. "But I needed a break. I hadn't taken a vacation in the two years I've been there."

She shifted on the sleigh and looked up at him through a fringe of long dark eyelashes, those sharp brown eyes shining bright. She shivered, and he put his arm around her shoulder and she didn't resist.

Oh yeah.

Her lips were so close to his, and her hair brushed the back of his arm, and she was wearing an adorable Santa hat and that silly elf costume that fit nice and snug around her gorgeous breasts.

"I want you," she said, surprising him.

"What?"

"I want you," she repeated, touched his inner thigh.

"Here?" he asked, thrilled by her boldness. "In Santa's workshop?"

"I can't think of a better place." Her fingers worked the big, black patent leather Santa belt.

Ryder groaned, wrapped his big hand over her small one, clutching her tight, making her stop. "Katie," he said. "You don't really want this. Not here. Not like this."

"It's not up to you to tell me what I do and don't want," she sassed, and he loved that sauciness. She snagged his earlobe between her teeth and used it to gently pull his head down.

"Yes, ma'am." He chuckled.

"It's late. The place is closed. There's no one else around."

"But the walls are thin. It's a plywood structure. We're on the town square. What has gotten into you?"

"What's the matter? You afraid of getting caught?" she asked.

Actually no, but it was as good an excuse as any. "Yes."

"Hmm," she said. "As I recall, when you were in high school you weren't afraid of getting caught doing the deed with Missy Kirkwood in the balcony of the Twilight Playhouse."

"My point exactly. I don't want to ruin your reputation the way I ruined Missy's."

"I think Missy's reputation ship had sailed long before you came along. Besides, you just let me worry about my own reputation." She touched him, placing her palm over the zipper of his jeans. "Ryder," she whispered. "Please."

Instantly, Ryder got hard.

"I know you want me too."

There was no question about that.

"What's holding you back?" she said. "You wanted me. Now you've got me."

What had gotten into her? And why was he holding back? Ryder had no idea and she wasn't waiting on him to formulate a kind, well-thought-out answer to her question. She was busy with that wicked mouth of hers, kissing his chest where his shirt was unbuttoned, running her hands inside the waistband of his Santa pants, making him harder than he'd ever been in his life.

"Katie," he barked. "Stop it."

She pulled back, startled, her eyes widening. "You really don't want me, do you?"

"God, woman! I want you so badly I fear going blind with it."

She wriggled back up against him. "Then what's the problem?"

"You're too good for this. And you're breaking your own rules and you're going to regret it. I don't want you to regret it. Regret me."

There it was. His fear. That at some point she was going to regret the rashness he seemed to ignite in her.

"I see." She pulled back. Straightened. "I'm sorry."

"Katie, it's not you. I promise."

"No worries." She shrugged, but there was hurt in her eyes. She didn't believe him.

Dammit. Fine. If she wanted him here, like this, then that's what he'd give her. He tugged her into his lap, and slipped his hand up underneath her sweater tunic, over the waistband of her tights and her thong panties. Using his hand, he pleasured her with his fingers, doing things to her that had her mewling helplessly, while he kissed her and pinched her nipples through her clothes and whispered her name.

And when she came, shuddering hard, he held her in his arms for a long, long time.

Katie couldn't stay away from Ryder. No matter how hard she tried. She was breaking her own rules and she had no idea why, other than when she was near him or thought about him, or dreamed of him, she got horny.

What a miserable state of affairs.

Time and time again, she found herself texting him, asking him to come over after ten at night and park the Harley in her garage.

And there he'd be.

Showing up on her back porch with a pizza or a Chinese takeout or tacos. They'd eat and talk and have sex. He'd tell her about his trying relationship with his dad, the financial shambles the ranch was in, how he spent his day. She'd tell him about how the prep for the wedding was going, or the volunteer work she was doing, and what was going on with her family.

They played with Harry, and baked Christmas cookies, and watched Christmas movies until three in the morning. Then Ryder would get on his Harley and drive away.

Every night, he'd ask, "Get your period yet?"

She'd shake her head. "Not yet. Not late yet."

He'd squeeze her hand, and she'd squeeze his back, and they would make love, and each time was better than the last.

"If we made a baby," he said. "I'll be here for you. You know that, right?"

"Shh," she'd whisper, and brush her knuckles over his lips. "Don't borrow trouble."

On December tenth, he said, "It's been a week since the condom broke. You said you were getting your period in a week. You haven't gotten your period yet."

"It's due today," she said. "So not late. Tomorrow it will be late."

The next day, her parents invited Ryder to Sunday dinner. It was the first time he'd had a chance to see her parents since he'd been back in town, and her folks had planned a big celebration.

The trick? How to get through the evening without tipping their hand that they were involved.

Katie thought they were doing a great job. They arrived separately. Made the rounds separately. Ryder mostly hung out in the kitchen charming her mother and shooting the bull with her dad and eating cookies. Katie spent time entertaining the kids, reading them Christmas stories in the den, or talking to Gabi about the wedding.

The evening grew later, and the couples with children started leaving. Gabi and Joe, Katie and Ryder ended up sitting around the kitchen table while everyone else was in the living room saying their good-byes.

"Are you guys going to Patsy and Hondo's Christmas party Friday night?"

"It's a couples-only party, why would Ryder and I be invited?" Katie asked, shaking her head.

"Give it up, sis," Joe said. "We know."

"Know what?" Katie plastered a palm to her chest, tried to look innocent.

"Let it go." Ryder shrugged. "The jig's up."

"Wh-what gave us away?" Katie asked.

"Oh, like, everything." Gabi giggled. "You two are as moony-faced for each other as Joe and I."

"We are not."

Joe rolled his eyes. "Look, I'm supposed to punch you on principle for dishonoring my baby sister." Joe leaned over and thumped Ryder lightly on the shoulder with his fist. "There. Consider Katie's honor defended."

"I can't believe you guys knew." Katie shook her head. "Why didn't you say anything?"

"It was fun watching you guys slip around," Gabi said. "We didn't want to ruin your fun. We remember what it was like to slip around."

Joe slung his arm around Gabi, kissed her until she giggled again.

Ryder met Katie's eyes across the table, "So since everybody knows, wanna spend the night together?"

Katie glanced over her shoulder to see if her parents were in earshot. "Not going to happen," she muttered.

Gabi leaned across the table to gloat at Ryder. "What that means, cowboy, is you struck out."

Ryder dropped a laconic smile. "Takes three strikeouts to end an inning."

"Throw as many pitches as you want," Katie said. "I'm not swinging at them."

"Wait a minute," Ryder said. "If I'm striking out, doesn't that mean I'm the batter?"

"I'm certainly not the pitcher," Katie said. "I'm not the one throwing around sexual innuendo."

"Maybe not intentionally." Ryder's gaze dropped to her chest. "But your body sure is."

Katie glanced down and saw her nipples were so hard they were poking through her bra and T-shirt like miniature missiles.

"Deny it all you want, Katie Cheek. But you

want me. You want me bad." He grinned, got to his feet, and sauntered away all long-legged and loose-hipped.

Gabi leaned over and whispered, "You do kind of want him pretty bad. There's no shame in going after him."

"Over, dead, body, my," Katie said, alarmed at how her jumbled thoughts came out of her mouth.

"Exactly," Gabi said. "He's reduced you to talking gibberish."

"I'm screwed, aren't I?"

Gabi winked. "Apparently in more ways than one."

"Who all knows about us?" Katie whispered, leaning back in her chair in order to see Ryder shaking hands with her father in the living room and thanking him for the nice evening.

"Everyone," Joe said.

She heard the front door close behind Ryder as he left, and the roar as the Harley engine popped into gear. "Everyone as in—"

"Your parents," Mom said, coming into the room. "What do you think, Katie, we're blind?"

Katie felt like she was going to hyperventilate. What did her parents think? She sneaked a glance at her mother's face. "Um . . . um . . ."

"We adore Ryder, you know that," Mom said, sitting down in the chair Ryder had just vacated. "But you need to be very careful, young lady."

"I know, Mom. He could break my heart." She was acutely aware of that. She didn't need anyone to remind her.

Mom blinked. "Oh well, that too, I suppose."

"Isn't that what you were warning me against?"

"No dear, I was warning you against breaking his. Ryder has had enough hurt for a lifetime. Don't you go toying with his affections. Hiding him like he's a dirty little secret. For shame, Katie Cheek. For shame."

CHAPTER 22

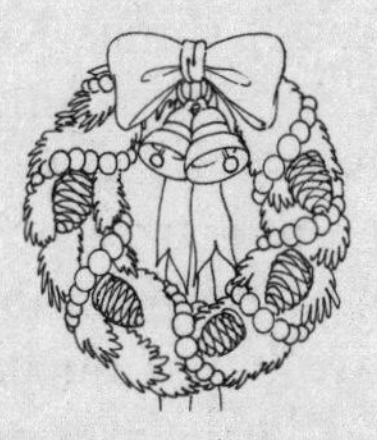

Her period was a week overdue. And it had been two weeks since the night the condom broke. Katie kept telling Ryder not to worry, that her periods were irregular, and they were often a week or more late.

"I'm sure it will start today or tomorrow," she'd told him every day since Sunday dinner at her parents'. "Stress can make it late. Stressing might be the very thing holding it back, so please stop asking. I'll let you know when I get it."

"And if you don't get it?"

"Let's not get ahead of ourselves." She worked hard to sound unconcerned. But she was worried.

So worried that she'd driven to the neighboring town of Jubilee to buy a pregnancy test, but she didn't know how accurate the test was so soon after missing her period. Especially since her cycle was irregular, so she'd not taken the test yet.

Luckily, she'd been too busy to dwell on it. Since she and Ryder had been outed as a couple, they started openly dating and doing group activities with other couples. They went ice skating with Gabi and Joe. Took in a live performance of *A Christmas Story* with Emma and Sam. Went caroling with Jenny and Dean and the kids.

The events were all things Katie had done numerous times, but so many of them, Ryder hadn't done before. At least not in Twilight. The ice rink hadn't been built until after he'd left town. And in high school, he'd been banned from caroling on the town square based on his reputation as a troublemaker. And he'd never seen a play in the Twilight Playhouse all the way through, because he got kicked out for "ungentlemanly behavior" with young ladies in the balcony.

And then there were her duties as Gabi's maid of honor. It was her job to make sure the other bridesmaids had gone for their fittings, had the right jewelry and the 411 on the pre-wedding activities. Write her toast speech for the wedding reception. Host the bridal shower, which was tomorrow, and make arrangements for the bachelorette party. Since the wedding was on Christmas Eve, the best time for the bachelorette ending up being today, Friday the sixteenth. The guys were having Joe's bachelor party the same day.

Thank goodness, she'd done her Christmas shopping months ago. Otherwise, she'd be in deep pickle juice. Between the demands of her spectacular sex life and the wedding, she was barely keeping her head above water.

"Did you hire a stripper for Gabi's bachelorette party tonight?" Jana asked when she came into the office with the mail.

"No, I did not hire a stripper." Katie picked up the mail and started sorting through it, but she couldn't really concentrate. Her mind was on what she and Ryder had gotten up to the night before. Chocolate body paint had been involved, and whipped cream.

"Aw." Jana pouched out her bottom lip. "You were my last best hope for a rocking bachelorette party. Everyone else around here is such a fuddy-duddy." She stared pointedly at Sesty, who ignored her.

"Just because I wouldn't let you eat sushi off a bare-chested waiter at my bachelorette party doesn't mean I'm a fuddy-duddy," Sesty said.

"Tell you what, Jana," Katie said. "When you get married, I'll hire an entire herd of strippers."

"Oh." Jana shook her head. "That's not happening. I'm never getting married."

"Famous last words." Sesty flashed her wedding ring for effect.

"Well, if I found someone as hot as Josh, maybe I'd reconsider," Jana said. "But there's no one here in Twilight who can live up to your man."

Mine can, Katie thought. Then she thrilled a little at the idea of Ryder being *her* man, and squelched any lingering doubts running around in the back of her mind.

"Do you need any help with last-minute party prep?" Sesty asked. "You look too calm. I'd be freaking out if I was in charge of six wild bridesmaids and an anxious bride."

Katie shook her head. "Don't forget, I've been to lots of bachelorette parties. I know my way around the block. It's all set. The limo will pick us up at six. Everyone is meeting here outside the office."

"And if anything goes wrong, you can bet she has a contingency plan," Jana said.

"Three actually." Katie smiled but tried not to look smug about it. "But who's counting?"

She turned her attention back to the mail, and saw an envelope with Marva Bullock's name on it. Marva had already paid her bill. What was this? A Christmas newsletter, probably. She opened up the letter and read:

Dear Katie,

I can't tell you how much you've streamlined my life. This has been a tough transition for G.C. *and me as we adjusted to our changes in circumstance and downsizing, but you made it as seamless as possible. What a joy it's been to watch you change from an uncertain teen into a competent, self-confident young woman running her own business. Just please don't let your gift for order and tidiness keep you from taking risks. Life can be pretty messy sometimes, and you can't always wrap everything up in a pretty bow. Remember, everyone needs a junk drawer.*

All my best,

Marva

A lump formed in her throat as she stared at the letter, her chest tightening strangely as chill bumps ran over the back of her shoulders. It was as if Marva had guessed at the indecision that held her back from fully committing herself to Ryder. Or maybe she was reading more into it than was there. But Marva was a smart cookie and she didn't miss much.

Please don't let your gift for order and tidiness keep you from taking risks . . . Remember, everyone needs a junk drawer.

Was that what she'd been doing? Using her skill for organization and her need for order to avoid taking chances? Was her fear of making a mess keeping her from fully trusting Ryder by telling him she was in love with him?

She chewed on that thought for the rest of the day, and by the time six o'clock rolled around she wished she could skip out on the party and go home, slip into something sexy, and invite Ryder over. Take the risk, lay it on the line, and just say it. *I love you.*

Things had been going so well between them. He might not be able to say the words to her, but he'd shown her in countless little ways that he did love her. She could tell him first, and that would open things up for him to say the words to her.

But what if he didn't say them back?

Katie bit her lip. Well, it was just a chance that she would have to take.

And she had to do it before she took that pregnancy test. Because if she took it and the test was positive, and then he said he loved her, she'd never know if it was because he really did or simply because she was carrying his child.

She wanted to do it right now. But instead, she was ushering six chattering bridesmaids and one exuberant bride into the stretch limo.

"I'm so excited," Gabi said. "With you in charge, I know it's going to be a wild and crazy but safe night."

"I've got you covered," Katie said, taking her iPad out of her purse to double check the schedule for the progressive party. First, dinner on the Brazos River at a new fine-dining restaurant that had just opened up.

"Put that away," Gabi scolded. "I want you to have fun too."

Reluctantly, Katie slid the tablet back into her purse, took a deep breath, and told herself to relax.

She leaned back against the seat of the limo, glanced around at the lively women beside her, all laughing and talking and teasing.

Gabi sat in the middle wearing a soft blue dress that accentuated the color of her eyes, and adorable cowgirl boots Joe had given her as a wedding present. She kept stretching out her feet to admire the boots, and when she thought no one was watching, surreptitiously texted on her phone.

Katie knew with certainty that she was texting Joe. Gabi would coyly glance at her cell phone screen, smile big, and press her lips together like she had a secret, before tucking the phone in the folds of her dress.

Her brother had hit the jackpot with Gabi. The woman adored him.

Katie's heart thumped strangely inside her chest. An achy longing that flipped her stomach topsy-turvy as she realized that she and Jana were the only women in the limo who weren't married or about to be. She didn't begrudge any of them their happiness, but, oh, she wanted that too!

Why couldn't she have that?

Because the man you're crazy about is Ryder Southerland. The lone wolf who would never settle down.

Is that true, whispered a voice that had had an epiphany when she'd read Marva's letter. *Or are you afraid that big ol' man will mess up your well-ordered life?*

Gabi's phone pinged with a text and when she looked at it, her face dissolved in a beatific smile. "Joe and the guys are going to join us at Chez Genevieve."

"Aw," Jana said. "This is supposed to be girls' night out. That's the point of a bachelorette party. No guys. Um, unless there are strippers."

Gabi looked besotted and she blushed prettily. "Joe said he can't go an entire evening without seeing me."

"Ugh, I think I'm gonna puke." Jana playfully slapped a palm over her mouth.

Jana might be down on love, but the way Gabi stroked the cell phone screen with her thumb as if stroking Joe's face, and smiled dreamily, tugged at Katie's heartstrings. She loved how kind and caring Gabi had roped her restless brother and brought him down to earth. It made her happy to watch the two of them together, Joe barely able to keep his hands off his bride-to-be. The endearing way he gazed at her as if the sun rose and set on her smile.

Emma and Sam looked at each other that way too. So did Sesty and Josh. Meredith and Hutch. And the two other bridesmaids, Sarah and Caitlyn and their men, Travis and Gideon.

And Ryder? He looked at her that way too.

Katie's heart clutched, and sweet, bright heat spread like a virus through her body. Could she and Ryder have what their friends had?

She nibbled her bottom lip, considering. They were working on it. No doubt. The possibilities were there in the lingering glances, shared whispers, and spiked pulses.

They could have something great. Problem was, because of that bad-boy image, he thought he wasn't good enough for her.

Which was so silly. The rascally things he'd done as a kid were bids for attention. He'd outgrown the behavior a long time ago. He was a good man, a decorated soldier. He'd given so much for his country. He deserved a little happiness.

With her?

Yes, please.

Briefly, Katie closed her eyes. Did she want this too badly? Was she misreading the signs? She was leaving herself open to a wide world of hurt. He could break her so easily. When it came to Ryder Southerland it was much safer to keep her feelings tucked away in a tidy decorative boxes and sealed tightly shut.

Except it was too late for that. Especially if she was pregnant.

God, her mind was a jumble scrambling from hope to fear and back again.

"It's getting really sappy in here." Jana elbowed Katie. "Know what I'm saying?"

Katie blinked, realized the other ladies in the limo were all on their cell phones texting their guys.

Jana gave an expressive eye roll, accompanied by a snort. "Ridiculous."

Katie fingered her own phone.

"Oh no!" Jana exclaimed. "Not you too!"

Katie shrugged helplessly.

"Ack!" Jana pretended to choke herself. "I need to get out of this love-struck town."

"Or," Sesty said, "you could just surrender and fall in love like the rest of us."

"And go around with those smug smiles? No thank you. I'd rather stick rusty nails in my eyes." Jana winked at Katie, then crossed her eyes. "Oops, forgot you'd moved over into the enemy camp."

"I never said that." Katie squared her chin as she realized everyone was staring at her. While she and Ryder definitely had a thing cooking, she didn't want the bridesmaids weighing in on her love life.

Not when things were still so new and uncertain.

"So you're with me?" Jana slung her arm around Katie's shoulder. "Love stinks."

"Keep that up," Emma warned, "and we're going to put you out on the side of the road."

"Who broke your heart?" Gabi asked Jana.

Jana looked startled. "No one. I'm the heartbreaker."

Everyone in the limo exchanged glances over Jana's head.

"What?" Jana growled.

"You're just trying to protect your heart," Meredith said kindly. "We get it. We were all there once. It's scary taking a chance on love. What if you let yourself fall and you discover there's no bottom to the abyss?"

The other women bobbed their heads in agreement. Katie's stomach dipped, but she had no idea why.

Jana snorted again, and crossed her tattooed arms defiantly over her chest, but for the first time she looked rattled.

And when the limo stopped at the restaurant, they stepped out into the December evening to find the guys standing outside the Chez Genevieve on the banks of the Brazos River, their hands stuffed in their pockets as if they'd been pacing and waiting on their women to arrive.

Katie struggled to keep from melting into a pile of goo at the sight of Ryder's endearing face.

He walked straight toward her and she forgot she was in charge of the evening's activities and that she was supposed to be playing it cool. When he wrapped his arms around her, and pressed his lips to the top of her head, Katie's stomach rose up to dance with her heart in a swoony waltz.

"I missed you," he murmured, pressing her close so she could feel exactly how much he missed her.

Katie would have felt self-conscious for the public display of affection if every other woman there—except for Jana, who huffed and sauntered off—wasn't falling into the arms of the men they loved. It was a sweet tableau, six couples nuzzling beneath the twinkle of Christmas lights.

Ryder tipped her chin up and kissed her tenderly, and Katie promptly forgot about everyone else. Her focus was on one thing and one thing only. Ryder and his dynamite lips blowing her self-control to smithereens.

"I want you," he whispered against her ear.

"Ahem." She giggled. "I can tell."

"Your fault," he said. "For being so damn hot."

Her face flushed and she dipped her head to hide a blazing smile.

"Katie." He rolled her name over his tongue as if it was the most beautiful sound in the English language.

"Yes?"

"There's something I want to give you."

"I just bet there is, buster." She laughed.

"Well." He chuckled, joining her laughter. "Besides that."

"What is it?"

"Come with me." He took her hand. "I got us our own table inside."

"Ryder, I can't. I'm Gabi's maid of honor."

"She'll understand," he said. "This is important."

Katie's heart faltered . . . stopped. Her heart bounced back into action. Was he going to be the one to say "I love you" first?

"Yes, okay, let me just tell Gabi."

"Joe knows. He'll tell Gabi. Although . . ." He nodded at the bride and groom-to-be, who were staring raptly into each other's eyes as they walked into the restaurant. "I doubt they'll even notice we're gone."

CHAPTER 23

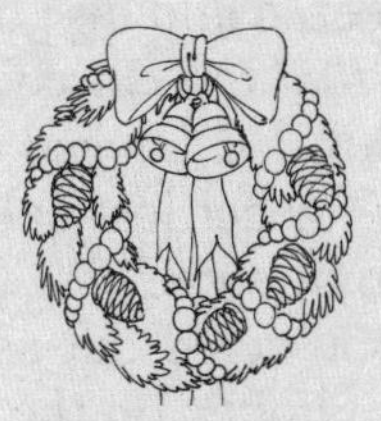

The waiter seated them in a corner table not far from the big table where everyone else was sitting, and brought them menus. But Ryder only had eyes for Katie.

This was an important night. He was going to tell her his story. The full story of how his mother had died to find if she still wanted him. And if she did, he was going to give her the heart necklace that had once belonged to his mother.

Over dinner, he started his tale.

She listened intently. Not interrupting. Her gaze never leaving his face.

Her breath hissed in over clenched teeth when he'd finished. She looked utterly stunned.

"Oh Ryder," she said. "I am so sorry. I had no idea you went through that. I mean I knew about your mom, but not the details. It wasn't fair for you father to blame you for her death."

"He was grieving her. My mother was the love of his life."

Katie reached across the table, placed her hand

over his. "Do you suppose that's why you've avoided commitment? On a subconscious level marriage represents death to you."

Boom!

His throat squeezed and his gut roiled. He didn't want to examine *that* too closely, so he kept going. Telling her how his dad latched on to Twyla, who was also grieving for her lost baby and failed marriage. "It was a toxic stew."

"No wonder you acted out as a child. Any kid would have. And phooey on the adults who didn't understand."

"Most people in town didn't. They deemed me 'bad' and I took that to heart. But your parents understood. Bill and Lois were so good to me, Katie. And kind. My one regret is the way I left town and never came back. Your parents deserved better from me."

"My folks don't judge you, Ryder. They just want you to be happy."

"Which is more than I can say for my own father."

"Jax is so unhappy himself. He has no idea what happiness looks like."

"I wish I could reach him, but even after almost two weeks of living there with him, I'm no closer to breaking through his crusty hide than I was the first day."

"He's been like this a long time. He won't change quickly."

"Or at all." Ryder hoped he didn't sound bitter. He wasn't bitter. More sad than anything. And scared that he could end up just like Jax.

"I wish we weren't in a restaurant. I'd take you in my arms and hug you so hard right now," Katie said.

"You can do it later." He quirked a grin, trying to lighten the moment that had turned so dark. "Since things with us are getting . . ." He pulled in a deep breath. "We're . . . Things are . . ."

"Yes?" She squirmed to the edge of her seat.

He took the black jewelry box from his pocket and her eyes lit up, and he realized too late she thought he was going to propose. He didn't know what to do. Quickly, so as not to lead her on, he cracked open the box, held it out to her.

"It's the necklace I bought for my mother. I . . . I want you to have it."

"This is what you found in your dad's room that first day we were together at the ranch."

"Yeah. It's not expensive or anything. But it means a lot to me and . . . please take it." God, he was mangling this. He should have bought her a necklace, not given her some cheap drugstore necklace he'd bought for his mother over twenty years ago.

Her hands were trembling. Was that good or bad? "Are you sure, Ryder? This was your mother's."

"I know. That's why I want you to have it."

Her face filled with tenderness and empathy. "I'd be deeply honored." She took the necklace from him and put it around her neck. It fit perfectly at the hollow of her throat. She fingered it lightly. "I'll cherish it always."

"Katie . . ." There was so much he wanted to tell her. His heart was full to the bursting, but he didn't know how to put into words how much she meant to him

"Yes, Ryder?"

"Thank you," he said. "You've made me come alive again."

She smiled softly.

The other group was breaking up, paying the bill, going their separate ways. The men came wandering over to his table, pulling Ryder out of his chair and telling him it was time for the bachelor party to begin in earnest, while the women captured Katie and took her away.

It was only when they'd been hustled to their respective limousines that Ryder realized he hadn't asked her if she'd ever gotten her period.

Watching the limo Ryder was riding in pull away reminded Katie that she'd gotten so caught up in the deeply emotional throes of Ryder's childhood story, she'd forgotten her mission to tell him she loved him.

She fingered the heart necklace at her throat. He hadn't said the words to her either, but he'd given her his mother's necklace. The necklace he'd fought for tooth and nail. The necklace that meant everything in the world to him. He wanted her to have it.

Touched. She was touched beyond measure.

But still, she ached to hear those three little words. *I love you*.

The bachelorette party progressed from winery to brew pub to dance club. Katie was there with a smile, making it the best night possible for Gabi.

She didn't drink in case she was pregnant, and when the others noticed, she laughed it off with an "I'm the designated grown-up."

Leaving everyone else free to live it up and be silly while Katie looked out for them. The party wound down at two A.M., the limo driver dropping the women off at their houses, one by one. Katie was last.

Harry met her at the door, hungry for loving. She'd already left food out for his dinner. She set her purse down on the table and it tipped over, raining the contents onto the floor.

"Fudge," she said, and bent to clean up the mess. She picked up the items, stuffed them back into the purse. Her hand hit upon the pregnancy kit she'd bought in Jubilee the day before.

She'd planned on taking the test with Ryder, but she couldn't wait anymore. She had to know. Now. Tonight.

Five minutes later, she was in the bathroom holding her breath while she waited for the results. A plus sign meant positive. Minus sign negative.

Please, she whispered. *Please.*

And in that moment she did not know if she was pleading for a plus sign or a minus. In a perfect world, she'd want nothing more than to have Ryder's baby. But they weren't married. And she didn't even know if he loved her. She loved him. More than life itself, but could she be satisfied with a one-sided relationship?

Or worse, what if he decided to head on back to LA?

No. She remembered what he'd told her. *I'll be*

here for you. Believed it because she believed in him. Banked on that promise because it was all she had.

What if she was pregnant? What if she had an adorable baby boy just like Ryder with dark brown hair and mischievous green eyes?

Wait. Don't skip ahead.

Emotions assaulted her in those quick seconds. So many feelings. Clawing at her. Hope and fear. Joy and sadness. What if? And what might be? And *What the hell am I gonna do?*

Katie checked her phone, counted off the seconds—three-two-one. Closed her eyes. Opened them. Stared at the stick.

And fell to her knees crying.

Saturday morning after the bachelor party, Ryder was in the barn trying to deal with the remainder of the junk they'd cleared from the house and stuffed in the barn. He had three flatbed trailers loaded with three piles—trash, keep, donate. Katie had taught him well.

He heard a noise from behind him, turned to see Katie striding into the barn. He smiled, thrilled to see her.

Being around her settled him, made him feel whole in a way he hadn't felt since . . . well, since his mother had died. He didn't know why. He couldn't explain it, but he accepted it. For whatever reason, Katie was his touchstone, and damn was he aching to touch her.

"I was just . . ." He paused at the look on her face.

Her eyes lacked their usual sparkle, her mouth

was turned down, and she had her arms crossed tightly over her chest, shoulders tense, body language hollering, *I'm upset.*

He leaned the shovel against the stall, came toward her. "Hey, what is it? What's wrong?"

She shook her head, moistened her lips, eyes clouded, going from brown to almost black as her pupils widened. A thick strand of dread grew like an instant tree root from his stomach all the way down through the floorboards. She looked absolutely distraught.

His legs felt heavy as redwood stumps, his knees gone to cement. He clumped toward her, a clumsy Frankenstein, but she squeezed herself tighter and stepped back.

Okay, he was officially scared now.

He pushed his palms downward; hell, they were heavy too. They swung to his sides, chunky sandbags dangling. "Please," he said. "Just tell me. What's happened? What have I done?"

She shook her head vigorously.

Finally, he dragged his legs over to where she stood. "Talk to me, Katie. Stop shutting me out. What is it? What's wrong?"

Shit, Southerland, calm down. Don't make a mountain of it. Probably her mood was related to some woman thing he didn't understand, and didn't really want to know about unless he had to.

She peeped at him over the edge of her palm she splayed over her mouth, two terrified brown eyes.

Okay, for sure he was worried now. "Katie?"

She hauled in a breath so deep he could feel the updraft of air as she sucked in. She raised her head, met his gaze, eyes now the color of a hot gas flame. "I'm pregnant."

His mouth dropped open.

"The broken condom did it." She shook her head. "One time. One measly time. You've got wonder sperm, Southerland."

He thought he'd been braced for the impact of the possibility. He was not.

Ryder's head swirled, struggling to process it. He could make split-second decisions on the battlefield, and as a bodyguard for the safety of his clients, but this was different. Here, now, he was frozen.

A baby? He and Katie were having a baby.

This was for real.

A kid, huh? A baby he could carry on his shoulders, and bounce on his knee. A boy he could teach how to ride and hunt. Or even a girl. He wouldn't mind a girl who looked like her sweet mama. There would be bedtime stories and camping trips and Little League games and recitals and Fourth of July fireworks shows and amusement parks and birthday parties.

Involuntarily, a dopy grin overtook his face as the sappiest feeling in the world swamped his stomach. A baby. Yeah. That wouldn't be so bad.

"This is a mess," she said. "An utter mess. How can I do my job when I'm out to here." She pantomimed patting an imaginary extended belly. "I crawl in attics and cellars on a regular basis."

"You . . . you're considering keeping it?" He heard the hope in his voice, felt his spirits take wings.

She looked at him like he was the dumbest man on the face of the earth. "Don't you know *anything* about me, Ryder Southerland?"

"I know you're a neat freak. Kids are not neat. Not in the least. They're messy and loud and break things."

"So is Harry." She pressed a protective hand over her womb. "And I'm keeping this baby whether you're happy about it or not."

"Of course I'm happy about it, woman. Don't you know anything about *me*, Katie Cheek?"

"I know you had a crappy childhood and you don't get along with your father. I know you live a solitary life in Los Angeles. I know you have trouble expressing your feelings. I know you are not father-of-the-year material. The famed lone wolf, who is so determined not to have people ride with him that the only vehicle he's ever owned is a Harley. You can't take a baby on a Harley."

"I know that," he mumbled.

Ouch. Shit woman, kick a man where it hurt, why don't you? But she was right. Every word of it. She was twisting her fingers around each other, knotting them up, worrying back and forth.

"How are *you* doing?" he asked.

She gulped, fear in her eyes. "Not the best in the west."

"Morning sickness?"

"Terror," she said.

Ah, those feelings he wasn't so good at. "What are you scared of?"

"Anything. Everything. How am I going to handle this? My business is still new. What if I'm a terrible mother? And you . . . Where do you come in? Will you be a long-distance father? Are you coming back to Twilight for good? What about your father? How is this all going to work out?"

She sank down on a bale of hay, all the air leaving her body like a deflating balloon. She looked forlorn. Her chin trembled as if she were on the verge of tears.

It killed him. He'd done this to her. Discouraged his spunky Katie.

"Hey, hey." He rushed across the floor to her, but she held up two palms. Clear statement. *Stop!*

"Don't touch me," she said. "You've already done enough."

"Katie."

"Don't talk to me like that."

Confused, Ryder crouched in front of her. "I only said your name."

"It wasn't what you said, it was your tone."

"What tone?"

"That macho man I'm-in-charge-listen-to-me tone."

What? Okay, she was just lashing out. She was upset and obviously, anything he said or did or didn't say or do was going to piss her off. He was behind the eight ball and there wasn't anything he could do about it except wait for the thundercloud feelings to pass. Hormones. It was her hormones.

"How did this happen?" she moaned.

"Um . . . the condom broke, and you weren't on an alternative form of birth control."

"I was speaking rhetorically. I was so careful.

My whole life I've been careful. I took the safe jobs. Dated the safe guys. Keep things neat and clean and tidy. Until LA. Until you. And now, boom! The biggest mess of all. You."

Shit. Ryder didn't know what to do. It tore him up to see her like this. In so much distress. And he was the cause of it. He might not be good at talking about his feelings or confronting emotions, but there *was* one thing he was good at.

Taking action.

Ignoring her stop-sign hands, he wrapped an arm around her waist, tugged her to her feet, pulled her up tight against him.

She gasped, stared up in his face looking affronted, but behind the irritation he saw relief. As stubbornly independent as she was, Katie wanted him to take charge. To tell her everything was going to be okay. That he was in the driver's seat and he'd make sure nothing or no one ever hurt her. That she was forever safe in his arms.

That look went straight to his head, and before he could think of a more romantic way to do it, he blurted, "We're getting married."

"No," Katie said.

He reeled backward, blinked as if she'd slapped him hard across the face. "What?"

"I'm not going to marry you just because I'm pregnant. This is the twenty-first century. All those old-fashioned ideas fell away a long time ago. You don't have to marry me just because you knocked me up."

"I know I don't have to marry you. I want to marry you."

"Now you do. After you found out about the baby."

"Of course. I'm not going to let my kid grow up without a name, or his father."

"You can give him your name, and you can be around him. We'll share joint custody, but we're not getting married."

"Give me one good reason why not?"

"Because I want you to love me for me, not just because I'm having your baby."

"Katie, I want you."

"But do you love me, Ryder? Because that's what I need. Someone to love me."

"I do."

"Do what?"

"You know." He shifted uncomfortably.

"Love me?"

"Yeah."

"Then say it."

"Katie—"

"You can't say it, can you? What's wrong with you that you can't say the word?"

She was right. He loved her more than he loved breathing, but he couldn't actually speak the words. They got hung up in his mouth like dry crackers. He'd not ever told any woman—other than his mother—that he loved her.

Things had gotten twisted up in his mind when he was a kid. He loved his mother and he told her he loved her every day. In fact, had told her that the very day he'd gone off to school and left the Tonka dump truck on the porch, and she'd fallen off and broke her neck. *I loved her and she died.*

It wasn't rational. He knew that. But somehow part of him believed that if he actually said the words "I love you," the universe or fate or God or whatever would know he was happy and take it all away.

Just like it had taken his mother.

"I love you, Ryder Southerland, with all my heart and soul, but until you can stand in front of me and say those words to my face, we cannot be together. Because that's what I deserve. A man who loves me for all he's worth, and can tell me so. I refuse to settle for anything less."

Chapter 24

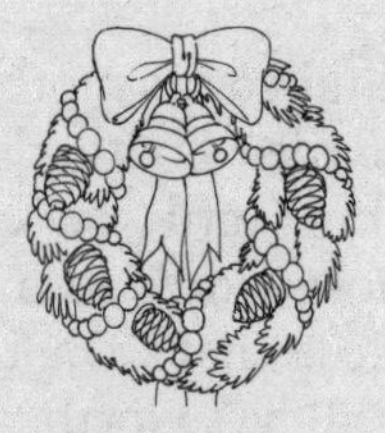

She was being irrational, Katie knew it. But the minute she'd seen that plus sign, a fierce protectiveness came over her and she was determined to do whatever was right for this baby, and that meant putting all her own wants and needs aside. This baby deserved a mother and father who loved each other. And if they didn't love each other, then they shouldn't get married. They could still be great parents without being married. They could love the baby, even if they didn't love each other.

But could Ryder love the baby? Could he love anyone at all?

She felt wretched because she loved Ryder so very much. Had loved him since she was fifteen, but she didn't know if he loved her. Yes, he liked her. Yes, they had chemistry. Yes, the sex was off the charts. Yes, he respected her. Yes, he treated her kindly.

So why couldn't he say that he loved her? All she could deduce was that he did not.

She turned and fled from the barn, anxious to

get to her car and get away before he could see that she was crying.

"Katie!" he hollered, and ran after her.

She didn't go to him, but kept walking as fast as she dared. She didn't want to risk tripping and falling and hurting the baby.

"Katie." Ryder caught up to her, grabbed her elbow, spun her around to face him. "Miss Priss," he said in a desperate tone, as if using the name to get through to her.

Her lips were trembling, her eyes damp.

"Katie Cheek, I want you, dammit."

"Not enough."

"I can't say it."

"Why not?"

"Because you're Joe's sister. Because I can't betray your mom and dad like that. They took me in. How could I fall for their daughter? So I stuffed my feelings down inside. Until that day you kissed me and I knew I couldn't stuff them down anymore, so I joined the army, because I couldn't stay in Twilight and be around you but not be with you."

"Let me get this straight, you could have sex with me, that was fine, but you can't love me because of my brother and my parents."

"I'm making a mess of this."

"Yes. Yes you are."

"I've always liked you. I liked you when you were fifteen and kissed me," he said.

"I was an ugly duckling and you were the most handsome boy in school. Why did you like me?"

"I could see how beautiful you were going to be

without the glasses and the braces and the frizzy hair, and the guys that couldn't see that were flaming idiots. But more than that, Katie, I admired your heart. You're so kind and generous and giving. And I respected your sense of order and the way you keep things neat and tidy. It made me believe in a better world."

"Oh Ryder," she whispered. It sounded so good. How she wanted to believe it. But how could she believe him when he'd never even hinted at any of this until now? Until he discovered she was pregnant, and he wanted to convince her to marry him?

And while he'd danced all around it, he still had not actually said the words she so badly needed to hear.

How easy it would be to close her eyes, let him take the reins, and believe that he loved her the way she loved him, and that he didn't need to say it. He could just show it. It would be that easy to get swept away. She'd done it before. With Matt. And she hadn't loved him half as much as she loved Ryder.

"Marry me, Katie. Let's get married."

She placed a hand on his chest, peered deeply into his eyes. "No."

"Shit." He tore at his hair with his hands.

"Calm down. Let's take a deep breath and back up a minute."

"Okay." He eyed her suspiciously.

"We're getting ahead of ourselves. Sometimes home pregnancy tests give false positives. Let's cool our jets. The wedding is next week. Christmas is next week. I'll make an appointment with the doctor for the week after that. When the doctor confirms I'm pregnant, we'll revisit your proposal, but for now, let's focus on first things first. Getting Gabi and Joe married off."

He cocked his head, studied her for a long moment. She saw an emotional tug of war going on behind his eyes, but had no idea what it was about. "All right."

Wrong answer! She wanted him to say he wanted to marry her no matter if there was a baby or not.

He chucked her lightly under the chin, pulled her into his arms. Held her head against his shoulder and rocked her gently back and forth. As she listened to his rhythmic breathing, felt his body heat radiating through her, she couldn't help feeling her heartfelt dreams, which had seemed within fingertip's reach just yesterday, were rapidly drifting away.

Thankfully, there was so much holiday/wedding activity, Katie didn't have much time to dwell on her situation. During the day, she could turn it off, shift her thoughts, stay busy. But the nights were a different story.

At night she dreamed of babies. Chubby ones. Skinny ones. Boy babies. Girl babies. Happy babies. Sad babies. She couldn't control her dreams. And several times that week, she woke in the middle of the night, thinking she heard the sound of a baby crying, or with her hand on her womb and a smile on her face.

She didn't see Ryder much. He'd learned the ranch was about to go into foreclosure and he'd been working with the banks and financial adviser to come up with a solution. She understood that the ranch and Jax took top priority right now, and actually, she was a little relieved. If Ryder was around a lot, they'd end up talking about the baby, even though they'd both promised to hold off until after the wedding when Katie had a chance to see her doctor.

But he would send her texts. *If boy, what do u think of Luke?*

As in Luke, I'm your father? she texted back.

Scratch that. Followed by: *Harley?*

No!

Spike?

We're not doing this.

Right. 2 B continued next week.

She laughed and turned off her phone. He was a persistent man. She would give him that.

They saw each other at the wedding shower. The guys had congregated at one end of the house to watch a boxing match, while most of the women hung out in the kitchen drinking wine, eating Christmas cookies, and watching Gabi open presents.

At one point, he pulled her aside to say, "How are you feeling?"

"Fine."

"No nausea?"

"It's way too soon for that."

"You know, you shouldn't be emptying Harry's kitty litter. Cat poop is dangerous to pregnant mothers. I'm coming over to empty the litter box for you."

"I can get Jana to do it."

"Does your health insurance have a good maternity plan?"

"Ryder," she muttered. "Cool it. Did you know almost thirty percent of all pregnancies end in miscarriage?"

He looked shocked. "That high?"

"That high."

"Oh." He bobbed his head. "Next week. After the wedding."

"After the wedding," she echoed, and they went back to their respective areas of the house.

Ryder didn't know what to do.

He wanted to be with Katie, to touch her, hold her, talk about the baby. But she was throwing up "yield" and "cautious" body language and he wanted to respect that. He knew she was working through something, so he held back when everything inside him urged him to go over to her house and tell her he was moving in whether she liked it or not.

But he respected her too much to ignore her desires.

Besides, he had his hands full at the ranch. Things between him and Jax had gotten marginally better. At least the old man was saying, "Good morning" now, which was something. They argued about everything, but nothing new there.

Ryder had staved off the foreclosure from the second mortgage his father had taken out on the place. From what he could gather, Jax had done that a few years back to pay off the credit cards

Twyla had run up then, but she'd just run them back up again.

But his efforts were just a stop-gap measure. He'd used his own funds to pay the overdue payments, but Jax didn't have the income to keep paying on the property. The only solution Ryder saw was to sell the place. Jax, however, wouldn't hear of it.

He'd bought his father some time. For now, the wedding and Christmas took center stage.

Friday, December 23, following the church rehearsal, the dinner was being held back at Chez Genevieve on the Brazos River, where they'd had dinner during the bachelor/bachelorette party.

He'd bought a special gift for the baby, and brought it along. Maybe he'd have a chance to slip it to Katie when no one else was around. Yes, he'd told her he would wait until next week, but he'd seen it in Jessie Calloway's motorcycle shop in town and he'd just had to buy it.

When he walked into the restaurant with the present tucked inside a holiday gift bag, he spotted Katie standing in the waiting area. She looked so beautiful with her hair tucked in an upsweep with a silver ornament, his mother's heart pendant at her throat, and wearing a shimmery red dress that it took his breath away. A year ago on this very day, she'd been wearing another red dress. His pulse beat an insane rhythm and his heart literally lurched in his chest.

"Hey there." He smiled. "Are we the first ones here?"

"No," she said. "The parents are in the banquet room with the bride and groom. Still waiting on the other members of the wedding. But I needed to get you alone before we go in." She looked solemn and her expression struck a chord of fear in him.

"Okay," he said, glancing around. "Where can we go?"

"Out on the patio." She gestured to the outside deck along the river where no one was.

"It's cold."

She reached for her coat on the coatrack, draped it around herself. "We won't be out there long."

He hurried ahead of her to open the door leading to the deck. A cold draft of air blew in around him. Her legs must be freezing. He took her hand, positioned her against the outside wall and moved to stand in front of her to block the wind coming in off the river.

"I got something for you. I wanted to give it to you in private, but since we're not getting much alone time these days . . ." He inhaled deeply. "I miss you, Katie."

Her smile was halfhearted, but her words were warm, and she said it like she meant it. "I miss you too, Ryder."

"Go ahead and open it." He pushed the sack toward her.

She opened the sack, looked inside at the little leather Harley jacket, pressed her lips together in a firm line.

"Like father, like son." He waited for her to smile. He expected a smile. "I know, I know, I'm jumping the gun, it might be a girl, but I couldn't resist."

Katie's face froze into an unreadable mask, her

skin blanched pale as snow. She thrust the jacket at him. "Take this."

"Ah, come on, sweetheart. I know you're irritated that I didn't wait after I promised I'd wait, but I was so excited—"

"I got my period," she said crisply.

Ryder stood holding the tiny baby motorcycle jacket in his big hands. Took the first hit of emotions like mortar fire. On his feet and scared shitless. No baby. No need for the jacket.

I can sell it on eBay, he thought. *For sale: Baby jacket, never used.*

Salt flooded his mouth, and he realized it was tears that hadn't reached his eyes.

"I was bleeding a lot, so I called my doctor and she got me in this morning," Katie went on matter-of-factly, her voice steady and clear as if she was reciting the Pledge of Allegiance.

Her calmness amazed him. He felt as if he'd taken a cannonball to the gut and she looked as if butter wouldn't melt in her mouth.

"My doctor confirmed that I had been pregnant but lost it early. It's called a chemical pregnancy. That just means it's a very early miscarriage. She said most women who have a chemical pregnancy don't ever even know they were pregnant. I probably wouldn't have known except the condom broke."

"How are you?" he croaked, rooting his feet into the floorboards in order to hold him upright, keep his knees from buckling. He wanted to go hold her, but he was afraid he would fall over if he moved. So he just kept standing there squeezing the little scrap of leather in his fist.

"I'm fine." She pressed a hand to her womb. "The bleeding is a little heavier than normal, but—"

"I meant emotionally. How are you feeling?"

"Numb." She nodded. "But I'm okay. I mean it was only a few weeks. It wasn't like . . ." She gulped. ". . . months. My doctor said not to be surprised if it all hits me later. Right now it doesn't even feel real."

"It was real to me," he said.

"I didn't mean the baby wasn't real. It was such a mental adjustment, I'd barely settled into the idea of a baby, when whoosh, she's gone."

"It was a girl?"

"Ryder," she said kindly. "It was way too soon to tell. I just thought of her as a girl."

"I would like to have called her Lucy after my mother."

"Ryder . . . please. Don't. Just don't."

He swallowed, felt as if a wrecking ball had smashed in his chest. He was dazed. Confused. "Well . . . well . . ."

"It's going to be all right." She reached out to rub a palm over his upper arm. "Look at it this way. You don't have to marry me now."

She looked so calm about it. Relieved even? Was she glad she didn't have to marry him?

"Yeah." He nodded, his hand clenched so tightly around the baby jacket he didn't know if he'd ever be able to unclench it. "Sure."

"Are *you* all right?" she asked.

"I'm sick to my stomach, but I haven't eaten today. I should have eaten."

"I don't mean physically," she said. "I mean emotionally."

"No," he said. "I'm not all right. I had this image in my head, you know? Of the baby. Of being a dad. Of taking the kid to the park and teaching him how to tie his shoes and ride a bike and throw a baseball. And I liked the idea. I liked it a lot."

"I did too," she said softly.

They looked at each other. She was a strong woman. A lot stronger than he'd thought, and damn if he didn't resent her for it. He needed her to need him. He needed to comfort her, but she was holding on without him.

It was all so sad, and if Gabi hadn't come out onto the patio and shooed them inside, Ryder had no idea what they would have done next. Hugged? Kissed? Ripped into each other? Walked away?

Didn't matter. They were members of the wedding and they had a rehearsal dinner to eat.

Chapter 25

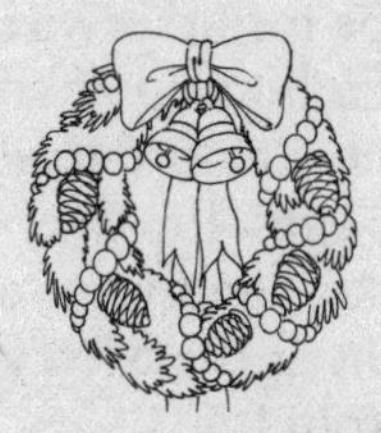

Ryder spent a restless night. After he got home from the rehearsal dinner, Jax was in a particularly pissy mood and they had it out. A Realtor had dropped by and left his card. Jax, who'd had hours to work up a head of steam, accused Ryder of trying to steal the ranch and sell it right out from under him.

Following on the heels of Katie's news, Ryder was in no mood for the old man's crazy shit. "If you're losing the ranch, it's your own fault," he said. "I bailed you out this time, but I'm not doing it again. You're on your own, and I'm going to bed. Tomorrow is Christmas Eve and I've got a wedding to attend. Good night."

Jax said some choice words and stomped off.

Ryder went to bed. Looked up the ceiling, and wondered why he was here. He didn't belong in this town. There was nothing for him here. His father hated him. He wasn't a rancher. Even Joe was so wrapped up with Gabi, they hadn't had any time to hang out together. Understandable, but it only served to underscore that there was really nothing for him here.

Lone wolf.

That's what he was. What he'd always be. He'd been dumb to hope for otherwise.

The alarm woke him up at six A.M. on Christmas Eve. Those best man duties. He got dressed, made bacon and eggs for Jax, who surprisingly mumbled, "Thanks," and went over to Joe's. Gabi had spent the night at the Merry Cherub with her parents in town from LA.

Joe was a nervous wreck, pacing and memorizing his vows. Ryder double checked everything he was responsible for. Secret getaway car so when Joe's prankster brothers and friends shoe-polished his truck, they could thumb their noses at them. Practiced his toast. Made sure he had Gabi's wedding ring secured.

At eight o'clock, Gabi called him in a panic. "Ryder, where's Katie?"

"I don't know."

"She's not with you?"

"No."

"Ask Joe, is she with Joe?"

"I'm with Joe," Ryder said. "She's not here."

"She's supposed to be with me. Where is she? I called her phone and she's not answering. I called her parents and they haven't seen her. I called Jenny and Sam and Mac and Ben and everyone I can think of and no one has heard from her. My dad drove by her house but her car isn't there or if it is, it's in the garage and she's not answering the door. Ryder, I'm flipping out. You've got to find her! I can't get married without my maid of honor."

"Gabi," he said calmly.

"Yes?"

"Breathe. Slow and deep. Joe is going to call you and talk to you. And I'm going to go find Katie. I'll find her and bring her to you and everything is going to be just fine. The wedding isn't until eleven. It's all going to be fine."

"Do you promise, Ryder? Promise me."

"I promise, Gabi. I'm hanging up now." Ryder hung up, turned to Joe. "Call your bride and talk her down. I'm going after your sister."

"Do you know where she's at?" Joe asked.

"No, but I'm going to find out."

Ryder drove to Katie's house. Gabi's father might have come over, but he didn't have a remote control for the garage. From all the times he'd hidden his Harley in her garage, Ryder did.

He hit the remote. The door rose. There was Katie's car. He went into the garage and closed the door, privacy from the neighbors. He knocked on the door leading from the garage into the house, got no answer, but he heard Harry meow.

Whipping out his phone, he called her. Voice mail. Dammit.

"Katie?" He tried the knob. Locked. But it was a flimsy lock. He took a credit card from his pocket and jimmied the lock. His stint as a juvenile delinquent was finally paying off.

He stepped inside. Harry eeled around his legs. "No time for a scratch, buddy."

Water running. Bathroom.

He moved down the hall, calling her name so he didn't startle her if she'd been in the shower and hadn't heard all the ruckus. "Katie? You there?"

He reached the bathroom, knocked on the door. "Katie?"

No answer. Just the shower continuing to run.

What if she'd hopped in the shower this morning, fallen and hit her head, and she was unconscious?

Fear ripped through him.

"Katie!" Ryder hammered on the door, his heart pounding faster with each passing moment that she didn't answer. "Katie, are you in there? If you're in there, answer me, dammit."

She didn't answer, but he thought he heard something besides the running water.

Ryder pressed his ear to the door. Crying. She was crying, sobbing as if her heart would break.

"Katie Cheek," he blustered in a bear growl. "Open this door right now or I swear to God, I'll smash it in."

"Go away," she blubbered so incoherently, he wasn't sure that's what she said. "I'm a mess."

"We have a wedding to get to. Gabi is depending on you. Now is not the time for a meltdown."

"I . . . I . . ." She was bawling so hard he couldn't hear what she was saying.

"Katie, I'm dead serious. This door is coming down in one . . ." He paused, raised his voice, and eyed the door. He wasn't afraid to smash it in. It wouldn't be the first time he'd knocked in a door. It was thin and he was big, but he didn't want to smash it in on her if she was crouched near the door. "Two . . ."

He readied his shoulder, lowered his head. "Get out of the way. I'm coming in . . . three!"

Ryder charged the door, teeth set, leading with his shoulder, ready for impact.

The door opened just as his shoulder touched it and he went flying in, smacked hard into the counter, momentum knocking him back into the wall. He slumped to the floor, staring at Katie who sat on the closed lid of the toilet, blinking at him bleakly, tears streaming down her face.

"Damn, honey," he said kindly. "You look horrible."

"I know," she howled, and blotted her eyes with toilet paper, little fluffs of white lint clung to her lashes. "I'm an ugly crier. Even my mother says so. You know you're an ugly crier when your mother says you're an ugly crier."

"You're not ugly," he said. "You just look like you've been put through the wringer. What happened? What's wrong?"

"I got my period!" she yowled. "I lost our baby, Ryder, and you bought that cute little jacket and I would have loved to name her Lucy after your mother."

"Oh sweetheart, oh baby. I'm so sorry." He crawled to her, pulled her off the toilet seat and into his arms. Held her and rocked her and cooed in her ear and when his cell phone rang, he grabbed it from his pocket, growled, "Got her, we'll be right there."

And ended the call.

"Baby," he said, stroking her hair. "Gabi's counting you on being there for her and I know you're not the kind of person who would let down a friend. Do you think you can do this? I know you want to do this for your friend, but if you can't do it, that's okay. I'll take care of it. Do you want to do this?"

Katie nodded. "I want to."

"Okay, I'm going to help you up. You ready to get up?"

"Uh-huh." But it was as if her legs wouldn't support her.

Ryder got underneath her arms, levered her to a standing position, but she flopped against him, limp and listless.

"I was trying to take a shower, but I couldn't stop thinking about Lucy."

"Shh, we'll shower. I'll shower with you."

He stripped off both their clothes and got them into the shower, but it had been running a long time and all the hot water was gone.

"Yowl!" Katie cried when the cold water hit her skin.

Ryder had taken many a cold shower when he was in the military. He just gritted his teeth and held on to her. "I know it's uncomfortable, but sometimes in order to grow we need to get out of our comfort zone."

"That's horseshit."

"Probably," he said. "But it woke you up and got some of your spunk back."

He soaped her up; she was shivering from head to toe but her skin pinked up and her eyes brightened. He helped her out of the shower, ignored his own chilled body, wrapped her in a big bath towel, and carried her to bed. He buried her under the covers, then went back to the bathroom to clean up and get dressed again.

When he returned to the bedroom, she was sitting up. He fetched the blow dryer, plugged it in, and brushed her hair while he blow dried it.

"Better now?" he said when he'd finished.

"Better."

"It's going to be okay."

Her smile was halfhearted, but at least it was a smile. "Ryder," she said. "Thank you for coming for me. Despair and inertia had such a hold on me I don't think I could have snapped out of it without you."

He leaned over and kissed her forehead. "Yes, you would have. You're tougher than you think. Do you need help getting dressed?"

"No thanks," she said. "I've got it from here."

"All right," he said. "But I'm waiting around in case you need me."

"Joe needs you."

"You need me more." He squeezed her hand.

"I'm a wreck."

"No you're not. You're amazing." He bent again, kissed her on the lips this time, soft and slow.

She slipped her arms around his neck, tried to pull him down on the bed on top of her.

"Not now, you little minx. We've got a wedding to get to. Rain check. This kiss will have to hold you until then."

The wedding was magical. A storybook affair for the ages. Gabi was the most beautiful bride. Joe the handsomest of grooms. And as they were leaving the chapel for the reception hall, a light sprinkling of snow drifted from the sky, which had everyone oohing and aahing.

They played Christmas music at the reception, and served a traditional turkey dinner. Toasts were made. Waltzes were danced. Party favors were given out. Hands were shaken.

Ryder put his arm around Katie's chair, leaned in close. "How you doing?"

"I'm all right." Her smile was brighter, improving, but there was still the hint of sadness. He wished he had a magic wand to wave and make it all better. They'd only had the idea of a baby in their lives for a short time, but the kid had already made an impact. It was startling how much it hurt.

The death of a dream.

"Dance with me?" Katie stood up and held out her hand.

"Gladly." He stood up, wrapped his arm around her waist, and led her out onto the dance floor.

He pulled her close to him, smelled the sweet scent of her hair, and for a moment it felt as if everything was going to be all right.

"Ryder," Katie whispered.

"Yes?"

"I know you're big and strong and decisive and domineering and you're afraid that admitting you have tender feelings will make you look like a wuss, but sometimes, a woman needs to hear her guy whisper sweet nothings. Maybe it's a failing for the fairer sex. I don't know. I just know it's a thing."

He scratched his ear. "Um, yeah. I think we've covered that."

"I have another question."

"All ears."

"Where do we go from here?"

"What do you mean?"

"Our relationship. The wedding is over. Your dad is home and doing as well as could be expected. You've saved the ranch, at least for the interim. You have a job to get back to in LA. We're not having a baby. Where does that leave us?"

Um . . . He had a feeling this was a loaded question. One he didn't really have an answer to. "I don't know. We still have to process losing the baby."

"Did you know that a lot of couples who lose a child get divorced?"

Booby-traps. Land mines. What was it with women and questions like this? Did they enjoy seeing their men blow themselves up? "They probably didn't have a strong marriage to begin with."

"Maybe, maybe not."

"What are you saying, Katie?"

"I'm saying what if we had gotten married and we lost the baby after it was born? Would we have made it?"

"This is a hypothetical question. I don't see the point of it."

"Do you still want to marry me now that there's no baby?" She stopped dancing, and he had to stop too.

"Absolutely," he said honestly. "Maybe not right away. A long courtship might be fun before diving headfirst into parenthood." From the look on her face he could tell he'd detonated one of those land mines. *Ka-blewy.*

"And there it is," she murmured. "The inability to commit."

"Hey." He notched up his chin. "I wanted to marry you. I was all in."

"When there was a baby. You were all in for the baby, but not me."

"That's not fair."

"No?"

"I committed to the army," he pointed out.

"Well hooray for you. I'm sure Uncle Sam appreciates that greatly. But hey, answer me this. If you were so committed to the army, why did you only serve two terms? Why not career military? Most people are either one-termers or lifers. Seems to me like you only half committed."

"You're mad at me."

"Oh really." She sank her hands on her hips, cocked her head. "What was your first clue?"

"It's okay." He made calming motion with his hands. "You've suffered a blow. Your hormones are all over the place . . ."

Even as the words slipped out of his mouth, he could see himself in slow motion setting off that huge bomb. *Ka-motherjamming-boom.*

"Oh no, you didn't." She ground out the words.

"Pretend I didn't say that last part. Erase, erase, erase." He painted on a pretty smile that stood a good chance of getting him slapped. "Joke. Hee hee."

Tears bloomed in her eyes. "A miscarriage is not a joking matter."

Okay. Throw himself in middle of the minefield. Kamikaze style. A sacrifice. A warning salvo for the entire male species. When dealing with an upset woman, sit down, and shut the fuck up.

"I wasn't joking about that," he said soberly.

"I hope you weren't."

All right. Enough wedding reception for him. The bride and groom were gone. Katie had a ride home. Best thing he could do, walk away. She was going through something and he was only making it worse. Best plan of action, let her be. Call her tomorrow, grovel profusely, send flowers. Fresh start. Just like her company logo.

He held up his hands in surrender and walked away.

"Are you walking away while I'm talking to you?" Katie came after him.

Ryder ducked his head, aware that people were staring at them. He moved a little faster.

"Don't run away from me when I'm talking to you."

He quickened his pace. He could see the Harley in the parking lot from here.

"Ryder Southerland," she yelled, trotting after him. "We're not done hashing this out."

He spun on his heels so he could walk very fast backward and glare at her, making his face a thundercloud, hoping to scare her off with a show of masculine bravado. "I'm *not* running away."

"You're moving in the opposite direction at a trot. What would you call it?"

"I wasn't trotting," he said. "I do not trot."

"Trotter."

His jaw tightened and he stopped. "Okay. Here I am. Standing still. What did you want to discuss?"

"You look like you'd rather be having a root canal."

"Well . . ." He shrugged. "Maybe."

"Is talking about your feelings *that* difficult?"

"What are you talking about? I'm not having any feelings."

"Of course you are. Everyone has feelings. All the time. Even hardheaded macho men who are so scared of expressing their feelings they pretend they don't have any."

He groaned. "Why do women do this?"

"Do what?"

"Poke and prod and try to get men to open up and when we do . . ."

"What?"

"You don't like what we have to say." He lowered his head, lowered his eyes, lowered his voice. Growled. Grr.

"You don't scare me. You ran out on me when you were seventeen and the going got tough, why would it be any different now just because it's thirteen years later."

"Whatever you say."

"Bye, lone wolf. Hope you find what you're looking for."

"I'm sure I will. Eventually."

"You know," she said, shaking a finger at him, "that's bullshit too."

"What is?"

"Wolves aren't loners. They're pack animals."

All right. Crazy town time. No judgment. She was

completely entitled. He loved her, even if he couldn't say it. He was just going to give her the time and space she needed to heal.

So he did exactly what she said he would do. He hopped on his Harley and sped away.

Chapter 26

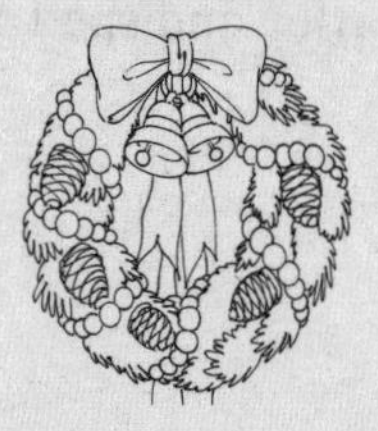

Ryder had a plan. He was going back to California until this blew over. Obviously he was agitating Katie. He'd lie low and see how things shook out. Might as well get on the road. He stopped at the ranch. Surprisingly, his father wasn't there. He left him a note, grabbed his gear, and headed west.

He'd be back. Hopefully.

If Katie ever spoke to him again. And yes, okay, maybe he was feeling a little sorry for himself, but he'd get over it.

Ryder crossed the Brazos River and was half an hour out of town as the sun was setting on Christmas Eve. Houses along the road lit up with decorations.

His cell phone vibrated in the pocket of his leather jacket. Katie! He pulled over on the side of the road, took out his phone, hopes soaring.

Those hopes floated back to earth when he saw Clara's name on the caller ID.

"Ryder?" Clara's voice sounded faint.

"What's wrong?"

"What makes you think something is wrong?" she asked.

"It's Christmas Eve. You're always with your daughter and her family on Christmas Eve. If you're calling me on Christmas Eve something must be wrong."

"You know me too well."

"What's happened?" His mind went in a million directions, dreading the worst. Had she broken her hip? Gotten swindled by a scam artist? Found out she had cancer? A lump of despair landed in his stomach. Normally, he did not immediately jump to worst-case scenarios, but when it came to people he loved . . .

Loved?

Yes, he'd never admitted to himself before, but he did love Clara. She was the grandmother he'd never had, and for the last two years, she'd been his only version of family.

"The most beautiful thing has happened," Clara whispered.

It took a second for that to sink in. Clara was calling because something good had happened, not something bad.

"But you're breathless."

"You'd be breathless too if the man you'd loved for almost fifty years just proposed."

"Wait. What?"

"It was the most beautiful thing," Clara said again.

"Who? What man?"

"Roger Fellows."

"Who is he?"

"Oh honey, back in 1967 it was the summer of love. I was rocking mini-dresses and literally wore flowers braided in my hair. And the music, oh my, the music was so wonderful! 'Light My Fire' was playing from the head shop that was next door to my father's print shop and they had the record player cranked so loud you could hear it through the walls. Could smell the pot fumes from next door too, but that's neither here nor there. It was the first time I ever heard 'Light My Fire' and the first time I ever laid eyes on Roger, who'd come in to have copies of flyers made about a Vietnam War protest. We were both twenty-one."

"You never told me this story."

"Well," she said. "There are some things people like to keep private, particularly when there's heartbreak involved."

Hell, he got that.

"It was one of those instant, dizzying love-at-first-sight things." She sighed dreamily. "Although at the time, because it happened so fast, I feared our chemistry was as much pot fumes and printer's ink as Roger's charm and good looks."

"So you reconnected," he said, hoping to speed her along so he could get back on the highway. He wanted to ride. Needed to ride. Craved the wind in his hair, and that long, empty stretch of open road to remind him of how free he was without commitments or community weighing him down.

"We did. But wait, I have to tell you how we separated. Roger got drafted. I wanted to run away to Canada with him, but he would have none of it. He didn't believe in the war, but he wasn't a coward. He didn't run out on his responsibilities."

"He sounds like a good guy."

"Yes. The best. Anyway, he got sent overseas and he was captured as a prisoner of war. The government thought he was dead. Told me and his parents he was dead. We grieved and moved on. I married Mr. Kincaid, and we had a nice life, but I never forgot Roger. Much as, I suppose, Katie never forgot you when she was engaged to Matt."

"How do you know all this about Katie? You only talked to her once, for maybe ten minutes. A year ago."

"There's a lot you can learn about a person when they replant your Christmas cactus and change a lightbulb for you. Consider the relationship you and I have, for instance. Most of the things I know about you came from when you were helping me."

That was true. Whenever he fixed things for Clara, he'd talk because she pretty much put you on the spot and forced you to talk to her.

"Clara, I hate to rush your story, but I'm sitting on the shoulder of the road on my Harley freezing my ass off in this cold snap on Christmas Eve. Eighteen-wheelers whizzing by."

"Oh," she said. "That's what that noise is."

"Could we cut to the chase, and you can fill me in on the details when I get home? I should be there by Monday morning."

"You're coming home?" Clara inhaled sharply. "Now?"

"I'm already on the road."

"But what about Christmas? What about Katie?"

"Bah humbug on Christmas."

"I see." She sounded disapproving.

"See what?"

"It's your usual attitude about the holiday. But what about Katie? I thought she'd straightened you out, and had given you a dose of Christmas spirit."

"It didn't take."

"You broke up!" Clara's voice hopped an octave on that last word.

"It was for the best."

"What did you do to her?"

"Back to Roger," he prompted, reluctant to dissect what had gone wrong between him and Katie. "How did you two meet back up again?"

"Facebook of all things," she said. "Now back to you and Katie."

"Look, Clara, I don't want to talk about it."

"Too painful?"

"Yes."

"All the more reason to talk about it. Tell me what you did to her. Maybe I can help you salvage it."

"I didn't do anything to her, Clara." *Beyond get her pregnant*. But he wasn't going into all that with his neighbor. "I don't belong here. I don't fit in."

"You don't fit here either, Ryder," she said sadly. "I'm your only real friend. Oh sure, you have guys you'll go get a beer or ride motorcycles with or take in a baseball game with, but no one who truly knows you. Except me."

"Yeah?" His voice came out acrid.

"Yes," she answered back, sounding like a prizefighter ready to talk smack. "I know you love

Katie with ever fiber in your body. I saw it in your eyes whenever I mentioned her name. I hear it in the anguish of your voice. She gives you what she needs most."

"What's that?"

"A place to call home. Whether you believe it or not, Ryder Southerland. You belong in Twilight. You belong with Katie."

"Easy for you to say. You're in LA. With Roger."

"That's why I'm saying it! I'm seventy years old and I found love again, and rekindling things with Roger has reminded me of the only reason us humans are put here on earth."

"What's that, Clara?" he asked, because he desperately wanted to know.

"To love, you ninny. We're put here to love. You have a wonderful woman who loves the dickens out of you. And I know you love her too. Stop letting your foolish pride and pigheaded beliefs that you're this bad man stand in your way. You are not a bad person. No matter what some people might have told you. Ryder, you're good to the bone, but you've been playing at being a tough guy for so long you've forgotten who you truly are. But Katie knows it. She sees it. That girl is your salvation and if you don't turn that motorcycle around and go back to her and fix things right now, I'm going to fly to Texas and kick your ass."

Clara was right. One hundred percent. Being near Katie made him feel like someone had returned a cherished keepsake he believed forever lost. And she was so connected to the community, whenever he was with her he felt drawn effortlessly into her world.

He knew people accepted him only because of Katie, but it didn't change the fact that the acceptance felt good. Because of her, the townsfolk were willing to give the bad boy a second chance.

Maybe Katie was right. Maybe people in Twilight really did forgive and forget easily. Maybe it *was* his guilt and shame that caused him to feel isolated and alone.

And maybe he needed to stop seeing himself through the old lenses. Hard to do when every corner he rounded held memories of his mistakes. He understood now why he had never returned to Twilight. It had as much to do with the stranglehold of the past as it did with his soured relationship with his father.

It was way past time he cleared all that up.

The Cheek family Christmas Eve was in full swing. Everyone in the world Katie loved was in this house. Everyone, that was, except for Ryder. She tried not to think about him. Tried to keep a smile on her face and her hands busy.

She helped her mother in the kitchen, ladling food in serving dishes and carrying it to the large dining room table for family-style eating. Joe and Gabi were canoodling in the corner, enveloped in newlywed bliss, eyes only for each other. They would spend Christmas in Twilight and then head to Hawaii for their honeymoon on Monday.

An image of Ryder's sexy face popped into her

mind, and she couldn't stop a sad sigh from slipping over her lips.

She couldn't believe how rude she'd been to him. Yes, she'd been hurting, but he'd been hurting too. She almost picked up the phone to call and apologize. She should have picked up the phone.

But she couldn't bring herself to do it. Even if she apologized, nothing would have changed. The man still couldn't tell her that he loved her. Nothing to do but put him behind her and start healing. It was for the best.

Ryder turned his Harley around and drove back to the Circle S. First things first. He had a few issues to straighten out with his father.

"Dad," he called, walking into the house with the pizza he'd stopped to pick up before the last pizza place closed on Christmas Eve.

To his surprise, his father was at the kitchen table with dinner prepared, and damn if there wasn't a small Christmas tree as a centerpiece.

"Hey," Ryder said.

"Thought we should do something special since it was Christmas Eve," Dad said.

"That's real nice, Dad. I bought pizza."

"Pasta Pappa's?"

"Of course."

"Probably better than this shit I cooked. Just one of those frozen dinners."

"We'll have both," Ryder declared.

They sat down to eat.

"Wanna beer?" Jax asked.

"Love one."

They drank beers and ate pizza and lasagna from the freezer case. They didn't have presents to exchange, but they exchanged conversation. Pleasant conversation, and that was the best Christmas present of all.

"I want you to know," Ryder said. "You're not going to lose the ranch. You won't have to sell it."

Jax looked suspicious. Hey, Rome wasn't built in a day. "Why not?"

"I'm staying," Ryder said.

"In Twilight?"

"Yep."

His father blinked at him as if he was speaking in a foreign language, but slowly a hesitant smile hitched up the corners of his mouth as his words sank in. "But . . . but you hate the ranch."

"I never hated the ranch, Dad, I just never felt welcome here."

"Because of Twyla." His dad's voice was brittle, thin and sharp and sad. So many colors of sad. "I married her so you could have some stability."

"We were just fine alone."

"We weren't and you know it."

"We weren't any better with Twyla."

"I know. But she was my wife, Ryder, and despite her problems, I loved her. Not the way she deserved. I couldn't love her with all my heart. Not after I lost your mother. Lucy was the love of my life. Twyla knew that, and I can't help wondering if that was behind her shopping addiction. Why she kept buying more and more stuff until we were drowning in it."

"I was a punk to her," Ryder said. "She wasn't my mother and I made her pay."

Jax nodded. "She wanted to love you, but you just couldn't let her."

"I was a kid. I was hurting. I'd lost my mom and I felt like I was losing you too."

"And I was too wrapped up in my own grief to see how I was hurting you."

"I judged Twyla instead of trying to understand her. I was a confused kid with his feelings sticking out like porcupine quills," Ryder said. "But I learned something about her this week that I never understood."

"What's that?"

"How losing a child can drive you mad with grief and make you do things you never thought you'd do."

"Like what?" Jax asked.

He met his father's eyes. "Hurt those you love most."

Tears trickled down Jax's face. "I'm so sorry, son. I wished we could have had this conversation thirteen years ago."

"I do too, Dad. I do too."

Katie had fallen asleep on her parents' couch, Harry in her lap. She'd not wanted him to miss out on the Christmas Eve festivities. He'd gotten tons of cat toys and special tins of Fancy Feast.

Her siblings and their children had departed, and it was only she and her parents left, and she was in no hurry to go home to that empty house. She could see her parents sitting at the kitchen table, their foreheads touching as they talked in low voices about the wedding.

Katie yawned and stretched. Harry followed suit. She glanced at the clock, saw that it was almost ten. It was either time to go home or make peace with spending the night here.

From outside the house they heard a loud clatter. She and Mom and Dad sprang up, as the sound of "Santa Claus Is Coming to Town" blared out over a loudspeaker. It sounded like it was coming from their front lawn.

"What the hell?" Dad said.

All three of them sprang to the window, threw open the sash.

And there, on the lawn, what indeed did appear, but a brand new minivan and Ryder Southerland sitting on the top of the minivan and holding the boom box over his head.

"Katieeeee!" he hollered.

"Romeo bellows," Mom said. "Best haul him in off the front lawn before the neighbors call the cops. With his reputation, he's likely to spend the night in jail. Your father and I are off to bed, but keep it down, will you."

"Yes, Mom." She kissed her parents good night.

"Katieee!" He bellowed again like Stanley bellowing for Stella in *A Streetcar Named Desire*.

Katie put on her jacket and went outside. "What is this?" She waved at the minivan.

"Traded in the Harley."

"You didn't!"

"Yep."

"You can't do that. The Harley is your pride and joy."

"No it's not. You are. And the kids."

"What kids?"

"Lucy and Spike and the other one."

She folded her arms over her chest. "We're not naming one Spike."

"Harley then?" Ryder slid off the front of the minivan and sauntered across the lawn toward her. "Since I had to give up my motorcycle for that rug rat?"

"Harley might be on the table," she said. "If you tell me how you got a minivan on Christmas Eve."

"Let's say there's a certain car dealer in town I used to run with back in the day and I know where the bodies are buried. I made him an offer he couldn't refuse."

"What's that?"

"My Harley and the full asking price for the minivan."

"You didn't!"

"I did."

"Ryder! Why?"

"To prove to you that I can commit. I want to commit to you, Katie Cheek. In frizzy hair or in straight. In ugly cry face or beautiful, beautiful kisser." He set down the boom box, leaned forward, wrapped an arm around her waist and pulled her to him for a long, hot kiss.

"Wow," she said. "Wow."

"But first, we need to get some things straight."

"Such as?"

"I can be a jackass some of the time."

"No kidding."

"I am not a poetic man, nor given to expressing my feelings in words. I would much rather take action and show you how I feel." He winked. "If you get what I mean."

"Subtle, Southerland. Real subtle. How will I ever figure out what that means?" Their breaths were frosty in the cold air. The Cheeks' house twinkled like the Griswolds' in *National Lampoon's Christmas Vacation*.

"I want you to be happy." He paused, grinned. "And naked. Naked is always good." He fiddled with the buttons on her sweater.

She slapped his hand away. "You haven't groveled enough."

"Good point." His voice was low-pitched, and she thought dreamily of moonlight, indigo, velvet. "Katie Cheek, the taste of your lips, the smell of your hair, the feel of your skin against my palms keeps me up at night," he said. "And when I finally fall sleep, dreams of you make it hard to wake up. And when I'm with you . . ." His voice grew husky. "I feel alive."

"And you said you weren't a poetic man."

"You might have taught me a thing or two."

"Hooray for me."

His jaw tightened and his eyes went cold. Chills raced up her spine and she rubbed her arms to warm herself.

"What?" she asked, unnerved.

He smoothed her hair from her face with his palm, peered into her eyes. "Don't you get it? I'd rather have bad times with you than the best of times with anyone else in the world."

"Really?"

"I'd rather have chaos with you than peace without you."

"Why not just have peace with me?"

"I was hoping you'd say that. I love you, Katie. I've loved you since I was ten and you were eight years old and I pushed you out of the way of that float. You are the driving force behind everything I do. You are the reason I get up in the morning. You are every fantasy I've ever had. And no matter what happens, each day I'm with you is the best day of my life. I'm yours, forever and always."

"Wow," she whispered. "Wow."

Her heart leaped, grimy with joy. Love was messy, yes. But worth it, so worth it. And as a wise woman once said, everyone needs a junk drawer.

Ryder Southerland it seemed, was hers.

"Marry me, Katie. Say yes and make me the happiest man alive."

"Hmm," she said.

"What's that?"

"Go get the Harley back. I never did get that ride you promised. But, oh, keep the minivan too. It might be a while before we have kids, but doesn't hurt to start practicing now."

"A woman after my own heart," he said, as he scooped her into his arms, and carried her to the minivan, where they christened it Sir Rocks-a-Lock as Christmas Eve drew to a close on the happiest night of their lives.

Here's a sneak peek at *New York Times* bestselling author Lori Wilde's newest Cupid, Texas novel

MILLION DOLLAR COWBOY

Available April 2017

Chapter 1

For the first time in a decade Ridge Lockhart was coming home.

He circled his Evektor Harmony over Silver Feather Ranch—the hundred thousand acre spread sprawling across Jeff Davis and Presidio counties—that had been in his family for six generations.

A cheery sun peeped over the horizon, greeting him jovially. *Hey buddy! Good morning. Welcome back to the fifth circle of hell.*

His jaw clenched and his stomach churned and the old dark anger he thought he'd stamped out years ago by working hard and making his mark on the world came roaring back, leonine as March winds.

He was in town for one reason and one reason only. Do the best man thing for his childhood buddy, Archer Alzate, and then get the mother-trucker out of Cupid, Texas.

ASAP.

Ridge took his time coming in, buzzing the plane lower than he should have. Taking stock.

Sizing things up. No matter how you sliced it, this was where he'd been hatched and reared. He could not escape his past.

Miles of desert stretched below his plane, land so dry a man got parched just looking at it. Land filled with cactus and chaparral flats; land teaming with rattlesnakes, horned toads, lizards, stinging insects, and roadrunners. Land that claimed lives and crops, hopes and dreams, in equal measure.

This land was a far cry from the cool, green country where he lived in Calgary. But damn his hide if he hadn't missed it. The Chihuahuan Desert. The Trans Pecos. Cupid. Silver Feather Ranch.

Home.

And that was his personal curse. To hate the very place that called to his soul, the place where he did not belong, but secretly yearned for.

Throat tight, tongue powdery, he reached for the gonzo size energy drink resting in the cup holder, and guzzled it down.

Ah. Much better. Thirst quenched. Caffeine buzzed. Cobwebs chased.

His chest knotted up like extra string on a wind-whipped kite. Ignoring the taut sensation, he cued up his MP3 player, drummed his fingers against the yoke in time to the rocking beat of "Homecoming" by Hey Monday.

The song wasn't a favorite. In fact, he didn't even much like it. An old girlfriend had introduced him to the tune. But the conflicted notes perfectly captured his complicated feelings, so he'd stuck it on his travel playlist. As the final note of electric guitar twanged out, the landing strip came in sight.

Ready or not, here I come.

He dipped the plane lower, coming in, coming down.

Their paternal grandfather, Cyril, had left all four Lockhart grandsons two-acre parcels of land on each four quadrants of the ranch, with the stipulation that none of them could sell their places without approval from the entire family. Which was the only reason Ridge had held on to his house.

To the North, he spied Ranger's place. Although he'd only seen it in pictures, his brother had built an eco-friendly, solar home out of reclaimed wood and recycled everything. Out of the four Lockhart brothers, he and Ranger were closest in age. Ranger was thirty-one to Ridge's thirty-two, but they were as different in temperament as wind and earth. Maybe it was because they had different mothers. Or maybe it was because Ranger was a legitimate Lockhart, whereas Ridge was the bastard.

Ranger was a brainy astrobiologist who worked at the MacDonald Observatory and thought everything through with cautious deliberation. Ridge was an act-first-ask-questions-later entrepreneur who'd built his own drilling company from the ground up, and he'd recently patented a new drilling method that promised to revolutionize silver mining and make him crazy rich in the process. China was clamoring for his business and after the wedding, he'd be headed to Beijing for six months to train silver mine employees in his patented drilling technique.

His two other younger brothers, Remington and

Rhett, had the same mother. Lucy Hurd had been his father's second wife and the closest thing to a real mother Ridge had ever had. He'd been devastated by kind-hearted Lucy's death from ovarian cancer when he was in junior high school, leaving him to comfort his younger siblings as best he could.

Army Captain Remington was twenty-eight and currently deployed in the Middle East. He had stuck a travel trailer on his parcel of land on the west side of the ranch for a place to stay when he was home on leave, but hadn't bothered to commit to construction. And the youngest, Rhett, was a PBR bull-riding rodeo star. He had built a rustic log cabin on the south end of the ranch in Presidio County.

Ridge carefully avoided flying to the east side of the ranch where his own house stood. The house he'd built, but had never lived in. The house he hadn't seen in ten years. Who knew what kind of shape it was in?

Dead center in the middle of the ranch, situated around the landing strip put in for crop dusting planes, were stables, bunkhouses, the foreman's farmhouse Archer lived in, three barns, numerous sheds, and the extravagant mansion where Ridge had grown up. The mansion his father lived with his third wife, Vivi.

Yep. Gossip of the decade. Vivi Courtland. Ridge's one time girlfriend was now his old man's spouse.

His stomach churned and deep-rooted resentment dusted over him, thick as the hard pack soil. Back. All the useless feelings he thought he'd conquered were back, as layered and nuanced as ever.

Anger. Shame. Fear. Guilt. Disgust.

"Damn it," he muttered, settled a straw Stetson on his head, and climbed from the cockpit, an unwanted lump in his throat and the morning sun in his eyes.

He forced himself to breathe. In. Out. Smooth and steady. Nothing disturbed him. He was the boss. In control. In charge. Tough.

Ridge pocketed the plane's key remote control, turned to the cargo hold to get his gear, and . . .

. . . that's when he spied her.

Lumbering up in a battered, blue Toyota Tundra extended-cab pickup truck and parking catawampus beside the tallest barn on the ranch.

Interest piqued, he cocked his head. Who was she?

The woman hopped from the tall truck with the fluid grace of a playful water sprite more at home underneath a cascading waterfall than smack in the middle of the Chihuahuan desert.

She wore faded blue skinny jeans that fit like spray paint, cupping rounded hips and a firm lush fanny. A neon-pink, V-neck T-shirt showed off a hint of sweet cleavage. Her flat-heeled cowboy boots were scuffed and dusty. From this distance, it appeared as if she didn't have on a lick of makeup, and her thick dark hair was pulled into twin braids. A gust of hot, lazy June air blew across the sand, and her nimble fingers reached up to tuck a tendril of loosened hair behind one ear.

Ridge had a sudden and startling vision of easing the elastic bands from her hair, undoing the braids, and watching that tumble of hair fall over his hand soft and smooth as liquid silk.

What the hell? Why the instant lust? Normally, he went for tall willowy blondes like Vivi. Not petite, shapely brunettes.

Why?

That was easy enough to answer. A) The brunette was smoking hot. B) There was something familiar about her, something warm and cozy and inviting. C) He hadn't had sex in so long he'd almost forgotten what it felt like.

Hope cut into him, gutted him open, leaving him raw and achy. Hey, who knew? There was a wedding this weekend—alcohol, food, music, slow dancing. Maybe they'd hook up.

Easy Lockhart, getting ahead of yourself.

He didn't even know her name, or if she was involved with someone, or if she'd even been invited to the wedding.

No, but that didn't stop steamy sexual fantasies from unspooling inside his head. Nor could he shake an odd feeling that he'd gone fishing for shad and managed to hook a mermaid instead.

The woman opened the extended cab's passenger side door, and bent over, butt wiggling as she ducked her head inside to retrieve something from the backseat. That round wriggly rump stole the air right out of his lungs, and highjacked his brain as effectively as a gun-toting bandit.

As the owner and CEO of Lock Ridge Drilling,

he made snap decisions on a daily basis and he'd honed the skill of sizing up people at a glance.

From the click-quick snapshot trapped in that breathless time of his mind, Ridge knew she was the spunky girl-next-door type. Able to climb trees, make chicken soup for a sick neighbor, organize a charity drive, spike a witty barb at smart-ass-know-it-alls, passionately root for her favorite sports team complete with face paint and logo jerseys, park her butt in the church pew every Sunday morning, and cheerfully answer three A.M. phones call from friends in need.

She was, in fact, everything Ridge was not—perky, happy-go-lucky, laidback, a rule-following, people-pleasing team player.

Not his type. Not in the least.

Which probably explained the pounding lust. He had a knack for picking women who were all wrong for him.

At this distance, with the width of the landing strip between them, he hadn't gotten a clear view of her face, but his initial impression was that she was more pretty than beautiful, while her body language exuded a come-sit-by-me friendliness that drew him. She was curvy enough to let him know that she enjoyed a good splurge meal now and again, but she was also healthy, and fit. Her skin was tan and supple, her eyes soft and bright, her teeth straight and white. She took good care of herself.

But it was the way she carried herself that totally wrecked him. Confidence mixed with humility. She had an authentic stride full of wholehearted openness. The last person he'd known who knew who'd possessed that special combo was Archer Alzate's kid sister, Kaia.

He hadn't seen Kaia face-to-face since she was sixteen and when she had attended his and Archer's graduation from the University of Texas. But two years ago, Archer called him to tell him that while working on her doctorate in veterinarian medicine at Texas A&M, Kaia had been in a terrible car accident and fractured her pelvis. Ridge had flown straight to College Station to see her only to discover she was in a medically induced coma.

The waiting room had been packed with her family and friends, and no one noticed him standing in the doorway. After so much time away he'd felt awkward and misplaced, an outsider. Not wanting to turn Kaia's accident into a stage for his return, he'd slipped quietly away without speaking to the family. But later he texted Archer to meet him in the parking lot to get an update on Kaia's condition. Archer gave him the rundown, including the fact Kaia had such a high medical deductible, he didn't know how she was ever going to afford to finish her degree.

Once Ridge knew she was stable and going to pull through, he went to the business office, anonymously paid the fifteen thousand dollar deductible toward her medical bills, and swore Archer to secrecy.

Later, when she was out of the coma, he sent flowers and a card and he'd gotten back a kind thank you note, and their correspondence had ended there. Archer kept his word and Kaia never knew Ridge had come to see her or that he was the one who paid her deductible.

Ridge slipped off his sunglasses for a clearer look at the provocative woman. From the back seat of the Tundra, she extracted an oversized present wrapped in gold foil. The package was so big, and the backseat so small, Ridge wondered how she'd managed to cram it in there.

She tossed her head, a triumphant smile on her face, and turned in his direction. Their gazes met across and empty desert.

For a split-second, his heart stopped.

Her obsidian eyes arrested him, a mysterious color that suggested hot summer nights and low, deep-throated whispers. Ripples of recognition jolted his nervous system, both shocking and delightful. He knew her.

Kaia Alzate.

Freakadilly circus, he'd been lusting after little Kaia Alzate.

Hot for the girl he'd once dubbed the Braterminator.

Ridge coolly slipped his sunglasses back down over his eyes. She'd pestered the hell out of him and Archer when they were kids. Tagging along everywhere they went, tattling if they stepped out of line, and generally being a run-of-the-mill pain-in-the-ass.

He might have hidden his eyes from her, but he couldn't hide the goose bumps spreading over his skin, pushing an insistent heat into his blood stream as he watched her from behind the safety of the polarized lenses of his aviator Ray Bans.

Her snapping black eyes sparkled with glee, as an enthusiastic grin split her mouth wide. She had recognized him too, and she looked more than happy to see him.

His gut dove the way it did whenever he'd practiced a stall in pilot training, spinning, whirling, and hurtling headlong toward the earth.

Thank God her hands were full because he had the distinct impression that if she'd been empty handed, she would have come flying across the tarmac to hug the stuffing out of him.

He didn't mean to do it, told himself he wasn't going to do it, but damn if he couldn't help sliding his gaze over her body. After all, she had no idea what his eyes were doing behind the sunglasses.

Thank you, Ray Bans.

She moved toward him, arms strapped around the oversized present. Stopped. Cast a glance over her shoulder at the main house. Swung her gaze back to him. She wanted to come over, but didn't seem to know what to do with the package.

He kept his face unreadable, but gave her a respectful nod. *I see you, but no need to rush or gush or make a fuss.*

Deliberately, he turned away, telling himself it was to chalk the plane's tires, and it had nothing to do with the fact his chest was tight and his head fuzzy. And a smile he could not stop was pushing across his face.

He was happy to see her too. So happy it freaked him out.

Once the chalks were in place, and he reined in his galloping pulse, Ridge raised his head, ready to dish up a slick greeting.

But she was gone.

Yay. Great. Perfect. He'd avoid her exuberant hug. Good work.

Why then, did he feel so bummed?

Holy tidal wave!

It was Ridge Lockhart, and he was more devastatingly gorgeous than ever.

Of course, Kaia had known he was coming home for Archer's wedding. She expected to see him. Thought she was braced for it.

Fat chance!

What she hadn't expected was that he'd be so damned sexy.

Her initial impulse had been to run to him and fling herself into his arms and tell him how thrilled she was that he'd come home. But she wasn't eight years old anymore, and he was no longer that lanky boy who'd yanked her braids and called her irritating names.

Her heart jackhammered, and she clutched the oversized wedding present tighter and hurried up the stone walkway to the mansion where the wedding party was assembling before the rehearsal. Instead of the traditional rehearsal dinner, Casey Hollis, the bride-to-be, had decided on a rehearsal brunch. As soon as everyone arrived, they would all head out to the cowboy chapel to rehearse.

Ridge included.

Kaia's pulse gave another sharp hop.

The gift was a crate for the German Shepherd puppy that Archer and Casey were adopting from the shelter when they returned from their honeymoon. But ugh. She hadn't fully thought it through. Per usual, excitement had swept her away.

Then again, she'd used the gift as a shield against Ridge's steely gaze. It provided a great excuse not to talk to him until she was prepped.

Seriously? She was not a silly teen with a monster crush on her big brother's best friend. Why did she need to prep to speak to the man?

Why?

Because just seeing him standing there in the sunlight sent her blood swirling the way it always had.

Darn it. Shouldn't she be over puppy love by now?

There ought to be a law. No one man had a right to look so handsomely heartbreaking.

The past decade had been kind to him. More than kind. He'd grown from the lean, skinny kid into full-blown manhood. Big-framed. Rugged. Untamed as ever.

He moved with the predatory grace of a mountain lion on the hunt. Intent, alert eyes and muscles, but with loose limbs and fluid joints. He looked like he should be on a high mountaintop staking in a pennant flag, claiming his territory.

Dressed in jeans, Stetson, suit jacket, tie, aviator sunglasses, and lizard-skin boots, he was part businessman, part pilot, part cowboy, and one hundred percent alpha male. Muscular fingers and scared knuckles hinted at his roughneck past.

He was both raw-boned and polished. Cheeks and jawline sharp, primal. Nose perfectly straight.

Eyebrows orderly. It was a dizzying combination of refined poise and rough-edged virility.

Everything about him caused her insides to quiver and her heart to flush. She couldn't have been more surprised if she'd unearthed pirate treasure in the desert.

Oh no. Oh damn. She was in trouble. Felt the truth of it overtake her. Nothing had changed. She still pined for him. How could she not even know it until now?

Stop it. Just stop it.

She was letting her imagination run away with her. All she had to do was steer clear of him until he went back to where he'd come from, and that would be that.

Turmoil over. Crisis avoided.

Except that she had to be around him for the wedding. He was her older brother's best friend and the best man and she was a bridesmaid. There was no way she couldn't avoid him completely.

Chill axe. No need to flip out. He would only be in town for three days. She could keep her hormones in check. All she had to do was make sure she was never alone with him. Considering all the people who'd been invited to the wedding that should be a piece of cake.

Armed with a plan, Kaia chuffed out a relieved breath, kicked on the front door with the tip of her boot in lieu of knocking and called out, "Open up. It's me, Kaia, I come bearing gifts."

Give yourself a Christmas present
any time of year with these delicious stories by
New York Times bestselling author

LORI WILDE

CHECK OUT HER E-BOOK STORIES FROM AVON IMPULSE:

The Christmas Cookie Chronicles: Carrie

The Christmas Cookie Chronicles: Raylene

The Christmas Cookie Chronicles: Christine

AND DON'T MISS HER OTHER JUBILEE, TEXAS, NOVELS:

The Sweethearts' Knitting Club

The True Love Quilting Club

The First Love Cookie Club

The Welcome Home Garden Club

Available in print and as e-books from Avon Books!

MORE ROMANCE IN CUPID, TEXAS, FROM *NEW YORK TIMES* BESTSELLER

LORI WILDE

Love At First Sight

978-0-06-221893-3

Natalie McCleary couldn't believe it—a lean-muscled, nearly naked man stood in her path . . . and then it hit her: love. But how can ex-Navy SEAL Dade Vega offer her his love, when he can't promise to stay in Cupid longer than a week?

All Out of Love

978-0-06-221896-4

When football star Pierce Hollister returns home, running the ranch in Cupid, he wonders how it all went so wrong. But one thing is right: Lace Bettingfield. The former plain-Jane has turned into a luscious knockout.

Somebody to Love

978-0-06-221898-8

Back home in Cupid, Texas, sexy cowboy-scholar Jericho Chance takes a new look at his bubbly best friend, Zoe McCleary. With her lightning smarts and luscious body, he realizes she's his somebody to love.

Love With a Perfect Cowboy

978-0-06-221900-8

Luke Nielson has come striding back into Melody Spencer's life, tempting her with the memories of long, lazy evenings and hot, passionate kisses. But that doesn't mean he'll get her in his bed.

NEW YORK TIMES **BESTSELLER**

LORI WILDE

**welcomes you to Jubilee, Texas—
where red hot cowboys look for love!**

The Cowboy Takes a Bride

978-0-06-204775-5

When out-of-work wedding planner Mariah Callahan learns her father has left her a rundown ranch in Jubilee, she has no choice but to accept it. Although she wasn't counting on ex-champion bull rider Joe Daniels stirring her guilt, her heartstrings, and her long-burned cowgirl roots . . .

The Cowboy and the Princess

978-0-06-204777-9

On the run from an arranged marriage, Princess Annabella of Monesta dons the guise of a hitchhiking cowgirl. But when she finds herself drenched, alone, and hungry, she has no choice but to trust the tall, sexy, Texas horse whisperer who offers her a ride.

A Cowboy for Christmas

978-0-06-204780-9

It's Christmastime in Jubilee, Texas, but Lissette Moncrief is having a hard time celebrating, especially after she smashes her car into Rafferty Jones's pick-up truck. Yes, he's a whole lot of handsome, but she's not about to let herself get whisked away by his charming ways . . . only to watch him drive away in the end.

AVONIMPULSE